# MANIFESTATION

WANDERING STARS VOLUME TWO

fourshadow publishing

Scripture quotations from the *Authorized King James Version*, Public Domain, 1611

Quotations from the *Book of Enoch*, Not in Copyright, Translation by R. H. Charles, 1917

Cover design and artwork by Mike Heath at Magnus Creative
www.magnus-creative.com

Maps, diagrams, and page layout by Jason Tesar
www.jasontesar.com

Copyright © 2014 by Jason Tesar
All rights reserved

Published by
4shadow, LLC

ISBN-13: 978-1505369977
ISBN-10: 1505369975

# ADDITIONAL CONTENTS

SENVIDAR

ARMAYIM

BAHYITH

SAHVEYIM

BADENA DEL-EDHA

KHELRUSA

MURAKSZHUG

ADVANYIM

SEDEKIYR

NAGAH

THE REALM OF TIMA

DA-MAYIM

S. A. 693-988. THE MANIFESTATION ERA

GREAT WATERS

NORDUR

VISTUR

AUSTUR

SUÐUR

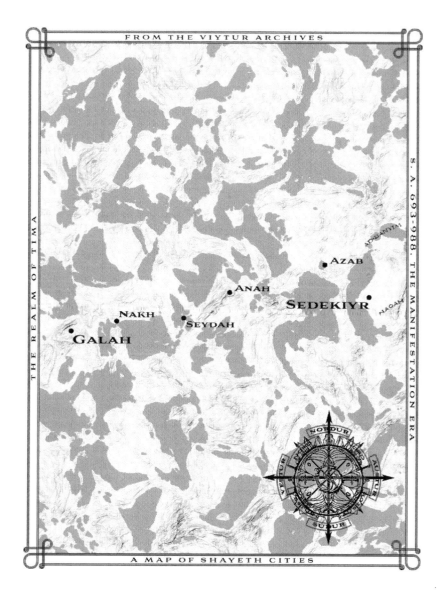

THE REALM OF TIMA

S. A. 693-988. THE MANIFESTATION ERA

AZAB

ANAH

SEDEKIYR

NAKH

SEYDAH

GALAH

ATLANTIA

MAQAM

NORDUR

AUTUR

VITUR

SUDUR

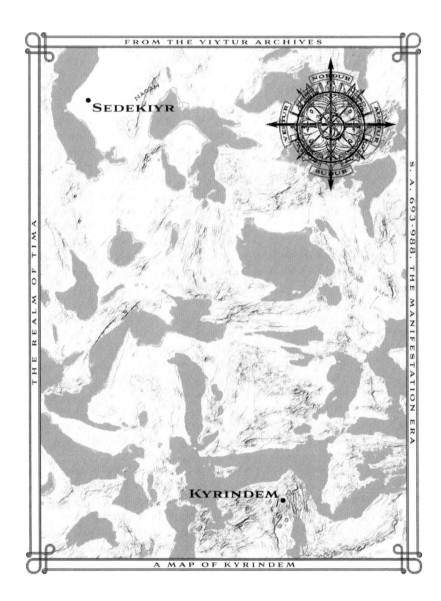

SEDEKIYR

KYRINDEM

THE REALM OF TIMA

S.A. 693-988, THE MANIFESTATION ERA

## Creatures of the Temporal Realm

## Creatures of the Eternal Realm

| Temporal Realm | MYNDAR (Shaper) | IRYLLUR (Air Soldier) | ANDUAR (Land Soldier) | VIDIR (Sea Soldier) |
|---|---|---|---|---|
| KAHYIN (Human) | N/A | IRIYL | ANIYL | VIDIYL |
| SHAYETH (Human) | MYNIYL | IRIYL | ANIYL | VIDIYL |
| CANINE (Wolf) | ULIYL | N/A | N/A | N/A |
| FELINE (Tiger) | KJOTIYL | N/A | N/A | N/A |
| RAPTOR (Bird of Prey) | ARIYL | N/A | N/A | N/A |

*... the angels which kept not their first estate, but left their own habitation, he hath reserved in everlasting chains under darkness unto the judgment of the great day ... **wandering stars**, to whom is reserved the blackness of darkness forever.*[1]

S.A. 693

# 1

*The angel's red eyes smoldered with lust, intensifying and subsiding like the coals of a dying fire threatening to burst into flame with each subtle breath of the wind. They hovered above her, faintly illuminating the surrounding skin—a face as dark as ash. The expressions almost looked human, vacillating between grimaces of pleasure and pain, only broken by one of slack emptiness that might have hinted of death if not for the determination behind each horrifying thrust.*

*Sweat glistened on the dark surface of the muscled arms that pinned Sheyir to the ground, immovable as the stone beneath her. Wings of smooth, black feathers spread above them both as though for privacy, but they were alone. The assault felt like a weapon, stabbing between her legs, killing her from the inside out. Pain crawled up her belly and into her chest, stealing the breath from her lungs and the screams that wanted to escape. Screams that had escaped an eternity ago, but to no avail. Sariel was gone, and Sheyir was helpless. She dug her teeth into the flesh of her lip and tasted the salty blood. She studied his face, concentrating on the details to distance her mind from what couldn't be stopped.*

*The angel lowered his head, hiding his face in shame as his body shuddered. When he finally lowered the rest of his body on top of her, his skin hot from exertion, she thought the worst part was over. Long seconds passed as his weight kept her from breathing. She began to gasp for air and shake with panic as he turned his head, his breath humid in her ear.*

*"If you tell Semjaza, I'll bleed you like an animal."*

*Embers danced through the air, appearing and disappearing as unconsciousness beckoned her. She considered surrendering to it when the angel shoved himself backward before standing.*

*There was a sudden void and a rush of cold air where he had been. Something trickled out of her. Was it blood? She didn't know, but she could feel through the pain that the soil was wet beneath her.*

*As the angel turned, his dark wings closed around his naked body—blending with the darkness until his eyes were all that could be seen. And then he was gone.*

*In the silence, Sheyir realized that the void he'd left in her was not just physical. The words he had whispered had also stolen her last hope of retribution. Semjaza may or may not hold him accountable, but the cost of exploring that possibility was her own life. Was it worth it? Could she endure just a little more suffering?*

*The ache between her legs was now a searing fire, and Sheyir began to weep as she reached down below her belly.*

*"...bleed you like an animal," the words repeated in her mind.*

Sheyir's eyes flew open and the dream vanished. She inhaled deeply of the cool night air, greedily drinking in the precious substance as though the dark angel were still on top of her. The wings that she had been staring at were now the underside of a conical, thatched roof—evidence that she was safe. But the pain in her abdomen remained, drawing her attention to where her hand lay. The skin of her belly bulged under her fingers as something moved beneath the surface. She knew better than to call it a child, for she had held the hands of several captive women as they had bled to death, their bodies torn open by such creatures clawing their way out. She would never forget the screaming or the helplessness she had felt as she repeated to them over and over again: "It will be over soon."

The creature moved again, causing a wave of nausea that passed over Sheyir in ripples of hot and cold, leaving her sweating in its wake. She winced before turning her head to look at Sariel sleeping next to her on the bed of woven grasses. His presence had once been comforting, but that feeling had become a distant memory. Before she had been stolen from Bahyith, she used to spend hours thinking about what her life would be like with Sariel. Now, she couldn't stop thinking about the fact that her rescuer had come too late to save her.

*   *   *   *

Sariel rolled over and stretched out his hand, but Sheyir was gone. He opened his eyes and shook off a yawn as he scanned the inside of their dwelling. Earthen pots lined the floor, filled with all manner of dried fruits and legumes. Bundles of drying plants hung from the support beams. A small fire burned under a hanging pot at the center of the room, warming the house as it sent a thin veil of smoke through the center of the two floors above, where it was vented through the apex of the ceiling. Sheyir wasn't in the house.

Sariel climbed to his feet and walked across the raised flooring, ducking under the overhanging thatch to step out into the cool of the night. The sky was just growing lighter to the east, revealing dozens of dwellings that encircled a central field of grass where the Aleydam gathered for nearly every work activity or social event. But the field was empty—still hours before sunrise when the villagers would awaken. The smell of damp soil was pungent as Sariel looked to the mountain peaks surrounding this high meadow. The mist, the mysterious substance that gave the Aleydam their identity, still clung to the higher elevations in the absence of the sun.[2] But as the air warmed with the day, the ethereal gray would descend upon the village and quickly pass by to fully blanket the valleys below.

Only then would the *People above the Mist* begin their work. If Sheyir wasn't inside their dwelling or sitting in the village center, there were only two other places she could be—gathering food on the slopes of the valleys around the village, or the isolated place she had discovered shortly after arriving here. Sariel suspected the latter.

Crossing the village center, he headed for a path that ascended into the trees. A handful of knee-high creatures, covered in gray fur, stepped casually out of his way and continued sniffing through the grass for anything that the villagers might have dropped. The path rose steeply into the mountains, winding back and forth between dense vegetation for almost an hour before it leveled out near the rough crags of the mountainside. The roar of falling water drowned out all other sounds long before the cascade of white could be seen through the trees.

Sheyir sat on a flat section of rock, overlooking a pool where the overspray collected before spilling over the edge to rejoin the main flow. Her back was toward Sariel, but she turned her head slightly as he approached and sat down next to her.

"When were you going to tell me?" he asked.

She stared out at the water with an expressionless face. "As soon as you rescued me. But then I saw that look on your face when you talked about bringing me here." She paused as her eyes welled with tears. "I didn't know how to tell you that someone had stolen from me what I wished to share with you." The tears began dripping over the edge of her lids.

Sariel reached around to her shoulder and pulled her close until she was rested against him. Although he couldn't deny the physical desire he felt for her, it wasn't the reason he had decided to stay in this realm. "I'm sorry that I couldn't stop them before they hurt you. But whatever grief you carry from that time, please don't let it be because of our physical love. In time, when you're ready ... It's not as important to me as the fact that we're together."

Sheyir's head dropped and she began to sob quietly.

Sariel put his other arm around her and tried to offer what little comfort he could. He hoped that her sobbing was from relief, but there was a knot in his stomach that said otherwise. He kept silent as Sheyir seemed to curl inward upon herself, until her head was lying in his lap. Sariel brushed strands of her black hair away from her face where it stuck to her tears.

Minutes passed before her sobbing receded and she stared out at the water again. "They have stolen more from us than you realize," she said finally, her words steady, as though rehearsed.

"What do you mean?"

"I'm with child. And my time upon this earth grows short."

Sariel stopped stroking her hair and leaned forward to peer into her eyes. "That doesn't necessarily ..."

Sheyir looked up. "The mothers always die."

Sariel closed his eyes and inhaled deeply. He didn't want Sheyir to see the rage that welled up inside of him. His body started to shake and he did his best to contain it. "Was it Semjaza?" he asked, eyes still closed.

"What does it matter? They're all dead now."

Sariel opened his eyes and tears spilled down his cheeks. It seemed that his earthly body would find some way to express what he tried to hold back. "It matters to me," he whispered.

Sheyir looked back to the water and her eyes grew distant. "It was the dark one ... with wings," she said. Her words were cold and without feeling.

"Azael," he replied, stroking her hair again to give his fingers something to do.

"Did you know him?"

Sariel shook his head. "I met him when I went to Semjaza to demand your release. That must have been around the time ..." Sariel trailed off as he suddenly wondered if his going to Semjaza had been the cause. Was Sheyir singled out on purpose? Had he sentenced her to death by giving the former Pri-Rada of the Amatru the benefit of the doubt? Was Sariel a coward to have thought of his future with Sheyir above anything else? He should have killed as many of them as he could on the road from the mines of Murakszhug, even if that meant forfeiting his own life in the process. He could still see Azael's red eyes. The way he had stood with confidence in front of Semjaza, protecting him. There was hatred in his gaze. Sariel wished that he could go back to that moment and tear every limb from that dark—

"Will you sing for me? I don't have the strength," Sheyir said, interrupting his thoughts.

Sariel blinked a few times and realized that she was looking up at him again. The sudden transition from memory to the present was disorienting. It took longer than it should have for him to realize that every second with her was now more precious than ever.

"I will," he replied, pulling her up to his chest with both arms.

\*　\*　\*　\*

KHELRUSA (KHANOK)
THE CITY OF THE KAHYIN

Ten Kahyin men stood in a line at the center of the training area. Their long, black hair fell in braids down their dark bodies, which were naked except for loincloths of animal hide. In the hands of each skilled hunter was a spear as long as he was tall. Fifty paces away were targets of hide, stuffed with leaves and stretched over a wooden framework. The sun was setting, and the mist that hung over the city during the day was being pushed farther down the valley by the cool air from the heights of Murakszhug. The hunters were confident and ready to demonstrate their expertise—the pride of their people.

The flat expanse of bare soil under their feet was dry, ringed on all sides with short walls of stone. Below the training area, the city of Khelrusa spread down the valley in a stair-stepped descent, ending at a curved wall that was now more stone than the wooden timbers of its original construction. The city had been undergoing a steady transformation since the gods had come down from the Mountain of Watching and taught them the crafting of stone. Only three had survived the war at Mudena Del-Edha, the *City of the Gods*, and they had returned to their chosen people.

Azael stood on the steps of the Kahyin temple and looked down upon the arena. He nodded to Luhad, the elder of the Kahyin tribe, indicating that the demonstration should begin. Luhad, the tallest and strongest of all the Kahyin, turned to his men and yelled a command.

The line of Kahyin hunters raised their spears and jogged forward a few steps before launching their weapons across the arena. Each one found its mark, and the targets jolted from the impacts. Luhad held up one hand as he jogged toward the targets. Azael descended into the arena with a casual pace and crossed the dry ground with long strides, reaching the targets at the same time as the Kahyin elder.

Five of the spears had gone straight through the thick animal hides and were embedded in the soil. Luhad quickly gathered them and offered the weapons to the god who towered more than four heads above him.

Azael accepted the cluster with one massive hand and inspected the newly-crafted iron tips. They were longer than a human hand, with a double-edged blade tapering to a point.

After removing the other spears from the targets, Luhad offered them up as well.

Azael took them in his other hand. Two of the stone tips had broken off inside the targets, which could be a useful attribute under some circumstances. But warfare was different than hunting, and the iron tips would allow his soldiers to continue using the weapons again and again.

"Good," Azael said.

Luhad nodded vigorously before waving to another man who waited patiently on the opposite side of the arena.

Tuval, the chief metalsmith, came running as soon as he saw Luhad's wave. He held something heavy across his chest that impeded his movements. When he neared, he knelt to the ground and bowed his head low before heaving a large, hide-wrapped bundle to Luhad.

Luhad took the bundle and lifted it to Azael with strained muscles. "A gift, my king," he grunted.

Azael took the bundle and began to unwrap the covering, finding a crude approximation of a vaepkir inside. The surface of the metal was dull, its color an inconsistent patchwork of earth-toned splotches. But Azael didn't care about appearances as much as function. He looked up and nodded to one of his only surviving soldiers, standing near the steps of the temple.

"Yes, my Rada," Rikoathel answered, walking down the steps and across the arena. He was larger than most Iryllurym, with dark brown skin that transitioned to even darker feathers along his wings. His golden eyes were less intimidating than those of his colleagues, but his height and thick build compensated for it.

"Hold this," Azael instructed, handing the weapon to him. "Reverse grip."

Rikoathel took the vaepkir by the handle and held the long, single blade out in front of him like a svvard.

Azael stepped back and unsheathed one of his own vaepkir from the scabbard at his lower back. Crafted by the Myndarym while they were still under Semjaza's control, the weapon gleamed in the fading sunlight. It was the temporal equivalent of the famed Iryllur weapon that had sent countless demons to the Place of Holding. Even at a glance, the difference in skill between the craftsmen was apparent. This one was a brilliant silver color, its surface perfectly smooth and free of any imperfections. Azael held his weapon in a standard grip, with the blade running upward along the outer edge of his arm. He tightened his fingers around the hilt, and with one swift movement, he lunged forward and attacked.

The vaepkir hummed as it cut through the air, then shrieked as it struck the Kahyin weapon.

Rikoathel blinked as the severed portion of the iron blade spun through the air beside his face. The crude hilt remained in his outstretched arm, which had never wavered from its position.

Azael resheathed his weapon and looked down to Luhad, who had terror in his eyes. "Your blade is weak."[3]

Luhad bowed low and skulked backward with his eyes staring at the ground. He turned to the metalsmith and cursed, belittling him with a string of obscenities. Tuval backed away and bowed, bobbing his head in agreement with each insult. When Luhad grew silent again, Tuval turned and ran away across the arena.

"My Rada," came a smooth voice from behind.

Azael turned to find his second-in-command standing behind him. In keeping with his stealthy nature, Parnudel had landed and approached without a sound. His mottled gray and brown colors kept him hidden among foliage during the day, and his soft feathers divided the air around his wings to give him silent flight. He met Azael's gaze with one of equal intensity in a golden hue. "The Myndarym are still here."

Rikoathel tossed the iron hilt of the inferior vaepkir to the ground and immediately stepped closer to join the conversation.

"The Myndarym? How do you know this?" Azael asked.

"I spotted one of them during my patrol. He was in his animal form, flying along the coastline of the Great Waters. I kept hidden and followed him northward, where I found a great forest city of theirs."

"So the Amatru let them live?" Azael mused.

"Or they evaded capture," Rikoathel suggested.

"Are they all in the same location?" Azael asked.

"I only observed six others in the city, my Rada. But there were humans as well. They've established themselves there."

Azael looked to the sky and considered this new information. After a long pause, he turned his attention back to his subordinates. "This situation could quickly become a liability if they realize we're still alive."

"We will kill them all if they come for us," Rikoathel said.

Azael grinned. He appreciated his soldier's defiant confidence, but he also knew that caution was needed. "You saw the tunnel under the mountains of Mudena Del-Edha just as I did. And you remember what they did to the sea gate? Those *Shapers* are dangerous, and we cannot take action without understanding the threat. We need more information. Both of you go to this forest city and assess their strength. I want to know how many reside there and if they have military capabilities beyond their *shaping*. Stay hidden, and if you are discovered, kill your enemy quietly and dispose of the body."

Parnudel's eyes narrowed. He looked offended that Azael would even suggest the possibility of him being discovered. "Yes, my Rada," he replied simply.

The two Iryllurym extended their powerful wings and leapt upward, rising farther into the air with each downward thrust. Within seconds, they disappeared over the forested mountains to the north.

When Azael turned his attention back to the arena, he noted that the Kahyin who were in the immediate area were all on their knees with heads bowed to the earth.

# 2

Mist floated across the plains in patches, carried by a southwesterly breeze. Every so often, a glimpse of Sedekiyr would open up on the horizon, and Enoch would feel his heart quicken inside his chest. Hundreds of small, brown huts stood out against the bright green grass like a cluster of fruit. And then the sight would vanish behind the veil of gray for long moments until it reappeared, closer than before.

The sun was past its zenith by the time Enoch was able to make out people moving among the huts. Many stopped their work and stared in his direction. Minutes later, voices could be heard above the steady swishing of his legs through the wet grass. Their shouting brought more people to the edge of the city so that a crowd had gathered by the time Enoch was close enough to begin recognizing faces.

A commotion developed on the left side of the crowd, and people began stepping to the side before Zacol pushed her way out. She stood there for a moment, looking on with disbelief until Enoch smiled back at his wife. Then she started running and didn't stop until she reached Enoch and threw her arms around him, nearly knocking him off his feet.

Enoch dropped his walking stick and traveling bag and held his wife tightly, cherishing the open display of affection for all the tribe to see. It was rare for her to do such a thing, which made Enoch wonder for the hundredth time this day what she had gone through since he had left.

"I didn't know if I'd ever see you again," she admitted.[4]

"I told you I would come back when my task was complete."

Zacol smiled. "You look thin. You're not eating enough."

Enoch immediately noted her changing of the topic, but decided to leave it alone. There would be plenty of time to share his stories with her. "Except for today, I've eaten plenty. It's just that I have traveled so far."

"Well, come and rest. I'll prepare something for you."

"Where's Methu?"

"He's taken to catching fish in the stream with some of the older boys. He should be back soon. Come and rest your tired feet."

The crowd parted and Enoch followed Zacol through the city. In addition to the crowd now following him, Enoch received stares from other Shayetham as they wound through huts and between short fenced areas. Most were stares of curiosity at seeing anything different than their usual daily tasks. But some of his people looked cautious, as if Enoch were from another tribe or as though they expected something bad from him.

Before Zacol reached the eastern edge of the city, she turned toward a hut and stopped outside the door. Enoch stopped short and glanced toward the eastern fields, noting that his dwelling was no longer there.

"The elders said it wasn't safe for me to be out there alone. They built us another here," she said, motioning toward the doorway.

Enoch was about to glance again at the fields when he noticed something moving inside the entrance of the hut.

"Ahva!" Methu exclaimed, running out of the doorway with his arms outstretched.

Enoch bent down and lifted his son from the ground. "Oh my! You've grown so tall. And you're heavier than I remember."

Methu was grinning from ear to ear. His face had lost some of it childish roundness, but his brown eyes were still large and filled with wonder.

"What are you doing back so soon?" Zacol asked her son.

"I caught three fish today, so I came back early," he replied before turning back to Enoch. "Want to see?"

"Yes, of course," Enoch replied, setting his son down again and following him through the doorway. Though it had been a little more than a year since Enoch had set out to deliver his message to the Wandering Stars, Methu seemed to have aged twice that amount.

"I've never caught this many before," Methu said, picking up a braided grass cord that was strung through the gills and mouths of three fish, each as long as his forearm.

Enoch knelt down and took the cord, lifting the fish to get a better look at them. In addition to the mud and blades of grass stuck to the water-going creatures, they were also bleeding from puncture wounds along their sides. "Did you trap them in the shallows, like I used to do as a child?"

Methu shook his head. "The other boys do that. But the fish know when they're coming. I stand still and use a stick," he said, jabbing his hand downward as if he were still knee-deep in the nearby stream.

"Ah, like a vandrekt," Enoch mumbled.

Methu's face went blank with confusion.

"A what?" Zacol asked from behind, a hint of tension in her voice.

"It is a weapon of the Anduarym, the angels of heaven."

Methu's eyebrows rose up. "You met angels?"

"I did," Enoch replied.

"Don't fill his head with nonsense," Zacol added.

Enoch turned his head to catch his wife's frown. "It isn't nonsense. I met the Anduarym and many others."

Zacol stepped forward and took the fish, inspecting them with a look of disapproval. "Well, there won't be much useable meat on these, but I'll do the best I can." She turned quickly and walked to an earthen pot filled with water to begin cleaning the fish.

It was plain to see that something was bothering her, but Enoch decided that it would be best to leave it until the happiness of their reunion had subsided. When he turned back to his son, Methu still had a look of wonder on his face.

"What were the others called?"

Enoch smiled. "Well, there are all kinds. The Anduarym walk on the land, like us. Some swim through the Great Waters like your fish. They are called Vidirym. And the ones that fly through the air are called Iryllurym."

"They can fly?"

Enoch nodded. "They even took me up in the air as if I were a bird of the sky."

Methu's mouth hung open in astonishment. "How did you meet them?"

"Well," Enoch replied, sitting down on the ground and crossing his legs. "If you'd like to hear it, I'll tell you the whole story."

\* \* \* \*

ALEYDIYR

The morning sun warmed Sheyir's back as she knelt in the fertile soil and lifted a vine to reveal a cluster of berries. The ones nearest the vine were still green and dull, but the cluster transitioned to a deep and glossy red at the bottom. She removed the ripest berries, reaching beside her to drop them into a woven bag hanging over her shoulder. The juice of the berries was slick between her fingers, an indication of her lack of skill.

*I must have squeezed too hard*, she thought, rubbing her thumb and fingers together and watching the way it stained her skin. The red seeped into the valleys of her fingerprints like miniature rivers through a land of flesh.

*The knuckles of her hands seemed pale against the darker backdrop, glistening in the firelight. But the rest of her arms, all the way up to her elbows, were bathed in crimson. The blood was everywhere. Splatters across the front of her clothing. A pool on the stone beneath her, footprints and other signs of struggle disturbing portions of its outer edge. Under her hands, the knees of her fellow prisoner were still in the air, even though the woman's skin had already gone cold. A still and pale face gazed upward at the cavern ceiling with lifeless eyes—a face that had expressed the most intense of human emotions only moments earlier.*

*From over her shoulder, gigantic hands reached down in front of Sheyir. She watched them with a childlike curiosity as they descended, moving between the knees of her friend. It wasn't until something pale and serpentine curled around one of the fingers that the curiosity gave way to fear.*

*"Take it out," a voice commanded from behind.*

*Sheyir blinked her eyes long and slow as if waking from a dream. When she looked again, she saw a tangle of pale blue and green vines writhing in front of her like a den of snakes. But there were no eyes or mouths. No flickering tongues. Just slender vines that reached out. Sliding through the blood. Latching onto the inside of her friend's legs. Curling around the fingers of the hands that were pulling it. Then a head and face that looked human, but the eyes were black. A torso, with arms, but more than there should have been. Blue and green skin, covered with blood.*

*A shrill screech echoed through the cavern, ending in a rapid series of clicking noises. The hands lifted the creature and Sheyir watched it being carried down the sloping rock toward the dark and still water. The surface churned, catching reflections of the firelight as if it were being consumed by the flames. The small creature, carried by the powerful arms of an angel, lowered toward the water until something broke the surface. Pale hands reaching upward. A wide face with black eyes. A large creature accepting the gift of its own kind.*

*Sheyir closed her eyes and turned her head away. When she opened them again, the body of her friend lay before her on the stone floor of the cavern. Though pale and lifeless, her upper body still looked normal. The rest of her was torn open. Gaping.*

*Sheyir lifted her hands in front of her face, turning them until she could see the creases of her palms. The blood had seeped into the valleys of her skin like miniature rivers through a land of flesh.*

"—if you don't work!"

Sheyir looked up suddenly, catching the stern eyes of an Aleyd female. It took her a full second to realize where she was.

"You said you would help. We will send you away if you don't work!" the woman repeated.

Sheyir nodded quickly before looking down again, searching for another cluster of berries. The juice was now sticky between her fingers, and she wiped them on her tunic before moving on.

\* \* \* \*

SEDEKIYR

"I thought He loves them," Methu said.

Enoch looked down at the grass between his toes as they walked. "He does."

"Then why did the Holy One say that?"

Enoch smiled and nodded. It was amazing to think about how quickly his son was developing. Methu had almost no ability to reason when Enoch had left for Khanok. Now they were sharing a conversation, however difficult it was to explain the subject matter. "Do you know that your mother and I love you very much?"

Methu nodded.

"How?"

Methu jabbed a stick into the ground as they wandered back toward the city. After a long pause, he suddenly looked up. "Because you tell me."

"That's right. And we show you as well, by feeding you and clothing you. And protecting you."

Methu pulled the stick from the ground and swiped it at a tall blade of grass. "I can protect myself."

"I'm sure you can," Enoch replied. "But what happens when you do something wrong?"

Methu stopped walking and looked up with a scrunched face. "Mother punishes me."

Enoch smiled awkwardly, suddenly realizing that his absence might have negatively affected his son's perception of Zacol. "Yes, we punish you," he replied, trying to subtly inject himself into the role of the household judge. "And why do you think we do that?"

Methu took another swipe at the grass and kept walking. "Because I did something bad?"

"Well, it's more than that. If you disobey, it could hurt other people as well as yourself. And we don't want to do either of those, right?"

Methu nodded, but kept silent.

"But more importantly, we don't want bad things to become part of who you are. Part of your character. Because if they do, then you will go on hurting people your whole life. Do you see?"

Methu shrugged. "Yeah."

Enoch looked up from the grass along the stream and could see the huts of Sedekiyr. He looked down at his son again, doubtful that Methu understood what he was trying to say. "Even though the angels are wondrous and beautiful ... even though their ways are mysterious to us," he explained, "the Wandering Stars have disobeyed the Holy One. They are hurting themselves and they have hurt many others also. The Holy One must punish them."

Methu nodded before throwing his stick over the grass and into the stream. "Why does He wait?"

Enoch was surprised by the bluntness of his son's question, but he tried not to show it. He didn't want there to be any shame in the conversation between them. As he opened his mouth to answer, he remembered his time in the Eternal Realm before the throne of the Holy One. He could still feel the blinding intensity of His radiance. And His words came into Enoch's mind.

*Now, Enoch, son of righteousness, I have another message that you will not speak to the Myndarym. You will teach it to your children and they will teach it to their children. Thus, it will remain with your household for generations to come. At the appointed time, it will be revealed to my Wandering Stars and they will hear and understand. Say to them, 'You will see your destruction from afar and will know it is coming. Because of your unfaithfulness, this judgment must come to pass. Therefore, I will raise up one from among those you despise ...'*

The words faded away and Enoch was left with the memory of his encounter with the Myndarym on the shores of the Great Waters several months ago. "In some ways, He has begun punishing them already. But I'm afraid the fullness of it will not come for many generations. I know that the Holy One is immeasurably patient with all his children, so I must also believe that there is purpose in His waiting."

# 3

The metal wheels of the carts groaned in protest as Hyrren pushed them along the rails. There were three carts joined end to end. Every so often a flat section of a wheel would slide instead of rolling, grinding against the metal rails and adding to the already oppressive resistance of the steady incline. Hyrren's arms were shaking from exhaustion, and it appeared as though embers of a fire were drifting across the tunnel in front of him. He inhaled another deep breath of the humid air and closed his eyes to stop his vision from swimming. Then he widened his legs and threw his steadily diminishing body weight against the loads of ore. His legs were considerably weaker today. Three days without food was taking him close to his limit. But the reason for the delay wouldn't matter one way or another to Luhad, the elder of the Kahyin. He was in charge of everything from the food distribution to the metal work. Explaining to Luhad that his failure in one area was causing Hyrren's failure in another would only invoke his legendary wrath.

Up ahead, the tunnel grew lighter. When the heat of the smelting room could be felt, Hyrren knew that the end of the passage was near. As soon as he began to feel relief from the chill in his fingers, another wheel slid along the rails and Hyrren stumbled, almost losing his grip. He quickly dug his feet into the soil and righted himself, pausing again until the embers dissipated from his vision. The rapid beating of his heart may have been induced by the fear of losing his carts. But after he caught his breath, it kept racing, fueled by his anger.

He was the son of a god, after all. And look how far he'd fallen in just a few moons—raised in his father's fortress, all of the food he and his siblings could eat, the Kahyin as their servants. Now they were starving, and the Kahyin ruled over them. Everything had been turned upside down when the gods attacked his father's kingdom. They had no right to enter this realm and destroy everything his father had worked so hard to build. Hyrren would remember that day for the rest of his life. The way the enemy gods took him and his siblings from their hiding place as if they were in need of rescue. How they gathered everyone on the peninsula outside of his father's tower and walked around them in circles with disgust on their faces. Hyrren remembered the vandrekt they pressed against his neck and the arrogance of their leader as he inspected them all.

That was the first time Hyrren had experienced the type of fear that could make his legs go weak. Wondering when the blade would be dragged across his neck. When would his own blood flow? It was such a normal part of his life now that it was hard to remember what it felt like to live without it. It didn't make his legs go weak anymore. That sensation was saved for starving. Now he just felt angry, and it fueled him—giving him a strength that was independent of nourishment.

Hyrren dug his feet into the soil. He leaned on the carts overflowing with ore. He pushed with his arms that were nothing more than bone and muscle. And the crudely made vessels gave in to his anger, yielding before him as they ought to.

*I am Hyrren, son of Semjaza*, he repeated to himself, over and over again until the ground leveled out and the tunnel widened to reveal the bright and hot smelting room.

The cavern was wider and deeper than most under the mountain. It was circular in shape, with furnaces around its perimeter. The Kahyin men were doing the light work, loading the heated chambers with small batches of ore from the pile at the center of the room and keeping the fires roaring as hot as possible. Hyrren would have loved to see one of the humans push even a single cart from the mines up to the smelting room. Or even a group of them. For just one day, he and his brothers could stoke the fires and load the furnaces. And the weak humans would see just how valuable the Nephiylim really were.

The rails extended to the center of the room where Hyrren's younger brother, Imikal, was just beginning to unload his cart. There was another slight incline leading to the top of a metal slide where the ore would tumble down to the pile at the center. The smaller Nephiyl grabbed the edge of his only cart and began to tip it toward the slide, but it wavered. Imikal's leg stuck out to balance the cart, but it faltered under the strain.

Hyrren could see what was about to happen. He immediately left his carts on the flat terrain and started running.

Imikal's body went limp, and he fell sideways. The cart landed on him, and its contents spilled out across his legs, tumbling back down the incline instead of the slide.

"Imikal! Imikal!" Hyrren called out, but there was no response. By the time Hyrren reached his brother, he could see that the younger Nephiyl wasn't moving. He looked pale, and sweat stood out on his skin in large droplets. "Water! Someone fetch water!"

There was shouting in the background, but Hyrren could only focus on his brother's face, held gently in his hands. "Imikal? Can you hear me? Imikal?"

The crunch of footsteps on the coarse soil grew near.

Hyrren reached out his hand to grasp the water, turning his head a second later to realize that it wasn't relief that was approaching.

*Crack!*

Luhad's whip snapped in the air.

Hyrren flinched with surprise.

"Get up, you lazy filth!" Luhad yelled, retracting his hand for another blow.

Hyrren raised his arm, but the whip unfurled past his hand.

*Crack!*

Imikal's body jolted. A welt appeared instantly on his chest.

"Get back to work before I take your head from your body!"

*Crack!*

Imikal's face twitched from the impact and his lip split open.

"NO!" Hyrren roared, throwing himself over his brother's limp body.

"Pick up your mess!"

Another crack, and Hyrren felt the sting across his back. A small cry escaped his lips, but he clenched his jaw to quiet himself. He wouldn't give Luhad the satisfaction of knowing the pain he inflicted.

"Get out of the way!" Another crack and another sting.

Hyrren's whole body tensed. Something inside him welled up like never before, an emotion that scared him as much as it empowered him. He wanted to kill. He wanted to see Luhad's body broken in pieces. He wanted to see the elder's blood spilled out on the ground. But his mind seemed to focus at the same time, sharpening to a point like one of the metal weapons that Tuval made. He knew that lashing out in anger would only bring more pain. So he channeled the urge into words. "He fainted because you starve us!"

*Slap!*

The whip lashed across Hyrren's back before it was able to snap. The pain was duller than before, but spread over a larger area.

"Then hunt your own food, you lazy beast."

*Snap!*

Hyrren kept his head down and his arms spread wide to cover his brother, who still hadn't regained consciousness. "We have no time to hunt when we're doing all of your work!" The next blow had some extra effort behind it, catching Hyrren across the back of the head and burning like fire.

"Work? Is that what you call it, when you're lying down?"

Hyrren couldn't take it anymore. He slowly rose to his feet as several more blows tore into the flesh of his back. He turned to face Luhad, towering over the Kahyin elder.

Luhad's eyes flashed with hatred, and his dark skin trembled with rage. "You filthy abomination!"

*Snap!*

Hyrren's chest began to bleed, but he didn't even blink.

"You came to us, remember? When they killed your father?"

*Crack!*

Hyrren's face burned.

"You think you're special? Not anymore!"

*Snap!*

"If he doesn't pick up this mess and get back to work, I'll throw him out with the refuse."

*Crack!*

Hyrren couldn't see out of his left eye anymore, but he wouldn't let Luhad break him. "I'll pick it up."

"Oh? And who will do your work while you do his?"

*Snap!*

"I'll do it all!"

"And how will you make up for this lost time?"

*Crack!*

Hyrren could taste blood. "How will you explain this lost time to your gods?"

Luhad's eyes narrowed at the defiance, and his body suddenly erupted into a spasmodic fury. He struck again and again, as fast and as hard as his body could move. And with each lash, his anger grew more intense.

Hyrren smiled and spread his arms, letting each strike of the braided animal hide open his own. The gnawing hunger pains were gone now. The weariness that he had felt only moments ago had been consumed like dry grass in the fire of his anger. The pain seemed to him like the furnaces of the smelting room, extracting from his weakened body a hidden strength that was more powerful than anything he'd felt before this day. He began laughing, welcoming each blow as it tore him open—his weakness and fear draining down his face and chest in streams of red.

Luhad's attack slowly abated. The rage in his eyes cooled, and was replaced by a look of disgust.

Hyrren had stopped laughing. And though he had lost all the feeling in his face, he suspected that there was still a smile there. "What's the matter, Luhad? Have your weak arms failed you? Or is it your weak spirit?"

Luhad raised his hand again, the bloodied cord dangling below it, the tip coiled like a snake on the ground behind him. But the serpent didn't strike. It knew that its fangs were dull, its venom impotent.

"I am Hyrren, son of Semjaza. And you will not break me."

"Get back to work!" Luhad yelled before stepping away. With a wary gaze, he turned and marched toward the exit.

Hyrren looked around the smelting room with only his right eye, seeing that every Kahyin man had stopped working to watch the confrontation. Normally, they would have received a lashing from both tongue and whip for stopping, but Luhad seemed to have dispensed all the punishment he could muster for one day. As Hyrren's heart slowed and his anger dissipated, the pain in his body intensified. But he smiled anyway. A great victory had been won. This was a turning point in his life. He knew it. He could feel it, even without the cycles of experience that would allow him to look back at this moment with confirmation.

Turning around, he noticed Imikal staring up at him, eyes wide with disbelief.

"They will never break us," he assured his little brother. "We are the sons of Semjaza."[5]

Imikal nodded.

\*   \*   \*   \*

KHELRUSA

Azael stood at the entrance of the temple, looking down upon the city that spread across the narrow valley between spurs of Murakszhug. The first stones of the temple's foundation had been laid where the Kahyin used to offer their animal sacrifices to the gods. Semjaza had chosen the Kahyin for their strength, and they worshipped him and his armies in return. Now they were far too busy to bring sacrifices. The altar behind Azael was cold and bare. Instead, the Kahyin brought their problems. They came to the highest point of the valley in order to give an accounting of their efforts and the hindrances that kept them from making progress. It was a worthwhile trade, for Azael cared nothing for worship. His status as a god among the Kahyin was already established. But his kingdom wasn't. It needed stability. It needed to be strengthened. And then it would need to grow. This was where Semjaza had failed and where Azael would succeed.

Instead of inspiring the worship of humans, Azael contemplated more practical matters—the most pressing being how to feed his population. Apparently, the Kahyin were struggling to provide food for themselves and the Nephiyl children under the mountain. "The forests of Khelrusa are stripped bare," Luhad had said. "My hunters search far and wide, but these monsters consume everything we give them. They cannot be satisfied, and they are more trouble than they're worth in the mines."

Azael had seen the blood stains on Luhad's whip. He had known the Kahyin resented the Nephiylim, whether because of jealousy or the fact that breeding the Nephiylim required so many of the Kahyin females. But it seemed that the animosity was growing between the two groups, and Azael had to figure out how to stabilize the issue in order for his kingdom to grow.

As he pondered this issue of social concerns, he watched the brume flow down from the dense forests above. It blanketed large portions of the city, the stone and wood structures disappearing behind wisps of gray. Though it was midday, the sun was also obscured, leaving the sky darker than usual.

A pale shadow passed over the steps of the temple before him, and Azael looked up to catch a glimpse of Rikoathel's silhouette descending through the haze in a wide spiral. The Iryllur soldier, who was larger than most, came to a soft landing inside the training area before coming up the steps of the temple. Azael instinctively scanned the area for Parnudel, finally noticing him approaching on foot from the left and only a few paces away. Having left their armor and weapons behind during their reconnaissance, both angels' movements were quieter than usual.

"My Rada," Parnudel announced, stopping before Azael and bowing his head.

Rikoathel did the same.

"What news do you bring me?"

Parnudel looked briefly at Rikoathel before answering the question. "The Myndarym believe that they are the only ones left in this realm. Those who prefer to go about in their natural forms are gathered in the city to the north. I listened to their conversations, and it is clear that they are seeking to expand their rulership. They are discussing issues of jurisdiction and how to divide the earth among them."

Azael crossed his arms and nodded for Parnudel to continue.

"There are two among them who prefer to go about in their animal forms. They are being sent out as messengers to the others who also roam the earth as animals."

"What is the message?" Azael asked, though he already suspected the answer.

"They are inviting their brethren to return to the city and participate in a rulership Council."

Azael squinted, and Parnudel immediately offered an explanation.

"I overheard one of them say that conflicts are inevitable as they each establish their own kingdoms. They see wisdom in gathering everyone to address these issues before they arise."

"And how are the invitations being received?" Azael asked.

Parnudel glanced at his fellow soldier, and Rikoathel took over the reporting. "My Rada. The messengers are continually going out and returning. We tracked five of these missions, and none of the animal Myndarym accepted the invitations. They seemed reluctant for reasons we couldn't discern."

Azael smiled. "Though your news of this growing kingdom might seem troubling, this division between them is a weakness that we could exploit. After they *shaped* the fortress, it was clear to me that the animal Myndarym resented Semjaza and wanted nothing to do with his kingdom. Scmjaza represented their opportunity to come to this realm and nothing more. They sought freedom from authority and unrestrained individuality, which is what they found living as the animals they *shaped*. They won't be enticed to join the Council because it only represents what they wish to avoid. It has nothing to offer them."

Azael's soldiers nodded at their leader's assessment.

"How many of the others are gathered in their city?"

"I counted ten, my Rada," Parnudel answered.

Azael unfolded his arms and rested his hands on the hilt of the pair of vaepkir at his lower back. The feel of the weapons helped him think. "The animal Myndarym are in the majority, which makes them a liability. The others are right to think that conflict is inevitable. For now, there is enough territory in this realm for all to go their separate ways. But they will cross paths again at some point, and when they do they will have greater interests at stake. What of the Council Myndarym? Do they possess any military strength to enforce their position? You said they have humans in their city."

"They do have humans, my Rada," Parnudel answered. "But not an army. I saw only females, and they were working throughout the city—happily, it seemed."

Azael frowned in confusion. "Happily? Are the Myndarym using them to build?"

"No, my Rada," Rikoathel answered. "The city is fully constructed. They have *shaped* it from the living trees of the forest. It spans the flatlands between the sea and higher elevations, all the way to the mountaintop where the Council meets. The women were gathering food and tending to animals."

"There were a few Nephiylim as well," Parnudel added. "But they were quite young. And I didn't see any evidence that they were breeding them like they were doing with the animals."

Azael held up a hand to halt the conversation. "What kind of food?"

Parnudel glanced at Rikoathel before answering. "All kinds, my Rada. Within the borders of their city are vast groves of trees, fields of shrubs and vines, and all manner of plantings. They collect what grows and use it as food. And they're doing the same thing with animals. They've gathered herds of creatures, but they aren't hunting them. They're collecting what the animals produce."

"And this sustains them?" Azael asked.

Parnudel glanced nervously at Rikoathel. "It must, my Rada. I did not observe them hunting."

Azael nodded, satisfied with the intelligence that had been gathered. Already, a plan was forming in his mind. Ages of warfare had taught him to see the weaknesses of his enemies and contrast them with the strength of his own resources. On the surface, his present situation was different than the grisly battles he'd waged in the Borderlands. But beneath the surface, the similarities were startling.

Azael turned his wandering eyes to Parnudel. "The intervals between training will need to be shortened. Inform Luhad that his soldiers are to conduct all exercises within the city, in plain view. Have him transport the entire contents of the armory out into the training area as well."

Parnudel nodded, but his eyes narrowed in confusion. "My Rada, are we preparing to attack the Council?"

Azael smiled. "Not yet." Then he turned to Rikoathel. "Locate one of the Myndar messengers of the air. On his return to the city, reveal your presence to him ... discreetly. Pique his curiosity and make sure he follows you back here, but do not let him believe it is anything other than his good fortune."

Rikoathel raised his head as he realized Azael's strategy. "Brilliant, my Rada."

Azael met his subordinate's intense gaze. "He must believe that you are unaware of his presence, or it won't work."

"Yes, my Rada!" Rikoathel replied, clearly eager to get started.

# 4

The breeze moved gently over the plains, the long grass waving in ripples like the surface of the Great Waters. Beads of dew clung to each blade like precious jewels sparkling in the first orange rays of morning light. Enoch's tunic was soaked from brushing past the droplets. The skin on his legs was on the verge of being uncomfortably cold. But the sun's warmth on his back countered the sensation, preserving him like an embrace from the Holy One.

His family's new dwelling was just ahead on the eastern edge of the city where the previous one used to be, but this one was surrounded by several others. Enoch was pleased to see this as another type of embrace—a connection that the Holy One had just pointed out to him. With a smile on his face, he approached the dwelling and circled around to the western side.

Zacol was leaning over, tending to a small fire outside the hut. "You were up early," she said.

"I wanted to get out into the fields before the sunrise," he replied.

Zacol nodded before standing up and walking through the doorway.

Enoch stood watching the flames for a moment. His interactions with Zacol had been awkward ever since his return. He hoped it might improve with time, but there had been no progress to confirm this hope. When the fire crackled, it stirred him from his thoughts. He inhaled deeply, suddenly noticing the nervousness that fluttered in his chest.

*Holy One, please help me with this. She was your child before she was my wife. Once again, I find myself lacking wisdom.*

Walking into their dwelling, Enoch found his wife's back turned as she cleaned up the remains of a meal that Enoch had missed. He watched her in silence, hoping that the right words would suddenly pop into his head. It occurred to him how humorous it was that only months ago he had confronted angels, even the smallest of which were twice his height. Most were soldiers who could have crushed him with one blow, or creatures that could have ended his earthly life with one bite from their vicious jaws. And here he was trembling with fear about speaking to his own wife. Had he learned anything during his time away?

"Didn't you get enough time with Him during your journey?" she asked, breaking the silence without turning around.

The words cut through him just as swiftly as the blades of Semjaza's soldiers through the bodies of the Speaker's angels. Enoch's heart sped, but he tried to envision his fear floating away from him like the mist on the breeze outside. He decided to reply before his imagined relief could actually be felt. "Hearing Him requires an ongoing relationship. It is not something that can be picked up and set down at will."

"Much like a marriage," Zacol mumbled.

Enoch felt his chest grow hot as if there were fire inside. "I didn't ask to be taken away from my family," he replied, louder than he intended. When he continued, it was softer and with more control. "The Holy One spoke, and I listened. Should I pretend that I cannot hear these things? Do you believe it would go better for any of us if I ignored him?"

Zacol stopped working and dropped her head. "Yes, I do … sometimes," she whispered.

Enoch walked over and stood beside his wife, who seemed ashamed to make eye contact with him. "You're jealous of the time I spend with the One who created me? The One who created you and everything else in this world? That's absurd!"

Zacol turned slowly toward him, her eyes floating upward until she was looking her husband in the eyes.

Enoch reached out and took her hand. "He is the only One worthy to receive all the honor and glory we can offer Him."

Zacol's head dipped almost imperceptibly, the faintest of nods.

"You are my wife, and I love you dearly. But my relationship to Him is completely different. The honor that is due Him can never be replaced, by anyone." Enoch's words were almost a whisper now, and their hut seemed painfully quiet.

Zacol pulled her hand away from Enoch and turned to walk across the room.

Enoch let her go. He knew how impassioned he could get when discussing the will of the Holy One, and he didn't want to unleash that upon her as though she were one of the Wandering Stars.

An awkward silence developed as Zacol lingered near their bed, looking down as if she were contemplating curling up there for the rest of the day. It would have been uncharacteristically strange for someone who rarely sat down until the sun was setting.

"You're right," she said, abruptly turning around. "I will never fulfill that position in your life, nor do I want to. But you just referred to it as a relationship, which means it's not entirely different from what we expect of each other. There are similarities. I just wish you would talk with me as much as you do with Him. Share yourself with me."

Enoch frowned. On the surface, Zacol's plea seemed genuine, but there was too much history between them to simply accept what was on the surface. "I truly wish I could, but you don't seem to care. You haven't even asked me about what happened when I was gone. When I tell Methu the things I saw and the places I went, you call it nonsense. You cannot imagine what I've witnessed or how I've suffered. You used to be the only one in this world who listened to me. And now I have all of these experiences that I want to share with my only friend and when I try to include you, you're always busy and distracted. I wonder if you even—"

"Someone has to work around here!" Zacol yelled suddenly.

Her words seemed to reach into the soil beneath him, unearthing years of buried tension. Enoch gritted his teeth and felt his fist slam down on the table next to him before he even realized what he was doing.

Zacol flinched.

Shame descended upon Enoch like a dense fog, curling down over his shoulders and around his chest. "I'm sorry," he offered, but he couldn't take back his demonstration of anger.

Zacol's hand was over her mouth and her eyes were closed.

Enoch took a deep breath to calm himself. Though he had been wrong to lash out, Zacol was on the wrong side of this argument. He wouldn't be deterred from speaking the truth, whether she wanted to hear it or not.

"Your work is a convenient excuse to hide behind. And that is what work does. Everyone in Sedekiyr is concerned with all of their daily tasks. It is the tasks that receive all of our attention. No one but me gives any attention to what the Holy One would have us concerned about. His desires are unrepresented among our people. It seems to me that you would have me set aside the one thing that truly matters and pretend to care about all of the things that matter least. How does that help the Shayetham? Isn't our tribe healthier if at least one person is listening for the voice of Him whose wisdom has no equal?"

Zacol had tears in her eyes, but at least they were open. At least she appeared to be listening. "Then what is He saying? Do you have some pressing message to deliver?"

"No," Enoch replied, exhaling the word from his mouth. "It doesn't always work like that. But I can feel His disappointment. He wishes I wasn't the only one to listen earnestly for His voice."

"So, there is no specific message beyond what you've been saying almost every day of your life?"

Enoch's shoulders slumped. "No."

"Then why not help out with the daily tasks in the meantime?"

Enoch reached up to scratch his beard before replying. "Because those things divert my attention. And there is a never-ending supply of them. Work is continually demanding. If I don't consciously decide to focus on His voice, the tasks will consume all of my attention and redirect my life."

Zacol smiled.

"What?"

She just shook her head.

"What?" he repeated.

It was clear that she was trying to restrain herself. When she spoke, it wasn't what he expected. "You are right that we don't give Him enough of our attention. But we don't live in the White City."

Enoch's eyebrows rose as if they had a will that was separate from the rest of his body.

"I was listening when you described it to Methu," she added.

Now a smile spread across his face.

"We live here on the earth," she continued. "And as you said, there are many things that must be done. Too many. There is no way around them. So ... when you concentrate solely on listening for His voice, it leaves the rest of us with more work to do and no time to do anything else."

Enoch opened his mouth to object, but Zacol held up her hand. "But the opposite is also true. When we allow our work to consume all of our time, there is nothing left for Him."

Now Enoch frowned because he couldn't anticipate where his wife was going with this line of reasoning.

"Unless something changes, there will always be two separate ways. You will remain divided from your people, and they will never understand you. This doesn't seem right to me. Do you think this is what He desires?"

"No," Enoch had to admit.

"Surely the Holy One knows that we must work. So there must be a balance. If you cannot concern yourself with our daily tasks and listen for His voice at the same time, how can you expect anyone else to do the same?"

Enoch was speechless. And though he didn't want to admit it, his wife was absolutely right.

"You are an elder of the Shayetham. You must show them that such a balance is possible. If not you, who else is able to teach them?"

Enoch stared at the floor as Zacol's words repeated themselves in his mind. Before long, a smile spread across his face and he found a little of his old humor coming back. "Easy for a woman to say. Men are not made to do more than one thing at a time."

Zacol smiled.

"By the way, where is Methu?"

Now Zacol laughed aloud.

Enoch laughed as well, finding the situation all the funnier because he honestly couldn't keep track of the boy and do anything else at the same time.

"He went to help build the new dwelling for Bilaj," she added as soon as she composed herself.

Enoch squinted.

"... because Bilaj and Tullah are marrying in three weeks' time?"

"Oh, I didn't know that," Enoch admitted.

"That's because you spend all of your time fishing with Methu like the young boys. Telling stories while the rest of the tribe is working." The smile on her face said that she was just poking at him for fun now.

Enoch nodded. "I'm teaching him all the things that the Holy One has taught me, so that I'm not the only one in the tribe who cares about what He cares about."

Zacol walked across the room and placed both hands on Enoch's arms. There was a twinkle in her eyes now. "And you do it while fishing with him, which is something he cares about. That is how people get along. You must share their cares, or they will not share yours. It is the same with the adults. They will never care about what the Holy One says if you continually diminish their concerns. You must get involved ... and not just as an act."

Enoch nodded his agreement, remembering similar words spoken to him by Ananel after he had been to the Eternal Realm and come back to the Myndarym.

*... continue to live among us. It is safer for you to remain familiar.*

"I keep silent most of the time," Enoch said, "so that I might only speak the words of the Holy One. He alone deserves our devotion. If the Shayetham will only listen because of my compromises, then they aren't truly listening for His voice, but to mine. I want them to listen for themselves, to draw their own conclusions. Each person should stand alone before Him and live their life accordingly."

"Of course, that's the goal," Zacol replied, finally going back to her cleaning. "It's an ideal that you've been seeking your whole life. But the tribe isn't responding to it. And as time goes by, they're moving farther away from Him. Doesn't it make sense to try something new? Why not choose an intermediate goal, something closer, and start making progress toward it?"

Enoch lifted his eyes to the ceiling as the reality of his failure hung heavy on his shoulders. Zacol was right. After all these years, Enoch's own tribe wouldn't listen any more than the Wandering Stars did. Had that also been because of his approach? Would the angels of heaven have responded differently if he hadn't been so direct? Suddenly, the sight of the thatched roof seemed to communicate what Zacol had been trying to make him understand.

"They didn't make this dwelling for us. They made it for you and Methu," he stated.

Zacol set down the earthen pot that she had just picked up, turning to face her husband without a reply.

"My absence improved your social standing," he continued, saying it as bluntly as he could for his own good. "Now that I have returned, the respect you earned is at risk." Zacol's silence was all the confirmation he needed. How could he be an elder to the Shayetham when he couldn't be anything more than a hindrance to his family?

"Where is the new dwelling for Bilaj?" he asked.

A tear spilled down Zacol's cheek and she reached up to wipe it. "The south end, almost to his father's dwelling. Why?"

"I'm going to help," Enoch replied.

\* \* \* \*

Methu reached down and grabbed a handful of grass by the base of their stalks. He shook his hand back and forth, loosening up the soil before pulling. The grass, longer than his arm, came out roots and all. He slid the stalks into the last bit of space in the cloth bag over his shoulder and looked up to see how his progress compared to the other children scattered across the fields. Two boys were already carrying their loads back toward the city, but the rest were still harvesting.

Methu smiled to himself. Third out of hundreds wasn't bad, considering he was one of the youngest. He pulled the bag around to the front of his body and held it tightly as he began running north to where the adults were gathered. If he hurried, he just might reach the building site before the other boys. As he neared, he could see dozens of men driving the support poles for the new dwelling into the ground. One man stood on the ground, with a second man on his shoulders pounding the blunt end of the pole with a rock. The sharpened end plunged down into the damp soil with each blow, until the pole sat at the same height as the others. On the opposite end of the dwelling, where the building had first begun, two men were just beginning to bend the entrance support poles toward each other to form a rigid arch.

Methu reached the building site before the other boys and opened his bag, dropping his bundle of grass on the ground where the adults had told the children to keep them until they were needed.

A creaking sound drew Methu's attention back to the entrance.

The two men had just lashed the top of the poles together with a braided grass cord. Their work looked secure, but they were staring at each other as though something were wrong.

*Snap!*

One of the poles broke while the other suddenly returned to its straight, vertical position. The broken portion of the other pole swung upward on the cord and launched into the air, spinning end over end until it came down in the field a dozen paces away.

"It was too dry!" one of the men yelled. "Danush. Tell them to cut greener stalks!"

The other man was fingering the notch in the upright pole where the cord had slipped loose.

Methu looked from one man to another, taking in what had just happened. But his gaze eventually swung back to the field where the broken pole stuck out of the soil at an angle. He'd never seen anything this exciting before. While the adults were frustrated by the setback to their efforts, Methu couldn't get the image of the flying pole out of his mind.

"Is that all you can carry?" came a voice from behind.

Methu turned as another boy, much taller, walked past and dropped his bundle of grass on the ground. It was Zejuad. He was three years older, but his load was only twice what Methu had harvested.

"Is that as fast as you can work?" Methu replied.

Zejuad scowled and started to take the bag off his shoulder.

Methu wasn't sure if the boy was preparing to give him a beating, or just taking a break from working, but he decided to run anyway. He dodged around the nearest adult and then ran down the length of the new dwelling. He slowed when he got to the end, noticing his father up on someone's shoulders.

Enoch was striking at the end of another support pole, and he looked exhausted.

"That's good," another man said from the ground.

Enoch climbed down from the larger man's shoulders and wiped his brow before bending over with his hands on his knees.

He dropped the rock on the ground, then looked up. "Hello," he said, finally noticing Methu. "What are you working on?"

Methu smiled so large that it felt like his face might split. "We're gathering grass for the walls and roof."

Enoch nodded and wiped his brow again before standing up to suck in a breath of air.

"We're going to need saplings soon," one of the men suggested.

Enoch nodded, then glanced over to a procession of men and women walking single file out to the nearby forest. "Alright. I'll go help gather."

"Thanks. We're almost done here anyway," the man replied.

Enoch took another deep breath and then wove through the crowd and began heading toward the forest. Methu watched him go, suddenly feeling happy, as if he were fishing instead of working. He wasn't sure why he felt the way he did, but he knew he liked it.

The sound of laughing broke through his thoughts and Methu turned to find the cause.

"It took him three times longer than anyone else," one of the adults said, a huge grin on his face.

"Well, he's small, so I thought he would be better on top. Can you imagine if he tried to hold me up there?"

The other man let out a snort before his laughing became so intense that it turned silent, his body shaking in great spasms. When he gained control of himself, he wiped a tear from his eye and looked at the other man, turning serious all of a sudden. "He's too small and weak. Don't let him help with this anymore. He's better suited to do the gathering like the children, or we won't finish before the sun sets."

The other man shrugged his shoulders and turned to lift the next pole off the ground.

Methu's teeth were grinding together. His whole body felt tense, like a support pole bent over and lashed in place. Didn't they know it was his father they were making fun of? Didn't they care that Enoch was their elder? Methu stared hard at the men, but they went about their work and didn't notice, as if he were nothing more than an insect to be ignored.

After a long moment of silence, Methu turned and noticed that Zejuad was walking back out into the field. The majority of the other children were either dropping off their first loads, or heading back out to harvest the next. Methu gave the men a dirty look before clutching his bag tightly against his chest and running back to the fields. For some reason he could feel himself moving faster than ever, and he knew that he could harvest more grass than anyone—no matter how old or strong they were.

# 5

Far below, the shores of the Great Waters slid by. Dark blue colors yielded to the brown and gray of soil, then a bright green of grassy plains. Slowly, the greens darkened as the plains gave way to forests. The land rose in elevation and its smooth texture grew coarse, its details becoming more apparent as it reached upward to the sky. But even when the land had reached as far as it could, ending in the jagged peaks of its colossal mountains, Fyarikel was still looking down on them. The wind slid under his feathers, whistling along his sleek body with just enough resistance to give him control over his movements.

The Myndar, wearing the form of a great bird of prey, circled to the south and looked out upon the city of Senvidar, its majestic trees woven together like an elaborate tapestry that had been draped across the earth. On its western border it touched the Great Waters. It spread eastward across the plains and foothills, eventually climbing up the western face of the mountains. Its eastern border sat atop the peak of the mountains where the Council of Myndarym resided. As impressive as it was, the city was now as large as it would ever be. Its construction had progressed rapidly after the Amatru had *shifted* into this realm and defeated Semjaza. In the absence of his insatiable presence, and with the anger of the Amatru pacified, the Myndarym had put all their efforts into *shaping* the earth and forests. But their unfinished work had come to a swift end months ago, when a prophet of the Shayetham had proclaimed a judgment upon them from the Holy One.

The Myndarym, whose very name had become synonymous with their ability to *shape* themselves and others, suddenly lost what made them unique. Neither could they *shift* back into the Eternal. The realm they had *shaped* from the beginning of measured time had suddenly become their prison. But the attack against their identity had failed. The Holy One underestimated their resolve. They refused to see themselves as trapped. This realm, seemingly abandoned by the Holy One, held so many possibilities. It was now self-sufficient, because they had made it so. Everything they needed to thrive was here with them. And this realm was large enough for each to establish and rule over his or her own kingdom. All that was needed was to agree upon the rules of ownership, which required a gathering of the Myndarym. This had been their primary task of late, and though they had met with some resistance among those in animal forms, they had also made much progress. The number of Council members was growing, and the collective body would soon be ready to begin negotiations.

A new beginning was in sight, but what Fyarikel had just witnessed could undo it all. He pulled his wings inward and dove. The air sped past his feathered body while his talons stayed tucked, out of the flow of air. The mountaintop expanded to fill the vision of his keen eyes and he quickly sighted the stepped, circular meeting area where the other Myndarym had been spending the majority of their time. With the smallest of wing adjustments, he flattened his trajectory and approached the center of the meeting area, spreading his wings at the last moment to slow himself for a perfectly gentle landing.

As soon as his talons scraped the stone beneath him, he pulled his wings around himself and stood up to his full height. The eyes of all the Council members were on him. He could see in their expressions that they were alarmed by his less-than-formal arrival.

"Fyarikel, is something wrong?" a female voice asked.

Fyarikel turned and locked eyes with Danel. She had risen from her place on the steps. "Yes," he replied, his voice like the grating of metal upon stone. But like all the Myndarym in this realm, he retained a complex arrangement of vocal chords that allowed him to produce any sound he wished, despite his chosen form. "I'm afraid I bring troubling news."

The rest of the Council members either stood or leaned forward from where they had reclined.

"Have the rest of our brethren not accepted our offer?" asked Zahmesh, a tall Myndar in his natural form, with a long beard that spilled down over his bare, muscled chest.

"The answers continue to be mixed," Fyarikel replied. "But we have a bigger problem. Semjaza's forces were not completely destroyed."

Gasps of surprise sounded from every direction.

"Upon my return from the west, I caught sight of something large flying through the trees. It was only a glimpse, as it was keeping below the forest canopy, but I knew right away it wasn't one of the creatures we *shaped*."

"Where was this?" Danel asked, concern temporarily marring her otherwise flawless skin.

"Along the coast of the Great Waters. It was moving south." Before the others could ask more questions, Fyarikel proceeded with his recounting. "I changed course to follow it, coming down from the sky to just above the trees. I let it stay ahead of me at the limit of my vision, and when it left the forests for the plains, I landed in the trees and waited."

"Who was it?"

"It was Rikoathel, but I didn't learn this until I followed him all the way to Khelrusa. That is where I chose a vantage point and observed. In time, I also identified Parnudel and Azael."

More gasps of surprise.

"How did they survive?"

"Why didn't the Amatru finish them?"

Fyarikel glanced from side to side, rotating his feathered head to locate each questioner with his piercing eyes. "The

Amatru don't know, or they would have finished their task while they were here. This is now our problem to address."

"Are there more?"

"I only observed the three Iryllurym," he answered. "But it seems that they have resumed Semjaza's work in earnest. There were thousands of Kahyin men training in warfare. Azael was teaching them how to use metal weapons that were being transported out of the mines. It was clear to me that they were preparing for something."

"This changes everything," Danel said quietly, before sitting down on the dark stone steps.

"Not if we strike now," Armaros replied. The intensity in his eyes was contrasted by his statuesque human appearance.

"With what? Our Shayeth women?" Satarel countered. Though human in form, his light complexion and dark hair wouldn't have fit in with any of the human descendants.

"No. We'll do it ourselves," Armaros said. "We still have the weapons we *shaped* for the Amatru."

Satarel shook his head. "No. They were made for soldiers two and three times our size ... with a few exceptions," he said, gesturing to Rameel, who stood on the west side of the meeting area. Rameel was one who retained the height of his natural Myndar form, the temporal equivalent of his eternal body. But his black skin and featherless wings were stark reminders that most of them had strayed from their natural forms in some way.

"Perhaps if we were still able to *shape* ..." Satarel continued. "Without that, we cannot attack in such an obvious manner."

"What other manner is there?" Armaros asked.

"To diffuse Azael's power," Baraquijal offered. He also wore a human form and seemed just as aware as Satarel of its limitations.

"That's also what I was thinking," Satarel replied. "Here we are attempting to assemble a Council of equals. Why not include them under a banner of peace and integrate their efforts with ours?"

"You want to make Azael an ally before he can become an enemy," Turel stated, with a grin. He looked like the male version of Danel, with pale skin and hair.

"That's right," Satarel replied.

Rameel frowned. "What's to stop him from seeing our invitation as a weakness? Why wouldn't he just invade Senvidar with his Kahyin army?"

Arakiba was nodding in agreement. Like Rameel, he had dark skin and a thinly muscled body. But he lacked wings and Rameel's imposing height. The features of his face were distorted, like a Marotru soldier, and it was obvious that he had prepared himself to prey on the fear of humans to define his place in this world. "That's what I would do," he growled.

"He doesn't know we can't *shape*," Ezekiyel pointed out. He too wore a human form, but there was a confidence in the way he spoke, something intangible that likely came from his esteemed position as a master of *shaping* and *shifting*. "He won't attack us as long as he believes that we are capable of destroying him."

"And how long could that secret possibly be kept?" Armaros asked.

"As long as it takes," Danel replied. "Each one of us is capable of patience ... and of controlling our words."

Rameel and Arakiba both smiled at this.

Kokabiel was rubbing his forehead with frustration.

"In the meantime," Satarel continued, "we integrate ourselves into whatever he is doing, and we let him help us as well. We demonstrate that success requires our mutual involvement."

"We're moving in the wrong direction with this topic," Kokabiel finally spoke. "We've just rid ourselves of our Amatru authority and now we're discussing how to make ourselves slaves to them once more?"

"Not slaves," Satarel argued. "Equals."

"Ha!" Kokabiel barked. "Azael looked down his nose at all of us. He would never consider us as equals, unless we were soldiers."

"War may very well be in our future," Rameel pointed out. "And I would rather have his armies on our side."

"Against our own kind?" Danel asked.

"We've already agreed that those who don't join the Council are liabilities," Arakiba interjected. "If they choose not to participate in this Council, they also yield their rights of ownership of this realm. Conflict is inevitable."

"What incentive would Azael have to join us?" Danel asked. "It's one thing to speak in broad terms. It's quite another to have an actual plan."

Satarel nodded before standing up from his seat. "We'll find out what he needs, and then we'll make him see that we are his way of getting it ... but on a schedule that suits our needs."

Fyarikel glanced from one Myndar to the next before adding, "Their Nephiylim looked quite thin, and the Kahyin as well."

The conversation went quiet as everyone on the Council turned to look at each other. Fyarikel knew what they must be thinking, because the idea had just occurred to him as well. The Kahyin's reputation for hunting was well understood, but so was its inadequacy to feed large populations. Semjaza had already run up against this problem while they were still under his rule.

Finally, Zaquel leaned forward. She was known for seeing things clearly and from a more unique perspective than most. When she spoke, her fellow Myndarym usually listened. "There are several mutual needs to be exploited here. I'm confident that we can uncover more as we discuss this further. But what is needed now, Fyarikel, is for you to go to Khelrusa. Present yourself to Azael on our behalf before they discover we are here. Invite him to attend the Council. Carry yourself with all the honor that is due a Myndar, and let him see your confidence. Make it clear to him that he and his Iryllurym are not our equals, but we are inviting them to participate anyway, so that their interests will be represented in future endeavors."

Fyarikel glanced quickly around the circle. Everyone nodding their agreement, except for Kokabiel, who seemed silently reluctant. "Very well," he replied before spreading his wings.

\* \* \* \*

THE UPPER NEPHIYL CHAMBER
MURAKSZHUG, KHELRUSA

Murmurs and whispers grew to a chorus of talking and footsteps. Lying on his side near the back wall of the cavern, Hyrren stirred—lifting his head to see what caused the excitement among his siblings. Through the faint light of a torch on the wall, hundreds upon hundreds of bodies could be seen moving in the direction of the only passage in or out of this stone room. Was someone bringing food? It was too much for Hyrren to hope, so he pushed himself up to a seated position and waited while the younger children crowded around the metal gate, sticking their hands through and calling out to whomever was on the other side.

Slowly, the noises shifted from higher-pitched optimistic tones to downturned mumbles of disappointment. Faces turned in his direction. Whispers of Hyrren's name drifted through the chamber, echoing many times over. Someone was asking for him.

Hyrren glanced up. Where the wall of the cavern rounded to become the ceiling, several faces stared out of the opening of another cave. The winged Nephiyl children were watching the commotion from their high vantage, but Vengsul, the oldest, was looking directly at Hyrren. Though they shared no blood relation, Vengsul had also been born in Mudena Del-Edha, which made him a brother. The expression on his face mirrored what Hyrren felt—that these visits by the Kahyin used to be met with excitement. Not anymore. There was only sadness and pain down here in the depths of the mountain.

Hyrren stood, wincing at the way his coarse tunic stuck to the wounds of his chest and abdomen, pulling at the scabs that had formed. He cautiously adjusted his clothing as he walked across the cavern, towering over the other children. Though he had only lived through sixteen cycles of the sun, he was the elder of this motley tribe of forgotten creatures.

The crowd of earth-toned bodies parted, and Hyrren approached the gate of iron. Through the lattice of thick metal bars, a Kahyin man waited. By the torch in his hand, Hyrren could see that he was one of Luhad's closest men. He was tall and muscular, by human standards, but still short compared to Hyrren. Luhad, who usually accompanied his men on such visitations, was nowhere to be found.

"The lower chamber needs cleaning," the man said.

Hyrren frowned. "It's not used anymore."

The man didn't answer.

Hyrren looked over the man's shoulder into the passage behind him. "Where's Imikal?"

"He's busy with something else."

Hyrren looked back to the children behind him, their eager faces hoping for something to eat. Then he turned back to the Kahyin man. "No food today?"

The man didn't even bother to answer. He just reached up and unlatched the gate.

As it swung open, Hyrren walked through it and into the tunnel. There was no lock on the rusted metal bars other than the fear by which the Kahyin ruled them, but it felt just as effective. The clang of the closing gate sounded harsh in the narrow space, and Hyrren allowed it to jolt him out of his thoughts. He had learned that it was best not to carry anything into these times of work. He kept silent for the rest of the trip, following the man through the winding passage—always turning to the right, always down, farther under the mountain. Eventually, the passage widened, spilling out into a chamber with a low ceiling that seemed to stretch away to a black horizon. In the foreground, stalactites hung down from the ceiling, dripping into a calm pool of dark water. Something pale floated ominously in the water.

The Kahyin man turned and placed his torch into a hole in the wall. "Take care of it," he said before turning and walking into the dark tunnel from where they had just come.

Hyrren watched him leave, a sense of nervousness growing in his stomach. When the passage was silent again, Hyrren grabbed the torch from the wall and turned to face the cavern once again. His eyes came to rest on the pale object in the water, holding him in a trance as he carefully stepped down the gently sloping rock. The torch wavered and crackled as though it were warning him, but Hyrren kept moving. Whatever was in the water couldn't be ignored, so there was no use in trying.

As he neared the edge, two more pale shapes could be seen floating together, a few paces out. A stench drifted to his nostrils, and Hyrren suddenly turned his head, his eyes closing involuntarily. He concentrated on the crackling sound of the torch in his hand while he gathered himself, trying to suppress the memories that had come to mind. But it was no use.

He remembered the fish laid out on the underground shore. He could see their blood running down the smooth rock, following the cracks, gathering in the level places. The Nephiyl children crawled up the rock with their human arms and hands, pushing with their lower serpentine appendages, while their mouths dug into the scaled flesh. They weren't coordinated enough to control their movements in the water and eat at the same time, so Aifett had put the food on the ground outside the water.

*"I cannot feed my children and yours at the same time," she explained. "I've been hunting all day and this is not even enough for us."*

*"I know," Hyrren replied. "They should be free to hunt for themselves."*

*"So should we," Vengsul added. "My children were meant for the skies, not to be kept under the earth like monsters."*

*Hyrren nodded. Aifett was the only one who could leave and return without being seen by the Kahyin. Beneath the lake was a maze of passages that led under the mountain and all the way out to the Great Waters. It was how his father's Vidirym had been able to come here and mate with the human women. But the gods were gone now, and their orphans crowded the underground lake like a teeming school of fish. When Hyrren and the rest of the Nephiylim from Semjaza's* fortress had come to Khelrusa, Aifett had found her way in below the water. Though still a child herself of only fourteen sun cycles, she had become a mother to them all. She went out and hunted for them. She taught them the language that her Vidir father had taught her. But she couldn't continue providing for everyone. Hyrren and Vengsul knew it.

"Leave this place," Hyrren told her. "Take your children and let them swim the open water. The Kahyin will not realize it for a long time. And they cannot follow you anyway."

Aifett's human face scrunched into a look of pain. Her black eyes looked intently at both of her siblings. "But what about you?"

Hyrren looked at his winged brother.

Vengsul shook his head. "We can't get our children out of here without being seen."

"Perhaps at night?" his sister protested. "When the Kahyin are sleeping?"

"No," Vengsul replied. "Some of my children are too young yet to fly. They would have to be carried."

"And the gates at the entrance to the mines are locked," Hyrren added. "Besides, my children make too much noise. We'd never get there without being stopped."

Aifett bowed her head. Long, flat tendrils of blue and green slid off her shoulders and swung from her head where a human's hair would have been. "There must be another way."

"I'll figure out how to free the rest of us," Hyrren promised. "But you can save these children now."

Aifett lifted her head and faced them. "When you are free, look for us in the Great Waters. Call us with the signal," she said. If her dark eyes were capable of crying, there would have been tears there.

"We will," Vengsul replied, reaching up to gently touch his sister's cheek. "Now go, before it's too late."

Aifett's body pivoted, propelled by the many flat appendages that swirled effortlessly beneath the water's surface. She looked down upon the younger ones of her kind, some of whom shared her same father. A series of clicking *noises emanated from her throat, carried aloft by a mournful wail. Though Hyrren didn't understand the language of the Vidirym, he knew that she was telling her children to follow her.*

*The creatures obediently slithered backwards into the water, becoming more agile as soon as they were inside the liquid environment. Aifett fixed her eyes on Hyrren as she moved backward, her bare upper body seeming to hover over the surface until it slipped downward. The water barely rippled, and then she was gone.*

The smell of rotting flesh was strong in Hyrren's nostrils, but there were no fish on the shore. Hyrren let his gaze drop to the water, ready to face what he already knew to be waiting for him. A small body floated in the shallows. It was facedown, thankfully. Its arms were by its side, tiny human fingers curled upward out of the water. The tendrils from its head and those of its lower body drifted lifelessly in the water, no longer swirling but hanging limp. The skin, drained of its sea colors, was now a pale gray.

Hyrren exhaled as his lungs suddenly felt cold. He propped his torch against the dry stone and removed his tunic, laying it out on the floor of the cavern. His hands and arms seemed to move of their own accord, his body doing what his mind couldn't accept. They reached down into the water and held the dead child—the precious Nephiyl that the Kahyin had carelessly put there, with no one to accept and feed it. It was soft beneath his fingers, and he felt his legs go weak as he lifted it. Water dripped from its long tendrils, darkening the dry stone. He laid it upon the tunic, suddenly feeling sorry that he had to expose the child's flesh to such coarse material. He kept it facedown, unable to bear what might look back at him. Then he stood and walked down into the water, choosing his footing carefully as he waded in the deeper section. When he was waist-deep in the dark lake, he reached out with both arms. His eyes concentrated on the stalactite above him, glossy white stone that never dried out, always dripping. His hands touched soft flesh and his peripheral vision could make out the pale, floating shapes. He pulled them closer before lifting them to his chest without taking his eyes off the ceiling. The smell was everywhere now, and he couldn't avoid it. Instead, he turned and marched as quickly as he could to the shore, laying the other children on top of the first and wrapping the corners of his tunic over them. He rinsed his hands in the lake, then grabbed the torch in one hand and the tunic, now more of a sling, in the other.

He didn't dare stop to think about what he was doing. He just moved as quickly as possible, carrying this precious load into the tunnel and upward. With the flames lighting his way, Hyrren marched. His pace was quick. He wasn't pushing carts filled with stone. He was carrying a sling that felt lighter than it should have. Upward he went, winding to the left. He passed the chamber where his children were gathered, waiting for food. He kept climbing, passing through tunnels with metal tracks along the ground and chambers with walls of crumbling rock.

He marched as a soldier, fast and sure, until he reached the old smelting room. It was small, and most of the old furnaces hadn't been used in quite some time. But one roared with orange flames. A silhouette moved in front of it. Hyrren lifted his torch and moved his arm in front of his eyes to block the glare.

Imikal crawled across the floor like a spider, a look of fear in his eyes.

"Imikal?" Hyrren called.

"I'm sorry. I'm sorry!" his brother replied.

Hyrren picked up his pace, jogging the rest of the way to the furnace until coming to a dead stop. A human body lay on the ground, slumped against the open furnace door. Its skin was charred at the extremities, and there were hunks of flesh missing in many places.

Hyrren turned to his brother, cowering on the ground.

"I'm sorry," Imikal said again. His words were garbled.

It took a moment before Hyrren noticed the blood on his chest. And there was something in his mouth. "What are you doing?"

Tears streamed from Imikal's eyes as he reached up to wipe his mouth with the back of his hand. "I couldn't stand the hunger anymore. And they want us to just throw them in ..."

Hyrren looked back to the body on the floor, realizing now that it was female—one of the Shayeth descendants. She'd just died giving birth to a Nephiyl child. Such was the fate of all the *mothers*, as they were called. It was one of Imikal's responsibilities to dispose of the bodies.

Hyrren took a step closer to his brother. "Get up."

Imikal scooted backward, flinching as he covered his face.

Hyrren scowled at his brother. "When have I ever hit you? I am not a human."

Imikal looked up. "You're not mad, then?"

"No. Now get up off the floor. You don't belong there."

Imikal pulled his feet underneath him and stood, moving slowly as if he were still expecting Luhad's whip to come out of the darkness and strike him. His gaze shifted about, afraid to settle on Hyrren's confident stare. Instead, Imikal seemed to suddenly take notice of the wounds across Hyrren's face. He looked down at his brother's chest and then his eyes swung to the side, noticing that Hyrren was carrying something. "What's that?"

Hyrren moved the fabric sling behind himself and dropped his torch before reaching out to place his hand on Imikal's shoulder. "Look at me. I'm not mad at you."

The skin above Imikal's eyebrows wrinkled, but his gaze finally settled on his brother's.

"We are the sons of Semjaza. And we do not crawl on the ground like animals. Understand?"

Imikal nodded.

Hyrren kept looking deep into his brother's eyes until he felt sure that Imikal grasped how important this was. Then he proceeded, "If the humans will not feed us by their spears, they will feed us with their bodies."

Imikal's worried expression vanished.

"Take the meat down to the children and share it with them. Do not let Luhad or any of his men see you."

Imikal nodded. Then after a long pause, the worried expression returned. "Is this wrong?"

The answer came into Hyrren's mind immediately, but he gave it some consideration before he let it out. "They are not Nephiyl. The mothers are nothing more than wombs to us. And the rest of them are no better than animals."[6]

Imikal squinted. It was obvious that the words were both shocking and sensible to him at the same time. Finally, he seemed to accept what he'd been told. He stepped past Hyrren and bent down to lift the body of the woman from the ground.

Hyrren turned, keeping the bodies of the Nephiyl children behind him as Imikal walked to a cart and dropped the woman inside. The cart squealed until Imikal got it moving. He looked back over his shoulder one last time before leaving the chamber, and Hyrren nodded confidently to him.

The sound of the cart faded into the darkness. Hyrren was alone once more. He turned and stepped toward the open door of the furnace. The fire was still burning, but the intensity of its heat had lessened. Hyrren knelt before the door, clutching the bundle with both hands. He waited for a moment, struck by the contrast of how light the children's bodies felt while the weight of their wasted lives seemed immeasurable. His eyes welled with tears and he closed them to keep from losing control of himself.

"I'm sorry," he whispered. "I've failed you."

Silence was the only response. But Hyrren understood its message clearer than if the pale Nephiyl children had spoken. *It is time*, they said without words.

Hyrren opened his eyes and tossed the bundle into the blazing mouth of the furnace. Then he slammed the door and latched it before standing.

"It is time."

# 6

Fyarikel came down gently upon the valley floor, but his talons dug deeply into the soil nevertheless. Overhead, the sun was doing its best to break through the veil of gray fog. Beside him, a raised dirt road continued through the central gate of the city and wound its way up the stair-stepped valley to the temple at the top. It was the same road that stretched in the opposite direction, all the way to Mudena Del-Edha. But the Myndar wouldn't follow it into Khelrusa. He would do nothing to reveal his familiarity with this city. Instead, he waited as a stranger outside the gate.

The Kahyin were moving about the top of the stone wall which spanned the valley. Though still quite far away, Fyarikel could easily make out their facial expressions. He could see their concern and the tension in their body language, their frantic movements. He kept still, waiting for someone to approach him. Several minutes passed before a terrified Kahyin male came stumbling out of the gate. He walked down the road with uneasy steps, then veered off into the field where Fyarikel waited.

The closer he got, the smaller he looked. By the time the human stood before him, Fyarikel wondered if this is what rodents looked like just before the mighty raptors he had *shaped* dug their talons into the rodents' soft flesh.

"I have come to speak with Azael," he screeched.

The man bowed. "He waits for you in the temple. He has sent me to escort you," he replied, swallowing the lump of fear in his throat.

Fyarikel lifted his gaze and focused his large eyes upon the temple in the distance. "Tell him I come in peace. And I request that he leave the safety of his city to speak with me, as is customary."

The man's eyes grew large with surprise, but he quickly bowed and backed away. When he reached the road, he turned and began running.

Fyarikel smiled inwardly, but prepared himself for the next meeting. It was one thing to project your authority to a human; quite another to maintain your confidence among enemy soldiers. Long moments passed. The thin haze that had allowed visibility into the city eventually grew dense, pouring like water down from the forests on either side of the valley. Khelrusa was hidden, and Fyarikel straightened his posture, expecting Azael to arrive any second. It was standard procedure for ambassadors to take advantage of any opportunity to surprise the opposite side—to unsettle them before negotiations.

A faint whoosh of air sounded overhead.

Fyarikel settled his wings and waited.

A massive, dark shape materialized from the mist before him, landing upon the soil with a powerful thump. Rikoathel pulled his wings inward and strode forward. His vaepkir were sheathed but he was still intimidating, being outfitted in full battle armor. When he came to within a few paces, he stopped, removed his helmet, and stood at attention.

"No sudden movements," whispered a voice from behind.

It was all Fyarikel could do to keep from jumping with fright. But he maintained his steady posture and lazily turned his head, catching sight of Parnudel standing a few paces behind him— also in full battle armor. How he had gotten there without making a sound was a mystery.

Azael appeared out of the fog along the road. He walked casually, as though he had nothing to fear, but it was an act. If he'd inspected the battlefield after Semjaza's defeat, which was likely, he should have plenty of reasons to fear.

Fyarikel locked eyes with the Iryllur and tried to imagine him as prey, which only worked until the moment the former soldier of the Amatru stopped in front of him.

"You wished to speak with me." It should have been a question, but Azael stated it as though he were pointing out evidence.

"I come in peace with a message on behalf of the Myndarym."

"Do you?" Azael asked. "Now you come in peace … after betraying us?"

Fyarikel could feel the pace of his heart quicken, anticipating and fearing a confrontation. But he told himself that he could kill these soldiers anytime he wanted. He convinced himself that he could dismantle their physical bodies with just a few notes of *unshaping*. And his body believed the lie that used to be true. His heart slowed. "It was Semjaza who first betrayed us. But soldiers aren't known for their capacity to make logical connections. You're more … action oriented. So I'll forgive your inability to think the matter through."

Azael's red eyes flashed with rage, but his body was otherwise calm.

"What is your message, Myndar?" Azael said, almost spitting out the last word. "Make it quick before I'm forced to take your head out of an action-oriented sense of duty to my fallen soldiers."

Behind Azael, Rikoathel smiled.

Fyarikel smiled as well, hoping they would interpret it as such through his bird features. "Despite my desire to see you try, I have come with an offer."

Azael's head rose just slightly, but he didn't respond.

"The anger of the Amatru has been pacified. Semjaza and his soldiers were the sacrifice to achieve that. Now the Amatru are gone, and we are here. This is a new world. Whatever our past grievances might have been, we mustn't allow them to dictate our future. We have the opportunity to create an entirely new existence for ourselves, without the nuisance of the conventions that plagued our previous home. Here, there are no Marotru, so there is no need for the classifications of Myndar, or Iryllur. We are all gods."

Azael crossed his arms, but stayed quiet. His eyes softened a bit, hinting that he just might be intrigued.

"We are following through with what Semjaza promised us. On the evening of the fifth full moon from now, there will be a gathering. We are meeting to share the plans for our individual kingdoms. We will determine the boundaries of our separate territories, possibilities of overlapping jurisdiction, rules of interaction, and the division of physical resources. It is our desire that each would have a robust and prosperous kingdom over which to rule. So we will also discuss any potential deficiencies among the territories—in food resources, building materials, and such—to mitigate potential future issues. In the early stages, it will be a combined effort until all the kingdoms are established."

Fyarikel couldn't interpret Azael's body language, but something had changed inside him. Fyarikel hoped that he had put just the right amount of emphasis on the food-production issue. He wanted it to sound like an accidental but fortunate development for Azael. And he hoped that the soldier was warming up to these ideas.

"We, the members of the Council, invite you to join us so that your interests may be factored into these decisions. And it seems to me that you do, indeed, have interests," Fyarikel finished, glancing toward the city that was just becoming visible again through the mist.

Azael crossed his arms and considered the invitation. "The evening of the fifth full moon?"

Fyarikel nodded.

"Where will the Council take place?"

"I will give you more details as the time approaches," Fyarikel answered.

"How many have agreed to this?"

"Dozens, so far. And the rest are being contacted as we speak."

Azael turned his head to the side and stared at the ground for a moment. It appeared that he was weighing the pros and cons, which came as a relief to Fyarikel, who had thought that the soldier might reject it outright. And that would put them all at risk.

Azael finally looked up. "We accept your invitation."

Fyarikel nodded, masking his enthusiasm so that he wouldn't appear desperate. "I will return soon with a more complete list of the topics that the other Council members will wish to discuss. This will give us all time to prepare. And if there is anything you want to add, I will take it to the other members."

Azael nodded.

Rikoathel's rigid posture relaxed.

Fyarikel turned his head and saw that Parnudel had backed off a few steps.

"Next time," Azael added, "you may come straight into the city. The temple at the top of the hill."

Fyarikel inclined his head before spreading his wings.

\* \* \* \*

Azael watched the Myndar rise into the gray sky and head south, doing his best to keep from betraying the location of their city. But it was a wasted effort. Azael knew where they were located, and he also understood their hidden motives. He had laid a trap and the Myndarym had walked right into it. Now he understood why Semjaza took pleasure in strategy. It was warfare of a different kind, but no less enjoyable.

"You played your part perfectly, my Rada," Parnudel said softly. "He wanted very much to convince you."

Azael smiled. "Did you see his anger? He hates me almost as much as I hate him. It is a good balance ... for a time."

"How long, my Rada?" Rikoathel asked.

"Only until we shore up our weaknesses with their strengths. Then we will overthrow the whole traitorous lot."

Parnudel came closer to his fellow soldiers. "My vaepkir thirst for enemy blood. I hope the wait isn't too long."

Azael smiled. "We will wait as long as it takes. And the taste of blood will be all the sweeter for it."

* * * *

SEDEKIYR

The sun was directly overhead, and the blue sky was more visible than usual. Enoch took one hand off the walking stick across his shoulders to wipe the sweat that stood thick on his brow. With a heavy cloth bag slung over each end, the stick began to tip without equal support. Enoch quickly put his hand under it again, jumping awkwardly to the side for a few steps to regain his balance. When the bags stopped swaying, he hiked his old walking stick farther up on his shoulders and readied himself to start moving again.

His dwelling was only a short distance away and his task was almost complete. *No more wiping*, he told himself. It had cost him his momentum, and the momentary relief wasn't worth it. The sweat would just return anyway. He took one step, then another, until he was moving again. Clumps of grass passed beneath his feet, trying to turn his ankles at every opportunity. Enoch navigated around them, trying to maintain a steady pace without hurrying. Before long, he felt the presence of something large, and he lifted his head to see that he was standing just outside of his grass hut.

*I made it!*

He squatted to the ground, legs shaking from exertion. The walking stick slipped backward off his shoulders and he let it go. The bags landed on the grass with a dull thump, and Enoch turned to make sure they hadn't split open before he doubled forward with hands on knees, trying to catch his breath. Tiny puffs of grain dust swirled at his toes, floating over the ground and drifting between the blades of grass. It was as if he were a bird flying high over the land, looking down on the mist as it swam through the plains and forests. Each tiny particle was distinct, but moved in rhythm with those around it.

*The particles shared a luminescence, glowing as though they were embers from a fire. They spread out, each taking its own path, weaving in and out of the trees. Their movements, once lazily floating and drifting, now seemed to have purpose. They lurched from one place to the next, hiding in the dark crevices of the land before streaking across the open spaces like darting fish. Wherever they lingered, fires rose up and consumed the trees. Where they passed over the land, the grass withered.*

*Enoch studied them with fascination, realizing that they weren't the only things moving. As he squinted, he could make out something else, not drifting, but flowing over the land. It was like water, but darker—a mixture of many subtle colors. The embers seemed to be retreating from it. Whichever location they abandoned, the liquid flowed in to fill the void. Some embers were unable to move fast enough, and their light was extinguished when the liquid overcame them.*

*The other embers changed course and began to move toward one another. Some joined together and moved toward the liquid, only to be consumed by it. The rest fled, slowly converging until there was only one group—a swirl of light that represented every color imaginable.*

*The liquid seemed to break apart, suddenly reaching in every direction. Wherever it flowed, the fields and forests were discolored and wilted in its wake. It continued spreading until it had almost surrounded the embers.*

*Enoch looked across the land and was grieved by the destruction. Trees had fallen over, their roots rotted away. Fields of green grass had turned dry and brown. Streams and rivers had stagnated, their once clear waters now cloudy and smelling of decay. He looked down in anger upon the liquid poison and the embers that would soon be consumed by it. He wanted to yell down to them both, to make them realize what they had done. But he was distracted by something familiar.*

Among the glowing light of the embers, tiny dots were spread out across the fields. They weren't moving, and something about their arrangement caused Enoch's chest to tighten.

He dropped from the sky, suddenly feeling a sense of urgency. The wind roared in his ears. The land rushed up to meet him. The tiny dots grew in diameter until Enoch could make out the blades of grass that comprised their thatched roofs.

Sedekiyr!

The embers were gathered, and the heat of their presence began to wither the grass in every direction. The roar in his ears was now Enoch's own voice as he called out to his people, but there was no answer. The land rose up fast, and before he knew it he was running across the fields toward Sedekiyr, screaming at the top of his lungs. On the horizon, the liquid was still moving, paralleling Enoch, reaching around the city like two giant arms. Enoch's feet felt as though they were stuck in the mud of a stream. Each step seemed to require all of his strength. He would never make it in time. He lifted his eyes to Sedekiyr and saw the darkness on each horizon merge until the city was completely surrounded. They were trapped.

Enoch could only watch as the embers began to glow brighter, their heat intensifying. They moved in rapid, erratic jolts—streaking across the city and clashing into one another. Enoch could feel their heat on his face. He lifted his arm to block its intensity. A sudden burst of light took the air from his lungs and he fell backward. He feared that the city had burst into flames, but when the light was gone the city was still intact. Only then did he realize that the light had come down from above, stabbing like a spear of the Anduarym and leaving just as fast.

The embers now looked dull by comparison, and the liquid gathered on the horizon now seemed black. Silence passed over the land, and Enoch knew that the time for waiting was over. The blackness began to move, flowing into a wave. A deep rumbling sound rose to an earth-shattering cacophony as everything in its path was consumed. The embers flared and *burst outward, trails of fire rising up in their wake. The city and the fields were suddenly covered in flames.*

*Enoch was between them, looking first left, then right. They were coming at him from both sides, and the sound shook him and the earth beneath him. Enoch clamped his hands over his ears and fell to the ground. His skin grew hot. The grass around him withered, turned dry, then burst into flames. He closed his eyes and screamed at the pain. Then he felt the wave of poison wash over him, overwhelming his body as it tumbled him over and over again. It extinguished the heat but filled him with a nauseating sickness that ate away at his bones, replacing one agony with another. When the wave had passed, Enoch let go of his ears, knowing that it was time to die. He opened his eyes and lifted his gaze.*

*To the east, the mountains of Nagah seemed to loom over him, demanding his attention. There were no flames there, only tall forests that offered the coolness of their shade. There was no poison there, only fresh water running down from its peaks. It was so quiet there that Enoch could hear the gentle trickle of its streams, giving life and peace to everything around it. Enoch reached out his hand and could almost feel the soothing water on his scorched skin.*

"—bags at once?" Zacol asked.

Enoch looked up to see his wife standing in the doorway. "Huh?"

"Did you carry both bags at once?" she repeated.

Enoch looked down to the bags at his feet. His toes were still covered in grain dust. "Yes," he replied quickly. "I used my walking stick. It's something I learned during my time away."

Zacol bent down and grabbed one of the bags with both hands. "They're so heavy, I expected you to make two trips."

Enoch leaned forward and kissed her on the cheek. "Then you underestimated me."

"I suppose I did," she replied with a smile, before straining to lift one bag off the ground and carry it inside their dwelling.

Enoch's smile faded as soon as Zacol was gone. He exhaled the breath he'd been holding, then stood up and looked eastward across the plains. Somewhere beyond the limit of his sight were the mountains of Nagah. He knew what needed to be done, but the Shayetham weren't going to like it. And neither was Zacol. Disappointment pulled Enoch's head downward and his eyelids closed.

# 7

The pile of dry brush crackled as the flames licked up its sides. The warmth and light stood out against the clear night, darker and cooler than the lower elevations that were always shrouded in mist. Beyond the fire, dozens more just like it ringed the central gathering area where the Aleydam met every evening to share a meal, to tell each other stories, and to discuss anything that affected the tribe as a whole. But the concerns of the Aleydam were few and far between. And tonight, there had been nothing serious to discuss, allowing for an entire evening of entertainment.

A young boy of only five years stood in the center of the meeting area. His voice was shrill, easily heard over the fires and murmurs of the tribe. "I saw it from the corner of my eye," he said, crouching and turning his head. "It was watching me through the vines. Its fur was too dark to blend in. I moved slowly. I pretended to put something in my bag, but instead I grabbed some berries."

Sariel smiled. It was marvelous to see the skill of the Aleyd storytelling expressed so well, even in a boy as young as this.

"The cat shrank closer to the ground," he continued. "I knew it was about to leap."

Sitting cross-legged on the ground, Sariel glanced to the side to watch Sheyir's reaction to the story, but she was looking down. Her eyes were distant, as though she could see far below her, into the earth. The broad leaf in her lap still held a pile of berries and nuts. It looked as though it hadn't been touched. The curve of her belly was becoming more pronounced by the day, growing faster and larger than a normal pregnancy. The other women hadn't noticed the abnormality yet. They just congratulated Sheyir and went about their work. But they would know soon enough.

Sariel reached out and laid his hand on Sheyir's shoulder.

She looked up and turned, smiling apologetically.

"Aren't you going to eat anything?"

She laid her leaf on the ground. "I'm not hungry. I'm also very tired. I think I'll go lie down."

"You'll miss the story."

Sheyir glanced over the fire to where the young boy now had his hands out in front of him, fingers curled like claws toward his audience. "His mother already told me what happened," she whispered before getting up from the ground and walking away to their hut.

Sariel set down his leaf and watched her go, having suddenly lost his appetite. The dread that gnawed at his insides ever since he found out about her pregnancy could only be put off for short periods of time. It stayed with him throughout each day, interfering with his work, causing him to be short with the other men of the tribe. It clouded his ability to think and limited his usefulness to the Aleydam, which was why he looked forward to the shared meal every evening. It was the only distraction that worked.

"... but it grew angry," the boy said. "That's when I took off my bag and started swinging it as hard as I could."

Sariel stared into the flames. They wavered in an erratic, unpredictable dance. Beneath them and farther inside, the hot coals glowed with a dull luminescence that resembled the Amatru territory of the Borderlands. The coals on the perimeter of the fire had cooled and darkened. They lay against a ring of gray stones, the exhausted remnants of something that used to be alive. The image of Yeduah's body suddenly came to mind.

Sheyir's father was slumped over the rocks, a spear sticking out of his ribcage. The corpses of the Chatsiyram littered the central meeting area—death where there had been so much life. It was the moment that had changed everything.

*If only I would have known what would happen ...*

He imagined himself there, standing in the center of Bahyith.

*The Aytsam, with their stone-tipped spears, were coming through the trees, shouting like animals. The Chatsiyram were behind him, cowering in fear. The air swirled with golden embers that drifted outward and upward. When they reversed their direction and came back together, a powerful Iryllur stood where Sariel's weak human form used to be. He could see the expressions on the faces of the Aytsam, but he wouldn't show them mercy. He knew what they were going to do in his absence. He spread his wings and lunged forward, soaring over the ground toward the nearest enemy.*

The image in his mind dissipated and there was only the ring of small fires. The night sky. The peaceful faces of the Aleydam, their smiles reflecting the soft orange glow. A tribe beyond the influence of Semjaza. Of Azael.

*I never should have left her alone!*

The tribe was clapping. The young boy was bowing his head. His mother was leading him away with a hand around the back of his neck, making it clear that he'd told enough stories for one night. Others were getting to their feet. Sariel stayed where he was. He wouldn't be able to sleep this night, and lying awake next to Sheyir would only drive him mad. He needed some quiet solitude to think through the options for Sheyir. He had to find a way to fix what had been done to her.

Something touched Sariel's shoulder. He looked up to see one of the tribesmen with his hand outstretched. The man didn't say anything, but he didn't have to. His wife stood next to him, and the look of compassion on her face was enough. It was their quiet way of saying: *We know something is wrong. Just ask, and we'll help in whatever way we can.* Sariel patted the man's hand, and the couple walked away from the fire, disappearing into the darkness.

Silence descended on the meeting area after the villagers had gone. Sariel picked at the blades of grass in front of his crossed legs. The flicker of the fires eventually subsided until there was nothing more than a faint glow, and then only the glow directly in front of him. Long moments passed, but Sariel's mind was blank. He thought the quiet would allow him to think, but it seemed that his imagination had exhausted itself. It had gone to sleep even though his body wouldn't. The temperature of the air continued dropping. The coals could hardly be seen anymore.

Sariel looked out beyond the village. Stars were scattered across the sky, filling the areas of darkness above except where the black silhouettes of the mountains blocked their light. There were only a few places below the horizon where the features of the land were visible—a jagged ridge or the edge of a forest. Otherwise, it seemed an endless expanse of black.

Something caught Sariel's attention. He looked up and panned across the sky, seeing that the stars were blinking. Then it dawned on him that they weren't blinking, but something was moving in front of them, momentarily blocking their light. Something was flying over the village and heading east. He couldn't tell if it was small and close, or large and far away. He couldn't see the creature at all, only the stars that it blocked.

Sariel climbed to his feet and started moving east across the meeting area. He had a feeling this wasn't just a random occurrence.

The pattern of blocked stars seemed to shift to one side.

Sariel squinted, his exhausted mind trying to make sense of the movement.

*It's circling!* he realized.

He began running, following the path that led across the slope of the mountain toward one of the fields where the Aleydam foraged for their food. Short grass transitioned to knee-high shrubbery, and Sariel couldn't see the trail. The soil was uneven under his feet and he had to slow down to keep from tripping.

Whatever was moving through the sky suddenly dropped below the horizon. It happened so quickly that Sariel knew the creature hadn't just flown away. It had landed. He kept moving as fast as he could, following the narrow, rocky trail. The steep terrain gradually flattened out and Sariel found himself in the middle of a field covered in berry bushes. It would have been familiar territory for him during the day, but at night it was disorienting.

He slowed to a walk and picked his way through the vegetation, scanning left and right. After a few minutes, he noticed a tall silhouette on the ground at the edge of the field. It was far too big to be a natural creature of the wild.

"Who are you?" Sariel called out in a hushed voice as he continued moving forward with caution.

"Naganel. I apologize for coming at night," he replied. His voice was almost a screech, but still managed to convey composure. "I've been watching you. You haven't been alone long enough for me to approach."

The words were immediately alarming. Sariel didn't like the idea of being watched without his knowledge. And it wouldn't have been possible if he were wearing his Iryllur form. But this human body had many limitations, the most immediate being its weak eyesight. As Sariel neared, he could make out a feathered texture to Naganel's body. He was wearing the form of a bird of prey, and his size was the next attribute that Sariel became aware of. The Myndar towered over him by the time he was close enough to communicate without raising his voice. "I assume you all evaded being captured by the Amatru?"

"We did," Naganel replied.

"And the soldiers are gone?"

"They are."

"How did you find me?" Sariel asked.

Naganel's head pivoted to the side in a very bird-like manner. "We have our ways. But that is not important. I have come to offer you an invitation to join our Council."

Sariel looked up into the Myndar's large eyes, now able to see them clearly. "A Council? To decide what?"

"The rules for governing this world."

"Why does it need to be governed by anyone? I thought you all came here to live as free as the animals you *shaped.*"

"We are free," Naganel replied. "And whether or not we wear our animal forms, we still want what Semjaza promised us."

"To rule as kings?"

"To rule as gods," Naganel corrected.

Sariel crossed his arms. "There is no creature in this world above you in status or power. So what is the purpose of adding formality to it?"

"To prevent conflict. If we are to rule, we must all reach a common understanding about the freedoms available to us ... and the limitations where those freedoms overlap with others. If you would like to have your interests represented, then I encourage you to attend."

Sariel shook his head. "In the interests of preventing conflict, you're pursuing something that will certainly lead to conflict. Doesn't that sound like a contradiction to you?"

Naganel adjusted his stance before answering. "Only because of your perspective. The goal of the Council is peace, not war."

It was obvious that Naganel wasn't going to change his mind, so Sariel changed the course of the conversation instead. "Will this Council meet in Senvidar?"

"Yes, the first meeting will."

"When?"

Naganel lifted his head to the sky. "It will be the evening of the fifth full moon from now."

Sheyir was due to give birth four months from now, and there was nothing in the world that would cause Sariel to leave her again. Even though this Council seemed like a terrible idea, and they were inviting him to influence its outcome, it was out of his control. "I'm sorry, but I cannot attend."

"Can't, or won't?" the Myndar asked.

"Can't."

Naganel's posture relaxed, but there was still an intensity to his gaze. "I understand your reluctance to leave your woman in her last days, but there are more important things than the fate of one human."

Sariel's body tensed instantly—a warrior's response. He'd felt it so many times and had allowed himself to follow through with the feeling. But now it made him pause. He didn't want to act without thinking any longer. He controlled his body and channeled his anger into his mind, forcing himself to see beyond the alarming words of the messenger. Aside from the insult to Sheyir, there was something else in the Myndar's statement that was revealing. Naganel obviously knew of Sheyir's pregnancy and had watched them both long enough to assume that it was Sariel's child. But the fact that he assumed she would die, meant that he also knew Sariel could no longer *shape* others. The real question was how he had come to that conclusion. There was much more to this meeting than a simple invitation, and it was clear that Sariel needed to begin conversing with strategy. As all these things ran through his mind, Sariel gave the answer that was truthful, and the one that was expected of him.

"There is nothing else more important to *me*."

"Perhaps, right now. But you may come to regret your decision later."

"What do you mean?"

The shoulders of Naganel's wings spread outward as though the Myndar was fidgeting. "Only that there may be negative consequences for not attending."

Every reply gave him just a little more information. "So you mean to rule by intimidation? Will you *unshape* those who oppose you?"

The intensity of Naganel's gaze was suddenly diverted to the ground, and Sariel knew he'd found a weakness. "Or can you not *shape*?" he pressed.

Naganel turned to the side. "I will deliver your decision to the Council," he said quickly.

"Wait," Sariel said.

Naganel's powerful wings extended into the air before shooting downward, moving the bushes with a gust of wind. His intimidating presence rose into the sky in lurches.

"Wait! Can you not *shape*?" Sariel called out.

Within seconds, Naganel was too far away for further conversation. But Sariel had already gathered the information he needed. The Myndarym must have lost their abilities just like he had, which begged the most important question. If they were powerless, how could there be any negative consequences for failing to attend the Council? What made them think that they could enforce their self-appointed authority?

# 8

Zacol placed the last bit of prepared food in the satchel before tying the top closed. Then she turned to Enoch and held out her hand. Enoch lifted the end of his walking stick and Zacol began tying the strap to the end of the stick. "You're sure it won't fall?" she asked.

"As long as it's tied securely and there's one on both ends," he replied.

"Why do the elders gather?" Methu asked from behind. He'd been pacing in and out of their hut for the last several minutes, clearly anxious to get going.

Enoch kept a steadying hand on the stick and looked toward his son. "Well, I suppose to share with each other and learn from one another."

Methu nodded, but still didn't seem to understand.

"The other tribes have been around for longer than our own. And they're much larger, so they've experienced more than us. They have wisdom to teach us. So every year, the elders meet to share their wisdom."

Methu looked down at the strip of braided grass cord in his hand and began unwinding it from around a stick that he'd been playing with. "Will Great-Grandfather be your teacher?" he asked without looking up.

"Yes. That's right. He's already met with his father and now he's bringing that wisdom to us."

Zacol took the other end of the stick and began fastening another satchel to it. Enoch held it steady, while keeping his other hand on the first bag to prevent it from falling off the table. When he looked back at Methu, the boy was standing in the doorway, pulling on the cord until it bent the stick in his hand.

Methu suddenly looked up, evidently realizing something. "Is this what we did last year?"

"Yes," Zacol answered, "when you fell into the stream and muddied your clothes."

Methu nodded and looked at Enoch. "But you were gone."

"That's why uncle Neshil took your father's place," Zacol answered. "Alright. It should be ready," she told her husband.

Enoch lifted the stick by its center and carried it outside into the morning light where Zacol helped him put it up on his shoulders.

"Is that too heavy?" she asked.

"It's fine. Not as heavy as it looks."

"Let me get the other bag, and then we can go," she said, going back inside.

Enoch looked down and noticed that his son was standing next to him with another stick in his hand. Enoch wondered where the boy had gotten it from so quickly. "Are you ready?"

"Uh-huh," Methu answered.

"Alright," Zacol said, stepping out of the hut carrying a smaller bag in her hands. "We'd better get going or we'll be late."

The trio set off to the west, moving along a worn path that wove through other huts of identical construction. The grasses and support poles were all dark brown, having been in place for years. It was yet another indicator of seniority among the tribe, but it didn't bother Enoch that his own dwelling was still a pale green color. In fact, he liked it better that way—an indicator of change. Of improvement. As the stick across his shoulders bounced with the weight of the food bags, Enoch found himself missing the experience of his travels. With the exception of numerous life-threatening situations, it had been exciting to wake up every day and know that he would see something different. The earth under his feet was so much larger than anyone realized, and there were so many plants and animals that he could travel his entire life and still not witness them all. Enoch was also aware that the only reason his mind now followed this path of thought was because of his present anxiety over the coming meeting.

He turned to the side and watched Zacol's profile for a few seconds. There was a smile under her sharp nose. A gleam in her brown eyes that hadn't been there for longer than he could remember.

She turned her head suddenly, catching Enoch's gaze as she brushed a strand of black hair away from her face. "It's good to have you back ... and involved," she said. "The gathering is going to be more fun this year."

"Were the women rude last time?"

She looked down and shook her head. "They ... tolerated me. But this year is going to be different. I can tell already."

Enoch smiled as best as he could and turned to stare at the path in front of him. It felt like the lump of anxiety in his throat was large enough to be visible. But Zacol hadn't noticed it. She was clearly thinking of other things. It was an odd experience to be intimidated by her in one moment, only to see her fragility in another. It was her hope that made her seem vulnerable—the belief that things were different now and that their lives were finally taking a turn for the better. But Enoch hadn't told her about the vision. It would have destroyed that hope, and maybe her along with it. He glanced at her again and saw the young girl he fell in love with. He saw her confident optimism, and the years of tested loyalty that had followed it. She was the only person in his life who ever believed the strange things he claimed to have seen.

A husband's protective instinct pulled at him from one direction. A prophet's devotion pulled from another. The opposing loyalties felt as though they would rip Enoch in two pieces. He adjusted the stick across his shoulders and looked down at Methu to take his mind off his anxiety. "What is that?"

Methu looked up, then down again at the sticks in his hand. "It's something I made. See? The cord goes around this stick like this, and then you pull it back."

Enoch squinted, trying to make sense of the contraption.

One of the sticks began to bend. "You keep pulling, and then ..." Methu let go and one of the sticks shot up in the air, spinning wildly. He flinched, apparently expecting it to have gone forward instead of over his head.

Enoch smiled. "What is it for?"

Methu shrugged before bending down to pick up the stick. He ran his thumb over a notch carved near the end, then looked at the end of the cord. "I'm a firstborn too," he said.

It was amazing how quickly a child's thoughts could jump from one thing to the next. "That's right."

"When can I come with you?"

"When you are thirteen years," Enoch answered.

"Will my brother go instead of me ... if I'm gone?"

Enoch glanced at his wife.

Zacol smiled and laid a hand on her belly, where there would be a visible bump in another month or so. "What if this is your sister?" she asked.

Methu made a disgusted face.

"Are you planning on going somewhere?" Enoch asked.

Methu looped the cord around the notch in the stick and pulled it back again. "I'm coming with you when you leave."

Enoch's stomach lurched, and he felt a chill pass over his body.

"Your father's not going anywhere," Zacol stated quickly.

Enoch kept his eyes forward so Zacol couldn't see how uncomfortable he had become. "There's a crowd already," he said, thankful that there was something else to comment on. In the distance, nearly half of Sedekiyr's residents were clustered together on the edge of town. The women were laying out their food while the men stood talking. In between and around them, children were chasing each other.

Methu ran ahead a few steps before remembering his manners. "Can I go?" he asked, turning back to look at Zacol.

She nodded.

Methu took off at a full run and didn't even slow down until he met up with the other children, and then only to exchange a greeting before joining in the chase.

Enoch watched for a moment, smiling in the silence.

"It's been better for him also," Zacol said finally. "The other boys didn't use to play with him very often."

Enoch nodded, suddenly feeling an emotional weight on his shoulders that was heavier than the load of food he was carrying.

"Are you nervous?" she asked.

"Yes."

"Well, you're an elder too. Don't let them intimidate you."

Enoch smiled at his wife's encouragement.

"You've seen things that they never will," she added. "Remember that."

"I wish they saw it that way," Enoch replied. "But the wisdom only flows in one direction—from father to son."

"Maybe they will listen to you this time. You've been helping everyone since you got back. They have to recognize that."

"Perhaps they will," Enoch replied. He wanted to go on and say that these gatherings weren't constructed to share wisdom as much as they were about listening to those who've gone before you. He wanted to say that those two things were not always the same, and that he'd given Methu a sanitized explanation of what was going to take place. But he held his tongue. Zacol knew more than anyone how the previous years' meetings had gone. There was no use in repeating it. But there just might be some use in approaching it from an optimistic perspective, which is what Zacol would argue. And if she was right, Enoch might never need to tell her about the vision. If his father and grandfather took his warnings to heart, any decisions resulting from it would have their authority behind it. *One can always hope*, he thought.

As they drew near to the crowd, several of the women left their preparations to come and help Zacol with her food. They greeted her with gentle touches on her arm before untying the bags from Enoch's stick and carrying them back to where the other food had been laid out on the ground. Enoch returned his stick to an upright position and leaned on it.

"You'll do fine," Zacol said, waiting a few more seconds before joining the women.

Enoch caught sight of his younger brother, Neshil, over Zacol's shoulder. He didn't look mad, but neither did he look happy.

Zacol noticed it and stepped to the side to command Enoch's attention. "He's just jealous that he can't participate. Never mind him. This is your right. Remember that."

It was just what he needed to hear. "I love you," he replied, leaning forward to kiss her on the lips. And the look of surprise on her face was just what he needed to see.

"Go work up an appetite," she said before letting go of him.

"We're just talking."

"Then talk with purpose," she added.

Enoch took a deep breath, smiled, then turned away from the crowd and headed out into the fields west of Sedekiyr. His father and grandfather had already arrived. They were sitting in the grass within sight of the whole tribe, but out of earshot, as was the custom. Though Enoch wasn't exactly late, he couldn't help but feel like a child who was about to be scolded for tardiness.

*Holy One, give me the courage to speak.*

The meeting area was a small circle of land that had been cleared of grass, no bigger than a hut. A small fire ring sat at its center, a mostly customary feature. Enoch had never known any of these meetings to last into the night. Grandfather Mahalal-el sat on a rock on the west side of the circle, facing east. It was symbolic of the tribe's wisdom flowing eastward with the movement of their people. At two hundred and ninety-eight years, Mahalal-el was older than any other person in Sedekiyr. He simply nodded as Enoch approached.

Yered, Enoch's father, sat on a wooden stump to Mahalal-el's left. Though he was only two hundred and thirty-three years, there was hardly any way of telling that he was younger. His dark hair and beard were the same color as his father's, though he kept his beard trimmed shorter. He was thick with muscle, which was the biggest difference between them. Yered looked up at his son and simply said, "Welcome."[7]

Enoch took his place on the ground. Though they were all similar in stature, the descending heights of their seats emphasized the hierarchy of this meeting. At seventy-one years, Enoch felt like little more than a child.

"Now that we are all here, let us get started," Mahalal-el said.

Enoch tried not to cringe at the implication.

Mahalal-el began the meeting by recounting Keynan's journey from Anah to the city of Azab, where Mahalal-el lived. The better part of an hour passed as Enoch listened to every detail of that trip until the time of their greeting. Enoch's foot was falling asleep and he crossed his legs in the other direction as his grandfather continued, painstakingly retelling every word of their conversation. As the elder moved through various topics, such as how to properly plan for new structures of an expanding city and better food production and distribution techniques, Enoch found himself marveling at the depth of his grandfather's memory more than the point of his words. The sun passed its zenith before Yered was able to speak, and then only to offer his opinions about how to implement what Mahalal-el had learned from his father.

These discussions lasted more than an hour before Enoch started to feel the pang of hunger in his stomach. By then, both of his legs were numb. His back ached to the point that he wondered whether or not he would ever be able to stand up straight again. But something else controlled his attention, making his momentary pain seem unimportant. He heard the whisper of the Holy One's voice. It was subtle, but he had learned over the years how to detect it. It came into his mind as gently as his own thoughts, but there was confidence beneath it—something that he rarely felt about his own wonderings. The feeling descended upon him like a calm and reassuring presence, and when it left him, there were words in his mind like echoes of something that he had just missed.

*It is time, my faithful son.*

Enoch suddenly became aware of the present moment.

"... three times in the last month," Yered was saying. He pointed over Enoch's head. "They're always spotted to the south, and we've been fortunate that it hasn't been one of the children who has stumbled across them. The creatures are likely to drag them away as food."

Mahalal-el nodded, his eyes focused on the southern horizon. "The men of my father's city take turns watching over the fields. Their huts are strong enough to hold a man on the roof, where they can see well."

Yered nodded. "That is good. Perhaps we should make sure that children do not go out into the fields without an adult to scare away the creatures."

Mahalal-el laced his hands together and set them on his lap. "The safety of our people must be our highest priority."

"I agree," Enoch said, recognizing the cue that the Holy One must have prepared for him.

The other men paused their conversation to turn and look at Enoch with their mouths hanging open. It was obvious that they had expected him to keep silent, especially after being away from the tribe for so long.

"If something threatens the safety of our children, we are obligated to take action. Yes?"

Mahalal-el squinted.

Yered placed his hand on his knee, as though he were preparing for a long distraction from the important things they had been discussing.

Neither one answered his question, so Enoch tried to be more direct. "What would you do if you knew of something threatening not just our children, but the entire city?"

"What are you getting at?" Yered asked. The scowl on his face said that he had already dismissed what Enoch hadn't yet shared.

"What would you do?" Enoch pressed.

"We would try to prevent it," Mahalal-el finally answered.

"If the threat was real," Yered was quick to add.

"Tell us what you have seen," Mahalal-el instructed.

Enoch couldn't stay seated any longer. He rose on shaky legs and leaned on his walking stick. "I saw embers, as if from a fire, drifting across the plains from all directions. They were chased by a dark liquid that crawled over the ground as if it were alive. It was a poison that withered everything it touched. And wherever the embers went, the heat of their presence scorched the earth."

"What does this have to do with us?" Yered asked.

"I was watching this from above, as though I were a bird of the sky," Enoch explained. "And I saw the embers flee from the poison that chased them. When they gathered together, it was here in Sedekiyr. The poison surrounded us so that none could escape, and the embers burned us from within."

"You mean that we are to be wary of fire?" Mahalal-el asked.

Enoch shook his head. "No, Grandfather. I believe the embers are the angels of heaven, the Wandering Stars. I have seen them in other visions, and they are most often revealed to me as points of light. I believe that they will come here and that their presence will bring about the destruction of Sedekiyr."

"By poison, or by fire?" Yered asked, a hint of amusement at the corner of his mouth.

Enoch felt his shoulders slump. "These visions are not usually taken so literally."

"Usually?" Yered asked.

Enoch felt his temper rising, and he had to breathe steadily to keep it under control. "It matters not by what method our city will be destroyed. I saw the embers and the poison come against each other in these very fields, but I couldn't see if anyone survived."

"What is the purpose of this vision, then?" Mahalal-el asked. "Is the Holy One simply telling us in advance that we will all die?"

"No, Grandfather. I do not believe so. In my vision, I looked eastward to the mountains of Nagah. While our city was consumed with flames and flooded with poison, I saw there streams of clear water to quench our thirst. I saw forests to offer shade and protection. I believe the Holy One wants us to move our city to the mountains."

Yered's amusement transitioned into a blank stare.

A faint wheezing sound emanated from the circle, and it took Enoch a few seconds to realize that it was coming from Mahalal-el. It grew louder and broke into pieces as his body began shuddering from laughter.

Enoch was so stunned by the elder's reaction that he didn't know what to say. When he turned to his own father, he saw that Yered didn't share Mahalal-el's humor. He looked embarrassed. "Why do you persist in dishonoring me this way?"

Mahalal-el was still laughing.

Enoch opened his mouth to reply.

"No! Don't say another word. You've said enough. Do you have any idea what you're asking?" Tears began forming in Yered's eyes.

Enoch swallowed the lump in his throat and waited for his father to continue.

"We are a people of the plains. This is our home and our way of life. What would the Shayetham do in the mountains? It's too cold. Our crops wouldn't grow. Our animals would starve. There aren't even grasses for building. What would you live in?"

Enoch opened his mouth again.

"No!" Yered yelled before standing up. "You will keep silent among your elders. Do you think that you were allowed here because of your wisdom? You have nothing to offer but distractions."

Mahalal-el had finally recovered from his laughing fit, the expression on his face quickly transitioning to one of anger. He waved a hand of dismissal at Enoch. "We are not moving to the mountains. Leave us, son of confusion! Take your children's stories and be gone from my presence."

Enoch stumbled backward. He'd never heard his grandfather speak in this way. And the tears in Yered's eyes would have been heartbreaking under different circumstances.

"If you have nothing constructive to offer," Yered pleaded, "then take yourself away from here."

The plains seemed eerily silent. A breeze moved over Enoch's skin, driving the swirling fog across the fields behind the elders. Enoch suddenly felt alone. "But these are the words of the Holy One," he said. "Do you think I enjoy upsetting you? I only tell you these things because—"

"Be gone!" Yered yelled.

Enoch stared hard at his father before turning his gaze to his grandfather. Their rejection hurt him deeply, but the sadness that he felt wasn't for himself. It was for his people. Their fate rested in the hands of men who refused the only true wisdom to be learned.

*Holy One, you are now my father and my grandfather.*

Enoch turned away from the circle of firstborn Shayetham and began stepping through the tall grass. Voices could be heard in the distance, murmurs of confusion coming from the gathered tribe.

"Bring Neshil over," Mahalal-el said. "He is a practical man."

Yered's voice suddenly rang out, loud against the stillness of the plains. "Neshil! Neshil!"

Enoch looked back over his shoulder to see his father waving. Ahead, an arm waved over the top of the crowd. A few seconds later, Enoch's younger brother broke away from the tribe and began coming across the field.

As Enoch veered to the northeast, heading toward his dwelling and away from the crowd, he noticed the smug look on Neshil's face. Behind him, another figure stepped out from the gathered tribe. Zacol's face bore a look of utter bewilderment. Enoch stared at her for a long moment as he walked away. Finally, she began crying and turned her back. Another woman put her arms around Zacol and comforted her.

Enoch couldn't tell if his wife's tears were due to sympathy or embarrassment. Either way, he knew it was best to separate himself from the tribe for a short while.

\* \* \* \*

Methu had been lying in the grass south of the Elder's Circle. He and a few other boys had decided to sneak up on the men and listen to their conversation. And they had heard every word. Methu suddenly stood up to watch his father leave.

"Get down!" the other boys whispered as loud as they dared. "They'll see you."

Methu didn't care any longer about being seen. The only thing that mattered was his father. He watched Enoch go, feeling embarrassed for him and wishing there was something he could do to make everything alright.

Something latched onto Methu's ankle, and he looked down to see another boy lying facedown, arm outstretched.

"Get down," the boy mouthed, looking up.

Methu frowned at him.

"Then leave, just like *he* always does," another boy whispered. It was Zejuad, the oldest of the group. "You're just like your stupid father. You never do anything right."

"I'm not like him," Methu replied.

Zejuad and the other boys started to laugh.

Methu stepped through the grass and tried to kick Zejuad in the ribs as hard as he could.

The older boy rolled quickly to the side, only receiving a glancing blow. Then he was on his feet in an instant.

A large fist slammed into Methu's face, and it seemed like his senses of smell and taste had suddenly merged into one. When he opened his eyes, he was on his back and Zejuad was standing over him with a triumphant look on his face.

"You're just like him. You're stupid and crazy. And someday it'll get you killed."

The others laughed nervously.

"Hey!" an adult voice shouted. "Get out of here!"

The boys glanced to one side, then stepped over Methu and ran away in the opposite direction.

Uncle Neshil's face suddenly appeared against the blue sky above. "You shouldn't be here!"

Methu started to get up when he felt a pinch on his ear.

"You disrespect this meeting just like your father," Neshil said, pulling Methu up by the ear. "You should be ashamed of yourself."

For some strange reason, the pain felt more intense than Zejuad's fist against his face. Methu cringed and began to cry. His uncle marched him across the field, finally releasing him when his mother's face could be seen at the edge of the crowd.

# 9

Sheyir lay on her side at the edge of the bed, facing away from Sariel. Her belly, swollen beneath her long tunic, indicated that she was ready to give birth, though she still had three months to go. Patches of moisture soaked through her clothing, and where her skin was uncovered, it was pale and coated in beads of sweat. Every so often, a bout of shivers would pass over her, rustling the mattress of grass on which she lay.

Sariel sat on the bed next to her. The fan he'd been using to cool her skin now sat idle beside him. "Do you need a blanket?"

"Maybe just for my feet," she replied, her voice barely above a whisper.

Sariel stood and draped a blanket across her bare feet, now shaking as well. Then he wiped the tears away from his eyes and returned to his side of the bed.

"This is how it starts," Sheyir said.

Sariel didn't know what to say, so he just laid his hand on her arm.

"They kept all of us together down in that dark place," she said, her voice distant. "When it was time to give birth, they took the mothers into another chamber with a pond on the floor. I always went along to help, but some of them didn't want to see what would happen."

"You don't have to tell me this," Sariel replied.

Sheyir kept talking as if she hadn't heard. "I figured it was better to know. They were in so much pain. Blood everywhere. They usually died before those disgusting creatures even came out—"

"Was this where the Amatru found you?" Sariel interrupted to change the subject. "The chamber under the mountains?"

Sheyir nodded, the mattress beneath her head rustling.

"Were there only two chambers?"

"No. There were many others. We stayed in the largest one. There were tunnels also, but they were blocked with gates. One of them smelled of animals."

Sariel tried to keep the conversation going. "Yes. Semjaza kept his hunting beast down there. That's what he used when he tried to escape."

"How did he die?" she asked.

Sariel hadn't ever told her. In fact, they hadn't spoken much of those times. It seemed that they had both wanted to forget about it as quickly as possible. He wondered if admitting the truth would help or make her feel worse. He finally decided on the former. "I killed him myself."

Sheyir rolled onto her back, wincing before looking up into his eyes. "You?"

"I know it's hard to believe," he admitted with upturned hands. "But I wasn't in this body at the time."

"But he was so ... big."

Sariel nodded.

Sheyir turned her eyes toward the ceiling. "That's good," she said finally, with a look of contempt.

There was more in her expression than a general hatred, which made Sariel wonder. "Did he also ...?" He couldn't finish the question.

Sheyir made eye contact again. "Yes."

"Before or after Azael?"

"After."

Sariel's head suddenly felt heavy, and he let it drop to his chest. After a moment of silence, he reached out and gently laid his hand on her belly. "Are you sure this is Azael's child?"

Sheyir slowly shook her head. "I think so, but I can't be sure."

Sariel remembered the satisfying feeling of the vaepkir sliding upward into Semjaza's stomach. The grind of metal on bone as the blade glanced off his ribs from the inside. The way the massive Anduar went limp and fell over him to the ground.

He must have allowed the memory to show on his face, because Sheyir's hand was suddenly resting on his arm. "It was obvious that he was scared," she said. "We all knew something was wrong when he came into our chamber. He was walking quickly and wouldn't even look at us. The other angels dug at the ceiling of the tunnel with their weapons after he left. That's when the rocks came down and blocked it."

"He didn't suffer enough for what they did to you. None of them did."

Sheyir looked as if she was about to nod her agreement, but her head suddenly turned to the side. Her body followed a second later, tensing as soon as she was on her side. A loud retching sound filled the hut.

Sariel jumped to his feet and hurried around the bed at the sound of liquid splashing on the floor.

Sheyir pulled her head back and let it fall limp against the bed. Her eyes were closed and her face scrunched with pain.

Sariel looked around the room in a panic, searching for the earthen pot of water that he refilled each day. He found it nearby and picked it up, carrying it closer to the bed. Stepping around the mess on the floor, he dipped his hand into the pot and used the fresh water to clean Sheyir's mouth.

Her body began to shake with silent sobs.

Sariel watched her, feeling more helpless than all the times he had watched his fellow soldiers die. At least they had known what the risks of combat were. Each one had made a conscious decision to risk his life to defeat the Marotru. But Sheyir was innocent. She didn't ask for this. It had been forced upon her. The war that Sariel had thought to be confined to the Eternal Realm had spread across the void and claimed another victim.

But he refused to accept that conclusion. "I'll figure out how to save you."

Sheyir's face was covered by her hands. Her words came out muffled. "There's nothing you can do."

He set down the pot of water and knelt beside the bed where the floor was dry. "Do you remember what I told you about the time before the *Reshaping*? Most of the others were only allowed to sustain animals and trees and plants, but I was also given a turn at sustaining the first humans."

Sheyir's hands suddenly flew away from her face. "You can't *shape* anymore! You can't fix this."

"But I know how your body works. I can find a way to save you."

Her eyes, fixed on the ceiling, slowly rolled toward him. Her voice was softer this time. "I can't ... hope. It will drive me mad. It's better if I accept what's going to happen. I won't live like those other women ... in denial."

Sariel put his hands together and rested his elbows on the bed. "Tell yourself whatever you have to in order to survive, but I will find a way to save you. I promise you that."

Sheyir smiled, but sadness was still heavy in her eyes. Her hand came up slowly from the bed and clasped Sariel's clenched fists. "You are a better man than any I have known. I believe that you will try, but I also know that this is not under your control. Or else you ..." she trailed off, evidently deciding not to finish the statement. "As much as you want to help, there is nothing you can do."

\* \* \* \*

KHELRUSA

The screech of the tall gate was a welcome sound for Hyrren. He hid in the shadows of the uppermost cavern, watching the only entrance and exit of the mines. A torch flickered on the opposite wall, barely pushing back the darkness. The sphere of orange light revealed a single Kahyin guard who had just opened the crude door of metal bars. He ushered another man inside, leading a beast whose back was piled high with thick branches. The four-legged creature snorted in protest as the man pulled on the leather strap around its neck, leading it leftward toward a passage that led to the smelting room. The Kahyin were taking down the trees of the surrounding forests to feed the furnaces for their metal work. The deliveries came several times an hour, and the formality of unlocking and locking the gate again had become a nuisance to the guard, who left the main gate to run ahead and open the next one for the delivery of wood.

Hyrren burst from his hiding place and ran across the cavern floor, slipping silently through the unlocked main gate. The night air smelled fresh and strangely fragrant. Hyrren guessed that it must be the forest he was smelling, instead of the damp earth he was used to. Overhead, the sky was clear and black, speckled with stars. They seemed brighter and more plentiful than they had looked in Mudena Del-Edha. Hyrren noted all of this in an instant, as he moved with soft steps across the road and into the trees beside it. It would have been nice to stop and drink in the beauty. It certainly crossed his mind that it might be his last opportunity. But there were more pressing matters. Matters that defined not only his fate, but the fate of every one of his kind.

Hyrren moved quickly, paralleling the road as it descended toward the city. The soil underfoot was soft and muffled his steps. He kept scanning back and forth through the darkness, choosing his path carefully and occasionally glancing toward the road. It wouldn't be long before another delivery of wood arrived. But Hyrren was confident that the footsteps of the man and beast on coarse soil could be heard long before they would appear. As long as he kept inside the trees, he should be able to make it all the way down to the temple and back without being seen ... though his return depended on the outcome of the anticipated meeting.

\* \* \* \*

Azael stood at the laver, his hands submerged in the fresh water that filled the metal basin. Small bits of roasted animal flesh clouded the water as he rubbed his fingers together, clearing away the remains of his evening meal. To his right, the open doors of the temple looked out over a flat expanse of fitted stones. Wide steps descended into a training arena of bare soil that had been churned into mud over the course of the day. Luhad's men had made significant progress in their training, but the more important advancement had been the fear it had likely instilled in the Council's messenger, who watched them in secret. Though he had been careful to stay within the forests atop Murakszhug, no Myndar could ever hope to stay hidden from the trained eyes of the Iryllurym.

Azael removed his hands from the laver and shook off the water. He allowed himself a moment of reflection as he looked down upon his city full of human subjects. The narrow valley flickered with distant firelight. The occasional sound drifted uphill, a mournful cry from a woman or the angered shout of a man. But Khelrusa was mostly quiet this evening. The men were too exhausted from their training to fight with each other. The women too wearied from their labor to argue with one another. Azael had been pushing them to their limits, and they seemed to thrive when being ruled harshly. Whether the Holy One had intended them to be this way, or the Myndarym had *shaped* it into them, didn't matter. It worked, and Azael cared most about practical matters.

He smiled to himself and turned away from the doors. From the corner of his eye, he noticed something in the temple that shouldn't be there. His hands immediately went to his vaepkir as his body crouched into an attack posture.

On the opposite side of the room, something large knelt on the stone floor. It was still, and had arrived without sound. Azael watched it, gauging the level of the threat even as he scolded himself for growing comfortable in these safe surroundings. He saw bare flesh the color of red soil, and hair as dark as the night sky, but it took a moment before Azael could make sense of what he was looking at. "How did you get out?" he asked, finally realizing what it was.

"My king," it answered without lifting its head. "The mines are busy. The Kahyin come and go throughout the day. I am quick and silent."

"Indeed, you are," Azael replied. He could see now that the Nephiyl had both hands pressed flat against the ground in front of his knees, head down against his chest. It was a posture of total submission. If Azael rushed him, the Nephiyl wouldn't even have the time to get his feet under him to take a single step before his life was taken. The posture, along with the silent arrival, spoke volumes. "You have earned your audience with me. What do you want?"

"We are starving, my king." Its head remained bowed.

Azael kept one hand on the hilt of a vaepkir, but allowed himself to relax just a bit. "Yes. I'm told that the Kahyin can't keep up with your insatiable appetites."

"You can see by the thinness of my body that our appetites are not the problem," the Nephiyl answered. He had forgotten to address Azael as king this time, and his words were thick with bitterness. "There are many of us. The Kahyin won't feed us because of their jealousy, or else they can't because they lack the hunting skill."

Azael grinned. The boldness of this child was as refreshing as it was disrespectful. He decided to play along. "The hunting skills of the Kahyin are without equal. I'm told the forests and rivers have been hunted bare."

"Whether or not that is true, there isn't enough food for us, my king."

Azael's grin grew into a smile. Luhad would be furious if he heard what this Nephiyl was saying. "Then what do you want? To go hunt for yourselves?"

"We would welcome the opportunity, my king, as a long-term solution," he answered. His head remained down and his hands kept to the floor. "I seek a more immediate solution. The Kahyin mothers who give birth to us ... we are instructed to dispose of their bodies afterward."

Azael took another step forward. "Did you come to inform me, or ask something of me?"

"Their bodies could feed us," the Nephiyl clarified. "I ask that you grant us permission to use them as food."

Azael took his hand off his vaepkir and crossed both arms in front of his chest. "The fact that they are your mothers doesn't bother you?"

"No, my king. They are human. We are Nephiyl."

Azael's keen eyes could make out deep scars covering the Nephiyl's back and arms. "This would only make the situation worse for you. The Kahyin men already hate your kind."

"Yes, my king," he answered simply.

"Lift your face to me," Azael instructed.

The Nephiyl's head slowly came up. His eyes, the color of hot coals, fixed their gaze upon his superior.

Azael recognized him, though the flesh of his face was badly distorted by scars. "You look different than when I saw you last. You are Semjaza's son."

"Yes, my king. I am Hyrren."

"You were not born in these mines. How did you come to be here?"

Hyrren's eyelids lowered ever so slightly. "While we lived in my father's kingdom, my siblings and I heard there were others like us. Then the enemy attacked, and they left us without a home. We came here to find our own kind. Luhad took us in and put us to work."

Hyrren's sudden arrival, his posture, the scars on his body—it all suddenly made sense. "Your request is not about food, is it?"

"Not entirely, my king."

"You risked your life stepping foot into this temple with me. And you risked it again by speaking so boldly. It would be inconsistent to shy away from the truth now. So, tell me why you have come here."

The fire in Hyrren's eyes seemed to flare. "I come to plead for my people. The Kahyin starve us and work us like animals, but we are the sons and daughters of gods," he replied, lifting his head even further. "We do not deserve to be treated this way."

Azael nodded slowly. "If I give you permission, the Kahyin will treat you even worse than they do now."

"Perhaps. But we are strong enough to endure. Perhaps they would be relieved to have the rest of their females back—the ones who are not yet pregnant. I only ask that you give us the ones who are already going to die."

"So you wish to end the breeding operation?" Azael asked.

"No, my king. I want to see my people multiply and cover the earth. It was my father's desire to bring forth a new creation, and I want you to put me in charge of it."

Now Azael smiled openly. "Your father wanted to breed himself an army, but your siblings are not all as large as you. Are they?"

"Not yet, my king. I am the eldest, but the rest are growing larger every day."

Azael squinted. "Stand before me."

The expression that crossed Hyrren's face was one of surprise mixed with fear, but he obeyed immediately. His earthen-colored body, sickly thin, rose from the stone as though it were a dead body coming to life. The filthy loincloth hung from the bones of his hips like the limp flag of a defeated army. But when his head approached the ceiling of the temple, his face took on a look of pride.

"How do you intend to continue the breeding operation?" Azael asked, stepping to the side and beginning to walk around the Nephiyl. "Will you offer your females to the Kahyin men?"

Hyrren's jaw tightened. "They are animals, and they are not worthy of my sisters. The blood of our fathers should not be diluted. It must be strengthened. My sisters will lay with their own kind. And they are strong. They won't die giving birth to our people. Let us give you the army my father desired. And let the Kahyin men return to their menial labor, as animals should."

Azael completed a full circle around the massive creature, coming to stand in front of Hyrren again. Before the Amatru attack, Azael hadn't paid much attention to these hybrids of human and angelic copulation. But now that Hyrren stood so proudly before him, he understood the wisdom of what Semjaza had been doing.

"Your people are too young yet to serve me as an army. But I see potential in you. I grant you permission to use the Kahyin females as you see fit ... and the ones we've taken from other tribes. I am also putting you in charge of the breeding operation, effective immediately. But you must continue to support the Kahyin in the mines. Their work is also important to my goals. If you produce results for me, I will reevaluate these matters in time."

Hyrren bowed his head in acknowledgement, but remained standing. "Your judgments are fair, my king."

# 10

Fields of tall grass stretched to the east, the vibrant colors fading until the land and sky eventually merged at a pale horizon. The narrow path of visibility was a rare sight; the rest of the fields were obstructed by ethereal wisps of white and gray that rose from earth and drifted with the breeze. Enoch's eyes were fixed on the horizon where the mountains of Nagah stood, hidden on this clear day by nothing more than distance. His body, exhausted from the emotional toll of the elders meeting, rested heavily upon his sturdy walking stick. His mind drifted like the mist over the fields, swirling, occasionally brushing against a substantial thought.

The swishing sound of approaching footsteps wasn't enough to bring him out of his trance until Zacol spoke from only a pace away. "Why didn't you tell me about the vision?"

Enoch closed his eyes, now conscious of their weariness. He wondered how long it had been since the last time he had blinked. "I've grown tired of disappointing you."

The grass swished again and Zacol appeared beside Enoch. "I'm more disappointed that you kept it from me."

Enoch let his head droop until his chin rested against his chest. He had never noticed before how much effort it took to keep his head upright. It seemed that his entire body wanted to follow the example of his eyelids and his head—to keep going downward until it reached a final resting place. He didn't have the strength or desire to look Zacol in the eyes.

"When will Sedekiyr be destroyed?" she asked.

They were just words, but they were laden with meaning. Zacol's straightforward curiosity was apparent. Her confidence in the Holy One's message was woven into the words as well. But the ignorance of the Shayetham was what stood out the most. He decided to answer his wife before addressing the latter.

"I felt the city burning, and I experienced the pain. When the vision left me, it felt as though the threat was not immediate. But I see that the elders only heard what they wanted to hear. The vision was a gift for our deliverance, not just a warning of our destruction." Enoch's head was upright now. His eyes were fixed on Zacol. Defending the words of the Holy One seemed to have given him strength.

"Of course, everyone is talking about it. They all say how absurd it would be to move the entire city," Zacol replied.

Enoch just nodded before looking eastward again. The horizon was no longer visible.

"What will you do?"

Enoch slowly shook his head. "The Shayetham are a stubborn people. They have but one method of accepting wisdom, and it doesn't include an outsider like me."

Zacol didn't reply, but Enoch knew what she was thinking anyway. He could almost hear her say that he shouldn't think of the tribe as something separate from himself. *Not they*, she was thinking. *We*.

"If we are to receive this message," he replied to the unspoken correction, "it will have to come from within. It must carry the weight of a respected elder."

"Keynan?"

Enoch turned to make direct eye contact with his wife again. "No. Even my great-grandfather is subject to the same limitations that I faced today. He simply passes along what was given to him. I must go to Adam."

The skin around Zacol's bloodshot eyes tightened. "You're leaving again?"

"Our firstfather must have spoken with the Holy One before he was exiled. He will know that these are not just stories I'm making up. If I can secure his blessing, the Shayetham will have no choice. They'll have to listen to me."

The life drained from Zacol eyes. The change wasn't something specific that Enoch could have described. But in the space of a single breath, his wife was gone and an empty shell of her remained. It was only then that Enoch realized the meaning of her previous question.

"I want you and Methu to come with me," he quickly added.

It took five long seconds for the words to have any effect. Zacol's eyes glanced eastward. Her lips, which were partly open, suddenly closed. That intangible quality that had left her now reappeared. "Why don't we just go to Nagah ... the four of us?"

Enoch's mind came to a stop at the odd number. It felt like his thoughts had become bound up with a cord until he realized that Zacol was counting the child in her womb. Only then did he proceed to be shocked by the rest of her question. "The vision was for the whole tribe. I can't just save my own family and allow the Shayetham to be destroyed. I have to find a way to convince them."

Zacol was silent for a moment as she either considered Enoch's request, or else was just choosing her own words carefully. "Methu and I have struggled to build a life for ourselves here. And most of the time, it has felt like our efforts have been without your help. We made progress while you were gone. The tribe was starting to take care of us as if I were a widow. And now you're asking me to give that up? Leaving will only take us farther from our goal of integrating ourselves here. Why would we do such a thing only to come back and have to start all over again?"

"Because the Holy One is asking us to. And we wouldn't just be returning to start over. We would be coming back with a blessing that would change everything."

"No," Zacol protested. "This is not what He asked. This is your own idea. And it would probably kill our child. Do you realize how far away Galah is? Would you have me give birth along the way without the help of my sisters?"

"I'll take care of you."

"You don't even know what's required," she argued. "I can't risk the life of our child as well as my own."

Enoch gripped his walking stick with tight fingers. He scanned the field around him, as if the solution were hiding somewhere in the grass. "Please," he said, finally. "Please come with me." It was all he could think to say.

Zacol lowered her head and closed her eyes. "You know that I would follow you anywhere the Holy One led. But that's not what you're asking. Either take us to the mountains of Nagah, or go wherever you will ... without us." She didn't wait for a reply. She just turned and began making her way through the tall grass, heading back to Sedekiyr.

\* \* \* \*

ALEYDIYR

The late afternoon sky was clear through the doorway of the hut. A ridge of mountain peaks cut across the deep blue expanse, jagged and gray with patches of green climbing up their crevices. And below that, in the foreground, Sheyir could see half of a hut that sat opposite the village center from her own. From her perspective on the floor the scene looked like the intersection between two worlds. The one below was temporary and rugged—substantial. The one above was an endless mystery that couldn't be grasped. When she had been Semjaza's prisoner, she used to lie on the floor of the cavern and look up at the ceiling, wishing it was the sky she could see instead of the oppressive stone that kept her in prison. Now her world had been turned upside down. The earth was beneath her and the open sky above, and still she was imprisoned. The wave of nauseating pain that had brought her to the floor a few minutes ago had been a reminder of what was to come—what she couldn't escape.

The pain had passed, but Sheyir had decided to stay on the floor, looking out at what remained of a beautiful day that she hadn't been able to enjoy. The old woman who had volunteered to periodically check in on her had already come and gone, leaving fresh water and some pieces of fruit on the table. But Sheyir didn't feel like putting anything in her mouth. There wasn't room inside her body for one more thing. Instead, she lay still and let the coolness of the floorboards against her face relieve the heat underneath her skin.

A tingling at her toes grew into a prickle, and Sheyir lifted her head from the floor. The prickling sensation grew sharper, spreading to her ankles. She pushed herself up to a sitting position and stretched her legs out, rotating her feet to relieve the pain. For a moment, the prickle dulled. Then it shot up the inside of her legs like two torches pressed against her skin. She let out a shriek and began kicking, crawling backward across the floor on her palms and heels.

Her back came up against the edge of the bed just as the pain disappeared. Sheyir collapsed against it, her body suddenly lacking the strength to hold itself up. She slid down the edge of the bed until her body was once again on the floor. Her breaths were shallow and fast, the air feeling hot as she expelled it from her lungs.

The other women who had given birth in captivity had also experienced a great deal of pain in their final days. But theirs had been a constant, duller pain that seemed to accumulate gradually. A few seconds of reprieve allowed Sheyir to realize that a pattern was forming. What she was experiencing now was more like …

*It's too soon!*

As if it were a wild animal that could smell fear, the pain attacked again. This time it clawed at her belly, forcing her up onto her hands and knees. She crawled across the floor to get away from it, but it shot through to her back and took control of her muscles. Her body flexed against her will, bending her back so forcefully that it sent her forehead crashing to the floor. A yelp escaped her lips before her throat closed around it, choking off the sound. She reached out for help, but her arms seemed to have a mind of their own, flailing uselessly in front of her. Something solid touched her fingers and she instantly grabbed it, digging her fingernails into what she realized was the leg of the table. Her other hand flew forward and joined the effort, grabbing hold of the wooden surface and pulling it toward her.

The table slid across the floor.

Sheyir's body moved toward it.

The lip of the table seemed so far above her. She pulled again with all her might, feeling a sudden urge to get up on her feet. It was as if she were climbing a mountain and relief waited just above that edge. As she stared up at it, too weak to overcome the weight of her own body, something rolled over the edge and fell toward her.

She didn't even have the presence of mind to flinch as the earthen pot shattered on the floor next to her face. Cold water spread across the floor beneath her, soaking her clothes before it spilled through the spaces between the rough wooden planks. Droplets fell from her eyebrows and slid down her nose. It was refreshing. It was a sensation other than pain. Sheyir let go of the table and laid her face on the floor. Her outstretched arms felt heavy, as if someone were sitting on them. The pain in her abdomen was gone now, and in its absence she could feel the shards of the pot beneath the skin of her arms. It might have been painful before this moment, but now it was nothing more than a mild irritant by comparison. A nuisance.

Sheyir opened her mouth to scream for help, but the sight of something lying on the floor in front of her made her reconsider. It was curved. Its edges were sharp, converging at a deadly point. The large piece of broken pottery lay before her like an open invitation. Instead of the water that it used to hold, now soaking the floorboards of her hut, she could see the blood of so many women splattered across a cavern floor.

She reached out and grabbed the shard of baked clay. The feel of it in her hand seemed to give her strength. She rolled onto her back and took a deep breath before grabbing the hem of her soaked tunic and pulling it up. The skin of her belly glistened in the daylight coming through the door. Beneath the surface, a creature moved—a living being with a will of its own. It pushed out against the walls of its fleshly prison, searching for an escape even as those walls pressed back, directing it. Sheyir could make out the shape of its hand sliding under her skin, and it caused her to clench her teeth.

But not from pain.

*You don't belong here,* she thought. Her fingers tightened around the jagged pottery in her hand. Her eyes went to its curved point, longer than her clenched fist. Long enough to plunge through her skin. But could she kill it before she bled to death? This creature that was never meant to be—was it more fragile than she? How many times would she have to plunge the pottery into her belly? How much pain would she have to endure? And how would she know when to stop?

There were too many unknowns. It was too slow of a process. But she had to do something.

The muscles in her back began to tighten again, and Sheyir dropped the pottery. *Not this time,* she thought. *You're not going to control me!* She gritted her teeth and rolled onto her side.

The pain intensified.

She pulled her knees up toward her belly and took a deep breath before pushing herself off the floor.

\* \* \* \*

Sariel handed his bag of gathered fruit to one of the women waiting at the edge of the village. He and the other men were returning from the fields, but his bag wasn't as heavy as the others, an indicator of how distracted he had been throughout the day. Normally, he took his work seriously, as it was the basis for his and Sheyir's acceptance into the tribe. That had become even more important now that Sheyir was unable to work. But he couldn't stop thinking about how to counteract all of the challenges associated with removing the child from Sheyir's womb as soon as it was capable of living on its own. It was the only viable solution, but it posed numerous complications, all of which could end in Sheyir's death. Though Sariel hadn't produced much food for the tribe today, he had managed to construct a plan that addressed each of the risks to Sheyir, along with a few secondary options that would hopefully not be needed. It would take a little time to pull together the needed supplies and tools, or make the ones that he lacked. And the outcome couldn't be guaranteed. But even the possibility of her surviving seemed to lighten the emotional weight that he'd been carrying. Sariel hoped it would have the same effect on Sheyir. She'd been so negative lately, having given in to what she thought was inevitable.

As the rest of the Aleydam returned from the surrounding hills and converged upon the village center, Sariel spotted the old woman who had been taking care of Sheyir for the last several days. She had just set down a shallow pot of water next to a row of others that the gatherers were using to wash their hands. Sariel knelt down in front of her and dipped his hands in the cold water. "How is she doing?"

The old woman glanced over her shoulder in the direction of Sariel's hut. "I brought her some food a little while ago, but she wasn't hungry. She just wanted to rest."

Sariel rubbed his hands together under the water and then shook them off before standing up to wipe them on a clean part of his tunic.

"She's very big," the woman added.

Sariel looked up from his tunic to notice the woman's matter-of-fact expression.

"There will be more than one baby," she concluded.

Sariel wanted to smile at the woman's observation, but the truth only allowed him to nod. "Perhaps. Thank you for taking care of her," he replied, before stepping away from the crowd.

Crossing the central meeting area, Sariel picked up his pace to a brisk walk and ducked inside the doorway of his dwelling. The small fire that usually occupied the center of the hut was only a pile of smoking remains, the light from the coals barely bright enough for him to see.

"Sheyir?" he called quietly.

There was no answer.

He squinted as he moved toward the bed. Something crunched beneath his sandals, and he looked down to see broken pieces of an earthen pot scattered across wet floorboards.

"Sheyir?" he called, louder this time.

He stepped quickly to the bed and could now see that she wasn't lying there. His eyes were adjusting to the lack of light inside the dwelling, but there was nothing to see.

"SHEYIR?" he yelled.

It only took seconds for him to scale the ladder to the second floor of their dwelling where supplies were kept, but she wasn't there either. He leaped off the ladder and landed to the sound of floorboards creaking in protest and then rushed out the door. In the fading light of the afternoon sun, Sariel glanced in every direction. The central meeting area was still alive with people coming in from their day's work, but Sheyir wasn't among them. He caught the stare of the old woman and raised his palms. "She's not here!"

The wrinkles on the woman's forehead deepened.

Sariel turned away and scanned the perimeter of the village, hoping to find Sheyir lingering at the edge of the forest. Perhaps she needed to stretch her legs? Or maybe she couldn't stand being inside all day long. But that wouldn't explain the broken water pot. Perhaps she ...

Sariel's gaze settled on a narrow path that led northward into the trees. His eyes followed it uphill until it disappeared. Above the trees, the jagged peak of the mountain stood out against the early evening sky.

Sariel started moving toward the path before he even knew why. Something was very wrong. He felt it at an instinctual level long before any of the negative possibilities took form in his mind. He wove quickly through the crowd of alarmed people and headed up the path as quickly as his legs could move. His jog sped to a run and then to a sprint. As he had many times in the recent past, he regretted the limitations of this human body. In his Iryllur form, he could have leaped into the air and reached the waterfall in mere seconds. But those seconds seemed to stretch into hours. The silence of the forest was ominous, and each heavy footfall sounded loud against it. His lungs began to burn. The path seemed endless, weaving upward through the trees without any sense of purpose. If there was any point to it, it was to prevent him from going up. The dirt passed underneath him like a stubborn animal that refused to obey. He pushed harder. His legs were on fire. His heart pounded against his ribs, threatening to break out of his chest. There was nothing more important than reaching Sheyir before she could …

The thought was unbearable. And he would die from exhaustion before he let it happen.

The path finally began to level out. The pounding heartbeat in his ears was slowly overcome by the roar of water. And still he ran, angling away from the path and into the trees, taking a shortcut to reach her sooner. Leaves whipped at his face. He swatted branches out of his way, oblivious to the cuts that were forming on his arms. The trees thinned out. The soil turned to wet stone beneath his feet. The darkness of the forest suddenly fled before a torrent of white water, rushing down from the heights above.

"SHEYIR!"

His voice was lost among the roar of something far more powerful. His eyes searched everywhere, bouncing frantically from rocks to trees, patches of moss to dense shrubbery, and from shadows to calm pools of water. His chest heaved.

"SHEYIR!" he yelled again, choking as his lungs protested the waste of precious air. But she was nowhere to be found.

The roar of the waterfall overwhelmed all other sounds, creating an odd sense of peace and stillness with its raw power. The abrupt change of pace was disorienting, and Sariel stood motionless for a moment, suddenly feeling the need to move with caution. He eased forward across the stone, feeling the soft and inviting moss underfoot. He noticed how the spray from the waterfall collected in the crevices, running down to fill tiny pools that reflected a pale but darkening sky. Above him, the tops of the trees stood out as stark silhouettes.

His heart had stopped racing. The pounding in his ears had subsided. His lungs ached with a cold pain, but at least they weren't burning anymore. The steep and narrow gorge spread out before him as he reached the edge of the cliff. The momentary relief of failing to find Sheyir sitting on these rocks had drained away. And in its place was a stronger, more powerful dread that her absence was only a confirmation of what he feared more than anything.

With a resignation that can only come from running into inevitability, Sariel leaned over the edge and began scanning the rugged terrain. His eyes passed over jagged boulders in a serpentine pattern, systematically inspecting everything that was visible in the fading light. After only a few minutes, his gaze settled on something small and paler than the surrounding rocks, over a hundred paces below. It wasn't part of the natural landscape.

Sariel started moving again, leaving the impassible terrain near the water. He stepped back into the trees, where the soil and moss allowed him to make his way down the face of the mountain. He went from one tree trunk to the next, hands outstretched, nearly falling with each step. His hands clasped desperately to the damp bark of each tree. His sandals slid over moss and mud, his legs nearly useless for the descent. Every few minutes, he maneuvered back toward the rushing water to get his bearings before continuing downward. By the time the slope began to level out, the afternoon sun was well below the horizon, and the first stars were becoming visible against a faded purple sky.

Sariel moved out of the trees toward the turbulent river, at once pushed by a sense of urgency and slowed by a hesitant fear of what he would find. The foliage remained thick until rocks began to dominate the landscape, then it disappeared completely. As he scrambled forward, the rocks became boulders. His view was obstructed, but he knew he was in the right location relative to the waterfall, which was now muffled and distant. Angling back upslope, he began climbing from one boulder to the next, some as large as the dwelling that he and Sheyir had built together. Each time he crested, the higher vantage allowed him to look across the earthen debris that had long ago tumbled down from the heights above. Among the dark, angular rocks, was the pale object that he had seen from the cliffs. It was sticking up from a crevice between two boulders at the water's edge. And though it would take several more minutes to reach it, Sariel could see that it wasn't a tree branch like he had hoped. It was a human foot.

He scrambled over the rocks, jumping from one to the next. The fear of what he might find was gone, and all that remained was panic. He crawled like an animal, bruising his limbs against the unyielding stones. Their sharp edges cut his flesh. His feet slid across surfaces green with algae, repeatedly getting stuck in the places where they plunged down into the shadows. And then the foot was visible again.

It stuck out from behind the next boulder at an angle, like a standard propped up by the last soldier of a battle. The acid in Sariel's throat burned, and he swallowed to force it back into his stomach, where it belonged. He knew what was before him. All that remained was to verify it. With ages of warfare and death in his past, it should have been easier than this. But his body shook with fear. His vision blurred from tears. He'd never felt such utter hopelessness in all his life.

Pressing his hands and feet against the rocks on either side of him, he crawled out of a crevice and made his way around the boulder. The pale skin on the bottom of Sheyir's bare foot was covered in mud. Sariel stared hard at it, his eyes refusing to take in everything else. But it was useless. After a few seconds, his eyes began moving, taking in the horrendous vision that would stay with him forever. Blood. A trail of splatters defining the multiple places where her body had struck on its way down from the cliffs above. A dark swath of it running down the side of the rock on which her body had come to rest. Limbs twisted into contorted positions, bending in places they shouldn't. Her black hair, once smooth and straight, was now tangled atop a head that seemed deflated, lacking structure.

Sariel began to scream. It happened before he even realized what he was doing, as though his body and mind were two different things. He shook as the sound poured out of him. His muscles tensed, using the last shreds of their energy to expel whatever pain would come out in the form of sound. He stumbled forward, reaching out for Sheyir's foot.

Her skin felt cold.

He wrapped his fingers around her ankle and pulled, wanting to remove her body from the crevice where it had become lodged. Her leg began to move, but her body didn't. There was nothing substantial on the other end of it. The skin of her thigh stretched like thin fabric as blood and entrails slid out from underneath it.

Sariel immediately let go and tripped backward to land hard on the rocks. His stomach began to heave, and he turned away. What little contents he had in his stomach came out, followed by spasms that took control of his body for several minutes. When it stopped, he just lay still, feeling the cold stone against his body. The sound of the rushing river was still loud in his ears. He had seen more than he wanted to, so he kept his eyes shut even as the tears spilled continuously from them. But the images remained as vivid as if he were still staring at them. He tried to replace them, imagining his time with Sheyir in her own village. But the contrast only brought more sobs, and he began to moan uncontrollably. He opened his eyes, looking for anything else to occupy his vision. Night had descended. Another day gone. But this was one he'd never forget.

# 11

The morning was unusually quiet. Ominous perhaps. Even before the sun came up, the faint sounds of the tribe were usually drifting to his ears—hard-working people wanting to make the most of the coolest part of the day. That's why Enoch would go out into the fields to speak with the Holy One. To find solitude and silence. But even the fields had a sound of their own—the constant drone of buzzing insects, the faraway tweet of birds, the rustle of grass in the breeze. But not this morning.

The air was still and almost cold. The brume was thick. The insects were waiting for the heat of the sun. And the people of Sedekiyr had apparently decided to stay inside their huts until Enoch had left.

*Until the nuisance is removed from their presence,* he thought.

He stood beside his dwelling, looking eastward as Zacol moved around inside putting together his bag of supplies. He could hear the occasional bump as she set something down, the creak of their table, or the sniffling of her fighting back her tears. Every sound was like something sharp digging into his flesh, reminding him of the pain he inflicted on those around him.

Though he and Zacol hadn't spoken to each other since yesterday afternoon, he knew exactly what she must be feeling.

From the time of his return, she had gone through a range of emotions—from the cold, distant outlook that helped her survive, to the warm, hopeful expectancy of someone facing a bright future. And back again. It was enough to drive anyone mad. No sooner had the word expectancy crossed his mind than Enoch began thinking about the reality of missing the birth of his secondborn.

*Why does it have to cost so much ... obeying Your voice? Is it to test my resolve? You already know that I will never forsake You. Why must my family suffer?*

There was no answer, at least not one that Enoch could hear while he lived on the earth. Perhaps somewhere above, in the White City, all the questions that had ever been asked had answers. Perhaps they were being stored up like grain, to be handed out at the appropriate time.

"This should keep you for a few days," Zacol whispered. She was standing next to Enoch now, a full animal skin bag in her hands. "Then you'll have to gather what you can along the way."

It was the same thing she had said to him on their last parting. But this time was different. This time he wasn't naive about what the world was like outside of Sedekiyr. "Thank you," he replied, accepting the bag. He put the strap over his shoulder before leaning on his walking stick.

Zacol turned around and went back inside their hut. "Come on," she said a moment later, her voice muffled through the walls of bundled grass.

A moaning sound was Methu's only reply.

"You will get up and come outside with me this instant," Zacol continued. "He is your father, and you will show him the respect he deserves."

There was a shuffling of feet before Zacol and Methu came out of the hut. Methu's wrist was clamped in Zacol's firm grasp.

Enoch turned to face them as they came near. They were both reluctant in their own ways, and he smiled at them, desperate to ease the pain of their parting. "I know this is difficult for you both," he said. "And I hope you know that I don't want to leave. You two are my tribe. I wish you were coming with me."

Zacol blinked, and the skin around her reddened eyes wrinkled just a bit more.

"But I realize that is too much to ask," he quickly added. "So instead, I ask that you speak to the Holy One on my behalf. Ask that He would grant me safety in my journey, and success in my goal."

Zacol smiled through her tears.

Methu had a scowl on his face and hadn't looked up from the ground the whole time. He had matured so much from that little boy who had been trying to explain something about a rock the last time his father had to go away. And just like his father, he had also lost some of his innocence.

"I'll have more stories to tell you when I get back."

Beneath his brows, Methu's eyes glanced sideways.

Enoch knelt slowly to the ground. He ducked his head to look upon the bruised face of his firstborn son. "I know this doesn't make sense to you right now, but always remember the things that I told you. Understanding will come with time. The wisdom of the Holy One will guide your steps when you cannot see the correct path to take."

Methu's eyebrows lowered even more. He yanked his hand away from his mother's and ran off into the city.

"Methu!" Zacol called after him.

"It's okay," Enoch said, standing up again. "Let him go."

Zacol exhaled loudly before looking back at Enoch. "How long will you be gone this time?"

Enoch shook his head. "It will take many months to reach Firstfather, and the same to return. I don't know what else the Holy One has in store for me."

Zacol was motionless, and her eyes stayed focused on Enoch in an unnerving way, as if she wanted him to feel the weight of his own statement. "Do what you must. And then come back to us as quickly as you can."

Enoch felt lightened by her words, even though they only expressed an acceptance of something that couldn't be changed.

"I will. For all the uncertainty that lies before me, I know that I will come back to you."

She nodded.

Enoch took a deep breath, tightened his grip on the leather bag over his shoulder, and turned toward the fields. He hesitated before finally stepping into the deep grass to head north along the edge of the city. After only a few paces, he remembered that there was still one more thing that needed to be said. He turned suddenly and found Zacol standing in the same place, still watching him. "I love you," he said.

"And I love you," she replied, her voice almost lost to the sound of the buzzing insects that had resumed their natural chorus.

\* \* \* \*

ALEYDIYR

*The tiny hand stuck out, each finger curled to make a miniature fist. The bones were prominent beneath skin that was the color of dark ash, glistening with a thin coating of blood. It looked as though the child were reaching out from the tangle of Sheyir's remains, but it had been forced out from the impact like all the rest of the ...*

Sariel opened his eyes, hoping the memory would go away. But the sight of Sheyir's funeral pyre was only a temporary distraction. Black smoke rose into the clear morning air, curling inward upon itself before the wind swept it away. The flames had been burning for more than an hour and looked just as fierce as when the ceremony had started.

Over the sound of crackling flames, the wailing of several women flared and subsided, as if they were part of the fire. Louder still was the voice of one who stood at the center of the meeting area, telling the story of how Sheyir had comforted her shortly after arriving at the village. Though death was rare, it was the custom of the Aleydam to honor the dead with stories of life, and it seemed that there were many stories to tell. That was the effect Sheyir had on people. Even from the Eternal Realm, Sariel had seen that she was different. He used to spend hours just watching her as she sat by the water's edge and sang the melodies that made Laeningar such an inviting place—a place of healing. She had appeared then as a multi-colored tapestry, as if woven from individual strands of light. And now, all that was left of her in this realm was a darker section at the center of the fire. Even a few minutes ago, the outline of her body had been visible like a silhouette. But that was gone now also.

Sariel looked away from the flames and realized that the village center had gone quiet. The woman who had been speaking was now sitting with her family again. The whole tribe, arranged in a circle around the pyre, was staring at him.

"Do you have any stories that you would like to tell us?" a man on Sariel's left asked, for the second time.

Sariel stared at him for a moment before he realized that the question was something he was supposed to respond to. His head moved up and down, reacting without his conscious assent. Memories whirled through his mind in reverse order— the sound of her laugh as they sat beside the stream in Bahyith, the feel of her hand the first time they touched, the nervous look on her face when Sariel had been invited into her village, and the sight of her tiny body as she ran through the trees in terror when Sariel had *shifted* into this realm in his Iryllur form.

"There are so many ..." he managed to say before grief took control of his body. His face shriveled into something that he was embarrassed by. His head felt weak and suddenly dropped against his chest. And he began to cry all over again. The sobs shook him. The world around him faded into nonexistence, eclipsed by a shadow of sadness.

When he regained control of himself, he realized that somebody was touching him. He opened his eyes to find a hand resting on his shoulder, and the concerned look on the face of a man with whom he'd only traded a dozen words since coming to the village.

"You don't have to speak if it is too painful."

Sariel nodded before letting his eyes drift from one person to the next around the meeting area. Most of the men were solemn, their faces masks of stone. A few wore softer expressions of concern, like the man next to Sariel. The children were crying, as were most of the women. But the others had a different emotion in their eyes. It took a moment to recognize their fear. They were the ones who had taken care of Sheyir's body in the night. They had gathered her broken parts and wrapped her in tight garments before carrying her back to the village. They must have seen what Sariel had witnessed—the hand of a child that wasn't human.

The men had stayed back with Sariel, focused on consoling him by the light of the torches in their hands. Sariel couldn't remember much about the previous night, other than waking up to the sound of shouting. A procession of torches coming down through the forest toward him. It turned to chaos after they found him lying next to Sheyir's remains. Yelling. Crying. People pulling at him to see if he was alive. He wasn't even sure if he came back to the village under his own strength. It was like a nightmare too vague to remember but too powerful to forget. And now it was morning. Sheyir's broken body was turning to ashes. The faces of the Aleydam were still looking at him, waiting.

"I do have something to say," he began.

The man next to him smiled and patted him on the shoulder.

"I want to thank all of you for your kindness ... for taking us in when we had no home. You allowed us to be part of your tribe, and I will always remember that."

Many of the sad expressions were replaced by smiles.

"But I cannot stay with you any longer," he added.

"You're leaving?" the man beside him asked.

"Yes."

"But this is your home now. You will come back soon, yes?"

Sariel knew that he would never get over the pain of Sheyir's death, and that this village would forever be a reminder of his own failure to save her. He had *shifted* into this realm because everyone whom he had loved in the other realm had perished before his eyes. Sheyir had been the only person standing between him and utter hopelessness. And now he had lost her as well. He would never be able to face this village or these people again. But he didn't want to cause more pain by admitting it aloud. "Perhaps, someday," was all he could manage.

The man appeared to understand what Sariel was really saying. He glanced at his fellow tribespeople before turning back to Sariel. "We will miss you. You have taught us many things and have provided for our people like none other. We will remember you always ... the elder without a tribe who came to this tribe with no elders."

Sariel laughed at the ongoing joke, and the rest of the tribe joined in. It was a moment of relief from their shared pain.

"How soon will you be leaving?"

"Now," Sariel replied, struggling to his feet. The weariness of his grief had weakened him, but there was still just enough strength to start walking.

"No. Sit and rest a while."

"Thank you, but I have to go," he said, a new sense of purpose rising inside him.

"At least wait until we can gather some provisions for you."

Sariel shook his head and laid his own hand on the man's shoulder. "Take my hut, and divide my possessions as you see fit. The land will provide everything I need. I don't have any time to waste."

The man looked shocked. "Why? Where are you going in such a hurry?"

Sariel looked out to the southeastern horizon. A white blanket of fog covered the land as far as the eye could see, punctured only by the peaks of the tallest mountains. "Far away," he answered. "I began something that is not yet finished."

The man followed Sariel's gaze before looking back and nodding. He let go of Sariel's shoulder and stepped backward, releasing him.

Sariel looked around the circle of familiar faces and hoped that, in time, their kindness would be the second strongest memory from this moment. Then he stepped closer to the fire and extended his hand, feeling the heat against his palm. The blackened bundle at the center of the flames was all that remained of Sheyir.

*I could have saved you, if you would have given me the chance. Now you must wait a while longer. I have something I must do before I see you again.*

Sariel turned from the flames and began walking toward the path that would lead down the southern face of the mountain range. The cool air that he had become accustomed to felt even colder the farther he walked from the fire. And it was fitting. If he couldn't feel the warmth of Sheyir's presence, then this fragile human body should acquaint itself with the opposite.

# 12

Hyrren grabbed the lip of the ore cart and pulled, dragging its wheels across the crack in the rails that had been steadily growing wider. The three younger Nephiylim pushing from the other side almost lost their footing.

Hyrren smiled. "There's another one up ahead, but you won't need my help for it. Just keep your hands on the cart and don't let it get away from you."

"Thanks," one of them grunted.

Hyrren nodded in return before waving for the next cart to be brought up. Two males, slightly older than the previous group, pushed their cart forward until the wheel caught in the gap. The shudder caused a fist-sized chunk of rock to fall off the pile. Hyrren ignored it, grabbing the cart instead and pulling it across.

The procession of ore carts was longer than it ever had been. Azael's promise to reevaluate the status of the Nephiylim depended upon the results that they could produce. It was just the opportunity Hyrren had been hoping for, and it didn't take much to convince his younger siblings to join the effort. Their fate was now in their own hands. They had both the motivation and ability to change things for the better, and they were making the most of it. Old carts that had sat idle were now being used regularly. The Kahyin males had even constructed a few new ones to keep up with the pace of the Nephiylim. But they couldn't spare any more time away from their other tasks to repair the overused rails, so Hyrren was doing his best to work around the problem.

Eventually, the rails would become impassible, and production would come to a halt. But it would be the Kahyin who would be held responsible for that. It was a problem waiting to happen. And when it arrived, it would only emphasize the weakness of the humans by comparison. It was Hyrren's goal to put more pressure on the Kahyin by outperforming them to such an extent that Azael's wildest expectations would be exceeded. Then he'd have no choice but to reconsider the hierarchy within his kingdom.

Hyrren's brothers continued their march upwards, each one progressively larger until the oldest ones at the back of the line became visible. These pushed their own carts, and Hyrren smiled with pride as he helped them across the deteriorating rails.

Imikal came last, now strong enough to handle two carts on his own. The change that had occurred in him over the recent weeks had been remarkable. It wasn't just the way his body had thickened, responding to the new source of food. Something deeper had taken place. He walked straighter, held his head higher, and there was a new confidence in his eyes.

Hyrren reached out and pulled the carts across the gap. Then he turned and followed his little brother up the passage toward the smelting room. "Can I take one for you?"

Imikal shook his head. "You've done so much for me already. I can handle a few carts."

Hyrren just smiled in return and patted his brother on the back. "They've probably reached the top by now. I better run ahead to help unload."

Imikal just nodded.

Hyrren jogged up the passage, feeling exhilarated by the newfound strength in his legs. They used to shake beneath him, threatening to collapse at any moment. They had been unpredictable before, and now it felt as if he could push five carts or more if it was required of him.

The passage grew lighter until Hyrren crested the incline and entered the smelting room. Just as he suspected, the youngest of his siblings had just reached the piles of ore at the center of the cavern. Where there had been only one short pile before, there were now six. Each one was taller than the Kahyin men feeding the furnaces, and the sight of such progress was almost more satisfying than a good meal.

"Wait," Hyrren called out. "We need to start a new pile."

The youngsters looked confused, but stopped attempting to dump their cart.

"I'll help you take it off the rails," Hyrren said as he approached the group of four. "Then you can roll it over there and dump it."

"Doesn't it have to go back down to the mines?" one of boys asked.

"It will," Hyrren replied, grabbing the edge of the cart and lifting upward. "For now, just dump it and set it aside. Then help the others unload. When we're done, we can put them all back on the rails and move them down to the mines."

The boys nodded as they struggled with the heavy cart that was now moving sluggishly across the hard soil.

Hyrren reached out for the next cart, and just as his hand came to rest on the edge, a sharp voice cut through the din of the smelting room.

"Murderer!"

Hyrren turned his head.

Luhad was coming across the cavern with a quick pace and agile steps as though he were tracking prey. One arm was outstretched with an accusing finger stabbing toward Hyrren. The other was hanging at his side, a long spear balanced in a loose grip. A dozen of his most important men followed, also carrying their hunting weapons.

Hyrren turned back to the group of Nephiylim and nodded. "You push while I lift."

"Look at me when I'm talking to you!" Luhad shouted from closer this time.

Hyrren eased the cart onto the dirt. "It's not as stable off the rails, so keep your hands on it," he told his young siblings. When he turned to grab the next cart, he felt the point of Luhad's spear against his chest.

The next group of Nephiyl youth backed away from their cart.

The Kahyin leader was standing less than a pace away. Both hands were around the shaft of his weapon, knuckles white from the strength of his grip. "You're a monster," Luhad hissed. "Have you no respect for the dead?"

The other men had formed a semicircle a few paces back. Their spears were also ready to strike.

"We have work to do, Luhad. Leave us alone."

"You filthy abomination. You disgust me!" Luhad replied, his eyes flaring wider than Hyrren had ever seen before.

The point of the spear pressed even harder against Hyrren's flesh. A sudden burning sensation let him know that the metal had finally pierced his skin and drawn blood. He kept his breathing steady and shallow. "Our king gave me permission."

"For the other women, perhaps. But not the Kahyin!" he yelled. "You disgrace my people."

The smelting room had gone quiet except for the distant roar of the furnaces. Kahyin and Nephiylim alike were staring.

"Why does it matter to you?" Hyrren asked calmly, looking down on the human who had seemed so intimidating just a few moons ago. "They're going to die anyway."

"Because their bodies are sacred to us," Luhad said through gritted teeth. His hands were shaking now, the spear vibrating with his barely contained rage.

"Then bring us something to eat that isn't sacred. Your people are supposed to be mighty hunters ... so hunt."

A moment of silence passed while the skin of Luhad's neck rippled with veins and strained muscles.

Hyrren couldn't help but wonder if the flesh of Kahyin males would taste different than their females.

A bulge moved through Luhad's neck as he swallowed. "There is not enough food in this whole world to feed abominations like you," he finally said, almost in a whisper.

The incessant degradation finally broke through Hyrren's resolve. He couldn't ignore the offense any longer. "We are the children of the gods. And what are you ... humans?" he spat. "One day, we will rule every last one of you. It is our birthright. And then you will be exposed for what you really are—nothing more than talking animals."

Luhad yelled at the top of his lungs.

The blade of the spear shook, biting harder into Hyrren's flesh as it slowly moved upward toward his neck. But it stopped, held back only by Luhad's fear of making a mistake for which Azael would hold him accountable.

"Do it," Hyrren said, leaning into the spear. His flesh yielded to sharpened metal. His blood began to run freely down his chest. The exhilaration of strong legs was nothing compared to the power that came from transcending the illusion of pain.

The intensity behind Luhad's eyes faltered. He pulled the tip of the spear away from Hyrren's neck, but let it linger in the air. A long moment of silence passed before he took a step backward, then another. Defeated, Luhad finally turned and began walking away past the other Nephiylim. His men followed, while the other Kahyin just watched in disbelief.

Hyrren let out the breath he'd been holding. His body was still tense, but the absence of an immediate threat allowed him to take notice of his surroundings again. Imikal had a satisfied smile on his face. The rest of the Nephiylim were grinning with pride, even the youngest, who still involuntarily cowered whenever the Kahyin were present. It was more than a victory for Hyrren; it was a victory for his people. And he didn't want it to end.

"Run along like the little animals you are and fetch us something to eat."

Luhad stopped walking.

The other men with spears slowed to a stop and looked back at Hyrren as if their ears were deceiving them.

A young Nephiyl stifled a laugh.

Luhad's head slowly pivoted toward the crowd of Nephiyl children clustered around the ore carts.

Hyrren felt the pace of his heart quicken inside his chest.

Luhad lunged to one side and struck a Nephiyl child in the face.

Hyrren moved so fast he surprised himself, closing the distance to Luhad in only two long strides. He shoved the Kahyin leader from behind and sent him tumbling across the cavern floor in a cloud of dust.

As soon as Luhad came to a stop, he reached out and grabbed his fallen spear, climbed to his feet, and turned around.

Hyrren knew instantly that he had crossed a line. He could see it in Luhad's body language. The man's rage was gone. The emotion behind his eyes had burned away. All that was left was the cold stare of someone ready to kill.

Luhad began running.

Hyrren took a few steps backward, unsure of what the man would do or how to prevent it.

Luhad came straight on, thrusting his spear forward with all his might as soon as he was within range.

Hyrren flinched backward and to the side, his hand coming up instinctively. The blade had stopped short of his chest, the shaft suddenly clenched between his fingers. He stared at it, a full second passing before he realized what had happened.

Luhad's reaction was faster. He yanked hard on the spear.

The blade slid backward through Hyrren's hand, opening deep gashes across his palm and fingers. The wounds looked like nothing more than pale lines on his skin before they welled up with the deep crimson color of blood and began dripping profusely onto the cavern floor. Hyrren turned to Luhad, his mind suddenly blank. His body began moving as if someone else were controlling it. His fingers curled into a fist. His arm coiled backward like a serpent before it struck forward and down at the man's face.

Luhad jumped back.

Hyrren stumbled forward as his punch failed to reach its target. He struck again with the other hand, hoping desperately to connect with anything but air.

Luhad dodged to the side.

Hyrren yelled as he threw yet another punch, falling forward into the dirt with momentum that he couldn't control.

Luhad was quick on his feet, jumping backward again.

Hyrren was on his hands and knees now, scrambling across the cavern to reach the enemy that was too cowardly to stop and fight. He clawed at the air, wishing he could just grab hold of the tiny man.

Luhad was almost running backward, his spear tucked under his arm.

Hyrren got a foot underneath him and propelled himself forward, his enemy suddenly within reach.

Luhad sidestepped the attack and jabbed with his spear.

Hyrren's shoulder erupted with fire and he flinched at the pain, swinging his arm upward. The shaft of Luhad's spear snapped and both pieces went spinning through the air. The cavern grew quiet all of a sudden as Luhad realized that he no longer held a weapon. He appeared stunned by this turn of events. Hyrren saw the opportunity and lunged forward, bringing his fist down in an overhead strike. He slammed Luhad's head and felt a grinding sensation like when the ore carts bumped into each other. But this one was followed by a snapping sound. Luhad's head flopped to the side. His body went limp and dropped to the cavern floor.

The satisfaction of finally making contact with his enemy quickly transitioned to regret. *What have I done?*

The cavern erupted into chaos. Shouts rose up from the Kahyin. The workers at the furnaces raised their tools overhead and began converging on the Nephiylim from all directions. The men with spears turned toward the ore carts and the children cowering behind them.

"NO!" Hyrren roared.

Spears flew through the air.

Hyrren burst forward.

Children raised their arms in defense.

Metal blades punctured flesh without any remorse.

Imikal was in the air, leaping over the carts toward the enemy. The older Nephiylim were coming to the defense of the younger.

It all seemed to happen too quickly for Hyrren to stop it. His legs pushed against the ground with all their might. His hands clenched into fists. He flew over the hard soil of the cavern, aiming for the line of grown men who were plunging their weapons continuously into the mass of confused children.

When Hyrren collided with the flank of the Kahyin soldiers, his arms were swinging wildly. His fists began smashing everything without discretion. Bones crunched. Men flew sideways through the air. Spears snapped. In just a few seconds, Hyrren had gone through all of them and was leaping over the carts to reach the nearest of the furnace workers.

A sudden rushing of wind filled the cavern.

The shouting of the Kahyin and desperate cries of the Nephiylim suddenly plunged into silence.

A massive shadow dropped from above and landed between Hyrren and his enemies. It wasn't until he saw the glint of shining metal that Hyrren realized who was before him. And it stopped him in his tracks, cutting instantly through his rage to another, weaker part of him. He fell immediately to the floor and bowed his head. But his eyes remained fixed on his king.

Azael's huge wings were still flared wide. The weapons that encircled his wrists and seemed to crawl up the outsides of his arms shone with an otherworldly brilliance. His red eyes flashed with a dark wisdom that cut through the gloom of the underground chamber. And beneath skin that was dark as ash, battle-hardened muscles held his body deceivingly still. He was the god of death, and everyone was subject to his judgment.

Other than his own father, Hyrren had never been so afraid of anyone in all his life. And it was obvious they would all pay for the mistake they had just made.

\* \* \* \*

Azael slowly retracted his wings and stood up to his full height. He kept his vaepkir unsheathed so that his subjects wouldn't forget the threat of death. From the corners of his vision, he could see that Parnudel and Rikoathel had also claimed instant control over their sections. Despite the friction between the two groups of subjects, it was satisfying to see that they still knew who was in charge.

The smelting room was a mess. Ore carts had been turned over on their tracks, the bodies of several Nephiyl children scattered between their contents. Spears and metalworking implements littered the floor, alongside pools of blood. But the biggest disruption was the number of dead Kahyin, including Luhad. Azael stepped slowly between the fallen, surveying the battlefield. There had to be four dozen or more. The realization that this would negatively affect his weapons production was offset by the impressive show of force. Azael had only allowed the conflict to last a few seconds before he intervened, but what the Nephiylim were able to do in that time was incredible—even the youngest ones. There was a raw instinct to their movements, and an undeniable power. They were nothing more than children. But even the largest and strongest of all the human tribes, trained for battle, were no match for them. This was a turning point for Azael, and he was glad that he had allowed the situation to spiral out of control, or he might have missed this opportunity.

He and his Iryllur soldiers had suspected this was going to happen. When Luhad and his men had grabbed their spears and begun making their way up toward the mines, Parnudel and Rikoathel had been watching from inside the forests. They informed Azael, and the three of them followed in secret. They had witnessed the entire event, from Luhad's antagonistic threats to Hyrren's response. It had been a clumsy fight, leading to an inefficient and blundering battle. But Azael had witnessed everything he needed to know.

He looked across the cavern to Parnudel and Rikoathel. Both soldiers, stepping silently through the battlefield, simply nodded. It was clear that they had reached the same conclusion.

Azael stopped in front of Hyrren and looked down on the child, still bowed low in reverence. "What happened here?"

"I allowed my anger to control me. I'm sorry, my king," Hyrren replied.

Azael grinned. "Do you remember what I said about speaking the truth?"

"Yes, my king."

"Good. Then tell me again. Do you regret your anger?"

"No, my king," Hyrren answered. "I'm not sorry for what I did. I wish I could have saved all of my brothers and killed a few more Kahyin before you arrived."

"A few ...?"

"All of them, my king."

Azael lowered himself until his knee was resting on the ground and his eyes looking directly into Hyrren's. "I've been wondering when you would make your move, Hyrren. Your father was the most fearless soldier I've ever had the pleasure of serving with. And he was even more ruthless as a leader. That very same blood courses through your veins. I knew the spirit of your father would rise again; I just didn't know how long it would take."

Hyrren lifted his head, and the fear that had seemed to be a permanent part of his demeanor was gone.

"Rise, Hyrren. Son of Semjaza. Killer of men. General of my armies," Azael said quietly.

The two of them stood up slowly together.

Azael had to look upward now to meet the child's confident gaze. "The youngest children of the Anduarym will work these mines and the furnaces, for we cannot know strength unless we face trials."

"Yes, my king."

"The youngest children of the Iryllurym will take to the skies to hunt for their brethren," Azael continued. "Those of us with wings were never meant to live under the earth."

"Yes, my king."

"For you and the other eldest ... you will learn the ways of war. You will receive the heritage of your fathers, forged in the battles of the Eternal Realm, paid for by the blood of my kinsmen," Azael said, pounding his chest. "And in all things, the Kahyin will serve your people."

Hyrren's eyes, the color of fire, glistened with tears.

Azael resheathed his vaepkir and glanced at his soldiers, receiving nods of affirmation before he turned back to Hyrren. "Welcome to my kingdom."

# 13

Sariel could hear the breeze moving through the trees long before he was able to feel it on his face. When he left the dense foliage and walked out onto a rock outcropping, he could also see the effect it was having on the mist. At the higher elevations, the visibility was much better. He could look out over the land and see the moisture that came up from the soil, clinging to the low places like it was a living thing. Above, the blue sky gradually faded to a pale orange near the western horizon where the sun was no longer visible. But the moon stood out clearly against the darker backdrop. It would be full in another week, which gave him just over a month to reach Senvidar before the Myndarym met for their Council. He still had a long way to go, but if he maintained his current pace he would make it in plenty of time.

It wasn't that he cared to join their efforts to rule the Temporal Realm. His motivation came from what the messenger, Naganel, had revealed—something that Sariel couldn't get out of his head. He'd had more important things to ponder during Sheyir's last days, but ever since this realm had lost her presence and ceased to be a place of refuge for Sariel it was all he thought about.

Naganel had said that there could be negative consequences for not attending the Council, which meant that there had to have been other Myndarym who refused. Otherwise, there would be no issue to force such a strong position. So how did they plan on enforcing their authority over this realm? If the Council planned on using their *shaping* abilities in a negative way, the other Myndarym could just as easily fight back with the same methods. So that wasn't a valid explanation. And given Naganel's reaction to Sariel's question, it seemed obvious that the other Myndarym had also lost their *shaping* ability. If so, what other leverage did they have? Had they taken over Semjaza's rule of the Kahyin?

Sariel remembered the human armies that were stationed at the land gate of Mudena Del-Edha during the Amatru attack. He'd been the one to realize that the mass of living creatures receiving the brunt of the first Iryllur strike were not angels. It forced them to abandon their strategy because the Amatru weren't authorized to kill humans.

*Could that be it? No. Surely not!*

A human army wouldn't pose a threat to the other Myndarym who had scattered after the war with Semjaza. Unless they were also confined to human forms like Sariel. But he doubted that any others had the type of motivation that he had to confine himself in this way. He wanted to interact with Sheyir on an equal level, without frightening her. Love had been his motivation. But they had sought freedom and power. It was unlikely they would have done what he did.

What else would pose a sufficient threat to the Myndarym who had chosen other forms? Sariel remembered the forms of those who had fought at his side against the Anduarym who stole their weapons. Large birds of prey. Wolves with teeth like daggers. Tigers with claws that could kill a man with one swipe. If it was a human army, it would have to be larger than the population of Khelrusa.

All of this speculation had been repeating itself in Sariel's mind as he had moved quickly over the land, gathering food along the way. The only time he didn't wonder about it was when he slept for a few hours every night. And then, it was his dreams that were troubled by these questions. He would wake and set out again before the sun rose, pushing his human body to the limit of its capability. The terrain under his feet slowly transitioned from one type to another—from the bare soil of a forest to marshy plains of grass. From wading through streams of cold water to scrambling up the side of a rocky cliff. And all the while, only one conclusion made sense.

*Some of Semjaza's forces must have survived.*

But for all the questions it answered, it created so many more. The first of which was plausibility. Could the Amatru really have missed some? Sariel had assumed that all of them had been killed, but there was no way for him to be confident about that now. He had flown away from Mudena Del-Edha to attack Semjaza. And after escaping the Iryllur soldiers, he had returned with only one thing on his mind—to rescue Sheyir. There had been Amatru soldiers present when he picked her up from the road in front of Semjaza's tower, but he couldn't remember much else.

If some of Semjaza's soldiers had survived, why would they choose to work with the Council instead of killing them? And how could the Council possibly lower themselves to work with the very angels who had betrayed them? There were so many questions that needed to be answered, so many possible scenarios to explore. But Sariel was sure of one thing—if any living piece of Semjaza's kingdom had survived, he would destroy it. He had made that promise to Semjaza himself when the leader refused to give up Sheyir. And Sariel would not tarnish her memory by breaking that promise.

\* \* \* \*

NORTH OF DA-MAYIM
THE UNMOVING WATERS

The north end of the Unmoving Waters narrowed and curved like an errant tree branch, pointing east as though a reminder of which direction Enoch's people needed to move. This message from the Holy One strengthened his resolve and added a sense of urgency to his movement. Enoch had been traveling for weeks, reacquainting himself with the solitude and slow, deliberate progress that he had come to appreciate on his last journey. Though it would require millions of steps to complete this task, he could look down at his feet and see evidence that his efforts were producing something. He could look back upon the coast of the Unmoving Waters and see from a distance the land that used to be underneath him, proof that his millions of tiny actions added up to something larger. He wished he could say the same about his influence among his own people.

From atop the rolling hills north of the water, Enoch smiled and closed his eyes. The sun was warm on his skin. A breeze kept the warmth from becoming oppressive. It was a beautiful morning. He turned until the sun was at his back and began making his way down the gentle slopes of short grass. Somewhere beyond the western horizon were the tribes of his forefathers. Though he had never seen them, he'd heard enough from Grandfather Mahalal-el's stories to know what to expect. He would walk backward along the timeline of his people, each city serving as a milestone, each culture more advanced than the last. The firstborns had always left the city of their fathers to establish one of their own ... until Enoch. They had brought their wives and children, and anyone else who was ready to push farther into the wilderness. In this way, the Shayetham had multiplied and spread across the earth.

But Enoch wouldn't be stopping at any of these places. His presence would violate the customs of his people—it was the fathers who carried their wisdom to their sons, not the other way around. Enoch didn't need to create any more obstacles between him and his goal. He would keep to the uninhabited places and not seek the shelter of his people until he was standing before the firstfather. He wasn't sure what he would say when that day arrived, but there was plenty of time to think on that matter. For now, he would just enjoy the journey.

Enoch lifted his gaze from the gently sloping hill and looked out to the west. The mist was moving in clumps today, following the low terrain like herds of grazing animals moving from one field to another. Enoch smiled at the image of himself walking between gigantic lazy beasts who barely noticed him. He was just about to laugh when he felt a presence over his right shoulder.

He turned suddenly, but the hillside was empty. He was alone, but it didn't feel that way.

*Holy One?*

There was no answer.

Enoch looked up to the sky, remembering the terrifying creature that had chased him into a river on his first journey. But the sky was clear except for a few small birds.

"Ananel?" he asked aloud.

There was also no answer from the Myndar who preferred roaming the earth in the form of a massive wolf. Enoch had encountered him unexpectedly on several occasions, but it didn't seem to be the case this time.

With his heart beating loudly in his chest, Enoch scanned the terrain in every direction, wondering if the Holy One had alerted him to a threat that he just couldn't see yet. As his eyes swung northward, the unsettling feeling disappeared.

*Hmm.*

He turned east and the feeling came back, but this time he was able to interpret it. It wasn't an imminent threat that he was feeling. It was a sense of being lost, as if he were moving in the wrong direction.

He pivoted to the north again and the sensation went away.

*But Firstfather is to the west,* he argued. *Why would you want me to go north? I've already been there.*

In the foreground, a patch of fog drifted away, revealing an open line of sight to another body of water—the southernmost of the Great Waters. Just to the right of that would be a narrow section of land through which he had traveled on his last journey. Ad-Banyim.

*There is nothing for me in that land anymore. Did I not complete the task you gave me?*

The breeze moved over the grass. Nearby, a lone insect chirped in its foreign language. Three small birds took to the air, the sound of their beating wings swallowed up by the distance.

Enoch took a deep breath and let it out.

*Very well. It does not make sense to me, but if You lead me I will follow.*

Moving around the slope, Enoch headed north and began to retrace the steps that he had taken over a year ago.

S.A. 694

# 14

From a distance, the only indicator of Senvidar's presence had been the height difference of the trees. The forest canopy was thick in every direction, an expanse of leaves that mimicked the rise and fall of the land beneath. But there was an unnaturally tall section that stretched from the slopes of the mountains all the way down to the coast of the Great Waters to the west.

Sariel had used an unobstructed hilltop vantage to the north of the city in order to plan his approach. Now he found himself stepping quietly through the shorter, thinner forest, heading toward the transition that marked the boundary of the city. The trunks sprouting from the forest floor around him were more than an arm's reach apart. But the vertical columns of living wood farther ahead were packed tightly together, forming a wall. Each trunk was wider than ten humans standing beside each other.

*There it is!*

Sariel kept moving forward a few paces before turning east and walking parallel to the edge of the city. Shafts of light spilled down from above illuminating sections of the unusually quiet forest. The ground underfoot was moist, muffling his steps over a light blanket of decomposing leaves. There a steady incline to the terrain which lasted for almost an hour before it leveled out. That's when Sariel's gaze settled on a gap in the wall of tree trunks to his right. He stopped behind a nearby tree and cautiously peered around its rough bark.

The entrance into the city looked like an arched doorway, with two massive trees of smooth, white bark growing toward each other, their branches interlacing overhead. Behind it were more trees that followed the same unusual shape, creating a passage into the dense forest. The soil was perfectly flat and free of obstructions, but Sariel was paying more attention to the Myndar who stood just inside the doorway. He was slightly taller than Sariel's Iryllur form, with a thickly muscled body covered in loose-fitting white cloth below the waist. His upper body was bare, and his thick arms were crossed at the chest. With his pale skin, he resembled the massive trees that towered over him.

"Zahmesh," Sariel called as he walked out from behind the tree.

The Myndar's blond head turned, his eyes quickly fastening on the one who had called his name.

Sariel came toward the entrance with a casual stride, showing that he was neither afraid nor hostile. "Does Senvidar require guards now?"

The Myndar looked down, his eyebrows appearing thin in contrast to the long and unruly beard that cascaded from his face like a waterfall. "Who are you?"

"Sariel. I was invited to the Council by Naganel."

Zahmesh frowned. "You're very early."

"I wanted to speak with my friends here before the other Myndarym arrived."

Zahmesh's face revealed nothing. He simply stared down at Sariel before he finally replied, "Wait here." He turned and strode down the passage, his long steps carrying him quickly from view.

Sariel did as he was told, passing the time by inspecting the gigantic roots of the trees that spread outward from the wall, emerging from the soil like grasping fingers. The natural trees outside of the city looked small and weak by comparison.

*I know exactly how you feel.*

The sound of footsteps brought his attention back to the entrance just as Zahmesh returned. A dark-haired woman was at his side, breathing heavily from trying to keep up with the Myndar. She was dressed in a flowing gown of white cloth that contrasted sharply with her ruddy skin. At first glance, she looked like Sheyir. Sariel's heart began beating faster even though he knew it was just their shared ancestry. This was obviously one of the women that Jomjael had brought to Senvidar after Sariel had freed them from captivity. But she didn't seem to recognize him in his human form.

"This is your escort," Zahmesh said, gesturing with his hand. "She will take you to the Place of Meeting."

The woman bowed to Zahmesh before turning to Sariel. "Please come with me."

Sariel nodded to Zahmesh and stepped past him, entering the hall of interwoven trees. As the woman walked steadily and silently before him, he looked up to the ceiling of branches arching high overhead. The canopy of leaves was thick, blocking all but a few thin shafts of sunlight. The smooth, pale bark of the trees reflected it, illuminating the passage with a gentle and diffused glow that only added to the city's mysterious quality. Butterflies of every color clung to the ceiling of branches and leaves, gently opening and closing their wings. Rainbows of color seemed to ripple through the air above their heads. When he had been here last, Sariel had been looking through Iryllur eyes. Even then this city had seemed impressive. Now, gazing through human eyes, it was magnificent beyond comprehension.

They turned left at an intersection and began heading east toward the mountains. After a few minutes, the passage opened on its right side, revealing a wide meadow of short grass and a herd of grazing animals. A handful of women walked among the beasts, stroking their fur and singing softly to them.

The trees closed around them again and Sariel suddenly realized how quiet this forest city was. He could hear the faint chirp of birds in the distance, but the steady buzzing of insects was mysteriously absent. Light and sound were subdued here, as if Senvidar was an opening into another part of creation's spectrum.

The wall of trees to their right opened once more, revealing another area of the city exposed to the sky above. Row upon row of large bushes stretched into the distance, with thick clusters of fruit hanging between their leaves. More women, dressed like Sariel's escort, walked among the vegetation and removed the ripe fruit. Their soft melodies drifted lazily through the stillness, and there was something very familiar about it.

"Why do they sing?" Sariel asked.

The woman slowed her pace and looked back over her shoulder. "The gods taught us how to bring life to the trees and plants so they will grow strong. We sing to call forth their beauty, and they sing back to us with their fruits. It is the same with the animals. We work against the death and decay that infect this world. We must keep evil things away from this place if it is to survive."

Sariel looked back to the women in the field, recognizing the melodies now. They were the human translation of the Songs of Creation—simple threads of a tapestry that was far too complex for the limitations of the human voice. Sariel wondered if such a limited, deconstructed approach could have any effect on this world whatsoever. Without the ability to see into the Eternal Realm, there was no way for these women to know if they were succeeding or failing. But it was beautiful nonetheless.

Again and again, the passage entered the dense forest and opened into fields and orchards. Gradually, it began to climb in elevation as he followed his escort through the foothills. Streams of water ran down beside the passage, breaking into narrow channels that ran through the orchards or collected into pools around the pastures. It seemed that the collection of moisture from the mountains fed the entire city, even pooling in arrangements of rock beside the passage for the citizens to drink. As the passage steepened, the roots of the forest spread across the soil, their rounded shapes becoming more angular and serving as a staircase. Short bridges of interwoven roots arched across the streams that were also woven through the passage. Sariel realized that his tapestry analogy applied everywhere he looked.

Overhead, the canopy of leaves transitioned to that of blossoms. Like the butterflies that he had seen earlier, the flowers enveloped the passage with bands of color and texture. Sariel smiled as he looked up, letting his eyes follow the trail of beauty. When he turned around to look at the ceiling behind him, he saw an opening in the dense canopy of blossoms and leaves. Below him, and spreading all the way to the western horizon, the city of Senvidar was laid out. Countless pastures and orchards. Tall stands of trees that curved through fields of grass in intricate designs. Wide swaths of water that curved through it all, splintering into hundreds of smaller tributaries. It was a sprawling city of unimaginable beauty, invisible unless seen from above.

The Myndarym had been hard at work since Sariel had last visited. And though he suspected they had lost their *shaping* abilities at the same time he had, the scale of their accomplishments made him doubt it. He couldn't help but wonder if he was the only one in a position of weakness.

The passage began to level out, eventually entering into the side of the mountain. Sariel realized that the Place of Meeting must have been moved from its previous location among the trees. As the canopy of leaves disappeared from overhead, it was replaced by a dense tangle of roots glowing with luminescence. The soft stillness of the forest was gone. In its place was a deep silence, punctuated by the echoing sound of their footsteps. Sariel was feeling the strain in his legs and lungs, and he could hear the breathing of his escort growing labored. The stairs under his feet showed no signs of being worked with tools. The stone had been shaped just as the trees had.

After another hour of climbing, the underground passage widened and opened to a blue sky above. The sun was closer to the horizon than it was to its peak. The *shaped* stone beneath Sariel's feet began to flatten until it was a smooth path between walls on either side. As they continued forward, the walls grew shorter and eventually disappeared altogether. The city of

Senvidar spread all the way to the coast. The large body of water that had served as Sariel's reference point during his travels spread from there to the western horizon. If Sariel had been able to catch his breath, the view might have stolen it from him again. It had been far too long since he had seen the earth from this vantage point, and he regretted once again trading his wings for a human body.

As he tore his sight away from the horizon, he noticed that his escort had stopped walking. She was on her knees in the middle of the path. A giant bird of prey towered over her, looking both majestic and dangerous.

Sariel looked up to the bird's large and piercing eyes while he remained standing. He recognized the Myndar from when they had fought side by side against Semjaza's Anduarym. His name was Fyarikel.

"Thou, whose eyes search far and wide," the woman said, "I have been instructed to bring this human into your presence. Please forgive your servant for approaching the forbidden place."

"You are forgiven," Fyarikel replied. "Retreat into the mountain until he is ready to be taken back to the city."

The woman kept her eyes on the ground and scooted herself backward. Then she got to her feet and turned, walking past Sariel down the path.

"The Council is not for several weeks," Fyarikel pointed out as soon as the woman was gone.

Sariel looked up at his fellow Myndar once again. "I have a few questions before the Council convenes."

Fyarikel blinked—thin, transparent membranes sliding quickly across his eyes. He kept silent for a long moment before he finally responded. "Very well. Continue on the path until you reach the Place of Meeting. I'll see who's available." He spread his wings and leapt into the air with a gust of wind.

Sariel closed his eyes and waited for the swirling dust to settle. Then he proceeded along the path. Less than a minute later, he crested the gradual incline and began descending toward a circular meeting area ringed by concentric levels of stairs that were too large for humans. In the center stood Fyarikel and three others, one of whom wore a human form.

"Sariel. Welcome back to our city," said Danel. "You're early."

Sariel smiled at the Myndar who had kept her tall, female form. The only words he'd exchanged with her in the past had been filled with tension, and though she spoke with more courtesy now there was a condescending tone to her words.

"Senvidar has changed since I was here last," he observed.

"And so have you," Turel replied. His pale skin and hair made him look like Danel's twin.

"I was under the impression that there were more of you. Are you the only ones who live here?" Sariel asked, making his way onto the floor of the meeting area.

"No," Danel answered. "I am told you have a few questions for us?"

Sariel had finally reached the center of the meeting area and approached the group. He could see now that Ezekiyel was the one wearing a human form. The master *Shaper* just nodded as Sariel came to a stop and looked up at the other Myndarym. "I would like to speak with everyone at the same time." In reality, he just wanted to know which of Semjaza's soldiers had survived.

"The others are busy with various tasks at the moment," Turel replied.

"But we can speak for them," Danel added. "We are in agreement about most things."

"What have you come to say?" Fyarikel asked.

Sariel looked at each of them in turn, his eyes finally settling on Ezekiyel, who hadn't spoken yet. "Naganel's invitation was odd ... to say the least."

Fyarikel's head tilted to one side in a very birdlike manner.

"How so?" Danel asked.

"He addressed me with the courtesy I would expect from a messenger, and then he proceeded to threaten me."

The look that passed over Danel's features was one of uncomfortable confusion, not about Sariel's claim, but of how to respond. It was exactly what Sariel's statement was designed to produce.

"What do you mean?" Turel asked, coming to her rescue.

"He said there would be negative consequences for not attending. But, as I observed on the way up here, it does not seem that my Myndar brethren have taken up the Marotru practice of *unshaping*. So I am confused about his comment."

Turel nodded. "I apologize on behalf of the Council if Naganel's manner lacked ... tact."

"Thank you," Sariel replied. "I am still curious about his comment, though."

"Well," Danel jumped in. "Some of our brethren wish to avoid the responsibility that we have taken upon ourselves by coming to this realm. They are showing themselves to be short-sighted, and it has required us to be less than polite ... when the situation demands. Again, we apologize if you received such a message unjustly."

Sariel could see that they were taking great care to avoid the actual meaning of his question, but he decided to play innocent a while longer. "Oh, no offense was taken. I suspected that much already. What I mean is ... what is the basis upon which this threat is being made?"

Turel inclined his head. "It is an appeal to their logic and their desire to remain free. Unless we all agree to mutually beneficial terms, this realm cannot be ruled by more than one of us without conflict."

Sariel smiled. It was clear now that as long as he kept being polite, they would keep avoiding answering the question. He needed to drop the act and use a direct approach. "Did any of Semjaza's forces survive?"

"Why should that matter?" Fyarikel asked.

Sariel turned to look up at the giant bird. "If you would have me participate in this Council, you will stop avoiding my questions and answer me truthfully. Or else I will know that you do not intend to have me, or any others, here as equals."

Danel looked offended, even confused by Sariel's accusation. "Some of his soldiers survived, but I don't see how that is relevant to this—"

"How could you even think about making allies out of them?" Sariel asked.

Turel crossed his arms. "I understand your concerns. But if we are to move forward in a constructive manner, we must forget about what transpired. It was Semjaza who betrayed us. His soldiers were just following orders. It is understandable that they were not as willing as we were to break away from him."

"Because soldiers are not as intelligent as Myndarym?" Sariel pushed.

"That is not what I meant ... of course. It is just that soldiers are trained to see things from only one perspective. It is what gives them their strength—the conviction that their leader is without fault. We cannot hold Semjaza's soldiers to the same standard by which we judged him."

Sariel shook his head slowly. "You forget that I have the unique privilege of both perspectives, as a Myndar and a soldier. So I will extend you the courtesy of not being offended by the way you have portrayed us soldiers as though we are human children. And in return, I would like you to answer me this—if soldiers are so single-minded as you have described, why would they ever agree to work with traitors like you ... from their perspective, of course? Why wouldn't they take revenge on the Myndarym who betrayed them to the Amatru and killed their leader?"

Turel straightened his posture, and it seemed that his look of offense was genuine.

"Azael has demonstrated that he is the exception," Danel offered. "To his credit, he understands the value of reaching a consensus before we all move on."

Danel's words hit Sariel as abruptly as a fist to the nose. Azael! The comment brought all of his wandering thoughts together into a fine point, focused on one thing. He had to compose himself before opening his mouth again, and he refused to let it show on his face. "Who are the other soldiers?"

he asked, managing to speak without revealing the rage that welled inside him.

"Parnudel and Rikoathel," Fyarikel answered.

*Would three Iryllurym be enough of a threat to the other Myndarym to force their participation?* he wondered, while outwardly he just nodded. "And they control the Kahyin, I assume?"

"Enough of this!" Danel almost barked. Apparently she had also lost her patience with pleasantries. "If you wish to be a part of this Council, you will do so as an equal, extending the other members the same courtesy. We cannot build a system of mutual governance while maintaining this concept of enemies and allies. Your very language betrays your polarized perspective."

Clearly, Azael's military strength was his leverage over the Myndarym. It explained why they would choose to work with him. But it didn't explain why he wouldn't just attack them and take over everything. Though Sariel had only spoken with the Iryllur once on the road below the mines of Khelrusa, the meeting had been very informative. He knew that only the threat of annihilation would keep Azael at bay, which meant that Azael didn't know about their loss of *shaping* power—it was their leverage over him. And the strength of Danel's reaction hinted that this truce went even deeper, but Sariel had learned everything he needed. He knew who was left, and he knew where they were. Now he just needed a good excuse to get out of Senvidar alive.

"I'm sorry. You're right. It's just ... very difficult for me to think of Semjaza's soldiers as equals. I was the one to go before the Amatru and plead our case. And then I fought alongside the Amatru against Semjaza. You did not. You helped, of course, but you didn't go to war against them."

Turel nodded.

"That's true," Fyarikel admitted.

Danel just squinted.

Ezekiyel didn't bother replying.

Sariel exhaled loudly and looked at the ground before finally glancing up again. "I'm going to need some time to ... accept this."

"You have until the Council convenes in twenty-three days. After that, latecomers will not be afforded the same status or liberties."

Sariel nodded. "I understand. I'll just ..." he mumbled, looking out over the city. "Well, thank you for your time. I'll see you again soon." He hoped his apparent confusion made him seem like less of a threat.

"Your escort should be waiting for you inside the mountain," Fyarikel reminded him.

"Yes. Of course," Sariel replied, jabbing a thumb over his shoulder as he stepped backward.

Turel nodded.

Sariel spun around and walked out the way he had come.

# 15

"I can understand his position," Turel admitted. "It would be difficult for me to accept it as well."

Danel shook her head. "I still don't like it. He knows we can't *shape*, and that makes him a liability just like the rest of them. He's either on our side, or we treat him as an enemy."

"The trouble is we don't know which," Fyarikel screeched. He hadn't been able to read the soldier's body language when Sariel was standing before him.

"We'll know soon enough," Turel replied. "I, for one, hope he comes back. He'd be a great addition to the Council with everything he's experienced."

Danel frowned and looked down at Ezekiyel. "You haven't said anything this whole time. What are you thinking?"

The master *Shaper*, who had chosen—for reasons only he knew—to restrict himself to a human form, looked up into Fyarikel's eyes. Though he was physically inferior, Fyarikel was still intimidated by the Myndar's intense gaze and the unfathomable depths of wisdom behind it. "I think you need to take to the skies and watch the exits of the city. If he goes south toward Khelrusa, kill him. If he goes any other direction, leave him alone but keep him in sight."

"If he heads south, it doesn't necessarily mean he will betray us to Azael," Turel argued.

Ezekiyel glanced up without moving his head. "That's not what I mean."

"You saw something that we did not," Danel prodded. "What was it?"

Ezekiyel stared straight ahead, his eyes distant, as if he were still looking directly at Sariel. "I saw revenge in his eyes. If he goes to Khelrusa, it will not be to speak with Azael."

Danel frowned and turned to look at Turel.

Turel crossed his arms, with one hand on his chin. "He could jeopardize our entire plan if he does something foolish."

Danel turned and fixed Fyarikel with a pleading gaze. "Go, please. Do as he says."

Fyarikel nodded and spread his wings.

The city was so far below Fyarikel that he could see its entirety without moving his head. But his eyes were powerful, able to take in even the smallest details. As his gigantic wings made use of the updraft coming off the mountains, he circled above Senvidar to give his eyes an ever-changing perspective. It had been hours since Sariel had left the meeting area, but he hadn't yet left the city. Fyarikel was trying to think through the possible explanations when he noted erratic movement in one of the orchards below. He pivoted his head and trained both eyes on the movement, realizing that it was Zahmesh waving up to him.

Fyarikel rolled to the side and pulled his wings inward, pitching forward until his beak was cutting through the humid air. The wind whistled as it passed over his sleek, feathered body. The orchard seemed to grow exponentially until he slowly unfurled his wings to flatten his approach. Just before the ground came up to meet him, he flared his wings to the extent of their reach and brought his downward and forward movements to a halt. When his talons came to rest against the dark soil between the fruit trees, his landing was as gentle as if he had done nothing more than hop a few paces. But he had descended many hundreds of paces in just a few seconds.

"Sariel evaded his escort," Zahmesh yelled as he ran over.

"He hasn't left the city yet," Fyarikel assured him. "I've been watching the whole time. He must be hiding inside."

Zahmesh turned and looked across the orchard as he contemplated what to do. "Alright. You keep watching from above. I'll alert everyone else to start looking."

Fyarikel spread his wings.

"When does Naganel return?" Zahmesh asked as an afterthought.

"Not until tomorrow evening."

"We could sure use his eyes right now."

"Don't worry," Fyarikel assured him. "Sariel can't leave this city in any direction without revealing himself. You just concentrate on finding his hiding place."

Zahmesh turned and began running.

Fyarikel reached upward and grabbed the air with his feathered wings.

\* \* \* \*

THE WESTERN SHORES OF THE GREAT WATERS
SOUTHWEST OF SAHVEYIM

Water stretched to the horizon on Enoch's right, rolling hills to his left. If he turned in either direction, the feeling of disorientation would return. It was a gift from the Holy One, but the strength of it had been fading for the last few days. Perhaps he was becoming accustomed to it with time. Or perhaps it was the strength of another sensation that was overpowering it. Hunger. The fruit and nuts that he had found along the way helped, but the gnawing in his stomach had become a constant warning. It no longer came and went in waves. He needed something more substantial.

Enoch kept moving northward over the uneven terrain, keeping near the tree line where his footing was more solid. Out on the beach, the smooth stones would turn under his feet as he took each step. It had been deceptively difficult. The lack of trees didn't necessarily mean that it was easier to travel through.

Climbing another short hill, Enoch wove through a sparse stand of trees and came out into a wide meadow. Flowers were blooming everywhere in clusters. A wide stream cut through the field of short grass. It reminded him of Sedekiyr, which in turn reminded him of something else.

Enoch picked up his pace to a jog, moving quickly but carefully over the soft cushion of green under his feet. When he reached the stream, he followed it uphill to a deep pool where the water collected after spilling over the edge of some rocks. The surface was smooth, and the clear water allowed him to look all the way down to the sandy bottom. It was as deep as he was tall. And there were fish everywhere.

Enoch smiled and knelt in the grass. He laid down his walking stick and dropped his pack. Then he untied the thin spear that he had made less than a week ago. It seemed that he would finally get the chance to use it. It was nothing more than a thick reed that he had split into four strips on one end, then carved into barbed points. A cord of woven grass kept each point away from the others, and kept the reed from splitting further. It wasn't quite as robust as what he would have used at home, but it was easy to carry and would serve its purpose.

Enoch stood with the spear balanced in his hand. He moved closer to the edge of the stream, his eyes focused on the long and narrow shadows that hung in the depths, slowly moving from side to side as they swam against the gentle current. The sun was still halfway between the eastern horizon and its peak, so he crouched low and moved to the west of the pool, where his shadow wouldn't disturb the fish.

Insects hovered above the water, moving in erratic but coordinated swarms. Every so often, one would dip down to the surface. They were so fast that it wasn't until rings spread outward across the water that Enoch could tell any contact had been made. He waited patiently, keeping one eye on the dipping insects and another on the fish. Minutes passed without activity until an insect dipped once, then stayed close to the surface.

A fish took notice and began drifting upward.

Enoch raised his spear over his shoulder.

The insect dipped again.

The fish darted to the surface with amazing speed.

Enoch thrust his spear. His foot went forward for balance, but discovered that the longer blades of grass spilling over the edge of the pool had nothing underneath them. Instead of watching his spear tip dive into the clear water, he watched the surface of the water coming quickly toward his face. Before he knew it he was submerged with flailing arms and legs, trying to get back to the edge he had just slipped from.

His spear floated downstream until it got stuck on a rock. Enoch watched it while clinging to the grass at the edge of the pool. Then he pulled himself out of the water with a great deal of effort and rolled over to lie back in the morning sun and laugh aloud at himself. Zacol would have frowned at him for acting childish. Methu would have talked about it for a week. But the only beings to observe Enoch's foolishness had been the birds who took to the air at the first sound of splashing, and the fish who had already resumed their previous positions in the water— the large intruder of their domain nothing more than a momentary distraction.

Enoch lay still for a few minutes, enjoying the sun on his face and the prickly feeling of his skin drying, the hairs on his arms popping up one by one as they freed themselves. He sat up again and looked down into the pool. It was just as tranquil as when he had arrived. He looked downstream and saw his spear pressed against the rocks, held by the gentle but steady current.

*Something is different!*

Enoch rose to his feet and looked southward to the trees he had passed through earlier. The feeling of being lost was gone. He turned to the north, then east to look out over the Great Waters visible through the gap in the surrounding trees. No matter which direction he faced, he felt at peace, as though he were safe.

*Have I reached the place you prepared for me?*

He looked around again, this time with a different perspective. Where he had seen a stream, now he saw fresh water to drink. The beautiful meadow was now an isolated location with trees on every side except to the east, where there was an impassible body of water. The meat of the fish would sustain him. The purple clusters hanging from the bushes at the edge of the forest weren't flowers but fruit. It was bountiful ... and protected. He could live in this place for quite some time.

*But why here? I'm all alone.*

Enoch suddenly remembered sitting on a rocky point on the other side of the Great Waters. It was a place where the Holy One had led him, and he had been just as confused. But when he observed the gathering of Myndarym, all of his waiting had made sense, even before he had delivered the message of judgment.

*Ahh!* Enoch smiled. *I will wait as you have instructed.*

∗   ∗   ∗   ∗

KHELRUSA

The ranks of Kahyin males began to lengthen, spreading out into a double-file formation that looked more intimidating than when they were all clustered together. There were two hundred of them, enough to convey Azael's strength, but not so many as to give the impression that Khelrusa had been emptied of its military force. In front of the Kahyin, Hyrren and ninety-nine of his largest siblings were already standing at attention—both the Anduar and Iryllur children, which he begun calling Aniylim and Iriylim respectively. To the untrained eye, these soldiers would be an unforeseen and intimidating presence. A shocking and upsetting revelation.

Azael knew better. He could see through their primitive armor and fragile weaponry to the human frailty and youthful ignorance of his combined army. But when he squinted to the point that his vision became blurry, he could almost see what the Myndarym would notice. The ratio of humans to Nephiylim was perfect. The mixed entourage of soldiers would have its intended effect.

"Not as impressive as a wing of Iryllurym," Rikoathel said under his breath.

"They never will be," Parnudel replied.

The two soldiers were walking behind Azael as he inspected the ranks of his army spread out along the main road through Khelrusa.

"I just wish we had more time," Rikoathel continued. "The Nephiylim aren't fully grown, and they require a great deal more training."

Azael kept his eyes moving up and down the ranks as he replied, "For now, it will be enough. The Myndarym know that the Kahyin population is large, and they will rightly assume that this is only a small representation of what I command. They will believe the same of the Nephiylim. All we have to do is march this force to the edge of their city, and the overactive imaginations of those *Shapers* will be what erodes their own sense of pride and confidence. I want to reach Senvidar before the others arrive, so that each and every one of them will see our strength and carry that memory with them into the Council. This is what will define our position, and what will make our participation valuable."

The citizens of Khelrusa were cheering at the sight of their fellow hunters and their gods together. The Nephiylim were still looked at with a mixture of disgust and envy, but Azael could feel that changing by the day. And this demonstration helped the effort. It was an awe-inspiring thing to see an army go out before you—to know that they fight for your interests. It had a unifying power that no one could resist. Azael was confident that one day, the Kahyin would respect the Nephiylim, perhaps even worship them. And moments like this one would serve as the starting point.

"I wish we could just kill the Myndarym instead of playing these games," Rikoathel said.

Azael looked away from his army to address his third-in-command. "I think we are all in agreement about that. But perhaps you could find some satisfaction in controlling them first? Let them serve us with their knowledge while we look for their weaknesses."

"And when they have nothing else to offer us?" Parnudel asked.

Azael smiled. "An unnecessary question, don't you think?"

All three of the Iryllur soldiers smiled.

# 16

Sariel kept absolutely still within the trees, keeping watch on the afternoon skies above. The Council would be starting in just twelve days, and he expected to see the last three soldiers of Semjaza's fallen kingdom flying toward Senvidar at any moment. Sariel's current location put him directly between there and Khelrusa, so he had found himself a high vantage point above the mist, with a thick forest canopy overhead for visual cover. Avoiding the passive gaze of the Iryllurym would likely prove more difficult than it had been to escape the surveillance of Fyarikel. But once he spotted his enemies passing by, Sariel would continue to Khelrusa and find a location that would allow him to study his enemies in their own environment after their return. There would be no way for him to successfully kill Azael and his soldiers while they attended the Council. There would be too many watchful eyes, and Azael would be on alert anyway. But when they returned to Khelrusa, they would let their guard down in the safety of their own domain. They would expose their vulnerabilities, and Sariel planned to be there, hidden and ready for that moment.

Unfortunately, he was at a vast physical disadvantage now. He couldn't just openly attack them as he would have done in his Iryllur form. He was no longer a soldier of the Amatru, and his tactics had to change accordingly, even if they were starting to resemble the Marotru—lying to the Myndarym, evading his escort, sneaking into Khelrusa to lie in wait and ambush his enemies. This was all new territory for him. But it couldn't be helped. Azael and his soldiers had to be released from their temporal bodies to face judgment in the Eternal. And Sariel was the one who would ensure it happened, no matter how convoluted the methods he used.

Sariel smiled as he noticed dark spots over the western horizon. Then his smile faded as he realized that they were circling.

*Why are there only two? And why aren't they coming from farther south?*

He watched intently as the winged creatures soared high over the fog with minimal effort, maintaining a wide circular flight pattern that was indicative of ...

*Moving sentries?*

Shifting patches of moisture below the creatures allowed a brief view of the land and something dark moving across it. It disappeared just as quickly, but it was enough for Sariel to see that the darkness undulated like a herd of animals. Sariel looked back to the creatures in the sky, wondering if they were just scavenger birds watching for an opportunity to steal something from the herd.

Minutes passed before they were close enough to confirm that they were, in fact, Iryllur. Sariel backed farther into the trees, knowing that Parnudel and Rikoathel had eyes that were far more capable than his own. With leaves covering his entire body, Sariel watched the mist drifting along the lower elevations, looking for the one enemy who really mattered. The sound of marching could now be heard—a disorderly tangle of many soft, rapid steps, mixed with deeper noises that occurred with less frequency.

The moisture parted again and Sariel witnessed something that he hadn't anticipated. An army of Kahyin soldiers with long spears was running before a group of other creatures much larger than the humans. Sariel would have thought they were Anduarym if their sizes had been consistent. It was difficult to tell from such a distance, but some were actually taller than Anduarym, and some much smaller. Then he noticed that several of them had wings, though these weren't flying.

*Nephiylim!*

He remembered what Sheyir had said about the other women giving birth in the caves beneath the southern mountains of Mudena Del-Edha. But her description made it sound like there weren't many of these creatures. There had to be almost a hundred in this group. Were there other chambers that Sheyir hadn't seen? Had Sheyir been part of a larger operation? The questions multiplied inside Sariel's mind as he watched the army approaching from the east. They were close enough now that the patches of mist swirling over the land failed to obscure them completely. And every time the air cleared, Sariel got a better look.

*They're children*, he realized. Their inconsistent sizes finally made sense. *But where did they come from?*

Suddenly, Sariel's entire body went rigid. His heart thudded against his ribs as if it wanted to break free of its cage. Just behind the Kahyin soldiers, an Iryllur walked with a casual gait, his long strides carrying him over the land as fast as the humans were able to run. He was shorter than some of the Nephiylim, which made him blend in at first. But his skin and feathers were as dark as the night sky, making him stand out as the army neared the flat terrain below Sariel's position.

*Azael!*

Sariel's couldn't take his eyes off the Iryllur. They were fastened in place as if they had become one with his enemy. His vision began to blur and he realized that he hadn't taken a breath for quite some time. He opened his mouth to suck in some air, feeling an intense cramping pain shoot through his jaw from having clenched his teeth so strongly. Never before had he felt such hatred, not even when going to war against the demonic hordes of the Marotru. It coursed through his veins, emboldening him with raw power that could not be tamed. It made him sure of something that would have seemed impossible only moments ago.

*You will die tonight*, he told his enemy quietly. *If I have to relinquish this human body in the process, so be it. But I'm taking you with me!*

Parnudel and Rikoathel passed overhead in sweeping circles. The Kahyin ran in formation across the ground, spears held upright. The Nephiylim marched behind, their erratic movements betraying their lack of maturity and discipline. But Sariel's eyes followed the dark one with a calm assurance that the sun would soon drop below the western horizon.

The sounds of the forest multiplied during the night. Chirps and screeches sounded from every direction. The creatures who had been sleeping during the day finally took their turn at roaming the land—all the better to conceal what little sound came from Sariel's movements. He looked for solid ground, damp enough to muffle the pressure of his footsteps. The base of trees offered concealment and were mostly clear of debris. He moved with the fog, drifting from one hiding place to another until the uneven shapes at his feet were no longer clumps of grass but the sleeping forms of Kahyin soldiers.

Without a sound, he confiscated two spears that were leaning against a tree, and he disappeared into the darkness again. His eyes had become accustomed to moving through the forest at night. During the long and lonely months that he had journeyed to Senvidar, he had sacrificed more than half of each night, trading sleep for the opportunity to gain more ground. He had become just as comfortable moving by the faint light of the moon reflected in the mist as he was in the sunlight. The ranks of Kahyin thinned out as he pressed on. There had been no one standing guard, which meant that Azael either feared nothing, or had chosen someone more capable for this task.

Larger shapes began dotting the landscape ahead. The Nephiylim slept closer to each other than the Kahyin, some in clusters, like animals trying to keep warm. Their bodies rose and fell with each breath, twitching as they dreamed. Some moaned and rolled over. Others stretched out their limbs without any warning. Sariel watched them from behind tree trunks, staying hidden between controlled bursts of movement. He wondered if their dreams were haunted by unpleasant memories, or if they were just less exhausted than the Kahyin from their travels.

As the slumbering bodies of Nephiylim slipped into the darkness behind him, Sariel approached a small clearing with only a handful of isolated trees sticking up from the grass at its center. On the ground, leaning against one of these wide trunks, was a silhouette. It appeared like a misshapen piece of fruit that had fallen from its tree, but it was darker even than the shadows left by the moonlight.

Sariel stayed within the tree line, seeing now the wisdom of Azael's defense. He slept in the open, surrounded by his army. And somewhere above, either Parnudel or Rikoathel was likely perched with a clear view of their Rada. They would be taking shifts, which meant that the other would be sleeping close by, perhaps just inside the tree line around the clearing. It was a good defense.

*How can I reach him?*

The most likely position for Azael's sentry was somewhere in the foothills of the mountains to the west. If he was looking down into the clearing from that direction, the tree line would obscure some of the clearing on the west side. Sariel would have the most concealment by approaching from that direction, but that was probably where the other sentry was sleeping. At least, that's how Sariel would have arranged it. And the fact that Azael's silhouette seemed to be leaning against the east side of the tree reinforced that suspicion.

There was no way that he would be able to kill Azael without alerting everyone else, which meant that he couldn't keep his promise of destroying Semjaza's kingdom. Azael would be his last enemy before his spirit was pulled back into the Eternal Realm and held for the Day of Judgment.

*At least I will avenge you, my love,* he told Sheyir.

Sariel decided to split the risk and approach from the south, where he was currently standing. He would be slightly closer to where he assumed Parnudel and Rikoathel would be, but he wouldn't be approaching Azael head-on. It might give him even a second's worth of advantage. He considered throwing his spears, but he wasn't confident that he could hit his mark from this distance. And if he missed, Azael would wake and the advantage of surprise would be gone. No, he would have to deal the final blow from up close, which meant getting across the clearing without being seen. The grass was too short for concealment. The only possibility was to move inside the mist, which was thinner at night than during the day.

*It will have to do.*

Minutes passed slowly. The sounds of the forest creatures blended into a discordant wall of noise that reminded Sariel of the songs used by the Nin-Myndarym to *unshape* the Borderlands. The position of the moon changed by a handbreadth before the spaces between the trees began to lighten with an approaching bank of fog. Sariel waited until he could no longer see the trees on the other side of the clearing, and the white orb of the moon was nothing more than a dull glow in the sky.

He stepped out of the trees and made his way as quickly over the grass as he dared, choosing each step carefully to minimize the sound. The few trees at the center of the clearing appeared as transparent, gray columns supporting a roof that undulated in the breeze. Their ethereal forms took on more substance as he approached, and the large silhouette sheltered beneath them seemed all the more ominous. Sariel was suddenly struck by the enormous difference in size between him and his enemy.

As he watched, with Azael's sleeping body so close now, a feeling of vertigo passed over him. He stopped moving to keep from falling over, and when he looked down at the grass in front of him, he realized what was wrong. What he thought was the sight of his enemy becoming clearer as he approached was actually the thinning of the mist. His concealment was dissipating all around him. Sariel looked up to the sky, the moon now clearly visible. Over the foothills to the west, moonlight reflected off the front edge of two flapping wings.

*I've been spotted!*

Sariel lunged forward and sprinted for the center of the clearing. He raised his right spear above his shoulder and kept the other by his side, prepared to impale his enemy from whichever angle presented itself.

A deep shout of warning from the western sky cut through the noises of the forest.

The silhouette against the tree began to change shape, the top portion lifting up and turning.

There was also movement inside the tree line to Sariel's left, but he ignored it. In seconds, he would be within reach of his enemy, and there was only one purpose in his mind now. He was moving as fast as he could, the spear in his right hand balanced over his shoulder.

In the blink of an eye, Azael was pivoting leftward.

Sariel tracked his movement and thrust his spear at the center of his enemy. The metal tip dug into the trunk of the tree as Azael came spinning around the other side of it, his wing unfurling in a backhanded motion.

Sariel angled left and tightened his grip on the other spear, but Azael's wing caught him below the knees and the world suddenly began to spin. He felt the weightlessness of flight while the sky and the land traded places over and over again. His body slammed hard into something and all of his movement came to an abrupt halt. The air had been knocked from his lungs and the muscles of his abdomen betrayed him, clenching so tightly that his lungs couldn't get what they desperately needed. When he lifted his head, Sariel realized that he was far away from the trees at the center of the clearing.

Azael was crouching, wings flared wide, moonlight reflecting off the vaepkir in each hand. His menacing red eyes glowed like the coals of a fire.

Sariel jumped to his feet. Somehow he had managed to hold onto his remaining spear, which he now raised above his other shoulder.

Deep laughter boomed from across the clearing in Azael's direction. The sound was so far outside the context of what had just happened that Sariel wondered if his ears were playing tricks on him. Perhaps he had damaged something in his head when he landed.

Azael's body shuddered with amusement as the laughter continued to roll across the meadow. Parnudel stepped from the shadows and into the moonlight from Azael's right.

Sariel now realized that he had been thrown far to the north side of the meadow, and some of his disorientation began to evaporate.

Rikoathel dropped from the sky and landed gently on Azael's left side with vaepkir drawn. The tree line around the meadow was alive with movement. The Kahyin and the Nephiylim were forming a perimeter, but were waiting for the approval of their king before attacking. The glint of moonlight from their spears looked dull compared to the weapons of the Iryllurym.

Azael's laughter slowly faded. "It looks like the Amatru failed to kill you as well. Or was your freedom the payment for betraying us?"

Sariel stepped forward and threw his second spear as hard as he could. It seemed to arc slowly through the air as if the whole thing were made of heavy stone.

Azael's arm came across his body in a blur. The vaepkir cut through the spear without any perceptible resistance, the two halves of the shaft spinning in opposite directions. His body came back to a ready position before he spoke. "Are you still trying to finish the war you started?"

Sariel kept silent. Rage still boiled inside him so fiercely that he considered running at Azael and attacking with whatever this human body had available—hands, feet, even teeth.

"Ah. You've come seeking revenge for your woman," Azael continued.

Sariel lifted his head with a mixture of pride and disgust, then spat on the ground in front of him.

Murmurs of disapproval swirled around him from the edges of the clearing. Apparently the Kahyin and Nephiylim could tolerate an act of violence against their king, but not a show of disrespect.

Azael just laughed in response. "I assure you, you will not get your revenge by playing these games. *Shape* into your Iryllur form if you want me to take you seriously."

Sariel couldn't think of anything to say. And for the first time since the sun had set, his rage began to wear off enough that he knew he had failed, and death was only seconds away.

Azael's outline straightened up to a standing position. "Tell me, how much did she suffer?"

The question dug into his flesh like a weapon, but there was a stronger force at work inside him now. He didn't want to die. He wanted to survive, at least long enough to finish what he started. Azael was just trying to provoke him into *shaping* so they could attack him with honor. Sariel had to change the course of the conversation as quickly as he could without revealing his own weakness. He took a deep breath and let his enemies see him trying to calm himself. "You will know how much she suffered when I make you endure the same. But I will do it in this form. I have to make it challenging for myself or it won't last long enough."

"Yes. I remember now that you were fond of jokes. Semjaza appreciated that about you, but I was never amused by it. You see, it is the way of the Marotru to hide behind something. I would rather be direct, so here is a question that gets right to the point. Was it my son or daughter who ripped your woman in half?"

Sariel wanted to charge at Azael and accept whatever consequence awaited him. But he noticed an opportunity to strengthen his position and buy more time, so he did his best to shrug off the antagonistic words. Despite the tension that held his body in a rigid stance, he smiled. "She killed that abomination before it could be born, and she had the courage to forfeit her own life in the process. So I will take my revenge in this form to honor her."

Azael slowly shook his head. "As much as I would like to take the head of the one who betrayed us to the Amatru, there is no honor is this for me. I refuse your challenge on the basis of your woeful inadequacy. But there are some who would gladly accept. Sons of Semjaza! Come forth!"

The sound of heavy footsteps drew Sariel's attention to the east side of the clearing. Ten Nephiylim stepped out from the gathered crowds. They were armed with spears like the Kahyin, but theirs were sized appropriately for their height, some looking like the trunks of saplings.

Azael turned his glowing eyes in their direction. "This Myndar is the one who killed your father."

Ten pairs of glowing orange eyes turned in Sariel's direction.

It was obvious where this was going. Sariel took the momentary distraction to get the largest head start possible. He began running southwest across the clearing. The confused Kahyin soldiers glanced at each other before parting to make way for him. A few of them were clearer minded, lowering their spears and starting to converge on him.

"Leave him for the Nephiylim!" Azael shouted.

The gap in the perimeter of soldiers widened and Sariel ran through it as fast as his legs would carry him.

\* \* \* \*

Azael could see Hyrren shift his weight forward onto the balls of his feet, ready to burst into a run. The young Nephiyl was eager to go after Sariel, but he remembered his training and waited for the order. It demonstrated that he was learning to control his emotions and channel them, which was a mark of significant progress.

Azael turned first to Rikoathel. "Go with them and make sure it's a fair fight. If Sariel *shapes* into his Iryllur form, cut off his wings, but don't interfere further."

"Yes, my Rada," the soldier replied before taking to the air.

Finally, Azael turned to Hyrren. "Take your brothers, and hunt him down. Torture him. Eat his flesh. Make it a ceremony if you wish. I don't care what you do with him, just be back by sunrise when we set out for Senvidar."

Hyrren's eyes narrowed, and the muscles of his forearm bulged as he tightened his fingers around his spear. "Yes, my king," he answered.

His brothers, gathered beside him, were staring intently at his face, waiting for his signal.

He turned to look at them and nodded, and the group set off at a run for the trees.

# 17

Sariel stopped running just long enough to listen for the sounds of pursuit. But his heartbeat and loud breathing were the only things he could hear. Because of their size, the Nephiylim could cover more ground in less time. There was no way to outrun them, so Sariel used the only advantages he had. He was smaller, and could move through dense foliage faster than his pursuers. While they had to plan their movement to track his, Sariel was free to run in any direction. He exploited these to the best of his ability, choosing terrain that amplified his strengths and their weaknesses.

The sounds of the forest seemed to grow louder as his heartbeat slowed. But there was no indication of where the Nephiylim might be. He couldn't have evaded them already, so he looked uphill and considered his next move.

The faint sound of wind moved through the sky overhead, and Sariel kept absolutely still.

Beyond the canopy of leaves, Rikoathel's silhouette glided westward and began banking to the north.

It didn't appear that he had spotted anything, but there was a distant shout directly downhill from Sariel's position. The Nephiylim were getting closer. Sariel looked back to the sky and waited until Rikoathel was beyond sight before continuing to climb through the thick foliage, angling south across the foothills. The land descended into a shallow ravine that looked like water had flowed through it at some point. Glancing uphill, Sariel could see that it was clear of obstructions, a channel running through the dense shrubbery that covered an open meadow. It was the opposite of the terrain that he had been looking for, but it presented him the opportunity to get away from the immediate area without being seen from above.

Sariel took it, moving quickly uphill along the bare soil in a hunched posture. Where the terrain grew steep over sections of rock, he scrambled on his hands and knees like an animal. Finally, the ravine entered another forest, and Sariel stopped to listen and watch. When he caught his breath, he could hear distant voices to the north. Through the shrubbery he could see Rikoathel's outline against a starry sky, circling over where the voices had come from. It appeared that the Nephiylim hadn't followed him south and were still moving uphill from their last position.

It was good, but Sariel needed more distance. He waited until Rikoathel's eyes were facing away, then he left the ravine and began sprinting directly south through the trees. A few minutes later, he came upon another ravine, this one deeper and narrower than the last. He changed course and followed it uphill where it left the trees and cut across another meadow of bushes and tall grass. Scrambling over the rocky soil, he kept low beneath the overhanging foliage. His legs and forearms were bruised by the time he was again concealed from above by the leaves of tall trees.

Sariel rolled onto his back and lay still, allowing his racing heart to recover. He sucked in air as quietly as he could and kept his eyes moving. But there was nothing to see. The canopy of this forest was extremely dense. Only tiny pockets of the night sky were visible. And now that Sariel was looking, he noticed that the sky was growing lighter to the east.

Dawn was approaching. He would soon lose the darkness as an ally in his escape. He climbed out of the ravine and glanced around in all directions. The forest was still and silent. Beneath the canopy, there was no indication that the night was disappearing.

Sariel took another deep breath before moving uphill with long strides. The sense of panic that had been with him since he first started running had changed its form as if it were being *shaped*. The desperation remained, but there was regret underneath it now. He was far enough away from his pursuers that he could finally think about his actions. He had been naïve about killing Azael. He could still see the red glow of the Iryllur's eyes, and the imposing silhouette of his angelic body towering above him like a mountain. Sariel had never gone into battle in a human form before today. He had been overconfident until the moment when Azael had sent him spinning through the air with a brush of his wing. In this fragile body, there was no hope for success through a direct fight.

Now he just wanted to survive. To hide and escape until he could figure out another way to finish what he had started. His original plan of going to Khelrusa could still work, but he'd have to take into account his own vulnerability now. That, at least, was something to be learned from the mistake of this night.

A snapping branch sounded to his right.

Sariel paused in mid-step and turned his head.

The forest was silent again.

But Sariel knew someone was there, less than fifty paces away. If he had been able to *shift* into the Eternal Realm, he might have been able to detect the swirling colors of a Nephiyl spirit against the dull backdrop of trees and rocks. But he had lost that ability, and now he was confined to a human body with only the senses of sight and sound to aid him. And if the breeze had been moving in the right direction, perhaps smell could have helped in some way.

Sariel glanced to his left and noted some steeper terrain that might offer a place to hide. It was farther away than he wanted, but there wasn't a better option at the moment. Carefully, he took a step to the side. Then he listened.

There was only silence.

He took another step. And another. Minutes passed without any indication of pursuit until Sariel found himself at the base of an outcropping. The soil had eroded from around the stone, revealing jagged fins that ran up the terrain like spines along the back of a reptile. Between them were deep crevices cloaked in shadow. Without any hesitation, Sariel crawled far up into the largest crevice and turned around. Hopefully, the Nephiylim wouldn't come in this direction, but he wanted to be facing the enemy just in case he was discovered.

Sariel held completely still. The pounding in his chest faded, and the forest grew quiet except for the muffled sounds of insects. It was a consistent backdrop of noise that became mesmerizing over time. And Sariel's ears stopped noticing the details. His eyes took over, staring at the night sky and comparing its color to the silhouettes of the few trees he could see from his limited perspective.

Suddenly, there was another noise present among the muffled cacophony. Was it footsteps? A scraping of soil against stone? Sariel couldn't be sure, and the noise stopped just as soon as his ears detected it. His eyes shifted from side to side, looking for some visual confirmation of what he had heard. But the scene was the same as before—a sky growing lighter with the approach of dawn, trees that blocked almost all of it, and a narrow strip of forest floor visible between the two walls of stone on either side of him.

Sariel looked down at the rock on his right side, noticing that the edge of the shadow had changed position. It had retreated into the crevice, leaving his right arm exposed. He stepped back to keep within the cloak of shadow, and his foot slipped off the side of a loose rock. The quiet grinding of stone upon stone may as well have been the shriek of a wild animal in the silent forest.

Sariel winced at the sound, and knew that if anyone were close, they would have heard it. He quickly bent down and felt along the floor of the crevice for the rock. When his hands settled around it, he realized it was almost the size of his own head. He picked it up and held it close to his chest, then waited for what seemed inevitable.

Long moments passed, and just when he had begun to hope that he was alone, someone passed slowly in front of the crevice opening.

The dim light of a sun not yet risen carved out the silhouette of a small Nephiyl, though he was still a full head taller than Sariel. He carried a long spear and moved in a crouching posture. His body language alone confirmed that he had heard Sariel's misplaced step. He glanced from side to side, then moved forward and beyond the edge of the crevice.

Sariel was alone once again, but wasn't yet safe. He took advantage of the moment and raised the stone quietly above his head, resting his arms against the side of the crevice for support. Then he waited.

Less than a minute later, the Nephiyl came into view again, from farther downslope. But this time his attention was focused on the crevice where Sariel was hiding, as if he had just realized it was there. He stalked uphill, weaving his head slowly from side to side as he tried to see through the shadows.

Sariel still had his arms above his head and was leaning against the crevice wall, but he readied himself to attack.

The Nephiyl was at the crevice opening now, hunched over and peering uphill with his head turned slightly to one side. He looked cautious, perhaps even nervous. His spear came forward, slowly probing the emptiness of the shadow. He stepped inside, reaching out with his weapon.

Sariel waited in the darkness, watching the point of the spear come closer and closer with each second. When the bladed tip moved slightly to the left, Sariel knew that he could get by it without being impaled. He burst from his concealed position and brought the rock down on his enemy.

The Nephiyl only had time to flinch and bring his other arm up before the rock crashed against his skull with a dull thud.

Sariel's momentum carried him downhill until his body collided with the Nephiyl. He tripped over the creature and tumbled head first out into the forest. But the soil was soft, and he quickly rolled to his feet and spun around.

The Nephiyl had fallen backward from the crevice and collapsed just outside the opening. Whether dead or knocked out, Sariel didn't stop long enough to notice. He ran back to the Nephiyl, stepped over his body, and picked up his spear. Then he rammed the long, metal blade down into the chest of the creature and punctured its heart.

It didn't even flinch, which meant that it was probably already dead.

Sariel stared at its face for a moment, seeing a resemblance to Semjaza as well as the human features of the woman who had birthed it. Then he took off to the north, and rounded the rocky terrain before turning west again and seeking higher ground.

The sky was now a dull gray color. The sun would be up above the horizon in just a few minutes. And Sariel knew that he had to be far away from this place when that happened. The trees began to thin as he went upward, but their size also increased. Trunks as large around as an Anduar soldier stretched up to the sky. The air came alive with the sound of running water. Eventually, Sariel crested the hill. He glanced behind him to ensure that he wasn't being followed, then took his first few steps down the other side of the hill when he heard someone shout. He reacted quickly, dodging behind a tree.

Another shout cut through the forest, and this time Sariel could make out the word. It sounded like someone's name.

*They're looking for the one I killed!*

Another shout came through the trees, this one from farther north.

*They're closing in!*

Sariel looked down the hill in front of him and saw bare soil between sparse trees. He bolted, running as fast as he could, hoping that the Nephiylim were still too far away to hear his footsteps. The sound of rushing water grew louder. Sariel's strides lengthened. The terrain was steep, but clear, and it seemed he was able to descend in minutes what had taken him hours to ascend during the night.

Through the trees below, the dark brown color of soil was replaced by the swirling white and green of rushing water.

Seconds later, Sariel skidded to a stop at the bank of a deep and fast- moving river. He turned and looked uphill behind him, then took off along the bank. He followed the flow of the water as it moved east and south, searching for a place to cross.

"Over here!" Rikoathel shouted.

Sariel looked up and noticed the Iryllur soaring high overhead to the west.

"He's over here!"

Sariel dodged back under the cover of the trees and kept moving along the bank, trying to think of how to get out from under Rikoathel's gaze and avoid the Nephiylim at the same time.

*Think!* he challenged himself. *What would they not expect?*

He veered away from the water and began moving uphill again. Just then, something passed between the tree trunks a few paces away. Its shape was obscured, but Sariel noticed that its skin was ruddy and lighter than the dark brown soil of the forest floor. He quickly came to a stop and dodged behind a cluster of smaller tree trunks, holding the Nephiyl's spear close, its shaft upright and hidden behind the trees. His chest was heaving and he couldn't hear anything but his heartbeat and the rushing water.

*I can't fail now. I haven't avenged Sheyir!*

The coursing of blood pounded in his ears. The tired wheeze of breath whistled in his lungs. The river roared.

*This isn't how it's supposed to end!*

A Nephiyl stepped cautiously from behind a distant tree to Sariel's left. He was looking toward the river. His body was thin, but whatever wasn't bone was clearly muscle that had seen plenty of hard work. His forearm rippled as he held his spear near his hip, parallel to the ground. He moved with careful steps, his large stride covering much ground even though he wasn't hurrying. He was twice Sariel's height—a medium-sized Nephiyl judging by the group he had seen on the previous day.

Sariel leaned out from behind his tree and scanned the terrain in every direction. The Nephiylim had obviously spread out, because none of the others were present as far as he could see. He was alone with this enemy. He moved quietly around the backside of the tree, then sidestepped to the next one, slowly making his way closer to the Nephiyl.

The tall creature continued moving toward the water, glancing up and down its bank for any sign of its prey.

But Sariel was approaching now from the east, directly behind him.

Suddenly, the Nephiyl turned. Whether by sound or intuition, he realized he was being stalked.

Sariel rushed at him, lowering the point of the Nephiyl spear in his hand.

The enemy took a few surprised steps backward before he remembered his own weapon. He clutched it with both hands and stepped into the attack, thrusting the blade at his enemy.

Sariel jumped from the ground at a full run. With his left hand he deflected the Nephiyl's spear downward while thrusting with his right. His own weapon drove deep into the abdomen of the creature and came to a sudden stop. Sariel's feet made contact with the ground again, and he used the leverage to push the enemy backward toward the water.

The Nephiyl stumbled on legs that had suddenly gone weak. He dropped his spear and looked down at the one now running through his own stomach, grabbing it with one hand as if he could undo what had happened.

Sariel continued pushing, eager to get his enemy into the river before he decided to call for help.

The Nephiyl looked up now and stared into Sariel's eyes. He was in shock and looked very much like a child despite his massive size. His mouth slowly opened, as if he were going to ask a question.

Sariel dug his feet into the earth and pushed against the creature who was larger than an Anduar and would not have budged under different circumstances.

The Nephiyl cried out in pain and stumbled backward, reaching out for something to stop his fall. His body folded forward and his other hand came down on the shaft of the spear, clamping around Sariel's wrist. His yell echoed through the forest as he fell backward against the trunk of a tree.

Sariel tried to yank his hand away, but he couldn't overpower the enemy's strength.

The look of panic drained from the Nephiyl's face until acceptance took over. And then his anger swelled.

Sariel planted his feet and gave the spear a sharp thrust, but it wouldn't move his enemy any longer.

The eyes of the Nephiyl suddenly flared. His body tensed. The cords of muscle beneath his forearms tightened. He leaned sideways away from the tree and flexed his back.

Sariel felt himself lifted from the ground as if he weighed nothing. His enemy spun and launched him into the air using the spear as leverage. Sariel held on to the spear with all his might, until he felt the cold impact of the river surface. And then he was under the water. His body slammed against something hard and he heard a crunch in his ears. He was experiencing too many sensations at once to know what had been injured. The spear was gone from his hand. Water was rushing around him. Or he might have been tumbling through it. He couldn't tell. The sound in his ears was both muffled and piercing at the same time. Bubbles and swishes sounded from all directions. Gurgles and screams, as if he'd fallen into the stomach of a gigantic monster.

The noise abruptly stopped as his head broke through the surface, but it only lasted a second before he was pulled under again. It wasn't until that moment that he remembered he needed air. His head poked through the surface again and he began waving his arms to keep himself in that position. He sucked precious air into his lungs, along with some water, before the noises surrounded him again. His lungs spasmed, wanting to expel the water, but he dared not open his mouth. He kicked with his legs and pulled with his arms, but the surface wouldn't return to him.

All of a sudden, something slammed into his back and Sariel felt his body jolt upward. His face came out of the water, and as he took a desperate breath his eyes captured the moment.

Something else was in the water upriver from him, its ruddy brown skin glistening in the pale morning light. Tall banks of mud and rocks rose up on both sides of the river. Above that, trees were passing by at an alarming rate. The terrain looked completely foreign, as if he had already traveled a great distance. And the roar in his ears suddenly rose in volume before he felt the water drop away from beneath him.

A sickening weightlessness was accompanied by the feeling of tumbling through the air with nothing to hold or grab. Trees and sky and water spun past his eyes. On instinct, Sariel extended his arms, but this human body lacked the wings of his Iryllur form, and he plummeted along with the water that carried him. Then his body was slammed again, this time so hard that it forced all the air from his lungs and the consciousness from his mind.

The water felt cold on his skin, but gentle. It was all around him, and he was drifting. Sariel didn't know how long he had been unconscious, but it couldn't have been too long because he was underwater and still alive. He kicked with his legs, moving toward the dull light. His chest seemed like it was on fire, and his arms felt weak and useless. Something firm but solid glanced off the top of his head just before he felt the springy collapsing of branches against his back. He wasn't drifting lazily through the water. He had been moving with the current, and he didn't realize how fast until his body had come to a stop against a submerged pile of debris.

The river suddenly felt as though it weighed more than a mountain. It pressed him against the branches and wouldn't let go. Sariel struggled, but he couldn't go up or down. His lungs begged for air.

The branches behind him began to snap, and his body fell into a void. Jagged wood poked at him from all directions, gouging his skin as he passed through it. And then the pressure was gone. There was nothing above him. Sariel frantically grabbed for the surface. Only his left arm seemed able to do what he wanted. The other was throbbing with pain and flopping limply beside him.

Finally, his head broke through the surface. He gasped for breath while kicking to keep his mouth above the water. He opened his eyes to find that there was only a handbreadth of room above his head. Dirt and roots hung low near the surface of the water. He was underneath an eroded bank, looking out on a swirling pool below the falls.

* * * *

Hyrren knelt beside Yelmur's body, his hand resting on his brother's cold skin. It was already pale. Hyrren wondered if the spear through his belly had done it, or if it had been the fall. He stood up and looked at the torrent of water cascading over the cliff above. It was high enough to kill a Nephiyl ... even more so a human.

"We have to get back," Rikoathel said to Hyrren from the western bank.

Hyrren ignored him and looked out across the multiple swirling pools of water that resulted from the sudden change in terrain. The force of the river was fractured here, made shallow and wide by the stone beneath it. Dozens of slower streams spread out from this point, and Hyrren looked downriver to where his brothers were searching. Several of them looked up and shook their heads.

"I've already flown down to the Great Waters and back. I didn't find anything."

"Where could he have gone?" Hyrren asked.

"He couldn't have survived the fall. He's probably trapped at the bottom of one of these pools. If he were alive, we would have found him already."

Hyrren frowned and looked downriver again.

"We can't wait any longer. The sun is up," Rikoathel added.

Hyrren had lost two brothers to this angel in human form. And the blood of his father cried out to be avenged. He at least wanted the satisfaction of seeing the small, pale body floating dead in the water. But Azael's instructions had been clear. This had only been a tracking exercise, and they had more important matters to deal with. "Let's go!" he yelled downriver.

A few of his brothers looked up.

Hyrren motioned for them to come back.

"I'll fly to Azael and let him know you're on your way," Rikoathel said as he extended his wings. "Move as quickly as possible."

"Of course," Hyrren said, bowing his head.

Rikoathel took to the skies with powerful thrusts of his wings, disappearing in seconds over the ridge of trees to the northeast.

# 18

The sense of falling made Sariel's body twitch, yanking him abruptly from a deep sleep. His mouth filled with water and he kicked with panic, thinking that his dark dreams had become a reality. But then he remembered where he was and reached up for the thick tangle of roots through which his good arm had been woven before he lost his grip and his head slipped under the water. He was still beneath the eroded bank, dangling in the river that had proven to be both an enemy and a friend to him.

From beneath the overhang of soil and roots, he looked out across the pools of water and saw that the light of the sun was coming almost directly toward him now. It was late afternoon, by the look of it. After watching his enemies pass along the opposite bank and hearing their footsteps above his head, he'd finally seen them leave the area as a group. Sariel had waited there for another hour before he'd allowed himself to relax. He lacked the strength to get himself out of this natural prison, so he found a place where the ceiling of soil above his head was high, and he waited.

Now he'd slept away the day and he still felt exhausted. His left arm was numb from being entwined with the roots above. His right one was throbbing with pain. He was sure it was broken, but he was more concerned about the sharp stabs of fire that shot through his midsection every time he took a breath.

His ribs were grinding on each other, now only held in place by the muscles around them. His legs ached as well, but at least he could feel them.

*How am I going to get out of here?* he wondered.

Though he had been disoriented after going over the falls, he remembered the submerged branches that he had broken through to get inside this place. He didn't have the strength to break through it again, or to fight the current on the other side of it. Going out the same way he came in would only lead to a watery death. So he began moving sideways, paralleling the edge of the pool. He reached for one root after another, ducking under the ceiling as it dropped almost to the water's surface in most places. It was painful, holding in enough breath to make it from one area to the next. But Sariel eventually found a section on the south end of the pool where he was only separated from the outside world by a thin tangle of roots.

With his good arm, he pulled on the sodden tendrils. They flexed without breaking, and Sariel's legs drifted out from underneath him without any leverage. The exertion caused a prickling pain to radiate through his abdomen, like a flock of birds pecking at him. The pain rose up through his chest and ended inside his head as a dizzying array of sparks floating through his vision. Sariel closed his eyes and took shallow, rapid breaths until he regained his full consciousness.

*Alright. I can do this. I just have to be smart about my movements.*

He tried again, but this time he put his feet against the roots just below the waterline. Instead of pulling with his hand, he pushed with his legs. A cold sensation spilled down the back of his leg and made his toes go numb, but it was better than his last attempt. He pushed until his legs began to shake. Finally, the roots began to snap. At first only one, and then the others in rapid succession. The numbness dissipated as his feet poked through the natural cage. Once the first hole was created, he was able to break the roots around it until it was large enough for his body to fit through.

With the sun now behind the trees to the west, Sariel pulled himself through the hole and out into the world above the water's surface. The trees on the east side of the pool looked healthy despite the fact that much of the soil beneath them had been washed away. Farther to the south, others hadn't fared so well. A dozen large trees lay along the bank, their roots sticking up in the air. Their branches were bare of any leaves, indicating that they had fallen long ago. But Sariel was more interested in the gentle slope that rose beside them and continued up into the forest. He let go of the roots and treaded water as the spinning current pushed him to the south. The rapid movement of his arms and legs brought another wave of pain, but it ended as soon as his hands and feet stuck into the mud along the bank.

Sariel looked up into the forest above, searching for any sign of an enemy before he exposed himself by returning to land. The trees looked just as peaceful and lonely as they always had. And other than the distant roar of the waterfall, there was nothing to be heard. It was time to move, and hope that Rikoathel and the Nephiylim were actually gone.

Sariel crawled from the water on his knees, with only one hand grasping. As his body left the liquid environment, the weight of gravity felt as though it were trying to crush him. His chest constricted. His lungs struggled to take in air. Pain coursed through his stomach and lower back in waves. The mud beneath him turned to dry soil and fallen leaves. Each movement took all of his strength. The terrain grew steeper. His muscles began to cramp and his knees slid backward without any traction. He continued forward, fighting through the pain.

He couldn't stop on the bare riverbank or he would be exposed to the skies above. He had to keep going until the trees protected him from sight. One crawling lurch at a time, Sariel inched his way across the land like an insect. Embers floated before his eyes, and the sight of the ground in front of him grew dark around the edges. The pain was catching up with him.

*Just a little farther!*

A wave of nausea passed through his stomach, and then his skin felt hot and cold at the same time.

*I'm almost there!*

Sariel's body suddenly went limp, and the world was drowned in darkness.

\*   \*   \*   \*

THE WESTERN SHORES OF THE GREAT WATERS
SOUTHWEST OF SAHVEYIM

Enoch yawned and stretched his arms. The cool morning air was refreshing in his lungs. The first rays of the sun felt warm against the skin of his face and arms. The sound of the stream entering the larger body of water over a bed of smooth stones created a gurgling sound that was gentle and soothing. It was as if the Holy One's creation were embracing him, caring for his every need like he imagined it must have done for the first humans.

With a smile on his face, Enoch set down his walking stick and stripped off his tunic. Then he slowly waded into the Great Waters up to his waist. Cupping the clear liquid in both hands, he brought it up to his face and rubbed, feeling the residual drowsiness rinsed away in an instant. It dripped from his eyebrows and beard, leaving behind a revived mind and alert eyes.

*Thank you, Holy One, for leading me to this place. If Your only purpose was to restore my soul, it has been worth every step to get here. I feel as though years of bitterness have been washed away by ...*

Out of the corner of his eye, Enoch noticed something out of place. He looked north across the outlet of the stream and saw something washed up on the shore. It was too far away to see what kind of animal it was, but Enoch was sure that it hadn't been there yesterday. He quickly waded back to shore and grabbed his tunic and walking stick before crossing the stream. Then he followed the edge of the water north until he stood close enough to touch the animal with his walking stick.

But it wasn't an animal, he could see now. It was a man. He was tall and thin, with shaggy hair and a beard, much like Enoch himself. But this man's hair was white in color, and his skin was much paler, like the sands of the stream that ran through Sedekiyr. He was lying facedown on the smooth stones of the beach, as though he had crawled out of the water.

Enoch knelt and watched the man's abdomen to see if he was breathing. The dirty tunic rose and fell so slightly that Enoch questioned whether or not it was imagined. In the end, he decided that he should feel the man's skin to make sure it hadn't gone cold. He reached out and touched his fingers to the man's outstretched arm. His skin was warm, too warm, in fact.

"Mmm ..." the man moaned.

Enoch pulled his hand away, startled by the sound. Then he suddenly felt ashamed of himself. It had been so long since he had heard the voice of another human that it felt like he was examining this strange event from a distance. He might as well have sniffed the man like a wild animal would have.

"Are you hurt?" he asked softly.

"Mmm ..." the man moaned again.

"I'm here to help you," Enoch said.

"Ffff ..." the man wheezed.

"Can you get up?"

"Fff ... ood."

"Oh. I have food nearby," Enoch said. "You can come with me."

The man tried to lift his head, but he looked exhausted.

"Wait. I'll help you get up," Enoch said. He stood over the man and grabbed him under the arms and began to lift.

The man cried out in pain, and his shriek echoed across the water. A bird took to the air from a tree nearby.

Enoch quickly let go of the man and stood up. "I'm sorry."

The man rolled from his side to his back, tears streaming down his face from closed eyes. His skin was flushed. The arm that had been outstretched on the rocks was now clutching at his stomach.

"I'm sorry," Enoch repeated. "I thought you needed help getting up."

The man began breathing loudly through pursed lips.

Enoch just watched, feeling helpless and stupid.

Finally, the man's breathing calmed, and he opened his eyes.

Enoch stared into blue irises that were more brilliant than either the sky above or the Great Waters below—eyes that he'd looked into on a handful of occasions, but never in human form. Once recognition arrived, the rest of the man's pale appearance suddenly made sense.

"Hello, Enoch," Sariel breathed. His voice was as thin and weak as his body appeared to be.

"You look very different from when I saw you last," Enoch replied.

Sariel attempted a smile, but his face looked like it refused to obey. "Everyone keeps saying that." The words came out with a wheezing sound.

Enoch couldn't help but smile in return. "How long have you been here?"

"Since last night. I'm ... traveling."

"You're obviously injured. What can I do to help you?"

Sariel closed his eyes and took a few careful breaths. "Can you bring me food?"

"Of course," Enoch replied.

"Good. After that, I'll need help getting back into the water. My ribs are broken, and so is my arm. I can't move unless I'm in the water."

Enoch nodded and then looked south along the shore, seeing the stream. It had only been a source of food to him until this moment. Now he saw it through the eyes of the Holy One—the One who had led him here just for this purpose. "My camp is nearby. I can take you the whole way through the water."

Sariel nodded.

Enoch stood and looked along the shoreline of the Great Waters in both directions, wondering how far the angel must have crawled through the shallows to get here. "You came up on land to sleep?"

"Yes."

"How long have you been like this?"

Sariel let out a gentle cough that seemed painful. After a few seconds of silence, he answered, "Two days, perhaps?"

"How did you become injured?"

"It's a long story," he grunted.

Enoch nodded. It was obvious that Sariel didn't want to speak about it yet, which was fine. Perhaps he would listen instead. "The Holy One has not given up on you. He led me here to find you. This is a safe place, and you will heal in time."

Sariel squinted. "There's one more thing that would really help."

"Of course."

"Can you put your clothes on?"

Enoch realized that he was still wearing only a loincloth. His walking stick and tunic were clutched in one hand. As the sudden embarrassment passed, he realized that Sariel had a smile on his face. Only then did he recognize the request as a joke.

# 19

Fyarikel's talons made clicking and scratching noises on the stone as he landed at the center of the meeting area. Rameel and Arakiba were sitting near each other on the first level of stairs speaking to Zahmesh, Turel, and Baraquijal, who were all standing. The small group halted their conversation and turned as soon as Fyarikel touched down.

"Azael marches on foot with an army. They are less than a day's journey away," the raptor announced.

"How large is the army?" asked Zahmesh, folding his thick arms across his bare chest.

"Two hundred Kahyin and ninety-eight Nephiylim."

"Nephiylim?" Zahmesh mumbled, turning to the others with deep furrows across his brow.

"There were some in Aryun Del-Edha," Arakiba replied, "but not that many!" The worried expression looked awkward on his demonic face.

Zahmesh looked back at Fyarikel. "You called them an army?"

"The Kahyin and Nephiylim are armed with spears and marching in formation. I think they've all come from Khelrusa."

Rameel stood from his seat. The bones beneath his wings of skin vibrated with tension. "You only observed humans when you watched over their city."

"Yes," Fyarikel admitted. "But I only observed from above. I never saw into the mines. I knew they made and stored their weapons inside, but I didn't think any more of it until a short while ago. It is possible that Semjaza's small harem was not the only group to give birth to Nephiylim."

"How many Kahyin soldiers did you observe in Khelrusa?" asked Zahmesh.

Fyarikel tilted his head as he remembered what he'd witnessed while hiding in the forests above the city. "I can't be sure, as they didn't all train at the same time. But I would estimate just over a thousand men."

Zahmesh nodded. "As I suspected. Azael comes with only two hundred, so it's likely that he also travels with only a small representative army of Nephiylim."

Rameel pulled his wings tightly around his body and crossed his arms like Zahmesh. "Isn't this exactly why we invited him ... for his military strength?"

"Yes," Zahmesh admitted. "But I don't like the fact that we obviously underestimated him. We still don't know exactly the size and configuration of his forces in Khelrusa."

Baraquijal, standing far below the others in his human form, looked up. "This is why we must all establish separate kingdoms and take his soldiers with us for protection. We must decentralize his power."

"That won't stop his soldiers from turning on us," Arakiba countered.

"Won't it?" asked Turel. "By the time Azael figures out that we can't shape, his army will be separated and spread across the earth, far away from his influence and command. We will include his soldiers in the establishment of our kingdoms, making them princes and rulers under us. Then they will have ownership and purpose far beyond anything Azael has ever given them. Fyarikel has told us what the conditions are like in Khelrusa," Turel said with a sweeping gesture of his hand. "His soldiers will come to cherish their new lives more than their old ones."

Baraquijal nodded his agreement.

"And soon," Turel continued, "our human wives will give birth. We will have Nephiyl children of our own.[8] In the years to come, we will give our daughters in marriage to his sons, and our sons will take his daughters. This will forge a strong alliance that will not be broken."[9]

"If our secret remains hidden for that long," Fyarikel pointed out.

"True. But in the meantime, we will make them dependent upon us. We will feed them. We will craft their weapons. But we will not teach them how to do these things for themselves. As we go out into the earth to establish our kingdoms, we will give his soldiers something to defend and protect, instead of endlessly training. This will be enough."

"It will have to be," Zahmesh added. "We don't have anything else to offer."

Fyarikel glanced from one to another of his fellow Myndarym. It seemed the conversation had come to an end. "I must go now. Parnudel and Rikoathel fly before the marching army. Naganel and I will meet them as emissaries so we can control their approach to Senvidar."

Rameel suddenly looked uncomfortable. "We're only allowing the Iryllurym into the city, correct?"

"Yes. Zahmesh and I have already settled the matter. Azael's soldiers will have to make camp outside of the city to preserve the peaceful nature and purpose of our Council."

Zahmesh turned to Rameel and took over the explanation. "Likewise, none of the Iryllurym will be permitted to bring weapons inside. If Azael's army tries to invade Senvidar while we are meeting, there are enough of us here to overpower them. We'll have to get through the Iryllurym first, but that shouldn't be a problem as long as they are without their vaepkir."

Rameel didn't look convinced.

Fyarikel curled his talons, scraping them against the stone. "When our distant brethren arrive, we'll also have more teeth and claws on our side."

Turel smiled, and Rameel reluctantly nodded.

\* \* \* \*

The chain of mountains to the east had been steadily increasing in height as the small army had marched beside it. Far to the north, its barren apex stood out from everything around it, a blade of stone stabbing upward through a fabric of trees. Along the northern horizon, a strip of darker green forest marked the edge of Senvidar. But this was as much as Azael could see from the ground. His vision was superior to most creatures in this world, but during the daylight hours, the advantage went to his scouts.

Parnudel and Rikoathel glided to a gentle landing on the soft earth to Azael's left. The Kahyin soldiers in front and the Nephiylim behind maintained their formation and their rapid pace.

"Their escorts have taken to the air," Parnudel informed. "They will be here in just a few minutes."

Azael nodded before turning his attention to his Nephiyl generals walking behind him.

"Yes, my king," replied Hyrren and Vengsul in unison.

"You and the rest of the soldiers will not be allowed into the city."

Hyrren nodded.

"Do you see the open field to the south of that outcropping there?" Azael asked with his arm outstretched.

"I can't see that far, my king," Hyrren replied.

Vengsul nodded. "I see it."

"After we leave, you will camp the army there in plain sight and wait for our return."

"Yes, my king," they replied.

Azael turned back to his Iryllurym. "Let's go."

The trio of angels took to the air and flew well ahead, but still in sight of the army, before landing in a clearing. No sooner had they touched down than Azael could see the dark shapes of the escorts approaching low against the horizon.

"As they take us inside, study the city for breach locations, choke points, and anything else that may be of use to us in the future."

"Of course, my Rada," Rikoathel replied.

Parnudel simply tilted his head, his lips curving into a grin.

The two massive birds of prey approached from separate angles, banking towards each other at the last second to end up directly north of Azael. Their wings flared upward, stopping their gliding and allowing them to touch down with only a few forward steps to use up their momentum. And now that they were side by side, Azael could compare their differences.

Fyarikel's plumage was a mottled mixture of warm brown tones, lighter on his chest and belly. His darker wings were thin and tapered, which would allow him to fly fast and turn sharply. His large, round eyes were so dark that they appeared black when they weren't catching the sunlight at just the right angle, reflecting a reddish brown. Naganel, on the other hand, was gray. His wings and body were thicker, implying more power than speed. A wide and sharp beak protruded between eyes that flashed with green. What the two messengers of the Council had in common was their size—both equal in height to an Iryllur.

*At least, the average Iryllur,* Azael thought. He was anything but. And Rikoathel was simply an oddity among his kind, one of the largest Iryllurym Azael had ever seen.

"Welcome, guests of Senvidar," Fyarikel announced.

Azael and his soldiers nodded.

"I'm afraid your army cannot be allowed inside the city. It would be inappropriate for the context of our gathering."

"I understand," Azael replied.

"And we must ask you to remove your weapons for the same reason," Fyarikel added.

Azael had chosen to present himself and his Iryllurym in battle gear for the express purpose of reinforcing their role to the other Council members. He had expected to relinquish his weapons, but making the Myndarym ask for it was better than volunteering. He and Parnudel unsheathed their vaepkir and handed them to Rikoathel, who flew them back to the marching army before rejoining the group. They kept their breastplates, which weren't a threat to anyone, yet still visually conveyed the message that Azael wanted to project.

The messengers didn't seem to mind. "Follow me," said Fyarikel. He turned and spread his wings.

Parnudel and Rikoathel did the same, taking to the air behind their escort.

Naganel waited for Azael to follow before he finally said, "After you."

Azael smiled. From a security perspective, it was smart for them to have one in front and one behind. It seemed that the Myndarym were finally thinking like soldiers. Azael decided it was time to play along, taking to the air with just a few powerful thrusts of his black wings.

Senvidar was just as Parnudel and Rikoathel had described it. The escorts took them on a direct approach to the stone meeting area at the peak of the mountains, so Azael wasn't able to glean any information beyond what he already knew. But it didn't worry him; the Myndarym would play host to all the Council members over the next few days, providing food and shelter. The time for Azael to conduct surveillance would come, but it would have to wait until after the meetings.

"Welcome to Senvidar," said Turel with open arms as soon as they all touched down. He approached at a casual walking pace with Danel only two steps behind. And he looked just the same as Azael remembered—pale skin and blond hair, eyes of sapphire. "On behalf of the Council members present, we thank you for coming early."

Azael simply nodded in reply as Parnudel and Rikoathel came near.

Danel stepped forward until she stood beside Turel. She obviously preferred a female form with its long tresses, but she had kept her pale coloring and turquoise eyes. "The other members will be arriving over the next two days, and we wanted the opportunity to speak privately with you beforehand."

"Of course," Azael replied. He had found it was easier to be courteous to traitors if he kept his replies short.

"Firstly," Turel continued, "we want to acknowledge that you may have legitimate grievances against us."

Azael smiled. He liked the way Turel was getting straight to the point.

"After all, it was our *unshaping* that allowed the Amatru to breach Mudena Del-Edha and defeat Semjaza. We openly accept responsibility for our actions. At the same time, we hope that you will acknowledge our legitimate grievances against Semjaza which led to our reaction. He deceived us in order to bring his armies here and establish his kingdom. He wanted only to use our power, but his promises to us turned out to be lies."

*Ah, there it is—a reminder of their power woven into a defense of their position,* he thought. But he just nodded instead of speaking.

"All of us have done what was required by necessity. Wouldn't you agree?" Danel asked.

Azael tried not to smirk at her choice of words. "Yes."

"Good," Turel added. "Then we hope that you will also recognize that those are the problems of the past. The anger of the Amatru has been pacified, and we are living in a new age ... which requires a new perspective. We all came here to establish our own kingdoms, and that is exactly the opportunity before us."

"Well said," Azael replied. "But I have a question before we get too far along. Are you surprised that I made it to this Council?"

Danel squinted before turning to look at Turel. Turel didn't wear his emotions so openly, but Azael could see that the blank look on his face was also confusion. "I don't understand," said Danel, turning back. "What do you mean?"

"I was attacked on the way here. Sariel snuck into our camp in the night, and he tried to kill me."

Turel inhaled a quick, shallow breath.

Danel put her hand over her lips. "I assure you we had nothing to do with it. Sariel was acting on his own behalf."

Azael tilted his head and kept silent for a few seconds, letting their discomfort grow. "I sincerely hope so," he finally replied.

"Did you kill him?" Turel asked.

Azael glanced over his shoulder and made eye contact with Rikoathel. The soldier's face and posture remained as unmoving as the stone beneath his feet. It was a trained response, covering up a profound sense of failure. But the mistake had been Hyrren's, not Rikoathel's. He turned back to Turel. "He was dealt with, but his body could not be recovered."

Turel shook his head slowly. "You see, this is precisely why our alliance is so critical. There are many others who apparently do not wish to join us, and they will become liabilities at some point in the future ... possibly dangerous ones."

"To answer your question," Danel jumped in, "we are not surprised, but relieved that you are here. And we are very much looking forward to what the future will bring to us all."

Azael smiled. "I couldn't agree more."

# 20

The sky was dark, but not yet black. The first of the stars were out, but their light was eclipsed by the glare from the flames in front of Sariel. He was lying on his side in the grass. The fire crackled, and he was instantly reminded of the evening gathering times with the Aleydam. The stories. The laughter. No sooner had the happy memory entered his mind than thoughts of Sheyir's suffering and death began to contaminate it. There was a great hole through the middle of Sariel's soul, as though he had been impaled by a gigantic spear. His breath escaped him for several seconds, and he was on the verge of breaking down completely before his training took over. Ages of warfare and loss had given him the emotional weapons to fight back. But Sheyir's loss was different. He couldn't fight this pain that threatened to strangle him to death. It was too powerful. The best he could do was run away from it. Deny it. Hopefully, in time, it would tire of the chase and let him go.

Enoch rose from the grass and poked at the fish that was suspended over the fire by a stick running through its length. "Almost ready."

Sariel shifted his weight to relieve the cramping in his shoulder, but the movement caused a wave of pain to flow through his abdomen. He inhaled a quick breath through his teeth and kept absolutely still. It passed a few seconds later and he let out the breath he'd been holding.

"Are you alright?"

"Not really," Sariel replied, carefully rolling onto his back.

"Do you want me to put you in the water?"

"No. Thank you. It's good for me to dry out from time to time."

Enoch nodded and checked the fish again. Then he lifted the stick off its supports and leaned it against a rock to cool.

Sariel took slow, shallow breaths as he looked up at the night sky. Several minutes of silence passed before he turned his head. "You don't speak much, do you?"

"I've grown accustomed to being alone," Enoch replied.

"Isn't that odd for someone who speaks on behalf of the Holy One?"

Enoch just shrugged.

"How come you haven't asked me again how I became injured?"

Enoch poked at the fish until he was satisfied that it was cool enough to hold. Then he laid it on a rock and began to peel away the skin and scales. "Because that knowledge isn't a requirement for my obedience to the Holy One. He led me here to find you and help you recover. That is all I need to know."

Sariel stared at him for a long moment, watching him separate the meat from the other, less desirable parts of the creature. "You are a very unusual man, Enoch."

"You are a very unusual angel, Sariel," he replied without looking away from the fish.

Sariel laughed aloud before his chest and abdomen seized up with excruciating pain. He clutched himself and waited for it to subside.

Another long moment of silence passed before Enoch turned and extended a broad leaf with a pile of roasted meat in the center.

Sariel reached out and took it, setting it on the grass beside him. "Thank you," he said before rolling slowly onto his side to face his dinner.

"Do you want me to help you sit up?"

"No. This is as comfortable as I'm going to get," Sariel replied. Then he picked up a small piece of the white flesh and placed it in his mouth. "Do you mind if I ask what you're doing here?"

Enoch's eyebrows rose. "You already know. The Holy One led me here."

"You came all the way from Sedekiyr because the Holy One told you I needed help?"

"Not exactly," Enoch replied. "I left Sedekiyr because of a vision the Holy One gave me. I was interrupted on the way because you needed my help."

Sariel licked his fingers. "What was this vision?"

Enoch stopped eating and turned to make eye contact. "It is not for your ears. It was meant for the people of Sedekiyr."

"A vision for the people of Sedekiyr that took you away from Sedekiyr?"

Enoch frowned. "That sounds like something my wife would ask."

Sariel couldn't help but smile. "It sounds like she is the practical one."

Enoch resumed eating. "Yes ... along with the rest of my tribe." He continued eating in silence before he added, "I'm the only one who thinks of the impractical things. Life cannot be lived solely by our own wisdom."

Sariel looked up to the stars again. "Indeed. Perhaps the Holy One is directing my steps as well."

"You don't believe that. You're just saying it for my benefit."

"No," Sariel protested. "Actually, I mean it. I've thought quite a bit about what you said to me when we first met in Senvidar."

"That the Holy One sees you?"

"Yes. But specifically, that I believe I'm doing the will of the Holy One even though I abandoned my home and disobeyed my elders."

Enoch nodded slowly.

"I did leave the Eternal Realm to follow my own path," Sariel admitted. "But I don't believe that I am completely outside of the Holy One's plans. In fact, I've wondered whether I'm fulfilling them in some unique way."

Enoch tilted his head and frowned.

"The Amatru are persistent in their ways ... stubborn, you might say," Sariel explained. "Before I came to this realm, I survived many lost battles. And even though it made me feel guilty just thinking it, I found myself frustrated that the Holy One didn't seem as willing as the Evil One to do whatever was necessary to win. Now I wonder if perhaps there is more to this conflict than only what I witnessed. What if the Amatru refuse to change their methods because that is not their role? What if they are incapable of considering other tactics for a reason? What if my role is not opposed to their goals, but complimentary to them?"

Enoch set down his leaf now that his fish was gone. "Maybe it was easier for me to see, because I am not one of your kind. But there was a vast difference between Semjaza's soldiers and the Amatru who came here while I waited with the weapons. Even the Myndarym, for all their beauty, were nothing by comparison. And when I saw the White City, and stood in the throne room ..." Enoch grew silent all of a sudden, and a single tear spilled down his cheek.[10] He quickly wiped it away and composed himself. "I can't imagine that the Holy One would compromise his righteousness just to win a war."

Sariel considered these words carefully before responding, "That's just it, you see? He isn't. I am."

Enoch didn't reply. He just stared into the flames.

Several minutes of silence passed before Sariel continued, "I find it an odd coincidence that, of all the places I might have ended up, you and I just happened to meet here. Perhaps the Holy One wanted us to be together for a reason. Maybe this vision is for my ears also."

Enoch slowly lay back on the grass until he was also looking upward at the stars. "I was high above the earth as if I were a bird. When I looked down, I saw embers drifting across the land. Wherever they went, the grass and trees caught fire. It seemed that they were fleeing from something, and as I looked closer, I saw a dark liquid spilling over the earth. It quenched the flames left by the embers, but it also withered everything it touched, like a poison. The embers converged into a group for safety, and that is when I recognized my own city. They took refuge in Sedekiyr. I went down to warn my tribe, but when I touched the ground, it was already too late. The embers had set the city on fire and were coming out in all directions. The poison had completely surrounded Sedekiyr and was closing in. I fell to the grass as the two collided over my head. It was chaos. But when I looked up, I saw the mountains of Nagah to the east. I saw safety. That's when I knew my people would only survive if they moved to the mountains."

"Oh my!" Sariel exclaimed.

"Yes," Enoch replied quickly. "It was a terrible sight to behold."

"No. You don't understand," Sariel clarified. "We have both witnessed the same event from two perspectives. The Holy One showed you what would happen in the future, and I have just witnessed how it begins. That's how I ended up here."

"I don't understand."

Sariel rolled slowly onto his side again so he could face Enoch. "After the Amatru destroyed Semjaza's kingdom, the Myndarym and I scattered before they could turn on us. I assume the Amatru went back to the Eternal Realm. Months went by without any word from either group. I was living far away from here when a messenger from the Myndarym found me. He said that they were gathering everyone together again to discuss how to divide and rule this realm. Some of the scattered Myndarym didn't want to participate. And I didn't like the idea either. When I returned to Senvidar to discuss it with them, I found out that some of Semjaza's soldiers had survived. And they were being invited to join this Council."

Enoch frowned.

"Semjaza's soldiers have taken over where he left off. They have turned the Kahyin population in Khelrusa into an army. And there are other creatures under his command. Semjaza's soldiers fathered children with their human prisoners. They are already incredibly strong, and they haven't even matured yet. The Myndarym are aligning themselves with this military strength so that their scattered brethren cannot oppose them. I think the conflict between the Council and the scattered Myndarym is the meaning of your vision."

Enoch sat up on his elbow and nodded his head. "I can see now that our coming together was meant for more than your healing. The ways of the Holy One never cease to amaze me."

"I agree," Sariel replied.

\* \* \* \*

SOUTH OF SENVIDAR

Hyrren stood in the middle of the field, feeling the cool night breeze as it moved across his skin. Azael's army was camped in the distance behind him, the light of their campfires dim and flickering. The Kahyin kept their distance from Hyrren's kind, like they had done every night since leaving Khelrusa. And it was just as well. The Nephiylim shouldn't have to share their fires with lowly humans.

Footsteps sounded from behind, and Hyrren waited patiently until his winged brother came to a stop beside him.

"Is everything alright?" Vengsul asked. The armor that he had worn during the day had been removed, and he looked once more like the child that Hyrren had grown up with.

Hyrren nodded.

Vengsul placed a hand on Hyrren's shoulder. "They died with spears in their hands instead of starving to death."

Hyrren turned and smiled as large as his grief would allow. Even though Vengsul wasn't a son of Semjaza, he was still a brother. They'd spent many cycles together in Mudena Del-Edha, and there was no one who understood him better.

"I still haven't gotten used to sleeping in the open," Vengsul added, trying to change the subject.

"I know … it feels good, though. Doesn't it?"

Vengsul walked a few more steps out into the field before turning around to face Hyrren. "We've come a long way."

Hyrren inhaled a deep breath of the air, still amazed at how clean it smelled and tasted. "Yes, we have."

"And it's all your doing."

Hyrren didn't know what to say.

"I mean that. It was your idea to go to Khelrusa. It was your strength that stood up to Luhad. Without you, our people would have died out before we even had a chance to survive. I want to thank you for what you've done. We're all grateful for your sacrifices."

Hyrren suddenly felt embarrassed by all the praise. He dropped his head and stared at the ground. "I just wish Aifett could see how far we've come."

Vengsul nodded. "I miss her too. Do you think we'll ever see her again?"

"Someday. I wanted to signal for her when we marched along the shores of the Great Waters, but I didn't want to expose her and her children. Azael hasn't even asked about them, and I don't want to bring his attention to it."

"Yes. He wasn't too interested in the breeding operations while Luhad was in charge," Vengsul pointed out. "It's for the better. Aifett would have struggled to thrive under Azael's leadership, anyway. She was always the independent one."

Hyrren smiled as he recalled many memories that substantiated his brother's claim. Then he let his eyes drift across the fields, drinking in the beauty of the wide, open space that was evident even at night. "Someday this whole world will be ours."

Vengsul suddenly turned his head as if surprised.

"Your children will fill the skies, and their wings will not even know the touch of confining stone. Aifett's children will rule the waters and their domain will never be challenged. My children will walk across the earth, and build cities wherever they desire. There will be no humans to steal our food, and no gods to rule over us."

"Brother! Don't say such things. If Azael finds out what you're thinking, he will kill you."

Hyrren finally turned his gaze to Vengsul. "Do you not feel it? There is a strength within our people that cannot be denied. I don't say these things because I am disloyal. I say it because it is ... inevitable. The gods may be up there on the mountain making their plans, but this world is our birthright. I feel it as clearly as anything I've ever known."

Vengsul's worried expression slowly drained from his face, and he turned to look up toward the mountain peak. "I admit that I have felt the same. But for now, we serve Azael. And we need to stay vigilant in case the Myndarym turn on him. So be ready to invade if we get the signal."

Hyrren nodded. "I am ready. And don't worry; I'm patient enough to wait until our destiny calls to us."

* * * *

THE WESTERN SHORES OF THE GREAT WATERS
SOUTHWEST OF SAHVEYIM

"Now it is you who isn't talking much," Enoch said as he handed Sariel a cluster of yellow fruit and sat down on the grass.

Sariel smiled, holding the food in his hand without taking a bite. "I was up most of the night, thinking."

Enoch peeled away the leaves in his hand until the cylindrical cluster was all that remained. Stuffing a piece into his mouth, he waited for Sariel to continue. But the only sound was the gurgle of the nearby stream and the tweet of small birds as they jumped from one place to another on the grass, pecking for insects. The sun was just above the trees to the east, and the air was already warm.

"I need to go to Khelrusa," Sariel finally said.

"Why?"

Sariel tugged at the fruit in his hand while he answered. "The embers from your vision are most likely the scattered Myndarym. But there are two possibilities for the poison chasing them. It could either be Azael's kingdom by itself, or the Council including Azael's kingdom. One would imply that Azael turns against the Council; the other could mean that their alliance remains strong. Either way, it is their individual centers of power that will make these situations possible."

"What are centers of power?"

Sariel took a bite and chewed for a few seconds before he explained. "It is a term used by the Amatru. In battle, whether against an individual or a group, your enemy has a center of power. It is the foundation from which he launches his attack, and the thing he will protect at all costs. It could be a piece of information, an ability, or a weapon. One way to defeat an enemy is to identify the center of his power and determine how to use it to your advantage."

Enoch looked down at the grass and flicked away an ant that was trying to climb up his leg. "But they are not fighting each other."

"Their conflict isn't physical, but there is most certainly a war taking place at this very moment," Sariel replied. "Of negotiations and posturing. Promises and favors. It is more subtle than vaepkir and vandrekt, but it is a war nonetheless. Azael and the Council are forming an alliance, and their centers of power are the basis of that alliance."

"You said they're meeting in Senvidar. Why do you want to go to Khelrusa?"

Sariel turned to look out upon the Great Waters through the gap in the trees created by the stream. "I'm missing one critical piece of information. I've already been to Senvidar, and I've spoken to the Council. I know that the center of Azael's power is his military strength. The Myndarym cannot *shape* any longer, and they have no way of enforcing the authority they seek. I understand why they would want to align themselves with Azael, but I don't understand the other side of the relationship. What need does Azael have that the Council is able to meet? For this, we have to go to Khelrusa."

Enoch frowned. "We? I'm not going to Khelrusa."

"We have to. Unless we find Azael's weakness and expose that to the Council, we cannot turn the direction of this situation. Don't you want to prevent the things you saw in your vision?"

"That isn't how it works," Enoch replied, leaning forward to make eye contact. "If I learned anything from my last journey among you Wandering Stars, it is that the Holy One doesn't show me the future so that I can change it."

Now it was Sariel who frowned. "Why else would He show it to you?"

"So that my people can prepare ... and trust not only in their own understanding."

"Changing the situation is the most effective way to prepare for it."

Enoch shook his head. "No. When I journey across the land, I find a high place and I look at what is to come. If I see water, I go around it. If I see a mountain ... I go around it. I don't stand before the mountain and try to move it."

Sariel smiled. "This isn't a mountain. These are living beings with strengths and weaknesses and desires that shift as quickly as the mist. If we don't influence the situation, your city will be destroyed."

Enoch climbed to his feet again and stepped over to the ring of stones with cold ashes inside. "My city is already going to be destroyed. I have seen it. My task is to move as many of my people to safety as I can."

Sariel leaned forward as though he was going to attempt standing, then winced at the pain it caused. When he spoke again, his tone was lacking patience. "Then why did the Holy One lead you here? To just take care of me and then leave again? You know there is something greater at work here."

"Yes. I believe that. But perhaps you are supposed to come with me."

Sariel pulled his head backward as if avoiding a flying insect. "I can't just walk away from everything that is happening."

Enoch turned from the cold ashes. "What do you hope to accomplish? Look at you. You can't even stand up."

Sariel looked down at himself. "This is because I let my grief control my actions."

"What grief?" Enoch asked. "What do you mean?"

Sariel shook his head before shifting his weight to his left side. "Nothing. I made a mistake; that's all. It won't happen again."

Enoch came forward and knelt before Sariel until they were looking each other directly in the eyes. "None of this was a mistake. Do you know why you can't shape anymore?"

The skin around Sariel's eyes tightened into a squint.

"The Holy One led me to where the Myndarym had gathered after your war with Semjaza. I told them, 'If you desire, in the hardness of your hearts, to live in a place that is not meant for you, then so be it. You will have what you want ... for a time!' That's when they lost their *shaping* ability."

Sariel's expression changed into a scowl. "You did this to me!"

The accusation was so much louder than the rest of their conversation that Enoch almost lost his balance. But he kept his eyes focused directly on Sariel. "No," he replied calmly. "I delivered a judgment from the Holy One. And I don't believe it was an accident that it affected you also. You weren't even there, and yet it changed you. And now, here you are in front of me in the form of a man ... weak and broken. What can you possibly accomplish in Khelrusa? If you go there, Azael will kill you."

Sariel looked down at the grass in front of him. The morning sunlight created shadows on the side of his jaw where the muscles were bulging with tension.

"If you truly believe that we were brought together for more than just your healing, then come with me," Enoch said.

A long moment of silence passed, and Enoch finally stood and walked back to the fire ring.

"Where are you going?"

Enoch smiled before he turned around to face Sariel. "West, to the beginning of my people.[7] I will receive a blessing from the firstfather, and then I will return to Sedekiyr to move the Shayetham into the mountains. Come with me. And if you will not listen to my words, then hear your own. You said the Holy One might have a unique plan for you. What is unique about another battle? What is unique about throwing yourself into the midst of creatures larger and more powerful than you? Look at where it has gotten you. Come with me and help me protect my people. Perhaps that is why we were brought together."

# 21

It took forty-five days for Enoch to retrace his path along the western shores of the Great Waters, until he and Sariel stood on the rolling hills north of Da-Mayim. They only stayed one night there, at the place where the Holy One had diverted his intended route. As they had done since Sariel had healed enough to walk, they kept moving at a steady pace, this time westward. Enoch knew that the journey to his firstfather would be one of endurance, so he concentrated not on speed, but on reducing the time spent with unnecessary things. They slept without shelter on most nights and ate on the move as they came across edible things growing from the ground or hanging from trees.

Their new route took them through densely forested lowlands before they veered southwest through open plains. The terrain reminded Enoch of home, and the nostalgic feeling only increased as they came within sight of Azab—the city of his grandfather, Mahalal-el. Several thousand huts and other wood and grass structures dotted the shores around a circular body of water. The resemblance to Sedekiyr was obvious, but Azab was much larger. Its name, in the Shayeth tongue, meant to *forsake*, or *leave*. Mahalal-el had been determined to escape the troubles of his own father, and had established the city far away from where he grew up.

As Enoch and Sariel skirted around the northern side of it, Enoch considered the significance of the city's name in relation to his own desire to keep away from the sight of its citizens. Among the Shayetham, the purpose of the elders traveling was to communicate with the next city or to establish a new one. The fact that Enoch was avoiding his own people altogether only made his objective feel all the more foreign.

It took another thirty-six days of following shorelines, weaving through forests, and passing over wide plains to reach the city of Anah, home of Enoch's great-grandfather, Keynan. Anah would have been easy to miss, situated where it was, high between two spurs on the northeast side of a mountain. It was also small—about a third the size of Sedekiyr, if Enoch could trust his eyes at such a distance. The lack of lowland grasses and the age of the city explained why stone had been used as the primary building material. Structures of all sizes littered the base of the slopes, as if they had tumbled down from the heights above. One look was all Enoch needed in order to feel the harshness of the place. Anah, or *humbled*, was what Keynan had called it during its founding. And like the unyielding stone around it, the city's name echoed the bitterness of the man who had gone out into the world to take control of it, only to suffer one hardship after another. He had all but lost his belief in the Holy One when his wife gave birth to Mahalal-el. Only then did a small measure of his faith return. Keynan had looked into the eyes of his son and found a reason to praise again. And so he named his son, *Praise of God*.

Sariel kept silent on most days. Enoch could tell that there was much on his mind, and he didn't want to pry. And anyway, Enoch had his own thoughts to wade through. He recalled the stories he had heard from his father when he was a child—the history of his people. Their successes and failures, marriages and feuding, had all just been tales. But now, as Enoch walked backward through time, retracing the lineage of the Shayetham, the stories became real. He saw the land through a different pair of eyes. Forests were no longer obstructions, but reference points for memories. Mountains were monuments, named after significant events. And water was not just something that divided land, but something that brought people together.

Such was the case when they reached the city of Seydah twenty-five days later. Enoch's great-great-grandfather, Enowsh, had found a lowland peninsula with an abundance of growing food, and decided that his people could also thrive if they put down roots here. And they did. It was this reality that set Keynan's expectations when he had ventured out into the world. Unfortunately, Keynan failed to experience the abundance of his father or siblings. The remainder of Enowsh's family multiplied, spreading across the peninsula to create a vast array of interconnected villages. Their wood and grass structures covered the plains and even extended into the water, where they could reach the fish instead of waiting for them to come into the shallows. Even from a great distance, Enoch and Sariel could see people walking along the bridges of wood, throwing out their nets of woven grasses.

From the city named for the Holy One's provision, Enoch and Sariel traveled another thirty-nine days west to Nakh. Shayeth, the thirdborn son of Adam, had chosen to think of the earth itself as his inheritance and named his city in honor of this idea.[11] It was similar in size to Seydah, but was limited to the forest surrounding a cove on the north side of another body of water. The dwellings were built beneath the canopy of the forest, with wide and flat roofs of woven grass sloping down from the thick trunks of trees. It reminded Enoch of Aragatsiyr where the Myndarym lived, but crude by comparison. Given the number of years Nakh had been in existence, Enoch had expected it to cover more territory, which only made the size of Seydah—a younger city—that much more impressive.

The last leg of their journey took twenty-four days. In terms of distance, the city of Galah was relatively close to Nakh, but the terrain proved challenging. Plains turned to rolling hills. Rolling hills turned to steep faces of rock, cut by hundreds of streams and rivers. Dense forests covered every part of the land that wasn't rock or water. No matter which direction they turned, it seemed that they were always going uphill. The lack of forward progress and the challenging terrain brought Enoch and Sariel into close proximity. They had to help one another cross safely through water and climb over obstacles. And in doing so, the duration and frequency of their conversations increased. Sariel pointed out things about the land, explaining why trees looked a certain way or why the water had chosen the path it had. Enoch would share the history of his people, combining the things he had heard through many elder gatherings with his own observations. He was able to speak freely with Sariel. There were no interruptions or judgments about his words. The angel simply listened, and occasionally shared some experience from his own past if it related.

Finally, the trees began to thin. The air grew cool. The fog that had always been present in one shape or another had dissipated. Enoch could feel a sense of foreboding within him, and he knew his destination was near long before he could see it.

Sariel, too, seemed to know it was coming. He usually moved about with a calm confidence, his eyes taking in the surroundings without much effort. But as they climbed out of the mist and scrambled upward through increasingly rocky terrain, he could be seen looking around in all directions. The sadness that had been present in his eyes those first days on the shore of the Great Waters had returned. Enoch wondered if there might be something more to his traveling companion's strange behavior, but didn't want to offend him by asking.

And then they crested the peak of a mountain. The city of Galah lay directly west of them, filling a high and broad valley that was ringed by mountains to the north, south, and west. The size of Galah was unlike anything Enoch had ever witnessed. In all the stories handed down to him over the years, none of them contained so much as a description of his firstfather's city. His eyes explored it as though they were a child's, fresh and naïve, without the help or hindrance of an elder's perspective.

A massive stone wall stretched for miles across the opening on the east side of the valley. Stone buildings covered the land, thousands and thousands of them, arranged in orderly groupings with roads running between. From their wooden roofs, columns of smoke—some as thin as saplings, others wider than the thickest tree—rose into the air. The smoke hung dark over the city, trapped by the mountains like a veil. Water trickled down the face of the mountains from every direction, gathering into a river that flowed through the center of the city and out from a gate at the center of the stone wall. Enoch didn't know precisely how old Galah was, but he knew Shayeth had been born here, which made it at least five hundred and sixty years old.

"I've never seen such a place," he said aloud.

"That wall makes me think they won't be receptive to an unexpected visit. How are you going to get in?"

Enoch shrugged without taking his eyes off the city. "I don't know yet." The wind blew strongly across the barren peak where they stood, causing Enoch to steady himself on a rock to keep from losing his balance.

Sariel turned his head. "I suggest we observe from the mountains above the city."

"Observe? What for?"

The sadness was gone from Sariel's eyes now. He seemed confident and focused. "To locate Adam."

"Then what?"

"If you go to the front gate and announce yourself, you may not even get the opportunity to speak with him. It might be better to approach him when he's alone ... bypass the restrictions."

Enoch nodded. "What if we can't find him? Or what if we find him, but he's never alone?"

Sariel turned his attention back to the city. "If that's the case, then we'll find another way. For now, we'll just observe so we can understand what we're dealing with."

Enoch's relief came out as a smile. "I don't know what I would have done if you hadn't come here with me."

It seemed that Sariel wanted to smile, but his face remained rigid, as if some other emotion were holding it in place. "Remember ... you were face to face with Semjaza and lived to tell your family about it. You walked into a gathering of Myndarym and delivered judgment. And then you walked out again. You've been through worse and survived. Adam is one of your own. You don't need to be nervous."

Enoch nodded. All of it was true, but none of it made his heart slow its rapid beating.

"Most importantly, you are the only human being to ever set foot inside the White City or the throne room of the Holy One. Not even I have done that."

Now Enoch smiled. "You're right. My fear reveals my lack of faith."

"That's not quite what I meant," Sariel said, shaking his head slowly. "Just focus on what the Holy One told you to do, and don't worry about what could happen. He always seems to protect you."

Enoch felt his stomach go cold. "He didn't exactly tell me to come here."

"What?"

Enoch frowned. "He showed me that my people would be safe in the mountains."

"That's all?"

"That's all," Enoch admitted. "I tried to tell my father and grandfather, but they refused to listen. Getting Adam's blessing was the only way I could think to convince them."

Sariel's mouth was open in bewilderment, and his eyes were wide with surprise. A long moment of awkward silence passed before he began laughing.

Enoch frowned again. "What?"

Sariel's laughter got louder and louder until he was holding his stomach and shaking. Slowly, he regained control of himself, and when he finally stopped, his face was red. He reached out and clamped his hand over Enoch's shoulder. "I needed that."

"I don't understand."

"Let's just say it's a relief to know I'm not the only one who has a problem following orders."

"Why would that be a relief?" Enoch wondered.

Sariel laughed once more and patted Enoch's shoulder. "Come on. Let's go find your firstfather."

# 22

The scale of Galah was massive, rivaling even Khelrusa. Sariel had never seen so many humans in one place, and its age was obvious at a glance. The stone buildings were evidence of a more sophisticated people than those he and Enoch had passed in the months it had taken to get here. The huge quarry against the southern slopes, the irrigation channels running throughout, the orchards and pastures on its eastern side—all of it set Galah apart as not just a village or a city, but a civilization. And yet, its impressive sight was countered by a darkness that went beyond the haze of smoke hanging between the mountains. If Sariel had still been able to *shift* into the Eternal, he might have found traces of Marotru influence.

He and Enoch had been conducting surveillance for almost a week, hiding out in the mountains around the city. It had initially been an overwhelming and discouraging process due to the enormity of such a task. But after the first two days, they focused their attention on the largest of the buildings—a sprawling, multi-level structure with a wooden roof that sat at the approximate center of the valley. Given the number of primary roads leading to it, and that more water had been diverted to it from the nearby river than any other section of the city, it made sense that the first of all humans would likely reside there.

Sure enough, halfway through the third day, they had spotted a small group of people exiting the building and moving west through the city. Unlike the others who came and went throughout the day at random intervals, this group left and returned at the same time each day. Sariel had suggested they move around to the forests on the west side of the city to get a better look and hopefully observe what the group was doing. It turned out that four of the men always stopped at the edge of the forest, where the development of the city ended. The fifth man continued into the trees and would wander alone until the sun was halfway through its descent toward the western horizon. With the constant bustle of this city and a seemingly endless supply of tasks for its citizens to accomplish, it seemed obvious that only the city elder would be afforded this freedom. It appeared that they had located their objective.

Today the pattern was repeating itself, and though Enoch was ready, he looked nervous. "Do you know what you're going to say?" Sariel asked him as they hid among the dense trees covering the western foothills.

"Some of it. But I don't know how he'll respond, so I can't prepare all of my words in advance."

"Just remember what I told you before about standing in front of Semjaza. You'll do fine."

Enoch smiled nervously.

Sariel looked up at the hazy sky and the white disk of the sun, just visible through a thin layer of moisture. "It's time."

"Thank you," Enoch said. "I couldn't have done this without you."

Sariel nodded and watched his friend slowly disappear into the thousands of tree trunks that stuck out of the ground like old, dark columns of a building whose roof had rotted away. This forest was no older than any other Sariel had encountered, but the gray bark around him and bare soil under his feet left the impression of fatigue, as if this part of the world had grown weary.

Sariel climbed to a higher elevation, and once he was above the mist, he could observe the western edge of the city where the trees weren't quite as dense. When he reacquired his sight of Enoch, he sat down on a rock ledge to catch his breath.

*Never needed to do that before this body,* he mused.

His hands, now resting on his knees, looked so small and weak. The scars on his forearms that he had kept to remember losing his team of Iryllurym in the Eternal Realm were now just reminders of his human frailty. He closed his eyes to make the image go away, and felt the cold, humid air against his face.

When he opened his eyes again, he looked out across the city. Wisps of white and gray moisture curled around buildings and swirled over the surface of the river. He was above it now, as he had been in Aleydiyr. The sudden image of a tiny hand flashed through Sariel's mind—its dark skin slick with blood. He inhaled quickly, trying to steady himself.

*Sheyir, why didn't you wait for me?*

It was no use wondering. She was gone, and there was no way to change that fact.

*And now I'm trapped in this body. If Enoch had kept his mouth shut, I'd still have my wings. Azael would be no match for me. I'd kill him and his Iryllur soldiers, and then it would be over. But instead, I sit here in this weak and useless body while they strengthen their position. While their kingdom grows.*

The loss of Sheyir and the delusion of his own invincibility had led him to sneak into Azael's camp that night. But the delusion had certainly perished in that river below the falls. Though he had managed to kill two young Nephiylim, he had failed to accomplish his goal and had almost died in the process. His enemy was now well beyond his reach, and a physical confrontation was pointless. He'd had months to accept that conclusion, but it still felt unacceptable. Once again, his thoughts probed other options.

*The Council could overpower Azael and his soldiers, if there were enough of them. But how could I motivate them? What would cause them to overcome their own fears and see Azael as an enemy rather than an ally? Perhaps if they had their own army, they wouldn't need his. But they don't have the experience or training to create one. Azael is too far ahead of them in that regard. And the motivation to overpower him would have to come first.*

He let the thought linger in his mind for several minutes while he watched the forest for glimpses of Enoch's movement. But there seemed to be no solutions to this dilemma, no matter how many different ways he approached it.

*One way or another, Semjaza's kingdom must come to an end!*

\* \* \* \*

Enoch glanced at the sky again, wondering how long he had been waiting. Perhaps Adam had chosen a different route today? Or he might have suspected someone was waiting for him and decided not to come. A scratching sound drew Enoch's attention back to the trees. His eyes darted from place to place, searching. A small, furry creature clung to the side of a tree trunk, peering around it in Enoch's direction. But it was too close to have produced the noise Enoch had heard.

Then it happened again. Another sound to the left, a few dozen paces away.

Enoch watched intently, finally seeing movement beside a tree. He waited a few more seconds before a man stepped out into view. His skin was dark and ruddy, like the Kahyin. His hair was cut short against his scalp, but his beard, a mixture of black and brown with flecks of gray, hung down to his navel in a single braid. His tunic of white cloth hung almost to his knees, and was gathered at the waist by a belt of some unknown material. There was a regal quality to how he carried himself, and coupled with his groomed appearance, he looked out of place within the drab forest. The man moved slowly, but not out of fear or caution. He was looking up at the trees and seemed to be lost in thought.

*It has to be Adam,* Enoch said to himself.

The man took a few deliberate steps and then stopped again, reaching out with his walking stick to tap the trunk of a nearby tree. He looked it up and down, from roots to leaves, inspecting it before scratching a mark in the soil with his walking stick and moving on.

Enoch's heart thudded inside his chest. He wondered whether it would be better to call out to Adam or just approach him. And what if this wasn't Adam?

"Are you going to say something, or just stand there?" the man asked quietly without taking his eyes off the trees.

Enoch swallowed the lump in his throat. "I didn't want to startle you."

The man kept moving slowly through the trees, touching some and marking the soil. "Then perhaps you should reconsider sneaking up on an *old man* in the forest."

Enoch had never heard anyone refer to himself as an old man. "Are you Adam, the firstfather?" he asked, following at a distance that wouldn't seem threatening.

The man stopped walking and turned his eyes in Enoch's direction. Aside from their intensity, Enoch noticed that they were green like his own—a rare thing among his people. "Who are you?" Adam replied.

"I am Enoch, the seventh firstborn through your son, Shayeth."

Adam exhaled quickly through his nose. "Shayeth was not my firstborn," he said before mumbling something else that Enoch couldn't hear.[12] Then he turned his head in the opposite direction and began walking again.

Enoch didn't know how to respond, so he just followed, moving a little closer to the firstfather than before. He had known this conversation was going to be difficult, but he hadn't anticipated it being so awkward.

"I have heard of you and your strange ways," Adam said finally. "What do you want?"

"To speak with you."

Adam tapped another tree trunk, made another mark on the ground, and continued moving west. "You bring dishonor upon your family by coming to me instead of going to your father."

"My father will not listen to me. And neither will my grandfather."

"That is because it is you who should listen to them. Wisdom flows down from father to son, not upward. It is unnatural."

Enoch followed, glancing down at the mark on the ground and noting that it was a circle, whereas the last one had been a straight line. "Did the Holy One teach that to you?"

Adam whirled around with unexpected speed, clutching his walking stick as if it were a weapon. "How dare you ask me such a thing? What do you know of the Holy One?"

Enoch was startled by the sudden outburst and took a few steps back. He opened his mouth to respond, but Adam cut him off.

"I can see why your father and grandfather will not listen to you; you have no respect for your elders. Leave my city, son of Yered. Leave me in peace!"

Enoch could plainly see that Adam was not enjoying peace at all. He seemed to be greatly troubled, but he thought the conversation might proceed easier if he kept that to himself. Instead, he remembered how Zacol sometimes turned conversations with other people by bringing up something that they might want to talk about. It was indirect, and felt dangerously close to deceit, but Enoch was failing to make any progress with his natural inclinations.

"I am but a humble servant of the Holy One. I have the utmost respect for all matters concerning Him. If my elders feel disrespected, it is because they have gone astray. They cannot hear His voice as I can, because they do not believe He speaks at all. But you ... surely you know He is there? He created you. He must have spoken with you." Enoch hoped his curiosity would overshadow the slight to his father and grandfather.

Adam's disposition seemed to shift ever so slowly, like the mist on a windless day. The cold distance that was evident even in his posture drained away, and Adam turned his head. His eyes now looked sad, as though he longed for something. "You cannot possibly imagine what I've seen ... and done."

Enoch smiled apologetically. "I could if you tell me what it was like ... in the first days."

Adam shook his head slowly. "That time has passed. It's like a dream to me now—a beautiful dream that fades upon awakening. I lose a little more of it each day."

"You speak of Aden?"[13]

There were tears in Adam's eyes now.

"Shalakh Akhar. After Aden," Enoch continued. "The point when we began counting the cycles of the sun. But no one will speak of what Aden is, or why we didn't count time before it. I have asked my father about it, but he won't say anything. And my grandfather won't even acknowledge my questions. I wonder if they even know."

"They do not," Adam replied quickly.

"But you do. I can see it in your eyes."

Adam shook his head and looked away.

"*Galah* means exile," Enoch pressed. "This city was not your first home. Aden was a place, wasn't it?"

Adam didn't reply.

"What was it like?"

Adam slowly lifted his eyes to the leaves and the sky overhead. Tears streamed down his face, but his crying was silent. "I can hardly remember anymore. And if it were possible for me to look upon it again, my eyes would not be able to comprehend its beauty."

Enoch suddenly remembered the feeling of being in the White City. "I know what you mean. I have visited a place of such radiance ... such glory that I felt my body was not capable of experiencing it to the fullest. I wanted to look everywhere and remember every sight and sound and smell, but it so far exceeded my comprehension that, when it was over, I began to forget what it was like. Now I find myself wondering whether it was real or imagined."[10]

"Yes, exactly!" Adam exclaimed before his raised eyebrows dropped again. "But it could not have been Aden."

"I don't know. It was a white city far above the earth. The walls seemed like water standing on its side ..." Enoch remembered the white flames burning at the base of the city walls, and all the colors that shimmered inside of the watery surface. The memory slowly faded, and when Enoch realized again that he was standing in the forest, Adam's words suddenly held new meaning. "What do you mean? Why couldn't it have been Aden?"

"Because we are no longer permitted to go there."

"We?"

"Me. My wife. And anyone who is descended from us," Adam explained. "Our exile was complete and permanent. There is only one way in, and it is guarded by two creatures more fearsome than anything you have seen.[14] They have many wings and ... their faces ..."

"Faces like ours, but also like animals?" Enoch wondered.

"Yes! How do you know?"

Enoch smiled. "They are called Keruvym. I saw them in the White City."[15]

"And their weapons of fire? Did you see them?"

"No. The ones in the White City didn't have weapons. And I felt safe near them, but I can imagine how terrifying it would be to face them here on the earth." Enoch suddenly remembered the intangible contrast between the feeling of security when he was with the Speaker and his angels versus the fear of standing in front of Semjaza.

"They would kill us to protect the Tree of Life," Adam mused.[16]

Enoch had never heard of such a thing, and was just about to ask what it was when Adam suddenly looked up and opened his mouth, as if he were staring at it and about to describe it. Enoch waited, but Adam kept silent. "Was it tall?" he finally asked.

Adam's reply came out as a whisper. "It had the power to sustain all things for eternity."

Enoch found himself looking up at the sky, following Adam's gaze to nowhere. "What did it look like?"

The faraway expression on Adam's face slowly changed to a frown. Then he lowered his head and began rubbing his forehead. "It was ... I ... can't ..."

"I'm sorry. I didn't mean to—"

"It was light ... and the other was darkness," Adam interrupted.

"What other?"

"The Tree of Wisdom," Adam spat, exhaling through his nose afterward.[17] "As though it were something to be gained. But he lied. And she believed him. 'You'll be as wise as the Holy One,' he said."

"Who lied?"

Adam ignored the question. "But it wasn't wisdom we gained, just a different perspective. It was like hearing a terrible secret that you would rather not know. Or worse yet, a lie that only becomes true when you hear it. But it can't be unknown, you see? That's the trap of it!"[18]

"Do you speak of the Evil One?" Enoch asked.

"And now everything is dying. Slowly dying," Adam replied, looking around at the trees though his eyes were distant.

Adam's enigmatic rambling was frustrating to Enoch, but at least he felt comfortable enough to talk. It was progress.

Adam's eyes seemed to find their focus, finally settling on Enoch. "Yes, the Evil One. He corrupts. He destroys. He steals. This was all for us," he said with outstretched arms, "and now it is his. And we are but wanderers here."

The word *wanderers* jarred Enoch from the temporary journey through Adam's memories, reminding him that there was still a goal at the end of this conversation. "The Evil One is still at work, bending this place to his will. But we don't have to make it easy for him."

"Did you not hear me? It is inevitable."

"If that's true, then why does the Holy One bother to speak at all?"

Adam's eyebrows lowered into something between confusion and a frown.

"You see?" Enoch replied. "You don't deny that He speaks because you have experienced it yourself."

Adam slowly shook his head again. "In Aden, yes. He spoke with us. He walked side by side with us. But never since. Now there is only silence," he said, opening his arms to the forest as proof.

"He speaks to me," Enoch said bluntly.

Adam suddenly looked him up and down with a disapproving scowl, as if noticing Enoch for the first time. "What does He say?"

"He showed me a vision of my city being destroyed. But there was safety in the mountains to the east of Sedekiyr. He told me to move my people there."

Adam smirked now. "And your father didn't heed this advice?"

"No."

"Perhaps that is because you are not the elder. You are the only firstborn in Shayeth's line to remain in the city of his father and not establish his own city. If you had done so, the people of your city would follow you."

Enoch felt his shoulders slump. "That's beside the point. It was not some other city I saw being destroyed. It was Sedekiyr. They are the ones who must move."

"Destroyed by what?" Adam asked.

Enoch shook his head now, thrown by the abrupt change in direction.

"What will destroy Sedekiyr?" Adam repeated.

Now it was Enoch's turn to exhale in frustration. He didn't want to get into the details of his vision because he knew it would only distract from the goal—for Adam to give Enoch his blessing. But Adam's question was a direct one, leaving no room for argument. "My city will be caught in the middle of a war between the angels."

Adam's eyebrows rose as he inclined his head. "Between the angels and whom?"

"Among themselves. Some have abandoned the Eternal Realm to inhabit this one. They desire to be gods and to rule over us. There is a conflict stirring among them, and I believe the Holy One showed me how it will affect my people so that I might save them."

Adam's laugh came out in one quick burst.

"You don't believe me?"

"Why should I?"

Enoch breathed in deeply and slowly. "I have spent almost two years away from my family dealing with this problem. I have walked among the Wandering Stars of heaven. I have lived with them. I have seen them kill each other. I have carried messages for them. I have carried messages from the Holy One to them. And I have pronounced His judgment upon them. This is not a dream, nor is it some tale I imagined. It is real." The words came out in a steady cadence, as if he were scolding Methu.

Adam leaned on his walking stick, his forehead creased with skepticism. "What would they want with *this* place? Do they think they can take it from the Evil One as he stole it from us?"

Enoch shook his head and looked at the ground. "Their ways are far too complicated for me to know. But the Holy One told me to move my people to the mountains. And that is what I must do."

"What do want of me, then?"

Enoch looked up again. "I need your blessing so my people will listen to me. You are our firstfather, and your authority will mean a great deal to them."

Adam suddenly glanced up at the sky, then at the forest around him. "I must get back."

Enoch followed his gaze out of habit. "Wait."

Adam turned and began walking quickly to the east, toward the city. "They will be expecting me."

"Wait," Enoch pleaded, again thrown by the sudden change in the conversation. "Can we talk just a moment longer?"

"If I don't return on time, they will come looking for me."

"Can we talk on the way?"

Adam looked back over his shoulder. "Even if I was willing to give you my blessing, you would also need something to signify it to your people. Something of mine that would be recognized by the elders."

"Yes."

Adam continued walking at a brisk pace, staying silent for so long that Enoch wondered if he had missed something. Perhaps Adam had asked a question and Enoch had been lost in thought and failed to answer.

"I could give you my tunic," Adam said finally, "but you could easily make one for yourself, so that will not do."

Enoch doubted that he could ever make a tunic of such quality, but he was relieved that the conversation was still going. "What about your walking stick?"

Adam glanced at the gnarled branch in his hand. It was as tall as his shoulder, and Enoch thought it looked worn—ancient, even. "I use this when I travel to Nakh for the gathering of elders. Shayeth would recognize it, but it would be meaningless to your father."

Enoch stroked his beard and tried to think of something else.

"No," Adam continued. "There's only one item that would serve this purpose, but it cannot be given.

"Why? What is it?"

Another awkward moment of silence passed before Adam replied, "As soon as we ate from the dark tree, everything changed. But Eve wouldn't let go of the fruit. She held on to it even as we were being exiled from Aden. It rotted in a few days, of course, as all fruit does. But the seed remained. It is dark, like the tree it came from—a gathering of shadows even in the light of day. She won't part with it; I think she still wants what was promised to us, and she believes that it can make us wise."

"So Eve has it?"

"It is mine as much as it is hers."

"Then you have it?" Enoch tried again.

Adam shook his head slowly. "I would not give it to you even if I held it in my hands now."

"I wouldn't keep it," Enoch assured him. "I would only show it to my father to convince him of your blessing. Then I would return it."

"I cannot."

"Why? Do you also hope that it could still make you wise?"

Adam slowed his pace a bit. "There is very little I hope for anymore."

"Then why will you not let me use it? It's not going to give you wisdom; it's nothing more than a symbol of the lie. Wouldn't you like to be rid of it? Even more so if it could help save hundreds and hundreds of your people?"

Adam breathed a quick laugh. "There are over three million people in this city. They are the ones I concern myself with. The people of Sedekiyr are Yered's responsibility."

Enoch tugged hard at his beard. Adam's response revealed a mindset that seemed to contradict the whole process of elders passing down wisdom to their sons. The sharing of knowledge that helped sustain the next generation was a physical act of taking responsibility. And Adam was the one who had started it in the first place.

"Oh! That's it," he realized. "At the next gathering of elders, when you travel to Nakh, all you have to do is communicate your blessing to Shayeth as part of the passing down of wisdom. He will communicate it to Enowsh and so on until my father hears that you agree with me."

Adam continued walking without a reply.

"What's wrong?"

"I cannot do that."

Enoch suddenly stopped walking. "You won't give me your blessing, regardless of whether there is a physical object attached to it." His voice was loud against the stillness of the forest.

Adam kept moving without even turning his head. Beyond him, sections of a building could be seen through the trees.

"Why?" Enoch yelled. When no answer came, he starting running until he had caught up to Adam. Without considering his actions, he grabbed the firstfather's arm and pulled him to a stop. "Tell me! Why won't you give me your blessing?"

"Unhand him!" someone shouted.

Enoch looked east to see a man running towards them with a thick wooden club in his hand.

Adam suddenly yanked his arm away from Enoch's grasp.

The dull thumping of footsteps could be heard approaching from the north and south, but Enoch's eyes were fixed on the guard coming from the east and now only a few paces away. "Who are you?" the man yelled.

Enoch held up his hands to show that he wasn't a threat.

"Firstfather. Are you alright? Is this man trying to hurt you?" the guard asked as he came to a stop beside Adam.

"He is disturbing me," Adam replied.

The footsteps coming from behind Enoch suddenly grew in volume. Something slammed into his back, driving him painfully to the ground. Hands were suddenly grabbing at his arms and neck, restricting his movements. With his face in the dirt, Enoch watched another pair of sandaled feet and bare legs pass in front of his nose. The crushing weight on top of him doubled.

"No one is permitted in this area except the firstfather. Who are you?"

Enoch couldn't see who was asking the question. "My name is Enoch," he replied, struggling to make his words clear through lips pressed against the dirt. "I'm the seventh firstborn through Shayeth."

The weight upon his body lessened slightly.

"What are you doing here?" another voice asked.

Enoch was unable to turn his head, but he could see Adam and the first guard from the corner of his eye. They were already a dozen paces away toward the city. "I came to speak with Firstfather."

"Why didn't you come to the front gate?" the second guard asked.

The third guard chimed in immediately, "The protocol for official messages is to make your request first to the city guard."

"I didn't think you'd let me in," Enoch replied.

"Exactly," the third guard said. "And the fact that you snuck in like a thief is exactly why we would have turned you away. Now get up!"

When they pulled Enoch up off the ground, it took a few seconds for him to regain his balance. He was finally able to see who had been pressing his face into the dirt. Both men were taller than Enoch, and muscular, but far less intimidating than the Kahyin hunters he'd faced, though these men also carried wooden clubs.

"Start walking," the second guard said, nodding toward Galah.

Enoch held up his hands and started moving. "Where are you taking me?"

"Just walk and be quiet," the third guard replied.

# 23

A crowd began to gather as the guards led Enoch down a paved road through the middle of the city. The citizens of Galah were staring, and Enoch tried not to make eye contact with them. He kept his head down and watched the flat, square stones passing underneath his feet. The river running parallel to the road drowned out most of the city noise, but Enoch could still make out the occasional question yelled in his direction. The guards didn't respond either, and simply pushed Enoch forward whenever his pace failed to suit them.

The road led directly east to the center of the city, where it circled a massive stone building, transitioning to wooden planks as it arched over smaller streams that had been channeled from the river. Tall trees lined either side of the road and formed a ring around the center of the city. It would have been both impressive and intimidating if Enoch had never seen the impossibly tall spire of Semjaza's tower, or the woven trees of Aragatsiyr, or the White City itself.

They entered the building through a tall, arched passage and ascended many steps until the passage opened into a massive square room with fires burning in pits at each of the four corners. Against the far wall a raised stone platform held a tall, ornate chair that looked to be carved from the same wood that grew in the forest to the east. It was empty. Beside it, on a smaller chair, sat a woman.

Enoch assumed that it was Eve, the firstmother and wife of Adam.[19] Though sitting, there was a sense of importance about her, as if she were imitating one of the Myndarym. Her skin was paler than Adam's, similar to Enoch's own. Her long-sleeved tunic reached down to her ankles, with a fine weave that was as pale as the mist. Her hair—a dark brown color with streaks of gray—was pulled upward from her face, swirling around the top of her head in a gathering of braids that spilled down in front of her shoulder and reached all the way to the floor. But it was the object resting on her forehead that Enoch's gaze settled on. It looked like the dark and jagged stone from which Semjaza's throne had been made. But the smooth oval hanging from a braided cord around her head, no bigger than the first segment of Enoch's thumb, didn't reflect light. Instead, it seemed to gather shadows around itself.

Before they had gone halfway across the room, one of the guards pulled on Enoch's shoulder. "Stop and kneel," he commanded.

Enoch did as he was told, making a conscious effort to look away from the seed of the Tree of Wisdom.

"The debris must have come down from the mountains," another man said. He was standing at the base of the steps, looking up at Eve. Enoch could tell that he wasn't just an ordinary citizen, nor was he a guard. Though his clothes were plain, he seemed like someone important.

"The blockage is affecting all the crops and pastures southeast of the third storehouse."

"Can you dig it out of the water?" Eve asked.

"Yes. But I'll need plowing tools and animals ... and Father gets nervous when—"

"Never mind that," Eve interrupted. "How many men will you need?"

"Twenty," the man replied.

Eve crossed her hands and placed them in her lap. "Take the guards from the quarry, and get started. I'll make sure your father approves."

The man bowed his head without taking his eyes off her. "Thank you, Mother."

As Eve's son turned to leave the room, she looked in Enoch's direction and waved the guards forward.

"Get up," they said, nudging Enoch.

He pushed himself up and moved forward with one guard holding each of his shoulders. When they reached the bottom of the steps, the guards pulled him to a stop and forced him downward again.

Enoch complied, kneeling on the floor of stones that had been cut smooth and fitted together.

"Firstmother, this is Enoch, the seventh firstborn through Shayeth," one of the guards announced. "We found him in the forest to the east. He was with Firstfather, holding onto his arm. It appeared that he was trying to restrain Firstfather from returning to the city."

From the corner of his eye, Enoch saw Eve's son come to a stop and turn around. He had been leaving, but now seemed interested in this conversation as well.

"Where is Adam?" Eve asked.

"He is washing up after his walk," the guard replied.

Eve lowered her brown eyes and met Enoch's nervous gaze with one of intense scrutiny. "So, Enoch of Sedekiyr. We have heard of your foolish stories and strange behavior. Why do you trouble us with your presence?"

"I only wanted to speak with Firstfather."

Eve's eyebrows rose. "If that is all you wanted, you could have made your request to Yered, and he to Mahalal-el. That is the proper way to—"

Enoch wanted to roll his eyes, but he closed them and lowered his head instead.

One of the guards suddenly grabbed him by the hair and yanked his head upright again.

Eve was on her feet in an instant, and if her gaze had been intense before, it was nothing compared to the look on her face now. "You lay a hand on your firstfather, and now you disrespect me in this way?" Her voice cut through the air like a weapon.

Enoch cringed inside, but dared not let it show on his face.

"Both are actions punishable by death," she continued, quieter but with the same intensity. "Because you are a firstborn, and your people are so obviously ignorant of our customs, I will grant you mercy only this once. But I warn you— tread carefully from this point forward!"

"Yes, Firstmother."

A smile bloomed on Eve's face, then withered as quickly as it had appeared. "Now ... what was so important that you had to steal into our city?"

There would be no tolerance for vague answers, Enoch realized. He would have to be as direct as possible. "The Holy One showed me that my people will be destroyed if we do not move our city into the mountains. I told my father and grandfather at the gathering of elders, but they would not listen. I came here to receive Firstfather's blessing so that my people would listen to me and be saved."

Eve squinted. "And did your firstfather give you his blessing?"

"You see, Mother!" the other man exclaimed. "These are the ideas he entertains. He has lost his mind. He's not fit to rule—"

"Hold your tongue, Yahsad!" she barked.

Yahsad bowed his head and kept his eyes on his mother.

Enoch now realized who the man was—Yahsad, the fourthborn son of Adam.

Eve turned to Enoch again. "Well?"

Enoch was about to answer when someone on the other side of the room behind him cleared their throat. Eve's demeanor immediately softened. Enoch kept absolutely still, listening to the approaching footsteps without turning his head. After a few seconds, Adam came into view, slowly moving up the steps toward Eve. The distracted man that Enoch had spoken to in the forest was gone. In his place was someone altogether different. He moved with confidence, unhurried, yet with purpose.

Adam sat down upon his throne and moved the long braid of his beard to the side of his knees. "Answer your firstmother," he said without looking up from his lap.

Enoch took a breath before finally replying to Eve. "No. He did not give me his blessing."

To the left, Enoch noticed Yahsad shifting his weight.

Adam looked up from his lap and locked eyes with Enoch. "The so-called Prophet of the Shayetham. The one who claims to converse with the Holy One. To live among angels. To walk the streets of the White City in the Eternal Realm," he said, his mouth steadily widening into a smile.

Enoch had to admit that all of his experiences sounded very strange and hard to believe when condensed into a few sentences. But it was obvious that Adam was only maintaining appearances for the sake of his wife and son. There was clearly a struggle of authority taking place.

"I only entertained your questions so that I could see for myself if you were as troubled as they say you are."

Enoch wanted to look at the expressions on the faces of Eve and Yahsad, but he had to settle for noticing from the corner of his vision that they suddenly became very still.

"What I see," Adam continued, "is that you disrespect your elders and ignore the customs of your tribe. I know that you abandon your family for months at a time to wander through the world by yourself.[4] It is clear to me that you cause pain for everyone around you. If your father will not move his people, it is because he knows how much work goes into establishing and maintaining a city. And if you had done what you were supposed to do—move from Sedekiyr and start your own city—you would know this. But obviously, you think only of yourself. There is not much purpose for someone like that in the world. I wonder ..." he paused, looking now at Eve, "wouldn't it benefit everyone to execute him for his crimes?"

Lines of concern suddenly spread across Eve's forehead. "Perhaps it would be wise to show mercy ... just this once. He is a firstborn, after all."

Adam laid his hand on his beard and looked to Yahsad. "What do you think?"

"I think we should throw him and his troubles out of this city. We have enough to worry about without taking on the concerns of Sedekiyr."

In his younger, naïve years, Enoch might have been thankful for the compassion that Eve and Yahsad were now showing him. Being thrown out of the city was certainly better than being executed. But Enoch had seen too much in his short time on the earth. Eve and her son didn't care about Enoch. An execution would undermine the importance of firstborns and therefore their traditions, ultimately weakening their authority over the people.

"A wise observation," Adam concluded. "Enoch, son of Yered. You are hereby banished from the city of Galah under penalty of death."

The guards grabbed Enoch under the shoulders and yanked him to standing. As they steered him toward the exit, Yahsad fell into step behind them.

\* \* \* \*

As soon as Enoch had grabbed Adam's arm, Sariel knew that his friend had made a mistake. By the time the guards had come running, Sariel had already climbed down off the rocks to move in closer. When he arrived on the scene, careful to stay out of sight, the guards had picked Enoch up from the ground and were marching him into the city. Sariel followed and considered attacking the guards until he realized that they were taking Enoch toward the large building at the center of the city. It might have been a prison they were taking him to, but it appeared too elaborate for such a functional structure. And if Adam were truly in charge of Galah, Enoch's fate would have been decided immediately. Perhaps the true decision maker was not yet present, and Enoch had just earned himself an audience with him.

Sariel had decided to stay back and let this situation play out. If Enoch were to be jailed or executed, he could rush in and attempt to stop it ... as long as the punishment took place in some other location. If Enoch's judgment and punishment were carried out inside the largest building, Sariel wouldn't know until it was too late.

It had been a risk, but Sariel had resisted his urge to plan for every contingency. The Holy One seemed to go with Enoch wherever he went, protecting him every step of the way. So Sariel had made his way back to the outskirts of town and resumed his surveillance.

It had only been a few minutes before Enoch and the guards could be seen exiting the building, and Sariel was now watching the small group very closely. Two of the guards held Enoch by the upper arms and moved him steadily along the main thoroughfare running directly east through the city. Another man followed close behind, apparently supervising the prisoner. Sariel knew that as long as they were walking Enoch was safe. If they stopped, or entered another building, it would be time for Sariel to act. But nothing happened.

The group continued walking, drawing a large crowd of citizens by the time they neared the main gate of the city. Sariel moved quickly down from the foothills, keeping inside the trees until he was close enough to hear the yelling and jeers from the citizens of Galah.

"Leave us, troublemaker!"

"Take your stories somewhere else!"

"Wanderer!"

"You're no prophet!"

"Didn't your Holy One tell you you're not welcome here?"

Sariel peered from around a tree and watched as the guards walked Enoch through the stone archway. The third man stood at the gate with his arms folded. Most of the other citizens were hanging back inside the city walls, but a few were following the guards with rocks in their hands.

"Troublemaker!"

"Liar!"

The guards shoved Enoch forward, and he stumbled, steadying himself with one hand on the ground before he stood up again. As soon as he was a few paces away from the guards, who had stopped walking, the citizens raised their arms.

*Run, Enoch!* Sariel pleaded.

They began throwing their rocks and reaching down to pick up more from the dirt. Most missed the target, but a few hit Enoch in the back. He just ducked his head and started moving forward at a walking pace.

*Run!*

More citizens began coming out of the gate now, picking up rocks as they spread out.

Sariel left the trees and ran toward Enoch.

The crowd began yelling even louder.

Hundreds of dull thuds sounded all around as rocks pelted the earth.

Enoch flinched as one glanced off his head.

"Get out of there!" Sariel yelled as he ran to his friend's aid. He was close enough now that the rocks began hitting him as well. He shielded his face with one hand and grabbed Enoch as soon as he was within reach. "Go! Run!" he yelled, circling around Enoch's back and pushing him.

Finally, Enoch began to run.

Sariel stayed close behind, shielding the prophet with his own body. Within seconds, the assault ended as they moved out of throwing range. But they kept running, heading for the trees. None of the citizens followed, which was wise on their part. Sariel was still holding Enoch's walking stick and was fully prepared to use it as a weapon. He hadn't wanted to make the situation worse by inciting a riot, but if anyone had been bold enough to follow them, they would have regretted it.

Finally, the yelling of the crowds dwindled, and the two travelers found themselves standing in a sparse forest west of the city. The fog was thin and low to the ground. Enoch was breathing loudly and staring back at Galah.

Sariel watched him in silence, now feeling guilty about blaming Enoch for trapping him in this human body. It wasn't Enoch's fault. Sariel had chosen this existence for himself, and he had done so for love. Sheyir drew him into this realm, and though their time together had been short, and much of it filled with pain, it had been worth it. Enoch was not responsible for the messages he received from the Holy One, or the judgments he pronounced on His behalf. He was a messenger. It was as simple as that.

In that moment, Sariel felt a weight lift from his shoulders. He hadn't even been aware of it until it left him, but now he recognized his bitterness and resentment toward Enoch as the products of his obsession with killing Azael. He was ashamed that he held anything in common with the cruel citizens of Galah. Enoch was alone, even among his own people. And as he let go of what he'd been carrying, Sariel found himself filled with compassion. He wasn't alone in this world, as he had come to believe over the last months. He had a friend standing next to him. And his friend needed his help.

Sariel lifted the walking stick and held it out to Enoch.

\* \* \* \*

Enoch accepted his walking stick from Sariel without a word as his eyes remained fixed on the city. How different things appeared now that he was leaving. When they had arrived, moving west into the past of his people, he had been nervous but also filled with excitement and hope. His goal had been within his grasp. He had been on the verge of meeting the very first human being. What wondrous things awaited him, he had imagined. The answers to ancient secrets. Validation for all his years of frustration. Wisdom beyond measure.

*Oh, how things have changed!*

As Enoch looked out across the city of Galah, he didn't see wisdom and progress. He saw unhealed wounds. The connection between the seed from Aden and his people's tradition of passing down knowledge was obvious. All those disapproving looks and painful words from Yered and Mahalal-el during the gathering of elders each year had been the result of his own failure to accept tradition. To listen and not speak. To learn and not teach. Year after year of guilt. Of asking himself why he couldn't just be like everyone else. It was his greatest challenge—a battle that he fought constantly within himself. But he was standing in a very different location now. He could see the origin of his people's obsession with wisdom. Whether or not it benefitted the next generation, he could see how it controlled them and how they wielded it like a weapon. It was something that he would have to consider deeply in the coming months. This day had changed everything.

"Come on," Sariel said. "Let's get you home. You have a family waiting for you."

Enoch turned his eyes away from Galah and smiled at his friend. "Indeed," he replied before taking his first step east, into the future.

S.A. 695

# 24

Hyrren knelt on a shoreline of smooth pebbles, his hands submerged in the cold water. The opposite shore couldn't even be seen from here. There was little doubt why the Kahyin had named it the Great Waters. He scooped up the clear liquid and splashed it on his face, feeling relief from the heat of the midday sun.

It had been a cycle since the first Myndar Council, and so much had changed since then. Hyrren was even taller than before, but his strength was what had improved the most since the influx of food from Senvidar. His thin and gangly limbs, which he'd accepted as normal, were now thick with muscle. But the added weight hadn't seemed to slow him down. He could move quicker than ever before and was easily the strongest one in Khelrusa, even more so than Azael or the other gods. And no one looked upon him as a child anymore. He was a leader among his people, the general of a Nephiyl army.

As he looked back at the dozens of his brethren following him, marching in a single-file column, it filled him with a deep sense of satisfaction. His people had been starved and beaten, on the verge of extinction under Luhad's leadership. Now they were Azael's soldiers, respected and feared by the humans. No one dared to speak against them or show them disrespect. It was the way things were supposed to be, the natural order. And if that weren't enough, Hyrren's people would soon spread across the earth as an integral part of the Myndar plan for inhabitation.

The gods had divided the world into kingdoms of jurisdiction, with the boundaries radiating outward from Senvidar. Each god had negotiated for his or her own section and would travel from Senvidar to establish the first settlement as soon as their security forces were available. That was where Hyrren's people joined the effort. As soon as there was a sufficient quantity of Nephiylim who had achieved maturity and proficiency in their battle training, that army would be sent out to assist in the establishment of another Myndar civilization. The first armies would be led by Hyrren and his siblings from Mudena Del-Edha; they were the eldest among their people, and their training had included matters of strategy and management of soldiers in addition to combat. After this, the process would continue repeating itself, with the oldest remaining Nephiyl assuming the position of general. And on and on it would go until Hyrren's people had spread across the earth.

As the eldest Nephiyl, he was the first to head out from Khelrusa to Senvidar. His army of Aniyl and Iriyl males followed, accompanied by females who were honored to serve as the mothers of the next generation. Marching behind them were hundreds of male Kahyin who would serve the kingdom with their physical labor. And to ensure that this slave population would continue into the future, human females from Senvidar had already been chosen to join them. They were of a different lineage than the Kahyin, but were still compatible.

The first of the gods to be given this opportunity was one by the name of Kokabiel. He would manage everything that wasn't related to security, such as production of textiles and raw materials, construction, irrigation, and even food. Hyrren hadn't met him yet, and he wouldn't until they all reached Senvidar. But it didn't matter which god Hyrren would be serving; it was only a temporary assignment. Azael had reminded him of their ultimate goal before they had left Khelrusa.

"Be diligent in your work. Help Kokabiel, and keep the peace. But never stop looking for an advantage over him. And once you find it, maintain it. Then be patient and wait for your brothers to do the same. When the time is right—when our position is strong—we will overthrow the Myndarym and confiscate everything they have worked to establish."

It didn't matter that Azael was just using him as leverage over the Myndarym. What was important was that Hyrren's brethren were being sent out into the world, in all directions, with the resources needed for them to thrive. Hyrren had goals of his own, and for now they were aligned with Azael's.

Everything had changed. The world was now full of possibilities, which was why Hyrren should have been happy. But he wasn't. There was still something missing—a hole right through the middle of him, as if someone had run him through with a spear. The Nephiylim of the land and sky were multiplying, claiming their inheritance, but a third of Hyrren's people were unaccounted for—the Vidiylim of the sea.

Still kneeling at the water's edge, with his hands below the surface, Hyrren brought two large rocks together with a crash. Three quick blows that could even be heard faintly in the air above the water. He waited a moment and repeated the signal, like he used to do in the caves under Murakszhug. But this time, Aifett didn't come.

*Where are you, my sister?*

Over and over again he tried. But as the column of Nephiylim and Kahyin marched to the north and eventually left him behind, Hyrren was forced to conclude that she wasn't coming. Either she was too far away to hear the signal, or something prevented her from responding to it. Hyrren let go of the rocks and stood, wiping his hands on his tunic. He hoped it was the former.

*Farewell, Aifett. I go out into the world to multiply our people. As I go, I will carry a dream within my heart, that when I see you again, you will be a queen upon your throne. The seas will be yours. I will own the land. And the skies will be ruled by Vengsul. Until we meet again, farewell, my sister.*

\*   \*   \*   \*

OUTSIDE SEDEKIYR

Enoch stood with Sariel in the fields north of Sedekiyr. The huts that comprised the city were just visible along the southern horizon. Tall grasses waved in the breeze, a sound that Enoch wouldn't forget for the rest of his life, and one that would be dearly missed.

"We've come all this way, and you're not going to enter the city?" Sariel asked.

"No."

"What about your father? Should you at least tell him what you're doing?"

"I have shared many words with Yered," Enoch answered, "but few have resulted in anything useful. Besides, he'll find out soon enough."

Sariel nodded. "Indeed. I may not know as much as the Myndarym of Aragatsiyr, but I understand more than the combined wisdom of your people. I will do everything in my power to help you establish your city and make it prosper."

Enoch smiled. He was grateful for Sariel's presence and companionship. The angel had been a great comfort to him during their journey back from Galah. The first weeks had been difficult, mired by Enoch's failure to secure Adam's blessing and the associated feelings of regret and sadness. But Sariel's relentless strength eventually lifted his spirits, and Enoch began to see that this journey was anything but wasted time. He had traveled backward into the history of his own people and had learned more in one year than in all previous seventy-three of his life. He now possessed a perspective that included both the end and the beginning of the Shayetham, and he understood things that his father and grandfather never would. While this information would only alienate him further, Enoch cherished it. It was the other side of what the Holy One had been speaking to him all his life—the reasons for the messages, which provided balance for his troubled mind.

In their thirst for wisdom, the Shayetham had long ago abandoned the only true source of it. They had traded the transcendent for the immanent, which explained their preoccupation with practical things. The irony was that, in their attempt to discover more, they accepted less. The solutions to their practical problems were now limited to only what they could understand. And this presented an opportunity for Enoch. If he couldn't convince his father's people to move into the mountains, perhaps he could entice them.

Perhaps he could establish his own city in Nagah, one that would eclipse Sedekiyr and provide more of what his people desired—food, clothing, shelter, and security. Zacol's suggestion had planted this seed in his mind, but if he had never journeyed to Galah, the seed would never have taken root. If he had never set out from Sedekiyr, he never would have met Sariel, who possessed the transcendent wisdom to make it all possible.

"Is that her?" Sariel asked.

Enoch squinted, now seeing a person separating from the crowd that had gathered on the edge of the city to watch the strangers standing in the fields. It was a woman, and she was handing the baby in her arms to someone else.

"Yes, that's Zacol."

"Do you think she'll agree to come with us?"

"I don't know," Enoch replied. "I have put her through so much, and sometimes I wonder if she would be better off without me. But ..."

"Without her, our plan becomes even more complicated."

Enoch felt his shoulders slump. Sariel's observation only increased his anxiety.

"No," the angel clarified. "I just meant that if this is what the Holy One was planning all along her response will determine our next step, but it won't ruin the plan."

"Oh," Enoch replied, suddenly recognizing his own lack of faith.

Sariel smiled and laid a gentle hand on Enoch's shoulder. "I didn't mean it like that, either. Just forget I said anything."

Enoch nodded before looking back toward Zacol. She was outside of the city now and walking quickly, about a quarter of the way to where Enoch stood. "I guess it's time."

Sariel let go of his shoulder, and Enoch started out across the field. He waded through the grass in long, steady strides. The air was still and unusually clear. Though it only took a few minutes to reach his wife, the journey seemed to take days. With every step, Enoch's impatience grew. His palm sweated against the shaft of his walking stick. His heart thumped louder in his chest. His breaths grew shallow.

Until they were close enough to see each other's eyes.

Zacol had tears streaming down her face, but no expression to go with it.

Then Enoch began to run.

Zacol's face softened immediately.

Enoch dropped his stick and bag and reached out, taking her into his arms. "Oh, I've missed you more than I thought possible."

Zacol hugged him back with surprising strength.

When at last she finally relented, Enoch pulled his head back to see a look of pure joy on her face that he'd never witnessed before.

"Welcome home," she said.

Enoch stared at her as if she were a dream that might vanish. "Sedekiyr is my father's home, but mine is wherever you are."

Zacol tilted her head, but kept smiling. "I take it you found what you were looking for?"

"No," Enoch said, still smiling. "But I found exactly what I needed."

Zacol's smile shifted to a look of confused amusement, before she looked over Enoch's shoulder. "Who is that?"

"A friend."

Zacol stared for a moment and then finally looked into Enoch's eyes. "There's something different about you. What happened out there?"

"I have so many stories to share with you," he replied, "but there's something very important that I need to say first."

Lines of concern were now visible on Zacol's forehead. "What?"

Enoch smiled so big that it hurt his face. "You were right."

S.A. 986

# 25

Hyrren bent down and pressed his fingers into the soil beside the oversized imprint of a canine's paw. The ground was firm, but the imprint was deep ... and fresh. Whatever had produced it was not native to this world, which gave him hope that he might be close to his first meaningful conflict since he had killed Luhad all those cycles ago.

Hyrren stood up to his full height of twenty-one feet and looked back at his patrol, a small group of Aniylim that he had personally trained. Like him, they wore loincloths of animal skin, with other hides draped across their shoulders to ward off the chill of the higher altitude. He nodded, and his soldiers brought their metal-tipped spears into a ready position. At the slow gesture of an opened hand, they spread out their formation. Then Hyrren looked down again at the soil and began moving forward, looking for another track.

The breeze drifted through the coniferous forest, whistling in the needles overhead as it pushed the dense fog against Hyrren's face. Between the scents of pine and damp soil, he noted something that didn't belong, but he couldn't place it. Had the air been moving the other direction, his own scent and that of his soldiers might have scared away his prey. But Hyrren knew these mountains well and had long ago learned how to use the air currents to his advantage. When the patrol had gone another thirty paces, Hyrren held up his hand, bringing them to a halt.

The foreign scent was gone.

Visibility was now limited to a few spear lengths.

Hyrren kept his eyes forward while motioning in a circle with his hand. His soldiers shifted their formation to an outward-facing defense, their movement almost blocking the sound of rapid footsteps coming upon them from behind. Hyrren risked a glance just as a massive gray creature lunged out of the fog. It slipped beneath the spears and clamped its jaws down on the arm of the nearest soldier.

The Aniyl yelled out in pain as he attempted to pull his arm free.

The wolf, Hyrren could now see, began dragging the soldier backward as its head whipped from side to side, its teeth cutting through flesh.

The soldiers on either side pivoted toward the animal.

"Hold your position!" Hyrren warned. "It's a diversion."

The soldiers obeyed instantly, shifting to maintain the circular formation as their fellow Aniyl, now screaming, was pulled farther into the mist.

The Aniyl finally gathered his wits enough to free his spear from his paralyzed left hand and thrust it at the wolf with the other.

The wolf was quick, lunging to the side with a growl as he dragged the soldier a few more paces and they both disappeared from sight. A moment later, his voice came to an abrupt end, followed by the sound of growling coming from all directions. The soldiers' eyes were shifting nervously. The wolf pack had them surrounded, and by the sound of it, they were much closer than Hyrren expected.

"Keep your eyes on the trees and be ready! They'll only attack if they find a weakness in our line."

"It is you who attacks us, hunter!" came a deep voice out of the forest. The sound seemed to bounce off the trees, making its origin difficult to locate.

"Who is there? Show yourself," Hyrren challenged.

A dark shape materialized from out of the brume on Hyrren's right, keeping just beyond spear range. Though smaller than the previous creature, its back only as high as Hyrren's upper leg, this wolf was still much larger than any natural beast and plenty big enough to be a formidable foe.

"You killed one of my people three days ago, and now I've taken one of yours as payment. But we have done nothing to warrant being hunted by you," the wolf growled. His golden eyes seemed to glow like flames against the dim background of the forest. The skin atop his snout was bunched into a terrifying snarl, revealing long daggers of gleaming white teeth.

"You are Myndar, yes?"

The wolf didn't answer.

"These are Kokabiel's lands," Hyrren continued. "You and your ... pack are not permitted here."

More glowing eyes appeared around the group, hovering before their dark silhouettes.

Hyrren's soldiers tightened up their formation even more.

"No one owns the earth," the pack leader clarified. "We are free to roam where we wish." His teeth seemed to be a hindrance to enunciating his words.

But they were the only reason Hyrren hadn't already put a spear through the creature's chest. "Tell yourself whatever you must, but your only chance of surviving is to leave now and never return. My next patrol will be along shortly, and another after that." Hyrren didn't bother describing what would happen if the soldiers found their general surrounded; he'd explained enough already. In fact, he actually hoped the wolves would stay and that his Aniylim would finally experience their first battle.

The pack leader growled low in his throat and slowly backed away until his gray fur became one with the mist, and then the ring of golden eyes was suddenly gone.

\* \* \* \*

EL-BETAKH
THE CITY OF ENOCH

Enoch walked along the docks, counting the crates that his sons were securing to the raft. Grain and seeds, clothing, building tools, and cutting implements—the annual offering for the citizens of Sedekiyr. It was all accounted for, and the last preparations were nearly complete.

With Sariel's wisdom, and the Holy One's blessing, El-Betakh had become a city of prosperity. With twelve hundred and seventy-two citizens, it was similar in population to Sedekiyr on the day that Enoch and Zacol had left. But what it lacked in size was easily compensated for in quality. Food was abundant and varied. The citizens were happy and productive. And the efficiency of their work left the community plenty of time to listen for the voice of the Holy One. Aside from the presence of his flourishing family, this was Enoch's greatest joy. All of the struggles of his past didn't seem to matter here. The stubborn excuses of the people had been left behind, and Enoch found a great deal of satisfaction in life as it was meant to be lived.

By contrast, the city of Enoch's father had since grown to millions of citizens, but that growth had been steadily slowing. Life was difficult in Sedekiyr, hampered as it was by the so-called wisdom of the elders. A city of that size encountered many problems that even Mahalal-el didn't know how to solve. People had to work much harder there. As it was in the days of Enoch's childhood, practical matters consumed everyone's time. Yered's people were cold, serious, and tired. Then, in S.A. 930, the death of the firstfather had struck a blow to their confidence. Life had stopped being an unending stream of possibilities; it had suddenly become a limited and precious gift.

What had been Enoch's struggle while under his father's leadership later became an opportunity for him. El-Betakh was everything that Sedekiyr was not, and every year, a few more families made the decision to move east into the mountains and become part of Enoch's community. To maintain that growing momentum, he and Sariel made yearly trips to Sedekiyr to share their abundance with the people. At first, the gifts were resented. But the fruits of Sariel's wisdom broke down those emotional walls within a few years, and now the citizens of Sedekiyr anticipated the arrival of Enoch and his strange friend with great excitement.

Enoch pointed at one of the crates and yelled over the crowd to his fourthborn son. "That one is loose on this side. Tighten up the rope."

"He's done this hundreds of times," Zacol said from behind. "He doesn't need your instruction."

Enoch turned around with a smile on his face. "But I need yours?"

"Always," Zacol replied. "You'd be lost without me." Then she leaned forward and kissed him gently on the lips. When she stepped back, she tugged at the animal hide around her shoulders, pulling the fur higher up her neck. The morning chill hadn't yet worn off.

"It's almost time," Enoch said, glancing up at the blue sky visible through the branches of the trees towering overhead. "Will you gather the children to see us off?"

Zacol's expression changed in the subtlest of ways, something that Enoch would have missed in their early years.

"What's the matter?"

"Will you look for Methu while you're there? Give him my love?"

"I'll try, of course. But he doesn't want anything to do with us. The last several years, he's been out away from the city, hunting. His family wouldn't even tell me where he went."

Zacol lowered her head. "I should have taken him by the ear and dragged him the entire way."

"It's not your fault," Enoch countered. "Methu has always been determined. He is the only one to blame for how this ..." Enoch caught himself, suddenly realizing that he was about to say something untrue. Methu's behavior was partly Enoch's fault.

"Everything's loaded," Sariel called out as he stepped off the raft and onto the docks. Then his jovial face grew serious as he saw that he had interrupted their conversation.

Enoch held up his hand.

"I'll bring the children," Zacol whispered before turning to walk away.

Enoch stood on the docks and watched her go. The sound of the rushing river nearby was almost loud enough to cover the murmur of the crowd that had gathered to see them off. Enoch only wished that his wife's joy could be as complete as everyone else's here. But their eldest son was like a stranger to them, and there were already five generations of children under Methu. Zacol just wanted their family to be together in one place. It didn't seem like too much to ask.

Sariel jogged over to Zacol and laid his hand on her shoulder. He said something to her, eliciting a hug in response. Enoch couldn't hear the words they shared, but Zacol seemed relieved as she walked away.

Sariel looked across the docks and nodded at Enoch before walking back to their wooden raft and stepping aboard. He made his way to the bow and bent down to grab the rope and pole that would be used to alternately push and pull the front of the raft, leading it on foot down the narrow river and out of the mountains over the next two days. When they reached the flatlands, Sariel and Enoch would board the raft and use the poles to steer their wooden vessel all the way across the plains to Sedekiyr.

Enoch lingered for a while, taking in the surroundings and the moment before he finally wandered over to the stern of the raft. He grabbed his pole and rope, and when he looked up, the crowd was even larger than before. Zacol had returned along with his children, his grandchildren, and several generations after them. Enoch smiled as he looked from one face to the next, seeing their anticipation. The citizens of El-Betakh grew silent, waiting for the blessing from their elder.

"May you hear the voice of the Holy One with great clarity. May His wisdom guide your steps. And may your lives show the evidence of His love."

The crowd began to cheer at the words that they had come to expect each year.

Enoch looked to Sariel, now standing on the opposite side of the river with rope and pole in hand, and nodded. At the same time, both men pulled backward on the ropes and steered the raft away from the wooden beams holding it in place. The heavy vessel moved sluggishly against the current, but once it was free of the docks, it began moving downstream and picking up speed.

\* \* \* \*

KYRINDEM

Kokabiel's sprawling city was filled to overflowing with Nephiyl weapons and human eyes—no place for a wolf. Ananel didn't doubt that he could move undetected through such a challenge, but the risk was unnecessary. Instead, he waited in the forest. Multiple scent trails wound through the sparse trees, proof of Kokabiel's repeated passage over the years. The Myndar was evidently fond of wandering away from his kingdom and its responsibilities. And if the other scents that Ananel had discovered at the end of those trails were any indication, he guessed that Kokabiel also enjoyed escaping his human form.

A distant snorting noise came from the south, and Ananel waited. He'd already caught the scent of the bear earlier in the evening, and had circled around to the north where the breeze would announce his presence. Minutes later, a hulking brown creature walked confidently into Ananel's line of sight.

"Kokabiel," he said, stepping out into the moonlight.

The bear stopped and raised its snout, sniffing for confirmation that this was the source of the scent. Then, sparks drifted through the air away from its body like embers from a fire. They floated lazily before stopping, suddenly rushing back together until they illuminated the form of a human standing naked where the bear had been. It was a display of trust for Kokabiel to take a weaker form.

*Or is it a display of confidence?* Ananel wondered.

Many years ago, Ananel had lost his ability to shape into other forms. Though he preferred to roam the earth in the form of a wolf, it was unsettling to be confined to it. From the few interactions he'd had with others of his kind wandering through the uninhabited places, it seemed that this problem was widespread. But Kokabiel apparently didn't have this same limitation, leaving Ananel to wonder if the Myndar also had use of his other powers.

"Ananel," the man said casually. "It has been a long time."

Ananel took a few careful steps forward. "I understand these lands are yours?"

Kokabiel smiled. "They are. You must have met my army."

"The introductions were not friendly."

"And neither will any future interactions be. Hyrren takes his responsibilities very seriously."

Ananel lowered his ears enough to demonstrate a friendly appearance, but not so much to communicate submission. "Is it really necessary for your soldiers to hunt us? You are in no danger from us, I can assure you."

"It's the principle of the matter," Kokabiel replied. "You had the opportunity to join the Council, and you chose to disregard the warnings."

Ananel raised one eyebrow in what he remembered was a human expression. "There were no warnings."

"Come now. Everyone was made aware of the potential issues we'd face. That's why we wanted you at the Council, so these encounters could be managed ahead of time."

"I was not told that armies of battle-trained Nephiylim would stalk and kill my people. It seems to me that the ambitions of the Council have grown over the years."

Kokabiel shook his head. "Our plans have not changed from the first meeting. Perhaps you misunderstood the message, or it wasn't conveyed clearly. Either way, I apologize for your loss. It is not my intention to harm you or your kind."

Anael bowed his head. "I must ask, then ... would it be possible for us to hunt on your lands and not have to worry about our safety?"

"Are you asking for my permission?"

"Yes."

Kokabiel squinted. "If you stay far to the south and don't settle in one place for too long. Hyrren doesn't usually patrol farther than a week's journey from my city. And as long as you take a variety of prey and not too many from one species, I don't have an issue."

Anael nodded. "And what about Hyrren?"

"I'll speak with him, but it would be best if the two of you never cross paths. And make sure your hunting doesn't interfere with his, or he will come looking for you."

"Thank you, Kokabiel. We will do as you say."

"Now, if you will please excuse me ..." he replied, and then his body began to shimmer.

Anael turned and began trotting away through the forest. By the time the display of light had subsided, his long strides had already carried him over a mile to the south.

# 26

The river was the most efficient way to transport a large amount of supplies to Sedekiyr, and one that wouldn't leave a trail to be followed back to El-Betakh. From the beginning, Sariel had insisted that the trading of supplies and people between the two cities remain as invisible as possible. If destruction really was coming to Sedekiyr, it would need to stay confined there.

With the towers of Sedekiyr now visible to the west, Sariel could stop watching the other horizons for signs of danger. He reached out with his pole and pushed against the grassy bank, making a small correction to the raft's course. Then he watched as the tall, wooden constructions grew nearer and nearer. He had helped with their design a few years back, and it was always interesting to see how the city changed in the time between these visits. The towers now had roofs over them, presumably to block the glare of the sun for better visibility. Or perhaps the men assigned to the task of watching the fields just wanted some shade for comfort.

A low, breathy howl drifted over the water. The morning lookout, who had likely spotted them long ago, was now announcing their arrival with a trumpet made from the hollow stalk of grass that grew as tall as trees in these parts. It was the most plentiful and useful material in Sedekiyr.

As the lattice construction of the towers became visible, Sariel put his pole back into the water and readied himself. Enoch, who had been sitting for the last hour, now rose to his feet. His pole was already in the slow-moving river, acting as a rudder.

"They have roofs on the towers now," he remarked.

Sariel nodded while keeping his eyes forward, noting that the walls around the city had also grown a pace taller. From the green color of the new wood, it seemed that the section near the docks had only been added in the last few weeks.

The raft slowed even more as the river widened into a harbor whose construction had been a mild point of contention between Sariel and Yered. Instead of digging away the marshy, unusable land to the northwest to make room for the collected water, Enoch's father insisted they dig to the southeast. He wanted the harbor closer to the city, but the soil was firmer there, less suited for digging and more suited for building things on top of it. Now that the city had grown so large, firm and dry land was becoming harder to find. As a consequence, the city was growing taller than it was wider, requiring more complicated structures from those who handled the building tasks.

With poles against the sandy bottom, Sariel and Enoch nudged their long, rectangular raft out of the flow and toward the docks at the northern edge of the city. There were already several dozen men gathered there, waiting to help unload the gifts. A few of the men waved their arms in greeting, clearly excited about this wonderful interruption to their typically dull lives.

When the fore of the raft was only a few paces from the dock Sariel drove his pole to the sandy bottom and let the aft end swing around until they were parallel to the dock. Enoch tossed his rope to the waiting men, and Sariel did the same. In less than a minute the men of Sedekiyr had the raft secured.

"Welcome," one of them said, as he inspected the floating vessel that would soon belong to the city. It would have been too cumbersome for Sariel and Enoch to drag it against the current to the east, and impossible to do so up the faster-moving water in the mountains. Instead, they would leave it in Sedekiyr as they had always done—another gift to the people.

"How was your journey?"

"Peaceful," Enoch replied.

"What have you brought us?"

"Medicine," Sariel replied. A few of Yered's people had begun experiencing strange discolorations on their skin prior to last year's visit, and Sariel thought he understood the cause. He had promised Yered that he would return with something that could be applied to the affected areas.

"More seeds, as you requested," Enoch added. "And cutting tools ... of metal this time."

All of the men smiled greedily. One man looked directly at Sariel and said, "Thank you. We'll surely use them."

Sariel smiled and glanced up at the latticed walls on the other side of the docks. "Yes, I can see that you've been busy."

The man nodded before stepping down onto the raft to help Enoch untie the rope around one of the crates.

"Have there been any attacks?" Sariel asked.

"Only in the fields," another man replied. "Never in the city. The walls keep us safe."

Sariel smiled. Those, too, had been his idea. Large reptiles sometimes moved through the fields in search of small mammals, and it had been a constant threat to Yered's people. Sariel had picked up on their fear many years ago and encouraged them to put something in place that might also be useful if Enoch's vision ever came to pass. From there, the construction grew more robust as rumors circulated about roaming tribes of displaced Kahyin. No one had ever witnessed such a thing, but the possibility seemed to provide sufficient motivation.

The people of Sedekiyr had slowly grown accustomed to Sariel's presence as well as his input. Enoch had never told them who Sariel really was, as that would have ruined everything. They just thought of him as a human—one who possessed a wealth of wisdom. With the annual offerings on which to focus, the expectation for Enoch to be *practical* was somehow forgotten. This left Sariel's friend free to be the type of influence he wanted to be among his father's people. It was Sariel's nature to avoid attention, but in this case, he gladly accepted the burden.

Walking across the raft, he patted Enoch on the shoulder. "Why don't you go take care of that *task* you mentioned?"

Enoch handed a crate to one of the men before looking at Sariel with a furrowed brow. "Task?"

"Yes," Sariel replied. "Go ahead. The men and I can easily handle these crates."

Enoch continued staring for a few seconds until he finally realized what his friend was saying. "Oh ... yes. That task. Thank you. I'll be back before you know it."

Sariel smiled. "Take your time."

\* \* \* \*

KYRINDEM

Hyrren had received Kokabiel's summons earlier in the morning. It wasn't urgent, so he completed his day's responsibilities and then took some time to clean up his appearance. A cold bath washed away weeks' worth of patrolling the forests. His hair, usually free to blow in the wind, was washed, combed, and gathered into a single braid that fell down to the middle of his back. A freshly-sharpened metal blade removed the scraggly beard that had formed during his excursion. The animal hide that covered his shoulders and upper arms was new. Its long fur faced outward, as it wasn't needed for warmth inside the city, where the buildings were heated by fire. Soft leather boots covered his feet and lower legs. And in place of the spear that he usually carried, a long, metal knife hung from a leather belt around his waist.

Such adornments were cumbersome, and he only wore them inside the city where they wouldn't catch on branches or rocks and get him killed. And even then, he only wore them when absolutely necessary. He suspected this would be one of those times, and as he stood in the hall outside of Kokabiel's throne room, he knew he had guessed correctly.

The thick, ornately-carved door opened inward, and Kokabiel's oldest daughter stepped past the Nephiyl guard and into the hall. Hyrren felt his heart lurch as she neared ... without even acknowledging his presence.

Yllfae was a Myniyl; her mother had been from Senvidar—one of the descendants of the Shayetham who had taken refuge there. She had only been an infant when Hyrren had set out from the Myndar city with Kokabiel. But it hadn't taken long for her to become the object of Hyrren's fascination. She was fair of skin and hair, though not as pale as her father. Her eyes were green, like the moss that grew on the rocks by the water's edge. Her long and graceful nose was adorned on either side by brows and cheekbones less prominent than Hyrren's. But when she spoke, her words were bold—a contrast to her elegant appearance.

Everything about her had fascinated Hyrren, but he'd always kept those feelings to himself. He had eventually fathered his own children with several of the Aniyl females who had come with him from Khelrusa. Yllfae had grown up and done the same with the males who had been born to Kokabiel's other wives from Senvidar. Though the two groups were both Nephiyl, fathered by gods through human mothers, they never mingled with each other just as the Kahyin and Shayetham remained separate. The fair ones and the dark ones—two branches of the same tree that had grown in opposite directions.

Even now, Yllfae captured Hyrren's attention as she moved down the hall toward him, appearing to float across the floor. Her light brown hair rippled in waves down her chest with each step. Her long tunic, made of a supple, blue fabric, billowed around her feet. There was something about the way she carried herself that made all her gestures look like a dance.

Hyrren smiled and stepped aside, nodding to her.

Yllfae glided past without making eye contact.

"Is it my scars?" he asked.

Yllfae slowed to a stop and turned her head, but not her eyes. "Pardon?"

"Is that why you won't even look at me?"

The rest of her body turned as though driven slowly by a breeze. Her passive gaze came to rest on Hyrren's eyes, then drifted down to his feet before rising again with disapproval. She squinted for a moment, and then continued down the hall without a word.

Hyrren watched her go, wishing that circumstances could have been different. But sometimes sacrifices had to be made for important goals. He put those thoughts aside and walked through the doorway and into the throne room of Kokabiel.

Though it was called a throne room, there was no throne to speak of. Kokabiel didn't concern himself with such symbolic, useless formalities. There was no doubt as to who ruled this area of the world, and the presence or absence of a chair wouldn't influence that in the slightest.

Kokabiel was standing by the window, looking out upon the courtyard. "Ah ... Hyrren. Welcome back."

"Thank you, my king."

Kokabiel left the window and walked to the center of the room where Hyrren had come to a stop. "I wanted to speak with you about your patrol. I understand you encountered something?"

Hyrren frowned, wondering where Kokabiel's information had come from. "It was nothing, my king. We came across a pack of wolves. I lost one soldier, but we chased them off. Your land and your people are safe."

"Oh, I'm not worried about my land or my people. You see, the pack leader is an old friend of mine. He is Myndar, and he has agreed to keep his pack far away from here."

Hyrren was furious at the thought that the pack leader and Kokabiel had spoken with each other, and that he didn't know where or when it had occurred. The wolf had somehow slipped through his defenses. But Hyrren kept his composure. "I don't understand, my king. The whole point of my people coming here was to protect you from such enemies."

"That's just it, Hyrren. Ananel isn't an enemy. But by tracking and hunting his pack, you run the risk of turning him into one."

"He refused to participate in the Council."

Kokabiel smiled. "Yes, I know. And I know that others on the Council would disagree with my approach. But I don't see any utility in creating a conflict where none exists. If and when Ananel's interests ever compete with mine, we can discuss using a different approach. For now, I have given him and his kind permission to hunt on my land. As long as they stay far to the south and don't exhaust any of our resources, there is nothing to be concerned about."

It was a ridiculous decision, Hyrren thought, to allow such a potential threat to exist in close proximity, and then to give it the support it needed to grow. Hyrren had to make a conscious effort to remove the emotion from his face.

"Do you have a problem with this arrangement?" Kokabiel asked suddenly.

"No, my king."

"Good. You are excellent at what you do, Hyrren. And I appreciate the amount of care with which you perform your duties. I have the utmost confidence that if a true enemy were to threaten my kingdom, he would not last long against you."

Hyrren nodded without expression, accepting the compliment while rejecting the reasoning behind it. "Thank you, my king."

\* \* \* \*

SEDEKIYR

"This goes straight to the storehouse," Sariel instructed. The last of the crates had been unloaded from the raft, and now the men of Sedekiyr were standing in a line, waiting to take the supplies into the city. "Oh, and tell Benahn that I'll be there soon to speak with him. The seeds are wrapped differently this time. He'll want to know how we kept out the moisture."

The man nodded as he lifted the crate from the dwindling stack.

As Sariel looked to the next man, he noticed Enoch coming back across the docks, shaking his head. "One moment," Sariel said, leaving the unloading area.

Enoch held out his hands.

"What happened?" Sariel asked as soon as he was close enough for words.

Enoch seemed too agitated to respond.

"Was he gone again?"

"No," Enoch finally replied. "He was in front of his dwelling when I got there. But as soon as I opened my mouth, he said, 'I don't want anything from you, and I don't have anything else to say.'"

Sariel put his hand on Enoch's shoulder. "At least he was home this time. Maybe that's progress?"

Enoch's smile was forced. His relationship with Methu was wearing on him more than he would ever admit.

"I was just giving the men directions. Why don't you finish up and help move the raft over to the other dock?" Sariel asked.

"Why? Where are you going?"

"To deliver a gift."

By the time Sariel retrieved his leather bag from the docks and made it to the center of Sedekiyr, Methu was gone. His wife, Jurishel, said that he'd gone out to the western fields to think. But Sariel wasn't about to give up so easily. He'd promised Zacol that he'd do what he could to change the situation for the better. As he walked through the city and exited its western gate, he wondered if it was time for a completely different approach. Following a worn path, Sariel walked for almost an hour until he reached a grove of trees where the river bent into a tight loop before continuing its westward journey to the Unmoving Waters. Methu was sitting on a low branch looking out over the water.

Sariel stopped at the edge of the eroded bank, under the shade, just a pace below the branch on which Enoch's oldest son reclined. The man looked just like his father—the same build, the same color hair, the same face but with a shorter beard.

Methu didn't even turn his head.

"I have something for you."

There was no response.

Sariel continued as if Methu were a willing participant in the conversation. "I couldn't help myself, actually. I saw that hunting tool of yours last year. I couldn't stop thinking about it, so I went ahead and made one of my own."

Methu shifted his weight and the branch swayed, but he wouldn't look down.

Sariel set down his bag and untied it, removing a long wooden object. "The first one broke, right here at the handle. That's when I realized I'd need wood that was both strong and flexible. The next one lasted about a month before the cord unraveled. I used the braided grass like yours, but it wore down a little with each shot."

Methu was doing a good job resisting the urge to look.

But Sariel knew he had to be intrigued. "A tendon works great, as long as you keep it away from water. You'll never guess what happened next, though."

Methu didn't guess.

"My darts wouldn't fly straight. So I figured, why not make them more like something that flies? You don't have many birds here in Sedekiyr, do you? Well, there are all sorts of birds in El-Betakh. You can find their feathers everywhere, just lying on the ground. And when I put feathers at the back of the dart, it flew straight."

Methu glanced down.

"See?" Sariel said, holding up one of the darts that he'd taken out of the bag. "Oh, you're probably wondering about the tip too. Well, I was using fish bone, just like you. But the darts flew so straight and so fast that they would break apart whenever they hit something. The bone wasn't strong enough. I don't know if Enoch told you, but we've been using metal for many things now. We mine it right out of the mountain, and then we heat it to separate it from the stone. It's really strong, so I wondered if it might work for a dart tip. Did you know, if you make a flat tip, you can sharpen the edges like a knife? And then the dart just goes right in."

Methu frowned before looking back to the river bend.

"Have you ever shot anything besides fish? What about those furry things that gather in the trees?"

Methu didn't answer.

"You probably can't get close enough to them before they scatter, right?"

A breeze moved through the air, causing the grass to sway.

Sariel looked out across the river and identified a tree on the other side that was just about the right distance. "What if you didn't have to get close to them?" he asked, laying a dart across the hunting tool and pulling on it until the notch fit snugly around the string. He raised his arms, took aim, and pulled back, launching the dart across the river bend.

Methu sat up when the dart hit the tree and stuck without bouncing off. Then he glanced back at Sariel with surprise.

"I don't know if you gave it a name yet, but I call this a *bow*," Sariel said, holding up the wooden tool. "You see how the wood is bowed?"

Methu slid off his branch and jumped to the ground.

As he came near, Sariel handed it to him. "I'll bet you could even take down one of those reptiles with this."

Methu took the bow without a word and began inspecting it.

"It's brilliant, really," Sariel continued. "I'm surprised you invented it before the Amatru did."

Methu suddenly looked up, as if someone had struck him in the face. "What?"

"Well, it would certainly be useful in a military setting," Sariel continued. "The Smyda are responsible for developing the weapons, but they didn't have anything like this."

Methu's look of shock disappeared. "Oh. More stories from my father."

Sariel gave the most sincere look of confusion he could muster. "No, Enoch never met the Smyda. They only operate in the Borderlands where we fought with the Marotru. Your father went straight to the White City when he visited the Eternal Realm."

The conviction in Methu's eyes faltered.

Sariel pointed to the bow in Methu's hands. "Do you know how useful something like this would have been when I flew with the Iryllurym? We never would have had to dive into the ranks of those demons. We could have just stayed in the air and loosed our arrows down on them. Oh, yes, I've been calling them arrows instead of darts. It just seemed like they should be called something else because of the feathers." Sariel jabbed a thumb over his shoulder. "I should be getting back. The men at the docks are probably wondering what's taking me so long."

Methu nodded, not knowing quite what to say.

Sariel pointed down at the leather bag in the grass. "I think there are about ten more arrows in there. Try it out and let me know if there's anything that we can improve."

Before Methu had a chance to say anything, Sariel turned around and started walking back to the city.

# 27

The Council met every five years at a different location—frequently enough for each member to stay informed on the progress of the others, but not so often that it interfered with the growth of one's own kingdom. The point was to keep the members invested in each other's successes and even to learn from their mistakes. For Azael, it was an opportunity to assess the strength of his own position against that of the Myndarym. What he had witnessed over the last few days of touring Kyrindem side by side with his enemies was that his advantage was gradually slipping away.

"Will Parnudel and Rikoathel be joining us?" Hyrren asked.

"No," Azael replied. "I didn't want to alarm the Myndarym by having us all together in a private meeting. They are both speaking with other Council members."

As it was, meeting individually with Hyrren was a risk. Azael had chosen to speak with his former general in the middle of the day to minimize the appearance of secretive behavior, but there were too many things to discuss to forego meeting altogether. As they walked among the section of the city inhabited by Hyrren's Nephiylim, they found themselves away from Myndar ears and able to speak freely.

"We are almost two hundred thousand strong, my king," Hyrren said.

Azael was pleased as they walked along a wide street between stone dwellings. Thin columns of smoke rose into the air from many places. Male and female Nephiylim could be seen working everywhere he looked. It reminded him of the early days in Khelrusa, and Azael suddenly felt naked without his armor or weapons. Drawing attention to his military dominance was only for the purpose of getting invited to the Council. Now it would have been a liability among the Myndarym, but he missed it dearly, along with the hands-on work of preparing for battle.

"You have done very well, Hyrren. I wish I could say the same about the others."

"Are my brothers not faring as well?"

"Some are," Azael replied. "Others have lost the advantage over their masters. We started out strong, but the kingdoms of the Myndarym are steadily gaining ground."

Hyrren's face grew serious, and his eyes focused on the forest to the north of the city.

Azael continued, "The Nephiylim in Khelrusa grow strong and plentiful, but this has only made us more dependent upon Senvidar. There is no more human flesh for food, and our successes in raising crops and livestock have been modest, at best. It seems the Kahyin are not well suited to live like the other human tribes of the earth."

"And weapons?" Hyrren asked.

Azael shook his head. "Tuval has made progress experimenting with different alloys and purification methods, but the weapons from Senvidar remain superior. For now, they still arm your brethren. What about you?" Azael asked, looking down at the knife hanging from Hyrren's waist.

"We've been left to forge our own weaponry. Kokabiel doesn't seem interested in such things."

Azael nodded. That much had been obvious just from looking around the city. The Myndarym had long ago *shaped* Mudena Del-Edha from the earth, growing and forming its gates and towers as if they were nothing more than trees. But now that the Myndarym had their own cities, they had left the building of them to the humans, who quarried the stone or cut trees from the forests. It seemed that the Myndarym were enjoying the benefits of ruling over their own subjects, now content to have others do their work. Azael understood the mindset, but he didn't share it. He was still involved at every level of Khelrusa's development, and that would only increase when Parnudel and Rikoathel finally took their own kingdoms. Out of loyalty to Azael, they had chosen to be last on the Council's list in order to assist with the training of the Nephiylim.

"Have any of your kind mated with Kokabiel's children?" Azael asked, looking around at Hyrren's section of the city for confirmation. "It seems to be a strategy of the Myndarym to dilute our interests and divide our loyalty."

Hyrren smiled. "No, my king. Kokabiel's ... children ... see us as crude and unintelligent. I have instructed my people to encourage this misunderstanding at every opportunity. As far as they know, we are just brutes who patrol the forests. I don't even let them see our training. I would have them completely ignorant of our ability to wage war against them. And it has worked. Our blood lines have remained pure, and everyone on Kokabiel's side vastly underestimates us."

"Excellent work, Hyrren! I can see that you hesitate to call his children *Nephiylim*?"

"I prefer *Myniylim*, my king. They are tall, but in all other ways they are a different breed. To call them *Nephiylim* seems an honor they don't deserve. Had they grown up in Khelrusa under my command, I would have had them executed to keep their condescending influence away from my people."

Hyrren's single-minded devotion to Azael's strategy was refreshing after all these years. "So, Kokabiel's children will not be an issue. What about the humans?"

"There are over a million and a half of them now, but they are easily swayed. I have not been able to detect a distinction in their loyalty between us and Kokabiel. They know their place as slaves, and I believe they will follow whoever is in authority over them."

"Good," Azael replied. Hyrren's successes were steadily rebuilding Azael's confidence. "You are still ready, then?"

Hyrren turned to face his true king. "I have been ready to overtake Kokabiel since the day I met him. But there is, of course, still the unknown of Kokabiel's secret excursions. They continue to happen with regular frequency, and though my soldiers have never been close enough to confirm it, we believe he *shapes* himself into various animal forms to mate with many different creatures. I have to assume that there are offspring from these unions, though we have not found any during our patrols."

Azael nodded. "This is nothing new."

"No, my king. But there has been another recent development that does weaken our position."

Azael stopped walking and turned to face Hyrren. "Go on."

"Did you know Ananel when you served under my father?"

Azael felt the skin on his forehead grow tight. "Yes. He used to go about in the form of a wolf."

Hyrren nodded. "He and his pack hunt on Kokabiel's lands far to the south. I have known about it for some time, and we've focused our patrolling efforts recently on tracking them. We even managed to kill one of his kind a few weeks ago. I spoke with Kokabiel about it, and it turns out that he is allowing them to hunt on his lands. He told me, 'I don't see the utility in creating an enemy where there is none.'"

"You think he's formed an alliance with Ananel?"

"Perhaps it's just a loose agreement. But the possibility of an alliance should be considered."

Azael crossed his arms. "What is your assessment of Kokabiel himself?"

"He doesn't like me, but he trusts me. I can easily create a situation where myself and several of my soldiers are alone with him. I am fully confident that we can overwhelm him before he has a chance to fight back."

Azael wished that his other generals had garnered the leverage that Hyrren possessed. "If I gave the order today, what would the outcome be?"

Hyrren inhaled slowly, his posture suddenly becoming rigid, as though he were standing at attention. "Kokabiel and his children would be destroyed in less than an hour, with minimal losses. The citizens of Kyrindem wouldn't question the change of leadership, and the city would be ours."

"Excellent!"

"Shall I move ahead with our plan?"

"Not yet," Azael cautioned. "After this Council is concluded, I will send Parnudel and Rikoathel to get the latest assessment from your brothers before the Myndarym return to their cities. If enough of them are ready to move, you'll receive my orders."

"And if they aren't, my king? Can we afford to wait?"

"No. But neither can we move ahead at a disadvantage. The Myndarym—while they lack our strength of mind—can become very dangerous enemies. Given what they accomplished against Semjaza, I would rather not have those talents turned against us as weapons. We need to strike at a time when they still consider us allies."

"Very well, my king. I will await your orders."

\* \* \* \*

Turel and Danel appeared unimpressed by the throne room. They sat in large chairs near the fireplace, keeping warm as they inspected their quaint surroundings with looks of amusement. But Kokabiel didn't mind. Buildings were little more than a practical necessity for him—somewhere to eat and sleep when needed. His goals were much broader, encompassing both the past and the distant future. He didn't expect his fellow Myndarym to understand, which was why he kept his work to himself. They would understand its value eventually. And when that day came, likely many ages from now, Kokabiel would be the one amused by their short-sightedness.

"Can I get you anything to eat or drink?"

"Nothing, thank you," Danel replied, putting up her hand.

Turel just shook his head.

Kokabiel settled himself into a chair across from them. "I'm sure you have more questions than we have time for, so let's get started."

Turel cleared his throat. "The Council is ... concerned."

"Oh?"

"The other kingdoms are experiencing more integration," Danel explained. "But here in Kyrindem, the balance of power seems to be shifted in Azael's favor."

"Seems," Kokabiel emphasized. "As far as the humans are concerned, the distinction between Kahyin and Shayeth is gone. They are united as one, and my influence over them exceeds any from Azael. So you can remove them from the list of things that you're concerned about."

Turel nodded.

"But what about the Nephiylim?" Danel asked. "The distinction between their lineages remains as strong as it did the day you left Senvidar."

"It is not for lack of trying," Kokabiel pointed out. "My daughter rules her kind as if she were their queen. She refuses to mate with the crude and ugly children of the Kahyin, and her opinion carries much weight. It is an ongoing issue between us. I have told her that she needn't limit herself to one mate in particular, but she is still repulsed by the idea."

"Many on the Council have not encountered such opposition. Perhaps a heavier-handed approach is required?" Turel suggested.

Kokabiel smiled, and even allowed a faint laugh to escape his lips. "Clearly, you do not know my daughter."

Danel smiled at this.

"In fact," Kokabiel added, "she reminds me of you."

Danel's smile disappeared, and Kokabiel couldn't tell if she considered it an offense or a compliment.

"Anyway, you needn't worry about that. Hyrren's Nephiylim might be numerous and strong, but those are their only advantages. I have other plans in progress that will soon upset Hyrren's power."

"Would you care to elaborate?" Danel asked.

Turel leaned forward in his chair to hear the answer.

"No, I would not," Kokabiel replied.

*   *   *   *

SEDEKIYR

The gifts had been distributed. Instructions had been passed on—along with the provisions—to the appropriate citizens. Wisdom had been conveyed from one people to another, though that term was specifically avoided. Now that their short stay in the city of Yered had fulfilled its purpose, Enoch and Sariel were ready to return home. They had their own provisions in leather bags over their shoulders, and they stood just outside the eastern gate of the city, waving to those who had gathered to see them off. The sun was just above the eastern horizon, and already the day was warm. Enoch didn't need a vision from the Holy One to know that he and his friend would be greatly relieved once they reached the cooler, drier mountain air.

"See you next year," Sariel yelled with a wave.

Enoch swatted at a fly that buzzed before his face, and then he held up his hand in farewell. Just before he turned to begin his journey home, a man stepped out from the crowd at the gate and began walking toward them.

Sariel turned suddenly to lock eyes with Enoch.

Enoch just raised his eyebrows and looked back as Methu made his way through the short grass. His son had remained elusive since their arrival, and the fact that Methu was now voluntarily coming this way made Enoch's heart race. He couldn't help but wonder what kind of terrible news was about to be delivered. And as he watched, the slow process stretching out into an agonizing delay, he was struck by the way his son looked both familiar and strange at once. The smooth-faced little boy, who used to enjoy fishing with his father, had become a bearded stranger with his own children and grandchildren. It was a pain unlike anything else Enoch had ever felt.

Methu was now close enough for Enoch to hear the swish of his feet through the grass. It seemed to emphasize the slow passage of time.

Enoch leaned on his walking stick and did his best to appear calm.

Methu glanced quickly at Sariel before coming to a stop in front of his father. He looked even more nervous than Enoch. His mouth was open, as though he wanted to say something quickly before his courage failed him, but he just looked down at his feet instead.

"I didn't think you'd come to see us off," Enoch said, hoping to ease the situation by breaking the silence.

Methu lifted his head, but it took several seconds before his eyes came to land on Enoch's. "I just wanted to ..."

Enoch waited for whatever painful words were sure to be coming.

"Tell Mother I'll come to see her soon."

Enoch could hardly believe what he'd heard. He just stared at Methu, struggling to understand.

"Well, if he won't, I'll tell her," Sariel chimed in.

Methu turned his head and smiled.

"Uh ... of course. Of course, I'll tell her," Enoch finally managed. "Soon?"

Methu looked at his father again, his eyes lingering for several seconds. Then he nodded and turned around, walking back toward Sedekiyr.

Almost a minute passed before Enoch turned to Sariel. "What did you say to him?"

"I just told him the truth."

"That's all I've ever tried to do."

Sariel shrugged before tilting his head to the east. "We'd better get going."

Enoch looked toward Sedekiyr one last time and made a conscious effort to capture this moment in his memory—the moment for which he and Zacol had been waiting so long.

S.A. 987

# 28

It had been a challenge for Hyrren to follow Kokabiel out of the city without being noticed. It had taken all of his natural stealth, in combination with the tracking skills he'd honed over the cycles, to keep up with the man while staying out of sight and sound. And it required adjusting his relative position based on the constantly shifting breeze. When Hyrren's master had finally *shaped* into an animal form when safely away from the eyes of his citizens, Hyrren's challenges grew to include speed and endurance. To see Kokabiel assume the elongated form of an enormous reptile had been surprising, even more so when he had taken to the skies with great wings of bone and translucent skin.

Hyrren ran in pursuit, all the while choosing the path that offered the most concealment and the quietest terrain. Eventually, Kokabiel's form began to shrink into the distance of the night sky. And then, just before disappearing altogether, he saw it drop behind the peak of a mountain. It took over an hour for Hyrren to catch up and ascend the treacherous, densely forested terrain, but his efforts were finally rewarded. A great commotion of thrashing noises led him to a valley on the other side of the range. The snapping of trees echoed through the forest amidst powerful shrieking and hissing noises that sounded like hot metal being worked into the form of a blade and then cooled by water.

Hyrren seized the opportunity to approach under the cover of the noise, getting almost close enough to see the scales of the intertwined creatures as they thrashed about. Their serpentine bodies writhed over one another as if they were fighting, oblivious to anything else around them. When the disgusting convulsions were over, Kokabiel's mate separated herself and slithered through the water of a nearby stream, moving up to a meadow of short, lush grass. Her scales gleamed in the light of the stars, pale and reflective. Kokabiel lurched after her, crawling on winged forelegs as his great tail hovered over the ground behind him, balancing the weight of his wings. His dark body settled down onto the grass beside his coiled mate, and he laid his head parallel to hers.

Hyrren kept absolutely still. Though he was now above and behind them, away from their eyes, he was close enough to be heard if he made a mistake.

The two serpents were unmoving, breathing heavily for several minutes before growing quiet. Then a deep and clear noise cut through the peaceful meadow. "Will it ever be different?"

"Someday, perhaps. At least we have this."

It was the deeper tone of the second voice that revealed to Hyrren which words came from his master. Only then did he begin to understand the meaning behind their conversation.

"Come with me. Leave all of this behind and come with me," she pleaded, in a voice that was gentle by comparison.

"I would love nothing more, but I cannot. There is too much at stake," Kokabiel answered.

His mate lowered her head to the ground. "Our children would benefit from your presence. They don't move like I do. I can't teach them to crawl or fly ... because of my limitations."

"You're still the most magnificent creature on the earth."

"That's beside the point. I'm not what I used to be ... what I could be."[20]

"We all lost our ability to *shape*," Kokabiel replied. "At least I am still able to take different forms. Had I settled on a form in that moment, I would have become trapped inside it. I am grateful that our children are able to escape the limitations of the curse through me."

"But I cannot," his mate said, turning her head away.

"You know that I would continue *reshaping* you if I could," he pleaded.

"Then come away with me."

Kokabiel lifted his great serpentine head. "Your curse is precisely why I cannot. If I leave my work behind, there is no hope for you."

"I fear there is no hope for me anyway," she admitted.

Kokabiel looked down at her. "I will not accept that. You were the most intelligent and capable of all creatures, and you lost everything because the enemy exploited your abilities. It wasn't your fault. You deserve to have it all back, and more. I will not stop until I see you enthroned again over all the earth."

Kokabiel's mate lifted her head and looked into his eyes. "I am capable of that now, if you were by my side. Promise me this—if you ever reach the conclusion that I cannot be restored … if you come to accept it as I have—that you'll come away with me. Our children are strong and cunning. If they were also plentiful, this entire world would be ours for the taking."

Kokabiel didn't answer.

Though Hyrren couldn't see his reptilian face, he could imagine the emotional turmoil. But Hyrren had no sympathy for his so-called master. *Let his mind be consumed by such agonizing questions—all the better for the distraction it provides.* It was Hyrren's people who would rule this earth. It was their inheritance. Their birthright. For the two hundred and ninety-two cycles since Kyrindem's founding, Hyrren had been focused on that goal and nothing else. It was a game of subtlety. Of waiting. Serving. Following orders. Suppressing his feelings. Denying his instincts. Building and preparing.

Finally, all of the sacrifices were justified. With only a few words admitted in secret, Kokabiel had just yielded his kingdom and sealed the fate of his Myndar brethren. Hyrren was burning inside. The emotions he was feeling at this moment were indescribable. Yet, one challenge remained; perhaps the hardest of all—to remain still and quiet until the serpentine creatures left this place and went their separate ways. Only then would Hyrren move. Only then would he run faster than he had ever run in all his life. He would find the swiftest of his Iriyl brethren and give him a message for Azael. And then he would prepare himself for war.

*   *   *   *

KHELRUSA

Azael stood on the temple steps with his arms folded, observing the training taking place in the arena below. Rikoathel moved among the formations of young Nephiylim, demonstrating the proper two-handed grip for defensive spear tactics. Though he was one of the largest Iryllurym, most of the young trainees towered over him. His voice boomed across the silent field of dirt, while his dark brown feathers blended with the earthen skin of the Nephiylim.

Year after year they had trained these children. Azael and his Iryllurym took turns instructing, rotating the topics and responsibilities to keep it from becoming dull. But it was no use. Each new crop of students took eagerly to the new information, while the seasoned veterans grew bored. Azael wondered how long they could maintain this routine as his eyes wandered across the city.

Far below, a stone wall reached from one side of the valley to the other. It used to mark the northwestern boundary of Khelrusa, and now it had become a landmark at the center of the expanding Kahyin population. Azael had never paid much attention to the passing of time during the wars in the Borderlands. There had been no point. The Amatru and Marotru were locked into a never-ending conflict. There was always another battle to fight, or a piece of territory to defend. But in this realm, time seemed to move differently. Things changed here. People multiplied. Cities grew. Animals were hunted to extinction. And plans fell apart.

Azael could feel his patience wearing thin. He used to see the smoke rising from Khelrusa and feel a sense of satisfaction at what he was building. Now he noticed the layer of darkness hanging over the city like a swarm of winged demons. He used to take pleasure in the sound of trees being felled, and the sight of new structures being erected, the fresh wood looking pale in the sunlight. Now he noticed the bare slopes on either side of the city and the thinning forests along the surrounding peaks. The orderly city that had been hidden at the top of a narrow valley was now a haphazard tangle of wood and stone that spilled all the way down into the flat lands and around the base of Murakszhug.

Perhaps Azael would have been able to derive some satisfaction from what he had accomplished if it wasn't for Senvidar. That city of the Myndarym, far to the north and beyond sight, was still close enough to haunt Azael's thoughts. He had been there too many times, and the memories were vivid. The city was like a beacon fire, bright and mesmerizing, drawing the attention of everyone around it. Its forests were thick and tall. Its grasses green and lush. Water flowed and gathered and dripped, feeding the land. Creatures of unimaginable variety took shelter there, eating of its abundance while they did the bidding of the Myndarym. Wheeled carts carried provisions from one place to another. Boats floated along the western shores, driven by the breeze as the crops of the sea were harvested and collected upon their decks. And the Nephiyl children who called it home were fair and graceful.

Azael understood Hyrren's struggle—the longing in the general's eyes, even as his words contradicted it. It was the same festering wound that Azael suffered. There was something about the beauty and majesty of Senvidar that made Azael want to destroy it. To set it on fire and watch it come crumbling to the ground. Better yet, to put his vaepkir through the hearts of its founders, and take the city for himself.

The imagined scene disappeared from before Azael's eyes, and the dull sight of Khelrusa appeared once more. Beyond the thinning trees of the southern ridgeline, two silhouettes had just become visible in the sky. Azael recognized Parnudel immediately. The other creature was larger, obviously an Iriyl, but it took a few seconds before Azael was able to recognize it as one of Hyrren's captains.

"Rikoathel!" Azael called.

The Iryllur stopped in mid-sentence and looked up.

Azael nodded toward the southern sky.

Rikoathel turned and watched as the pair of winged creatures passed over the southern spur of Murakszhug and descended toward the temple. He instructed his students to remain at attention before leaving them and walking up the temple steps to join Azael.

The winged Nephiyl came down heavy on the pavestones, his posture flaccid with exhaustion.

Parnudel landed silently and bowed his head. "My Rada. Vidri of Kyrindem has an urgent message for you."

"What is your message?"

The Iriyl did his best to straighten up. "General Hyrren says that our time has come. In spying, he heard Kokabiel admit to one of his animal mates that all of the Myndarym lost their ability to *shape* others, and that Kokabiel is the only one who can alter his own form."

Azael squinted before glancing at Parnudel and Rikoathel. The message was short and simple, yet its meaning seemed to ring in his ears. He thought about all the interactions he'd had with the Council members over the years.

*Could it really be true? Did they ever shape in front of me?*

They hadn't—neither themselves nor something outside of themselves. Kokabiel had been the only one to alter his own form, but even his city had been built with stones shaped by the hands of his human slaves. Azael had always thought this to be a result of the Myndar being focused on more important work. Now that he thought about it, none of the kingdoms bore the mark of Myndar *shaping* ...

*Except Senvidar!*

As soon as the realization came to him, he saw through the lie that had deceived him all this time. Senvidar was founded during the Myndar rebellion from Semjaza, and they *shaped* it from the trees just as they had *shaped* Mudena Del-Edha from stones of the earth. The Myndarym lent their abilities to the Amatru attack that brought down Semjaza's kingdom. But since the first meeting of the Council, Azael had not seen a single demonstration of their power. He'd had no reason to think that they had lost it. Hyrren's message explained why they all carried on in their other forms, even when it didn't seem practical.

*And Sariel* ... he remembered. *That's why he wouldn't fight me in his Iryllur form!*

All of it made sense now. Azael had the true answer to hundreds of questions that he had already explained away as he stayed focused on his ultimate goal.

Azael looked up from the ground, suddenly aware of the smile on his face. "Return quickly to Hyrren. Tell him that he has brought us to the start of a new era. He should prepare for war and launch his attack on the evening of the next new moon. We will instruct his brothers to do likewise, and I will take Senvidar that same night."

Vidri grinned as his eyes narrowed. "It will be my pleasure, King Azael," he said before bowing. Then the Iriyl spread his wings and took to the sky with renewed vigor, disappearing swiftly over the ridge to the south.

When Azael returned his attention to his Iryllurym, both were standing at attention, ready to receive their orders. "Fly fast, but do not let yourselves be seen. Inform the generals. Then hurry back ... it is time for our vaepkir to drink their fill of enemy blood."

\* \* \* \*

EL-BETAKH

Enoch laid the bundle of arrows inside the crate, next to hundreds more just like it. Then he stood up and stretched his back before returning to the tools building to get the next bundle. During his sons' multiple visits over the past year, Methu had said that the men of Sedekiyr were increasingly interested in the hunting tools that Sariel had made. The fishermen had been fighting over who could use the limited supply of spears, and the bow had gone from being Methu's strange invention to the most sought-after possession in the whole city. Their annual journey to Sedekiyr was now only a month away, but Enoch could already see that they were ahead of schedule. They would need a larger raft this time for all the tools, in addition to the other supplies they had promised.

"Enoch!"

He turned around to see Zacol walking up the hill toward him. It was times like these, when he saw his wife from afar, that he realized how beautiful she really was. Not that she wasn't beautiful from up close, but Enoch was always too occupied by the moment to see it. When he viewed her from afar, he saw her as the one who had stayed faithful to him all these years. She was the only person who believed in him. The one who labored on his behalf, instead of against him. That's when her true beauty was most visible.

As Zacol neared, Enoch found himself distracted by her eyes, the color of rich and fertile soil. Her long, black hair swayed behind her as she walked. The smile on her face had become a regular sight this year. And then there were her lips ...

"The children are ready for you," she said, now that she was close enough to speak without yelling.

"Oh, is it that time already?" Enoch wondered, looking up to the sky. The sun was directly overhead. And far to the east, behind a seemingly endless expanse of blue, the white sliver of a new moon was just barely visible. "I lost track of time."

Zacol smiled as if she were keeping a secret to herself.

"Yes, I know," Enoch admitted. "I never used to get lost in practical work."

Zacol only raised her eyebrows in response.

"It's very different when the work flows out of obedience to the Holy One instead of distracting me from it," Enoch explained.

"Well, perhaps that could be today's lesson for the children?"

Enoch smiled. "I'll get someone to take over for me here. Tell the children I'll only be another minute or two."

Zacol nodded and turned back down the hill.

Enoch watched her go, noticing the outline of her body as well as the bounce in her step. Methu had promised to bring his family to El-Betakh when Enoch and Sariel returned. Soon, all of his children would be together in one city. Enoch suddenly wondered if his own steps had been a bit lighter in recent months.

# 29

Hyrren and ten of his soldiers walked casually down the hall toward Kokabiel's throne room. Torches burned in their sconces on the left. Through the windows on the right, Hyrren could see the gleaming white sliver of a new moon hanging against the black sky. This meeting with Kokabiel was supposed to be for the purpose of discussing the expansion of Nephiyl living quarters, or so his master was led to believe. For now, Hyrren and his soldiers would keep up appearances.

They came to a stop outside the door, and Hyrren rapped his knuckles against the thick wood. Normally, he would have waited to be let in by the guards, but Kokabiel had no other meetings prior to this one. Hyrren wouldn't be interrupting anyone.

The soldiers glanced nervously at each other.

Hyrren knocked again, much louder this time. When no answer came, he tried the handle before stepping back and kicking the side opposite from the hinges. The wood split apart near the handle and the door flew open.

The first thing he noticed was an Aniyl guard slumped against the wall to his right. The stones behind him were displaced and cracked as though he had been thrown against them with tremendous force. Hyrren instinctively pivoted to the left with his knife in one hand and a spear in the other. Half of his soldiers followed, while the others headed to the right.

Hyrren almost lost his footing on the massive pool of blood covering the floor. What was left of the second guard's body was scattered in pieces across this side of the room. Blood coated the nearest wall in two giant upward splatters that fanned out from a central position. Hyrren's eyes tracked the trail of blood to the far wall, where the pattern was horizontal, and then to the mangled remains of the guard on the floor. Immediately, Hyrren thought of the giant, winged serpent that he had tracked, and wondered if Kokabiel was even still inside the city at this point.

"General, this one is dead also."

Hyrren turned to look across the room. Five of his soldiers were gathered around the other body, which was now slumped forward. The back of the Aniyl's skull had been crushed.

At the opposite corner of the room was an open doorway into Kokabiel's living quarters. Hyrren took off at a run. He knew that he wouldn't find his former master in there, but there might be a clue as to where he had gone. Within seconds, he found confirmation of both assumptions. The living quarters were empty, but the beams which supported the roof over the open balcony had been gouged, as if something large and coarse had passed by them. Hyrren descended the steps and ran out into the open air of the courtyard. As his soldiers came behind him, Hyrren looked up into the sky, searching for a sign of which direction Kokabiel might have gone. But there was nothing.

Continuing across the courtyard, Hyrren ran down a long set of stairs and circled back toward the southern wing, beyond which was the section of the city where Kokabiel's children lived. Before he even reached the many hundreds of buildings that were elaborate compared to his own people's dwellings, Hyrren could see that something was wrong. Instead of fighting, he could see his soldiers entering and exiting the buildings, frantically looking for their enemies.

"General!" a voice called out.

Hyrren located one of his captains and altered his course, heading toward the doorway of a single-level structure to his left.

"They're not here, General," the soldier explained. "Not even the young ones. They're all gone."

Hyrren inhaled deeply before closing his eyes and raising his face to the night sky. Kokabiel had somehow figured out that this was going to happen, and he had managed to escape with his Nephiylim. *Children,* he corrected himself. The plan to keep the females for breeding would now have to be abandoned. This uprising had suddenly become a hunting endeavor. When Hyrren opened his eyes again, his mind was clear. The city that stretched across the rolling hills below Kokabiel's castle twinkled with the firelight from human dwellings. As far as the citizens knew, nothing had changed.

"The city is ours, Captain," Hyrren finally replied. "Move our people into these dwellings and make this castle the center of your operations. You will have a minimum guard to maintain control of the city. The rest of our forces will come with me."

"Yes, General," he replied, grinning before he left to disseminate the instructions.

\* \* \* \*

SOUTH OF KYRINDEM

"Father, we cannot keep this up," Yllfae whispered.

Even at her quietest, Kokabiel could hear the straining of her lungs. "I know," he admitted, looking over her shoulder. Behind her, visible in the pale light of dawn, were hundreds of his Nephiyl descendants either lying on the ground or leaning against the trees. Some were holding infants in their arms, others were comforting crying younglings. Beyond the limited visibility offered by the forest, several thousand more were spread out to the south. They had been running all evening, and Kokabiel had nearly worn himself out moving between the head of the group—to give directions—and the rear—for protection in case Hyrren's soldiers caught up to them.

"It shouldn't be much longer now before—"

Screams of surprise suddenly erupted from a cluster of females to Kokabiel's left. A large male scooped up his son and ran away from the edge of the denser forest to the north.

Kokabiel instantly began running toward the commotion, embers trailing through the air behind him as he *shaped* into his most dangerous form. But the sight of fur relieved his fears, and the embers subsided.

"Ananel!" he shouted.

The wolf stepped out into the open. Behind him, hundreds of others were becoming visible through the branches of the forest. All were significantly larger than him, except the dark female who cautiously stepped out from the trees and stayed behind her mate.

"Hyrren's forces are only hours behind you," Ananel said calmly.

"You saw them? How many are following us?" Kokabiel asked as he drew near to his fellow Myndar.

"Too many to count. We tried cutting across your trail to divert them, but they just spread out farther and kept coming."

Kokabiel let out the breath he'd been holding before looking again at his Nephiyl children. They were frightened and exhausted. There was no way they could ever hope to outrun Hyrren and his soldiers. "You know these lands better than I do, Ananel. What do you suggest? Is there another route that we could take to get around them, or at least out of their path?"

"Not one that they couldn't just follow."

Kokabiel crossed his arms. "What about a river? We could—"

"It won't be fast enough."

Kokabiel clenched his teeth and stared hard at the ground.

"You brought this upon yourself, my friend. The Council never should have—"

"I know!" Kokabiel snapped. When he spoke again, his tone was more controlled. "We had no choice. But that doesn't matter now."

A long moment of silence passed before Ananel said, "You can't turn and fight; their numbers are too great. But you might outrun them with my help."

Kokabiel looked up from the ground he'd been staring at. "How?"

"My children can take your youngest as riders on their backs."

"Ananel, we outnumber you three to one."

The wolf lowered his head. "Your oldest would still have to run, but we would take turns with the youngest."

"That would gain us ... a day ... at the most? What then?"

"If we can maintain it for two days, we can reach Jomjael. Then all of your younger children could ride, and perhaps some of your older ones as well."

Kokabiel remembered the feline form that Jomjael used to take and imagined what his children might look like. "Would he help us?"

"I don't know, but you don't have another option."

"Alright."

Ananel lifted his head and loosed a howl that was just loud enough to be heard in the immediate area. All along the edge of the dense tree line, hundreds of gigantic wolves stepped into the light of the morning.

\* \* \* \*

SENVIDAR

The battle had raged all through the night. Swarms of Iriylim, led by Parnudel and Rikoathel, had descended upon the Myndar city from the east. Azael had been leading the ground forces against the southern entrance of Senvidar when he witnessed the sky to the north turn completely black. An unknown enemy was approaching, and their masses blotted out the stars. The Iryllurym redirected their forces to meet the threat, and soon after, gigantic birds of prey began dropping out of the sky, along with the occasional winged Nephiylim.

Zahmesh's Aniyl guards had put up a good fight, but even their superior armor and weaponry eventually yielded to the proficiency of Azael's soldiers. They breached the gate and steadily pushed the enemy farther inside the city. Azael stayed back from the fighting and just watched, allowing his inexperienced soldiers to put their training to use. He would have liked nothing more than to dive into the fray, but he had ages of battle experience to his credit and they had none. It took his soldiers longer than it should have to fan out and flank Zahmesh's forces, but they eventually realized what had to be done. It took every bit of restraint for Azael to hold his tongue. There were hundreds of inefficiencies to correct, missteps to redirect, and blatant errors that cost some of his Nephiylim their lives. But he let the battle play out. There was only so many times that an instruction could be repeated. At some point, experience had to take over as the master.

By the time the sun was rising over the peak to the east, Senvidar had fallen. Dozens of Myndarym were dead, along with thousands of their Nephiyl children. Naganel and his entire flight of would-be defenders had been decimated. Their bodies littered the city, scattered over the fields of grain or hanging from the branches of fruit trees. The Myniylim who held specific areas of responsibility had been spared, according to Azael's orders. They would be useful in the near future for maintaining the city's production of food, weapons, and other resources. And to support that effort, as many humans as possible had been allowed to live.

When only Zahmesh and a dozen of his top guards were left, huddled together in the middle of a pasture, Azael instructed his armies to pull back and form a perimeter. Then he walked alone into the field and approached the group of enemies.

"Very impressive, Zahmesh. With no training or experience to speak of, you built up an entire defense force. You must have trained them from infancy."

"Why are you doing this?" Zahmesh asked. His blond beard was caked with dried blood. Spatters covered his bare chest, and the long, double-bladed weapon that hung from his hands was still dripping with it.

Azael ignored his question for now and continued forward.

The pale-skinned Nephiylim crowded around their leader, fitting their massive shields together into a protective ring that was more than a third taller than Zahmesh. Their spears stuck out over the top of the ring like the spines of a deadly animal.

Azael's view of Zahmesh was mostly obstructed. "Your weaponry is nothing short of amazing. Of course, I see the influences of skoldur and vandrekt among your work, but the svvard was only in development when we left the Eternal Realm. I didn't realize you knew anything about it. And what is that you're holding?"

"Why are you doing this?" Zahmesh repeated with a shout.

Azael stopped walking only a few paces from the huddled enemies. He casually pulled the vaepkir from their sheaths at the small of his back, holding them out in a reverse grip with the blades pointing outward like svvards.

"You see these? Normally I carry the ones you and your brethren *shaped* for us in Mudena Del-Edha. But not this day. Such a special occasion required different weapons. These I found on the road from the land gate to Aryun Del-Edha. They are from the armory that you amassed to help the Amatru invade and destroy our city. With the Songs of Creation entrusted to you by the Holy One, you sang these into existence from the elements of the earth."

Zahmesh's face grew even sterner than it had been, but fear was still obviously the foremost of his emotions.

"But you can't do that any longer, can you? *Shaping*?"

When Zahmesh didn't respond, Azael continued, "You made these. Then you gave them to the Amatru. And the Amatru used these to kill my Iryllurym. I realize that Semjaza was the focus of your betrayal, and you succeeded in removing him from power. But you made a very serious mistake. You crossed me and failed to ensure that I was dead."

"It was never our intention to—"

"I am doing this," Azael shouted, "to show you and your traitorous kind the depth of your misjudgment. I am doing this to show you that I keep my promises. You *Shapers* trade allegiance as often and easily as the shifting breeze. But I am a soldier. And I promise you that I will hunt down and kill every last one of you for what you did. As you lay dying, I want the last thought running through your mind to be a confident assurance that I keep my word."

Parnudel and Rikoathel could now be seen standing at the edge of the field. Their arms were crossed, and they appeared to be enjoying this moment as well.

Azael turned his vaepkir around into a standard grip with the blades running upward along the outside of his arms. "Now, before I get started, is there anything you need to refresh your strength? Water? Food?"

Zahmesh's fingers tightened around the shaft of his weapon.

"Oh. One of your soldiers is missing his spear," Azael suddenly noticed. "You there. Pick up that spear and toss it over," he instructed one of his own Nephiylim.

The young soldier of Khelrusa stepped away from the perimeter and lifted a spear from the grass, tossing it over to the group of guards as instructed.

Zahmesh's soldier bent down and grabbed the weapon, sliding it under the protective ring of shields.

"That's better," Azael said. "I want to make sure that the odds are with you. Now—"

"We could serve you," Zahmesh interrupted.

Azael smiled. "Spoken like the traitor that you are. Don't worry; your work and legacy will indeed serve my purposes. But I have no need for a coward among my ranks. So now that that's settled, shall we get started?"

The shields closed in tighter, and the spears of the guards wavered with anticipation.

It had been far too long since Azael had fought, and it was a pity that this moment would pass so quickly. He promised himself that he would pay attention and savor every stroke. Then he spread his wings to either side and lunged forward.

Spears stabbed at him, but their range of motion was inhibited by the shields. Azael ducked beneath them and cut the legs out from under two of the guards. As they began to topple forward, he sprang up from the ground and between their spears, with his right forewing coming over the top of their ring of shields. He used his carpal joint to drive their defenses into the ground, then followed it with another slash of his vaepkir. Then his other wing came down, and another slash. Within seconds, half of Zahmesh's guards were on the ground, writhing in pain.

Azael broke through their defense as if it were merely a training exercise, scattering the guards. And as soon as they broke away from each other, they lost the advantage of their combined efforts. He slashed and dodged, wings and blades flying so quickly that it might as well have been a full army opposing them. One after another they dropped, until Azael cut the legs out from under the last guard and reversed the motion to run his blade through the Nephiyl's chest. When he pulled it free, the guard dropped to the grass, and the sharp ring of metal faded until the field was silent once again.

Zahmesh was backing away with fear in his eyes.

Azael retracted his wings and stalked forward, all traces of amusement now gone from his face.

Zahmesh moved his hands to the end of his weapon's shaft. Then he nearly threw the double-edged blade at Azael in a two-handed stroke.

Azael pulled his head backward just in time, feeling a brush of air in front of his nose.

Zahmesh kept the momentum from his missed attack, allowing the weapon to swing wide and then up over his head, before adding more muscle to it. When he brought the weapon full circle into a forehand attack, it was moving at twice the speed.

Azael was already reversing the grip on one of his vaepkir. Ducking under the attack, he used his standard-gripped weapon to deflect Zahmesh's blade upward, while the other slashed forward with expert precision. In one fluid motion, Azael defended and counter-attacked, severing both of Zahmesh's arms, which spun out into the field along with the weapon to which they still clung.

The Myndar stumbled backward with shock as his twitching stumps sprayed blood in every direction.

Azael quickly stood and pivoted, slashing his other blade across the front of Zahmesh's throat. Then he halted the attack.

Zahmesh dropped to his knees, choking on his own blood while his eyes turned upward and filled with the dread of what would happen when his spirit left his body.

Azael said nothing, nor did he allow any expression whatsoever to cross his face. He simply watched his enemy suffer through the last few seconds of his earthly life before his body slumped forward and fell to the grass.

A long moment of silence passed before Azael's Nephiyl army erupted in shouts of victory. The sheer volume of the noise—immediately following such complete silence—was deafening.

As he had done many thousands of times in his life, Azael wiped the blood of his enemy from his vaepkir and resheathed them. Without a moment's hesitation, he turned and walked across the pasture toward Parnudel and Rikoathel. He was vaguely aware that his name was being chanted, but his mind had already moved on from the battle. The next step of his campaign was his focus now.

"I trust you didn't wear yourselves out?"

"No, my Rada," his Iryllurym replied.

"Good. Fly as fast as possible, and determine the status of Hyrren and the other generals. I am eager to know if their battles went as smoothly as ours."

# 30

Methu's hands were working, knotting the cords that held the support poles of the roof in place. But his mind was wandering. He imagined the great Anduarym, with their skoldur and vandrekt, marching across the plains. His father stood in the foreground, small and fragile by comparison, but confident in the Holy One's protection. Enoch was pointing west, where the angels would find the rebellious Semjaza. Row upon row of them passed by, each stride equal to several from a man. Their ranks were awesome and terrible to behold. The mountains of Mudena Del-Edha would shake with their fury. And the waters surrounding Aryun Del-Edha would toss and foam in fear. The time of Semjaza's punishment had finally come.

"Father?"

The imaginary sight vanished from Methu's mind, and the roof of the storehouse took its place.

"Father!" Lemek repeated, louder this time.

Methu looked down and realized that his eldest son was standing below, trying to hand him another support pole. "Sorry," he said, quickly grabbing the hollow grass stalk and dragging it up onto the roof before laying it across the other supports. They were repairing an old section of the roof that had begun falling apart. Each section of the city had a storehouse where food and other perishable supplies were kept. Though the building was only a single-story, the ground had been dug away inside to make more room, and to utilize the coolness under the soil to preserve the supplies.

"Isn't that what bothered you about Grandfather?"

"What?" Methu asked.

"Dreaming in the daytime," Lemek clarified. "Grandfather couldn't concentrate on work."

"That's when I thought he was crazy."

Lemek handed up another pole.

Methu set it next to the other and began tying them into place. "I was just thinking about one of the stories he told me when I was young."

"You don't think he was making it up?"

Methu paused for a moment. He thought about all of the bizarre locations, the names and foreign languages, the detailed descriptions of the people and their interactions. If they were just stories, then Methu's father was indeed crazy. "No. Not anymore."

Lemek was climbing up the storehouse wall now, with a coil of rope around his shoulder. "What changed?" he grunted.

"I think I met one of them."

"Who? An angel?"

"Yes," Methu replied, looking up from the roof to gaze over the northern section of the city.

"Are there angels living in El Betakh?" Lemek asked, suddenly sounding worried.

Methu smiled. "Just one, I think. Why? Does that frighten you?"

"I suppose ... yes. It doesn't seem natural."

Methu smiled. "Well, you don't have to be afraid. You've met him too."

Lemek frowned.

"Sariel," Methu clarified.

"What? Sariel's not an angel. He's just a man."

"Then how do you explain his vast wisdom? His white hair?"

"He's an *old* man."

"From which tribe?" Methu countered.

"I don't know. One of Yahsad's descendants?"

Methu just smiled. "He's an angel. But if you don't believe … ask him yourself. He'll be here soon."

Lemek finally lifted the coil of rope over his head and set it down on the roof. "I guess I shouldn't let it bother me."

"What do you mean?"

Lemek grinned. "I've *always* known *you* were crazy."

Methu smiled before grabbing a pole and using it to jab his son in the gut.

Lemek flinched before tossing his rope in response. When it hit Methu's head, the coils unwound and spilled down over him like a tangled spider web. The two men stood there laughing at each other for a moment before they grew silent and began picking up their mess.

* * * *

SOUTHWEST OF KYRINDEM
SATAREL'S LANDS

Ananel slowed near the top of a ridgeline. The trees were sparse, but grew in clusters that would still mask his outline in the moonlight. The Nephiyl on his back had been doing a great job of holding on and showed no signs of tiring. But he couldn't say the same for all of Kokabiel's children. The youngest ones lacked strength and endurance, requiring them to rotate their mounted positions more frequently. The older ones were heavier, slowing the wolves. Surprisingly, the sharing of their weaknesses had allowed them to hold out long enough to reach the lands of Satarel. With any luck, Hyrren's armies would abide by their agreements and stay on their own side of the boundary.

As Ananel looked down into the valley he'd just climbed, seeing his pack and Kokabiel's children weave through the sections of crumbling rock, he picked up a scent coming from the west. The wind carried the smell of feline, as well as Nephiyl. But the Nephiyl scent was subtle, not the pungent odor that went before Hyrren's armies. This smelled more like the children of Kokabiel.

Ananel walked away from the trees and gazed out over the western landscape. In the light of the moon, patches of fog were drifting among the trees, gray against a backdrop of black. But something else was moving. Thousands of smaller shapes were flitting through the trees toward him, faster than the mist. It wasn't the sharp glint of moonlight on weaponry as he had seen from the pursuing army. These were softer, duller reflections. Ananel loosed a howl to simultaneously warn his pack and announce their presence.

Seconds later, soft footsteps could be heard moving in his direction.

"Ananel?" came a snarling voice.

"Jomjael," he replied.

A large, striped cat of golden brown coloring stepped out into the open. The human riding upon his back began to climb down immediately, and it wasn't until the man turned to face Ananel that he recognized him.

"Satarel?"

The man of black hair and pale skin came forward with a grave look on his face, looking especially upset by the Nephiyl upon Ananel's back. "You are being chased as well?"

"Hyrren's armies turned against Kokabiel. We helped him and his children escape, but we can't carry all of them at the same time."

"I wish we could help," Jomjael replied. "But we're trying to escape Imikal's army."

"You were also attacked?" Ananel asked, looking at Satarel.

"Not just me. Imikal split his army into two and came after both of us separately. Jomjael was the first to be attacked."

The sound of rushing wind preceded the appearance of a massive reptile, flapping its wings as it came to land nearby. Jomjael instinctively crouched and his ears went back, but he calmed when Kokabiel's intimidating form began shimmering with the light of a million embers. When the *shaping* was complete, Kokabiel was in his angelic form and walking toward the group. "Did you say he attacked Jomjael first?"

"Yes," Satarel replied.

Kokabiel glanced quickly at each member gathered. "Then it's not just the Council members he's after."

"He?" Ananel wondered.

"Azael. He's coming for all of us. He wants revenge for Mudena Del-Edha."

"Why now?" Jomjael asked.

Satarel looked up at the giant feline he'd been riding. "We tried holding him off by making him an ally, but he must have learned that we can't *shape*. That was the only thing holding him back."

"Well, who told him?" Ananel wondered.

The others just shook their heads.

"Did Fyarikel warn you also?" Satarel asked, looking at Kokabiel.

"Yes. I wonder how many others survived."

The sound of their fellow refugees approaching from the east and west finally grew loud enough to interrupt their conversation.

"We have to decide what we're going to do," Ananel said, getting back to the immediate problem.

"You said Hyrren is chasing you from the east?" Satarel asked.

"His forces are spread out to the east and north," Ananel replied.

"Imikal is to our west. We only have three hours ... at the most," Jomjael added. His tigers were now appearing in the spaces between the sparse trees behind him.

Ananel could hear his own pack coming up the side of the valley. "That leaves the south."

"We can't run forever," Satarel pointed out.

Kokabiel nodded. "My children can't do this any longer. And I imagine yours can't keep it up either," he replied, looking over Satarel's shoulder at the dark-haired Nephiylim sitting on the backs of the striped cats.

"There's a mesa about a half-day's run from here," Jomjael suggested. "Its sides are very steep, but I know a way to reach the top safely."

"Wouldn't we be surrounded?" Kokabiel asked.

"If it's tall enough and steep enough, we could fight back with the advantage of higher ground," Satarel said.

Ananel raised his snout to the air and checked for signs of a threat. Then he looked to his fellow Myndarym once more. "If we can't run, we must fight back. This mesa sounds like the best location to do that. Let's get moving."

The others nodded their agreement.

Ananel turned to notice his mate and several of his children standing behind him. He wasted no time raising his voice to the night to communicate the change of plans.

\*   \*   \*   \*

THE MESA
SATAREL'S LANDS

Hyrren stood atop the flat expanse of rock, looking north. The sun was low on the western horizon, but waves of heat were still rising from the earth, fighting back the haze that was attempting to build up in the gaps between the sparse trees. Hyrren's spear and arms were coated in blood. And all around him, bodies were scattered.

"Brother," came a voice from behind.

Hyrren turned to see Imikal walking toward him, stepping over the body of a pale-skinned Myniyl. To his left, a giant tiger was lying atop one of Ananel's wolves. It looked like the one had tried to save the other, but both had been run through with a spear. Hyrren smiled and spread his arms.

Imikal walked into the embrace with enthusiasm, even lifting his older brother from the ground for just a moment.

Hyrren couldn't help but laugh. When his feet were on the ground again, he pulled back to get a good look at his younger brother, who was now just as tall as Hyrren, though still a bit thinner. He also wore his hair long, but the front section had been braided and pulled back away from his face. If Hyrren's own face weren't covered in scars, he might as well have been looking into a mirror. "It has been far too long, Imikal."

"Indeed. When Parnudel told me that our armies were approaching each other, I could hardly keep my mind on the task at hand."

"When this is all over, we really must sit down and share a meal. I want to hear everything that has happened since I saw you last."

Imikal smiled before looking around at the battlefield. "That may happen sooner rather than later, from the look of things. Parnudel tells me that Azael has taken Senvidar."

"Yes, I heard as much from Rikoathel. Apparently our brothers to the north and east have not encountered the trouble that we have."

"Not all of them," Imikal corrected. "Rameel and Arakiba are still alive for certain. Azael has emptied Khelrusa of all Nephiylim and he has his armies spread out all the way to the east behind them."

Hyrren smiled. "The noose is tightening. And thanks to this ambush, our enemies are now headed straight for it. It's almost too much to believe ... we're finally on the move."

Imikal nodded. "No more scheming. No more pretending to be weak. These are exciting times."

"Did you hear about Baraquijal?"

"Yes," Imikal replied, shaking his head. "I don't know how he found out it was coming, but it was apparently a slaughter."

"I think he must have teamed up with another of these animal Myndarym. Perhaps Fyarikel? There is no way his own offspring could have killed that many of our kind."

"I agree," Imikal replied. "But we'll avenge them all."

Hyrren looked around once more at the slain children of Ananel, Jomjael, Kokabiel, and Satarel. "This is just a taste of what they'll receive. When we finally have them all surrounded, it will be our turn to do the slaughtering."

Imikal stepped over to the edge of the mesa and looked down its northern cliff face. "Should we rest a while and let our prey gain some distance?"

Hyrren squinted into the sunset before looking at his brother again. "My soldiers have benefited from finally putting their training to good use, but they could use a short rest. Let's take an hour before we set out again."

Imikal nodded. "Good. I'll inform my soldiers." He turned and began walking southeast across the top of the mesa, but stopped suddenly. "It's a pity we're not hunting humans. I have not been able to acquire a taste for any other flesh. And these fruits and grains that we have to carry with us are just terrible."

Hyrren laughed again. He had forgotten how amusing Imikal's honesty could be. "Someday, brother. We must take our plans one step at a time."

# 31

The raft was much larger this year, and so was the crowd that had gathered to see them off. Enoch stood on the docks beside the river holding Zacol's hand, while he raised the other to quiet the citizens of El-Betakh.

"May you hear the voice of the Holy One with great clarity," he began, noticing how many of his people were mouthing the words to the familiar blessing. "May His wisdom guide your steps, and may your lives show the evidence of His love."

They erupted into cheering just as soon as he finished.

Zacol stepped around in front of Enoch and reached up to put her hands on either side of his face.

Enoch leaned forward and kissed his wife's soft lips, lingering there for longer than usual. There was a floral scent to her breath—the smell of the tea that Sariel had showed her how to make.

"I miss you already," she breathed.

"Not as much as I miss you," he replied, kissing her once more.

Zacol's lips curled into a smile, and she leaned forward until her forehead rested against Enoch's.

Seconds of silence passed. Enoch savored the moment, realizing how time had changed them both. These recent years had been the sweetest of their lives, better even than when they had first met. All those years ago, when he had taken his first steps away from Sedekiyr to deliver the message to the Wandering Stars, he had no idea of the strain it was going to put on them both. But the Holy One had restored their relationship. And not just restored, but improved upon it. Enoch was amazed when he thought about—

"You should get going," Zacol whispered, interrupting his thoughts.

Enoch opened his eyes. Now he was sorry he had to leave. He wanted to stay in Zacol's presence forever.

"Don't forget to bring Methu back to me," she added, her face suddenly serious.

"If he changes his mind, I'll grab him by the ear and drag him all the way up here."

"Good," Zacol replied with a grin.

Enoch suddenly realized that the crowd had grown silent. Many of them had amused smiles on their faces. He glanced back over his shoulder and noticed Sariel waiting with his arms crossed.

"Alright. Alright. I'm coming."

\* \* \* \*

SOUTHWEST OF KYRINDEM

Ananel stood on a rock outcropping, keeping watch to the south as Jomjael's tigers stumbled past him. These tigers weren't accustomed to traveling long distances with speed, let alone with Nephiylim on their backs. Even Ananel was breathing heavily from the exertion. The surge of fear-induced energy had worn off now, and their massive group needed rest.

As the last of the cats entered the meadow that Ananel's pack had scouted for them, Satarel climbed down from Jomjael's back, and the two walked over to Ananel. Kokabiel, who had been hovering in the night sky over the rear of the group, finally descended to the ground and shaped into his angelic form. The ragged group of Myndarym was silent at first, too exhausted for words. They just stared at each other or out to the southern horizon where their enemies were sure to be following. They had walked right into an ambush at the mesa. Somehow, Hyrren and Imikal had known which direction they would turn, and had circled around to the south to lie in wait for them. As soon as the first of their group made it to the top of the mesa, the Nephiyl armies came around from the backside and tried to surround them. Kokabiel had been magnificent, reacting quickly with his deadly jaws and powerful tail. He took to the air and attacked the Nephiyl ranks, buying time for the group to reverse direction and run north. The teeth of the wolves and the claws of the tigers were also deadly, but there had still been many losses. Each of the Myndarym had witnessed some of their own children being slaughtered, and the resulting emotions were both numerous and conflicting.

Ananel wanted to kill. He wanted to tear Nephiyl flesh from bone. He wanted to cry. To mourn. He wanted to howl so loudly that the entire world would hear his pain. He wanted to lie down by a river and listen to the passing of water and nothing else for weeks until he was too feeble to get up again. He wanted to die. So many emotions coursed through his body, like streams converging into a flood that choked itself. And the result was silence.

Long minutes passed. The Myndarym watched the lands to the south, looking for signs that they had to get up again and run, even though they didn't have the strength for one more step. Ananel heard someone crying and turned to see Yllfae, Kokabiel's oldest daughter, walking back toward them. There was blood on her hands and the front of her dress, but it wasn't hers. She was sobbing, her giant frame shaking with despair. Kokabiel turned to her and shaped into a larger version of his angelic self, one that was equal in size to a Nephiyl. Yllfae collapsed into his arms.

"Shh," he soothed, stroking her hair. Yllfae had children and grandchildren of her own, and yet she became a fragile child in the arms of her father.

Something about the sight of them together brought Ananel out of his silence. "We cannot do this on our own."

The Myndarym turned from their thoughts and stared at Ananel.

"Any allies to be found will be chased by still more armies," Satarel replied. "We cannot even do this with help. They are too strong for us."

"And there is no safe place to which we can run," Jomjael added.

"The Holy One can save us," Ananel replied. "There is no other way."

More silence passed as the Myndarym stared at him in disbelief. Finally, Satarel spoke, "Have you forgotten that He abandoned us?"

"No, we abandoned Him," Ananel corrected.

"What difference does it make?" Jomjael asked. "We're alone one way or the other, and we have no way to change that fact."

"Enoch," Ananel replied.

Kokabiel suddenly turned his attention away from his daughter. "What about him?"

"He lives in Sedekiyr. We'll go to him and ask—"

"He's the one who pronounced this judgment upon us!" Kokabiel shouted. "You want him to speak with the Holy One on our behalf?"

"That didn't turn out well last time, remember?" Satarel pointed out.[21]

"Why would Enoch help us anyway?" asked Jomjael.

Ananel looked slowly from one Myndar to another and shook his head. "I don't know. I can't argue with any of the things you say. All I know is he's the only person with access to the Holy One."

Satarel and Jomjael lowered their eyes to the ground. Kokabiel went back to soothing his daughter.

"Our children are being killed before our eyes," Ananel continued. "Under our own strength, we are without hope. If there is another option, please tell me."

* * * *

Azael stood in the center of the Place of Meeting, the highest point of the mountain range on the eastern boundary of Senvidar. From this stone amphitheater, one could see unobstructed views in every direction. It had been the seat of the Council's power, however illusory it had been. Azael had sat in this place many times over the years, pretending to confer with equals. The circumstances had been very different then, suffocated by lies and false peace. But now the truth had been revealed. Blood had been spilled. And a revolution was underway. Azael felt as though he could truly breathe for the first time in centuries, and with this newfound clarity, he wondered if the Place of Meeting was a suitable location from which to rule and if it would need to be altered.

When Parnudel came to a landing on the smooth stone, Azael felt it more than he heard it, silent as his fellow Iryllur was.

"My Rada. Hyrren and Imikal have successfully redirected their enemies. Kokabiel, Ananel, Jomjael, and Satarel are all heading north as we speak."

"Excellent!" Azael replied. "Inform the other generals to hold the eastern front, and continue advancing our northern and western forces. We'll drive the Myndarym toward each other and corral them like animals."

"Yes, my Rada."

# 32

The docks were alive with the excitement of the annual visit. Men were gathered, eager to accept the crates that Sariel and Enoch were offloading from their raft. They talked and joked among each other, guessing what was inside each box and discussing what could be done with the supplies from El-Betakh. The noise was a constant murmur in the background as Sariel wiped the sweat from his brow and continued working. What had slowly accumulated on the deck of the raft over several weeks in Enoch's city would be stripped bare in just a few hours by the men of Sedekiyr.

As Sariel directed two men to grab both ends of a wooden box, he realized that the murmur had grown into something more. When he looked up from the raft, he noticed movement among the crowd of men leading down from the gates of the city to the docks. A small group of men was pushing through as others stepped to the side, complaining about the interruption.

Sariel stood up to his full height and glanced at Enoch, who had a concerned look on his face. The commotion rippled through the crowd like waves, lasting several minutes until the small group of five men stumbled out from the densest gathering at the edge of the harbor and began running toward the raft. They each carried spears upright and fear was on their faces.

"Enoch!" one of them yelled.

The prophet glanced at Sariel before stepping from the raft to the dock. "Yes, I'm here. What is it?"

The men came to a stop in front of him. The leader of the city guard spoke in hushed tones, as if he were delivering a secret. "Something waits for you in the fields to the south."

"Some*thing*?"

"It is a four-legged beast ... tall and fearsome. It has gray fur and a long snout. We saw it approaching and considered going out to chase it away, until we realized how big it was."

"Why do you say it waits for *me*?"

"Because it spoke! It called out to us, saying that it wished to talk with the prophet, Enoch. And then we saw the fields behind it ..."

Enoch frowned. "What about the fields?"

"Thousands upon thousands of them. Creatures of all kinds."

Enoch turned to Sariel and breathed a sigh of acceptance. "It has begun."

"Please. The people of Sedekiyr are frightened. You must go speak with them," said the leader of the city guard. "Whatever they want doesn't involve us. Lead them away from here."

"Father!" came another voice from the crowd. Methu suddenly pushed his way out onto the dock and came running.

"I'll go," Sariel offered, stepping forward to lay a hand on Enoch's shoulder. "It looks like you have other matters to attend to."

"Thank you," Enoch replied. "It sounds like Ananel. Find out what he wants and I'll be there as soon as I speak with Methu."

Sariel just nodded and turned to the guard leader. "Take me to the southern gate."

The man looked nervously from Sariel to Enoch and back again before accepting the instruction.

Sariel followed the men back along the dock, moving through the parting crowds. Methu sidestepped the group and ran past, making eye contact with Sariel as he hurried toward his father. The look in his eyes was something between awe and utter hopelessness. Sariel realized in that moment that this was not how he expected this event to occur. He had discussed this very day with Enoch hundreds of times over the years. They speculated when it would take place, how it would unfold, and where they both would be when it happened. Neither of them expected it to take this many years. And though they knew it was a possibility, neither of them believed that they'd be in Sedekiyr during its destruction. But now that the event was unfolding, Sariel was also eager to discover what circumstances had prompted it.

Were Ananel and the other animal Myndarym running from the Council? Or was Azael the antagonist? Was everyone running from his armies? Perhaps there were three separate groups, and their conflict would converge here? A thousand questions flooded Sariel's mind, but one stood out above all else.

*What will I do when Azael comes?*

\*   \*   \*   \*

"Father!"

Enoch had already gone a quarter of the way down the dock when his eldest son arrived, grabbing him by both arms.

"Father! It's the Myndarym. They've come ... just like you said they would."

Enoch laid his own hands on Methu's shoulders, with a much gentler grip than he was being subjected to. "Methu, listen to me."

"This is it ... isn't it?" Methu continued. "This is the moment you foretold, and no one believed you!"

"That doesn't matter now," Enoch replied calmly. "Listen to me. You have to get your family to safety. Bring them to the center of the city and find somewhere for them to hide. Can you do that?"

"They just laughed at you. And I was so embarrassed," he said.

"METHU!" Enoch shouted. The sudden rise in volume seemed to shake his son from his thoughts. "Are you even listening to me?"

Methu's eyebrows lowered and his excitement disappeared. "I am now."

"Good. Is there a place that your family can hide? Somewhere close to the center of the city?"

Methu thought for a moment. "Uh ... yes. The storehouse! Under the ground."

"Alright. I want you to find all of them and move them into the storehouse. Can you do that?"

"Yes, but—"

"No. There's no time for anything else right now. Just get them to safety first, and then find Yered. Tell him that everyone in the city needs to move away from the walls. The women and children need to be hidden, and the men should gather at the Elder's Circle to await my instructions. Do you understand what I'm telling you?"

"Yes."

"Good. Now go. I'll find you after I speak with the Myndarym."

"Father?"

"What?"

"I'm sorry I ever doubted you."

Enoch smiled. It was the apology he'd been waiting to hear for almost three hundred years, and now there was hardly enough time to acknowledge it. "Just get your family to safety. That's all that matters."

\* \* \* \*

The afternoon sun was low in the sky on Sariel's right as he walked through the tall grass. Behind him, the walls of Sedekiyr were topped with the heads of curious and fearful citizens. Before him, all along the horizon, thousands of creatures stirred. At this distance, they were an indistinguishable mass, with the exception of some whose shapes looked like the Nephiyl creatures Sariel had fought so long ago.

The wolf, who had been alone in the middle of the field, was now being joined by a large feline, three humans, a bird of prey, and one Myndar in angelic form. As he neared, Sariel began to recognize them, as well as the disappointment on their faces. The wolf was indeed Ananel. The feline was Jomjael. Kokabiel, Satarel, and Baraquijal were in their human forms. Zaquel, in her angelic body, stood equal in height to Fyarikel's avian form.

"What are you doing here, Sariel?" Ananel's voice was deep, with growling undertones.

"That's a better question for you," he replied, finally coming to a stop in front of the group.

"We're being pursued by Azael's armies. Were you chased here as well?"

"No. I came voluntarily, to protect the citizens of Sedekiyr."

Ananel's expressive eyebrows suddenly became lopsided. "They have nothing to fear from us. We just came to speak with Enoch. Where is he?"

"That's him," Fyarikel said, looking over Sariel's shoulder. "He's just exiting the gate."

Zaquel shielded her eyes from the afternoon sun and gazed northward to the city. Her angelic form gave her an equally high vantage, though her eyes couldn't compete with Fyarikel's.

"What do you want with Enoch?" Sariel asked.

"That doesn't concern you," Kokabiel shot back.

"It most certainly does."

"Why? Are you his protector also?" Kokabiel asked.

Ananel stepped between the two, blocking their sight of one another with his massive canine body. "We want him to speak with the Holy One and ask for our protection."

"Protection from what you brought upon yourselves?" Sariel asked. "He turned on you, didn't he? You brought Azael into your Council thinking you could win him over, and he turned on you."

"We had no choice!" Satarel argued.

Sariel shook his head. "You underestimated him. You thought of him as an ally, while he used you to make his kingdom strong. I even warned you about him, but you wouldn't listen." This last statement was aimed at Fyarikel, who had been present in Senvidar during Sariel's visit.

"What were we supposed to do … fight him?" the raptor said.

"Yes," Sariel replied. "And I would have joined you."

"Suicide," Fyarikel concluded, turning his feathered head away as if he would not accept any more discussion on the matter.

"You tried fighting him," Baraquijal pointed out. "And we heard how that turned out. I'm surprised to see you here; I was told you were killed."

Sariel ignored the implied question and turned to Ananel. "So Azael is leading an army from the south?"

"Not exactly. The Council collectively decided to send out each member to establish separate kingdoms, using Nephiyl soldiers from Khelrusa as security."

"To protect against us rebellious objectors?" Sariel guessed. "And I assume they turned on their Myndar masters?"

"Yes."

"Then how did you end up involved in this?" Sariel wondered. "You weren't part of the Council."

Ananel exhaled through his snout. "My pack helped Kokabiel and his children escape. We assumed the conflict was no bigger than that … until we crossed paths with Jomjael."

The large feline simply nodded.

"The Nephiylim in Satarel's land attacked animal and Myndar alike," Ananel continued. "It seemed that Azael's war was not just meant for Council members, but all Myndarym."

"That was our assessment, as well," Zaquel admitted. "The winged Nephiylim came directly for Fyarikel. When Baraquijal and I met up with him, he was already fleeing for his life."

"And not just us," Baraquijal pointed out. "He wants our children dead as well. He means to cleanse this world of any trace of our influence."

"This was obviously a coordinated attack," Sariel observed. "How did any of you manage to escape?"

Everyone looked to Baraquijal.

The man, who looked like one of the Kahyin with his dark skin and hair, suddenly looked apologetic. "Uh … well. Some of us were fortunate enough to retain just a fraction of who we used to be. Just as Kokabiel still has his ability to shape himself, I ... have a limited connection to the Eternal Realm."

Sariel nodded. "You saw it coming?"

"Yes. I went to Fyarikel and asked him to warn everyone he could. These were the only ones he reached before his own children were attacked."

Sariel looked up to the sky in frustration. It had played out just as he feared. "I tried to tell them. Azael is a soldier. I know how he thinks. He will never forget Mudena Del-Edha."

Ananel lowered his head. "That is why we need to speak with Enoch. Only the Holy One can save us now.

Sariel turned and looked back over his shoulder. Enoch was now well across the field and approaching the group, just out of earshot. "You can ask him yourself, but I don't believe you'll get the answer you seek. The outcome of this conflict has already been shown to him."

"What do you mean?" Ananel asked. "Has the Holy One spoken to him already?"

Sariel held up his hands, leaving that matter for Enoch. "I don't think you can escape the consequences of your actions. And unfortunately, the people of Sedekiyr will suffer for them also."

Ananel's eyebrows lowered into a scowl, but he didn't pursue his ignored question. He waited in silence for the prophet.

\* \* \* \*

Of all the scenarios that Enoch had considered over the years, one that involved him and Sariel being in Sedekiyr seemed the least likely to occur. Still, he had considered it, and even remembered worrying about what he would say to the Myndarym when they arrived. He hadn't come to any conclusions, but certainly thought he would be more nervous than he was right now. With a supernatural confidence that obviously came from the Holy One, Enoch approached the group of Myndarym in their various forms and came to a stop beside Sariel.

"Enoch," Ananel said, lowering his head in a show of respect.

"It has been many years, my friend. I wish we were reuniting under different circumstances."

The wolf nodded. "So it is true ... what Sariel tells us? The Holy One has shown you how this will turn out?"

"Two hundred and ninety-four years ago, the Holy One gave me a vision. I saw the Wandering Stars of heaven fleeing a terrible enemy. You were surrounded, and there was a great battle."

"We are indeed fleeing a terrible enemy," Ananel replied. "Is there no possibility of our escaping?"

"All I know is what I saw."

"Do we win this battle?" asked Satarel.

Enoch turned to the angel in human form and answered with as much compassion as was in him. "Such things are hard to discern. I only know that there was death on both sides."

"Enoch," Ananel pleaded. "I don't believe we can win without the help of the Holy One. Will you go before Him, as you did in Senvidar so long ago? Will you ask Him to help us?"

Enoch stared deep into the large, golden eyes of his old friend. "Of all the trials that I faced during that time, there were a few moments that I remember with fondness. I enjoyed our discussions during my time in your city. And the last time I went before the Holy One was something that I will never forget for as long as I live."

Something in Ananel's expression changed, as though he knew the answer that was coming.

"Believe me when I say that I truly wish I could help you. But the Holy One has already spoken on this matter."

"Our children are being slaughtered before our eyes, and you won't even try?" Zaquel asked.

"The judgments of the Holy One are true and just. He did not cause this to happen, but He knew in advance what the fruit of your disobedience would be, and He showed this to me. Do you not remember the message I delivered to you so many years ago, how your children would destroy each other before your eyes and by your hands?"

"Perhaps He could restore our *shaping* ability ... then we could at least defend ourselves?" Baraquijal suggested. "Surely He wouldn't keep us from that possibility."

Enoch shook his head. "You have forgotten what I told you on the shores of the Great Waters. Some of you were there when I spoke His words. You abandoned Him. You sought to live apart from Him, and now you are on your own. Is it not the response of a loving father to give his children what they so desperately desire?"

"Not if He knew it would end like this," Zaquel argued.

"He did know. And you also knew that disobeying Him would only lead to pain. And yet you chose to come here anyway. You made your decision. I'm sorry, but this is your judgment ... and it is of your own making." Enoch didn't wait for a reply. He turned and began walking back toward Sedekiyr.

"Enoch. Please!"

It was Ananel's voice, and it brought Enoch to a stop. He turned back and looked again at his old friend. "I will always remember when you saved me from those creatures to which the Kahyin made their sacrifices. If it were within my power to do the same for you ... I would. But the Holy One has spoken. I'm sorry."

\* \* \* \*

Enoch had spoken with such conviction and compassion that Sariel had to wonder—not for the first time—if the judgment applied to himself as well. He was one of the Myndarym, and he had also abandoned the Eternal Realm. But he didn't think of it as abandoning the Holy One. He hoped it was possible that the will of the Holy One was broad enough to encompass what he was doing, which only led to the obvious question.

*What* am *I doing here?*

When his attention returned to the other Myndarym, he found looks of despair and a few tears. He hated to say anything more, but there was another matter that needed to be addressed. "The citizens of Sedekiyr are frightened by your presence. When you leave, would you be so kind as to give the city a wide berth?"

Ananel didn't reply. His eyes looked dead. Then he turned and began walking south toward his children, presumably somewhere among the creatures amassed along the horizon. The rest of the Myndarym followed him in silence.

Sariel turned back toward Sedekiyr and ran to catch up to Enoch. As soon as he pulled alongside his friend, he asked the question that was at the forefront of his mind. "Where do I fit into this judgment?"

"We've talked about this before," Enoch replied. "I don't know such things. I saw the embers and the dark poison coming at each other. I saw Sedekiyr in flames. Then I saw the mountains. The only thing I know for sure is that my father's people aren't safe here."

"You didn't mention that part to the Myndarym."

"No, I didn't. But the words of the Holy One are true, so that part of the vision will come to pass whether or not the Myndarym know about it."

Sariel nodded. A moment of silence passed as he watched the blades of grass bend and part before his legs with each step. "When we first met in Senvidar, you told me that you had seen me before. That the Holy One had showed you."

"Yes."

"Was it a vision?"

"I think so, but I was very young. I don't really remember."

"You remembered enough to know that you had seen me before."

"Yes," Enoch admitted.

"Do you remember—?"

"You still want to know what He thinks of you," Enoch interrupted.

Sariel waited in silence for the answer.

"I suppose it is time to share it with you. I don't remember the vision, specifically. But I do remember being left with the impression that you were important. Critical, somehow."

Sariel felt excitement rising within him, but he kept it hidden as Enoch continued.

"These impressions are difficult because they can be misleading. I can see that you would also like to know whether or not you will survive Sedekiyr's destruction. I don't have the answer. It seems that the Holy One does have a plan for you, but that purpose could just be to defend this city to your dying breath. I ... wish I knew more."

Sariel felt his hopes dashed, like an overeager child who is suddenly confronted by reality. All he could think to say was, "Thank you for your honesty."

# 33

"What are we supposed to do now?"

It was Fyarikel's voice from above, and the question wasn't directed at anyone in particular. But Ananel had already been going over their options. He looked back over his shoulder at Baraquijal. "What do you think? Can you tell where our enemies are?"

The angel in human form shook his head. "Hyrren and Imikal are still to the south of us, but even their presence is ... vague. I don't sense the same buildup of activity from the Eternal Realm as I did when we were first attacked."

Ananel lifted his snout to the breeze, but he could only smell the children of the Myndarym gathered in the fields to the south.

"It occurred to me that Hyrren and Imikal were steering us toward each other," Satarel observed.

"What's your point?" Zaquel asked.

"Well, if that is true, there must be some purpose in it."

"A purpose that doesn't end with our safety, I can assure you," Kokabiel added.

Ananel stopped walking and turned around to face the others who were following at a close distance. "You're right. They want to get us all in the same place to make their objective easier."

"Which means we need to do the opposite and split up," Satarel added. "Make them divide their forces."

"Obviously, we can't go south," said Jomjael, who was usually quiet during most discussions.

Ananel bared his teeth as he considered a new strategy. "These plains are bordered on the west by the Unmoving Waters, and to the east by the mountains of Nagah. If we move quickly to the north, beyond these barriers, the land will open up in many directions. We could each go our own way and force them to choose or split up."

"What if they decide to concentrate on one of us?" Baraquijal wondered.

"My children will keep watch from above," Fyarikel assured him. "If the Nephiylim don't split up, they will have our talons to contend with."

"Why do you even travel with us?" Zaquel asked. "You could fly away at any time."

Fyarikel glanced at Baraquijal before answering. "I feel responsible for what has happened. And I am no coward. My people will defend you, whatever the cost."

"So it is decided, then?" Ananel asked.

The other Myndarym nodded their acceptance of the new plan.

"Then we should leave immediately," he replied, noting how quickly the sun was slipping toward the horizon.

\* \* \* \*

INSIDE SEDEKIYR

The sky above was the darkest of blues, fading to a dusty orange on the western horizon. Only a few citizens could be seen, rushing from one place to another with terror on their faces. Otherwise, the streets of the city were bare and unusually quiet. Methu had obviously relayed the instructions. It was part of the plan that Sariel had worked out with Enoch so long ago, but it was still discomforting to see it in action. As they neared the northern end of the city, the tall and elaborate structure of the Elder's Circle loomed over them. Sariel had never seen it in the early days, before the roof had been erected over it, but Enoch described it as nothing more than a circular patch of bare earth outside of the city limits where the elders would meet at each annual gathering. It was hard to imagine it as such, now that its roof was nearly as high as the walls of the city that had grown around it.

As soon as they left the open air for the torch-lit circle, Sariel could tell that something was wrong. The gathering of able-bodied men was not even close to being as large as it should have been. Before Sariel could turn his observation into words, Methu came out of the crowd and ran toward them.

"They wouldn't listen!"

"Where are the rest of the men?" Enoch asked.

Methu came to a stop in front of them, shaking his head. "They came here, like you said. But then they grew nervous while they waited for you. Some of the men started arguing that they should do something. They asked why they needed to wait for you. I told them to just be patient, but—"

"Methu, where did they go? Where's Yered?"

"He left."

"What do you mean, he left?"

"He took most of the men and left for El-Betakh."

Sariel grabbed Enoch by the shoulder. "That coward is going to leave a trail all the way to your city! We have to go after them."

"No," Enoch replied.

"They'll lead the enemy right to your family."

"No!" Enoch repeated.

His level of conviction was unusual to Sariel, who knew the man to be indecisive at times.

"The Holy One said that the mountains would be safe, so El-Betakh cannot be in any danger. We're staying here."

Sariel looked his friend in the eyes and was at once amazed by the man's faith and ashamed by his own lack of it. But as quickly as the emotion came over him, it also dissipated. He had seen countless battles go the opposite direction from what he had confidently planned for. The Holy One had never actually promised a specific outcome to any of the battles Sariel had fought, but the Amatru marched to the orders of their Ad-Rada, who was one and the same. The outcomes were implied, and Sariel had seen too many angels die to continue making assumptions.

But how could he hope, in one conversation, to convince his friend of something that had taken ages for himself to accept?

\* \* \* \*

"Is your family safe?" Enoch asked.

"Yes," Methu answered. "Lemek and my older sons are here, but Jurishel and the others are hidden."

"Good. And the rest of the families?" he asked.

"In other storehouses around the city."

Enoch grinned. "I'm glad you did not go with Yered."

"I didn't want to leave you ... again."

Enoch gently squeezed his son's arm before walking toward the crowd, heading for the center of the building. The gathering of men parted before him and the murmur of conversation grew silent. A few paces away, under the center of the conical roof, was the stone where Grandfather Mahalal-el would sit and dispense his wisdom. Yered's wooden stump was also there on the right-hand side. The ground was no longer bare, but covered in a short and soft grass, and Enoch briefly pictured himself sitting on the ground at their feet. It would have been better than sitting on dirt as he used to do. But now the very idea of sitting before his father and grandfather seemed absurd. Their wisdom was tainted. Though Enoch carried on this tradition among his own people in El-Betakh, he did so as if he were the firstfather, with no one before him.

Enoch walked into the circle and climbed Mahalal-el's stone, standing on it to be visible to the whole crowd. There were some gasps of surprise at this show of disrespect, but Enoch ignored them and cleared his throat.

"Two hundred and ninety-four years ago, the Holy One showed me a vision of Sedekiyr's destruction and where my people could go for safety. I sat in this very circle during the gathering of elders, and I told my father what I had seen. I didn't know when it would happen, but I knew it would because the words of the Holy One are true. I told Grandfather Mahalal-el that we needed to move the city to the mountains of Nagah."

Enoch stopped talking for a moment to let them consider the significance of his words. And the silence from the crowd indicated that they were doing just that.

"They laughed at me. They ridiculed me. They told me to take my strange stories and leave the city. So I did as I was told. I wonder if any of you remember that day. Were you standing there on the edge of the fields, mocking me? Glad to be rid of me?"

The Elder's Circle was so quiet now that Enoch could hear the chirping of a grasshopper nearby.

"The time of Sedekiyr's judgment has come, and it cannot be escaped."

"Surely the Holy One would not judge you," came a voice from the back. "What will He do to save you?"

Enoch stood on his toes and looked into the crowd to find the man who had asked the question, but there were too many people. "I do not know if I *will* be saved."

"Can we go to El-Betakh now?" asked another man.

"No. It is too late. The safety of El-Betakh is for those who obeyed the voice of the Holy One, not those who are now afraid for their lives."

"What about Yered?"

"Yes. What about my father?" Enoch replied. "He has run away like a coward. He would not listen to the Holy One before, and now he runs for safety where there is none to be had."

"If we can't leave, then what should we do?"

Enoch left the question unanswered for several long seconds to make sure that everyone was listening. As he did so, he was filled with compassion for those gathered. Despite all the ways that these people had mistreated him during his lifetime, even as a child, he couldn't help but feel sorry for what was going to happen. "Go find your wives and your children. Tell them the things that I've said. Then quiet yourselves and listen for the voice of the Holy One. That is what I'm going to do."

\* \* \* \*

THE PLAINS EAST OF SEDEKIYR

The light of the moon was struggling to pierce the mist that had grown dense throughout the afternoon and evening. Without a visual reference point, Yered kept the gurgle of the slow-moving river on his left. He and the men of Sedekiyr, the thousands who had the courage to do something about their predicament, were making good time despite the difficulty of moving through the tall grass without the benefit of sunlight. The plains became the domain of all manner of creatures when the sun went down. It seemed that every few minutes, Yered would hear a rustling of the grass as something scurried away, or the cry of an animal warning its friends that humans were coming. As long as they didn't run into any large reptiles, the group would be safe. And when the sun came up again, they would all be far enough to the east that the mountains of Nagah would be visible ... if the mist allowed it.

A splash of water drew Yered's attention to the left. He stopped walking and listened, straining his ears.

"Fish jumping?" whispered Neshil, Yered's secondborn son.

Yered held a finger to his lips while the men behind him followed his example and came to a stop. There were still too many footsteps through the grass to hear clearly, and Yered waved his hands violently to get everyone around him to stop walking. Slowly, the nearest citizens gathered around their elder as the ones at the rear of the procession eventually caught up to the others.

Several minutes had passed, and the only sound was the steady gurgle of the river.

"Do you think it was one of the reptiles?" asked Neshil.

"Perhaps a herd," Yered replied. Then he spoke louder so that the other men around him could hear. "Everyone needs to wait for my signal. And then we will yell as one. Pass the word."

A murmur of whispered conversation passed westward through the group, taking another few minutes before everyone was informed of the plan. When the murmur faded to silence, Yered nodded to Neshil and turned northeast where he thought the splash had come from. He couldn't see anything through the dense fog, but it didn't matter. When the voices of thousands of men were lifted into a single shout, whatever creatures roamed the plains would scatter in fear.

Yered inhaled a deep breath and opened his mouth, but a sharp and sudden pain in his stomach caused his plans to falter. He winced and clutched for his gut, his hand unexpectedly closing around the shaft of a pole sticking out of his body. He stared at it for several seconds, failing to comprehend what he was looking at. Only when he followed the soft moonlight along the wooden pole did he realize that something was at the other end of it. A massive face, vaguely human but extremely large, stared at him through the grass to the east. Gigantic hands were holding the pole that Yered now realized was a spear.

The grotesque face grinned.

The hands tightened.

Powerful arms lifted.

Yered rose unwillingly into the air, screaming now as his abdomen exploded with pain.

First dozens, then hundreds, then thousands of voices joined the chorus. But as Yered craned his neck to look back upon his group, he could see that Neshil and many others had also been impaled upon the ends of spears. They were not yelling to scare away a herd of reptiles; they were screaming and writhing in pain as their bodies were also lifted from the earth.

Yered looked down in horror at the creature beneath him, watching his own blood flow like a river down the shaft of the spear and over the giant's muscled arms. The disgusting face was contorted into a wicked smile now. And as Yered's vision began to blur, death gathering as thick as the fog, he remembered the strange stories told by his son. The unbelievable things that Enoch had said—ridiculous things that he had dismissed as lies—didn't seem so ridiculous now.

The giant turned his head and shook his spear, causing Yered's body to dance on the end of it. "Tonight, we feast on human flesh once again!"[6]

Thousands of shouts rose in response. The cheering of the giants quickly overwhelmed the pitiful cries from the men of Sedekiyr. Yered wished he could weep for his people, but he was too weak for tears. As the last drops of life spilled out of his earthly body, all he could do was look at the gathered army of giants and think how much they now appeared like a flood of poison about to sweep over the earth and devour everything in its path.

\* \* \* \*

THE PLAINS NORTH OF SEDEKIYR

Ananel noticed the strange scent only a moment before Fyarikel's screech cut through the air. The giant raptor dove toward the earth in front of him, coming to a rapid landing amidst a flurry of wings and mist.

"Friend or enemy?" Ananel called out as he slowed to a stop. He'd been moving as fast as he could without leaving the two-legged children behind. But even with Satarel on his back, Ananel was nowhere near the limit of his strength or speed.

"Friend," Fyarikel replied. "Myndarym and others, traveling together. They are coming this way."

Fyarikel and his kind had been circling above the group of refugees, keeping a watch above the nighttime fog. Their keen eyes could see far beyond anyone else's, so if they believed the creatures to the north were friends, Ananel had to trust them. But the stench in his nostrils argued with this assessment.

"If it's another group like us ..." Satarel said before trailing off.

"Then they are fleeing another army to the north," Ananel replied, finishing the statement.

"What's happening?" yelled Kokabiel, his deep voice booming from inside his massive, reptilian throat as he passed through the air above and circled back to land.

"There are other Myndarym ahead," Ananel yelled his reply.

"Which way are they going?" Jomjael asked, coming to a stop beside Ananel.

"They are approaching," Fyarikel answered.

Baraquijal slid down off Jomjael's back, and Satarel also climbed to the ground.

Zaquel was the last to reach the gathering group, even though her two-legged form was one of the largest present. "Is there another army behind them?"

No one replied, as the answer seemed obvious.

Ananel's pack, always at the front of the group, began arriving where the Myndarym were gathered. Yelps of confusion sounded across the plains, and Ananel answered with a bark of his own.

"Then we're trapped," Zaquel said.

"We have no choice but to fight now," Satarel replied.

"How?" Baraquijal added. "What do we know of warfare?"

"Nothing," Kokabiel replied. "But Sariel does."

"Yes, we'll have to go back to Sedekiyr and make our stand there," Zaquel concluded.

Ananel exhaled in defeat. He had really believed that freedom was within their grasp. Now it had been yanked away like some cruel trick. The message of Enoch, it seemed, would not be proven wrong. He should have known, after all the time he'd spent with the prophet. But even harder to accept were the words of Sariel that still echoed in his ears.

*... the people of Sedekiyr will suffer.*

As Ananel considered the coming war, now inevitable in his mind, the sound of a multitude rose inside his sensitive ears—millions of footsteps in the grass, those of his own group behind and another approaching from before him. The mist to the north began swimming with movement. Dark shapes appeared inside the gray, transitioning from ethereal wisps into solid outlines.

Arakiba was the first recognizable face. His chosen form was supposed to look like one of the Marotru, and when his Nephiyl children came out of the fog behind him, they indeed looked like an army of demons. Though most of the other Myndarym wouldn't be able to detect it, Ananel thought Arakiba's children also smelled like Marotru.

Seconds later, Turel and Danel came running out of the fog, and Rameel dropped to the earth in front of them, his leathery wings retracting around him like a cloak.

# 34

It had been a restless night for Methu, down in the tunnels of the storehouse with his family. The questions came rapidly, and the answers brought tears. They tried listening for the voice of the Holy One, but silence eventually gave way to conversations that lasted well into the early morning hours. Everyone had trouble sleeping, but in the end, they succumbed to exhaustion. All except Methu, who watched each member of his family grow still and quiet until he was the only one left awake.

The hours dragged on and Methu only had his thoughts to keep him company. He tried hard to remember all the things his father had told him during his childhood. He remembered how innocent he used to be and how that innocence had died when Enoch left to speak with the firstfather. He thought about his father's words at the Elder's Circle.

*I wonder if any of you remember that day. Were you standing there on the edge of the fields, mocking me? Glad to be rid of me?*

Methu was ashamed to admit that he was one of those people. He had watched his father go and he remembered wishing that Enoch would never come back, despite the pain of that leaving. These were the kind of thoughts that ran through his mind all night until he couldn't take it any longer. Methu finally rose, as quietly as he could, and stepped carefully over the sleeping forms of his wife and children. He tiptoed along the tunnel, making his way back to the main section of the storehouse as he tried not to wake the hundreds of other families hiding there as well.

A ladder led upward from the main chamber to the first floor of the building where Methu exited into the cool, moist air of dawn. The sky was still mostly dark and Methu shivered as he wandered through the empty city, finally stopping when he arrived at the southern gate.

Sariel was standing in one of the lookout towers above the city wall. Enoch wasn't with him. It had been a year since the last time Methu was alone with Sariel. Even during his trips to El-Betakh, Sariel was either out foraging or surrounded by other people. But Methu had listened to as much silence as he could possibly stand, so he began climbing.

When Methu reached the lookout tower, Sariel didn't even turn his head. He just stared out at the bank of moisture drifting across the southern horizon. The sky was now a pale gray color, and the green fields of grass looked lush by comparison.

Methu quietly walked to the railing and leaned his elbows on it. He allowed a few seconds of silence to pass before he opened his mouth, but then he realized what Sariel had been staring at. A break in the fog allowed him to see far into the distance, where something dark stood like the wall of another city. But it was moving.

"Have the Myndarym returned?"

"No."

Methu squinted. "What is that?"

"The armies of the Nephiylim. You can't see it now because of the mist, but their ranks stretch east and west as far as your eyes will allow."

"Nephiylim. Those are the ... children of the angels?"

"Yes," Sariel answered without taking his eyes off the horizon.

"What are they doing?"

"Waiting."

Methu nodded, watching the bank of fog that had melded into itself again to obscure the fields. Several seconds passed before he realized how incomplete Sariel's answer had been. "Waiting for what?"

"I would guess that they're waiting for the rest of their forces to the north."

"But ... isn't that where the Myndarym went?"

"Yes."

Now Methu realized what was happening. He remembered what his mother had told him about the vision of Sedekiyr's destruction, and now he understood the significance of the embers and the dark flood that chased them. Sedekiyr was where the two would clash. "I'm not going to just stand here and let them kill my family."

Sariel squinted, but didn't reply.

"I want to fight back."

Now Sariel turned his head, a serious expression on his face. "A human is no match for a Nephiyl."

"I don't care. I'll fight anyway."

Sariel's face softened into a smile. "You have the spirit of a warrior."

"Will you help us?"

"Us?" Sariel questioned.

"The other men here are not cowards like Grandfather Yered. They will fight."

"Good. Of course I'll help you. I've already been thinking of a plan."

Methu stood back from the railing and looked again at the horizon, but there was nothing to see. "Alright ... what do we do?"

"Do you still have the bow I gave you?"

"Yes."

Sariel stood up from the railing and crossed his arms. "Wake the other men and have them assemble at the Elders' Circle. And tell them to bring whatever tools are left that might work as weapons."

"Oh, we have plenty. Everything you brought from El-Betakh."

Sariel's eyebrows shot upward. "I assumed Yered took them when he left."

"No. The bows and spears are still in the storehouses where we left them."

Sariel put a hand on his chin and began stroking his beard. "Interesting ..."

Shouts of alarm began sounding throughout the city. Methu looked northward across thousands and thousands of thatched roofs, straining to discern any words among the noise.

"Come," Sariel said. "It sounds like your fellow warriors are already awake."

"What's happening?"

Sariel smiled. "Reinforcements have arrived."

* * * *

Sariel and Methu found Enoch just outside of the northern gate, beside the docks. The Myndarym and their children had indeed returned, but there were more of them this time. Sariel invited Enoch to come along and meet them, but he declined.

"I've said all I need to say."

Sariel didn't reply and simply patted his friend on the shoulder before addressing his son. "Methu. Lock the storehouses, and tell the men to be ready to escort our visitors inside. With a group this large, we'll need to spread them out."

Without waiting for a reply, Sariel turned and headed out into the northern fields. As before, the Myndarym stood together a few hundred paces away from the city, while their children waited far behind them.

"There is another army to the north," Ananel said when Sariel was close enough for conversation. "We're trapped, and we need your help."

Sariel came to a stop in front of the wolf and looked around at his companions. Kokabiel, Jomjael, Satarel, Baraquijal, Fyarikel, and Zaquel were there. Some of them didn't look pleased to have come back to Sedekiyr. The rest of the group was comprised of Arakiba, Rameel, Turel, Danel, Armaros, and Ezekiyel.

Now that Enoch's words were on the verge of coming true, the work of the prophet was done. Sariel could feel that the weight of responsibility had shifted to his own shoulders, and there was no point in talking about judgment any longer. The many events that had to occur to bring about this moment had already taken place. All that was left to do was to survive it, which meant that this had become a military task. Armies were approaching from all directions. Sedekiyr was the battlefield. It had walls and resources that could be used for defense. Each of the Myndarym—whether in human, angelic, or animal form—represented a segment of the multitude that was now gathered in the fields to the north. A variety of forms. A variety of abilities.

Sariel was no longer seeing the argumentative, deceived fools of his past. He was seeing the resources at his disposal. Teeth. Claws. Wings.

"Bring your children inside the city. When the gates are closed, we'll discuss our defensive plan."

\* \* \* \*

When Methu left to give instructions to the men of Sedekiyr, Enoch went inside and climbed up into the lookout tower. The moisture that had gathered throughout the night began dissipating with the rising sun. Never before had Enoch seen the fields of Sedekiyr alive with so much activity. As far to the north as he could see, the children of the Myndarym covered the plains. They seemed as numerous as the blades of grass which they trampled along their way. If these were the embers, Enoch shuddered to think of how the poisonous flood would appear.

*Holy One, I beg You to protect us. Though we do not deserve it, I ask for mercy.*

# 35

"It won't work," Danel argued.

Sariel and the Myndarym were discussing the defense plan beneath the roof of the Elder's Circle. He had expected them to be grateful for his experience and more accepting of his advice, now that the other half of Azael's armies had arrived from the north and were converging with the southern armies along the eastern front. Sedekiyr was almost surrounded, and it was plain to see that the Myndarym lacked confidence in the outcome of the impending battle.

"I understand your hesitation—" Sariel began before he was interrupted again.

"Hesitation?" It was Turel this time. "I think you underestimate our aversion to this plan, as well as overestimating our position in this conflict."

Ananel tried to come to Sariel's defense, but the arguing only got louder.

Sariel held up his hand. "This is not accomplishing anything."

No one seemed to hear him.

"SILENCE!"

The Myndarym finally took notice and stopped talking.

Sariel breathed deeply and continued with a quieter tone. "How dare you talk of war as if you know something of it? You don't. If anyone is overestimating our position here, it is you. This is not a war we can win. If you were holding onto that hope, you can let it die now."

The group seemed to be listening.

"You go on and on, while the enemy gathers outside. Soon you will learn that war is not about what *could be*, but what *is*. When the Nephiylim come charging at our walls, you will understand that the best we can do is to use the one advantage we have. Their forces will grow denser and slower when they reach the walls. If you must hope in something, hope that we can hold out long enough and kill enough of them to weaken their resolve. Hope that one segment of their lines falters more than another—that we might break through and escape. But do not withhold your commitment until you hear a plan that leads to victory. There is no such thing. And if that reality causes you to shrink back from this fight, then you will finally understand what separates warriors from everyone else."

The group was silent, and those who had been arguing with the plan were now looking at the ground.

Ananel locked eyes with Sariel and nodded.

"Now, as I was saying," Sariel continued, "the biggest obstacle for their ground forces is the wall around our perimeter. That will be the focus of their first attack, which will come from the sky. That's why we'll need Fyarikel and Rameel to lead the air defense. After we're done here, I'll go over Iryllur tactics with your—"

"Perhaps there is another way," Ezekiyel interrupted. He rarely spoke, so despite his quiet tone, all of the other Myndarym turned their attention to him. He looked up from the ground and stared at Baraquijal.

"What?"

"Your connection to the Eternal Realm is stronger than you're comfortable admitting."

Baraquijal looked nervously around.

"What is he talking about?" Danel asked.

Ezekiyel grinned. "I know what you were doing for Semjaza. Perhaps there are others who would come to our aid?"

"No. The cost is too great."

"What are you talking about?" Danel repeated, her voice now approaching a shout.

"Yes. What *is* he talking about?" Sariel asked.

Baraquijal's shoulders slumped. "Before we came to this realm, I served with the Viytur on an ... unconventional mission. They wanted to infiltrate the Marotru intelligence organization."

"What?" Jomjael snarled.

Baraquijal's eyes were deep with remorse. "I made a few contacts among them by pretending to be a traitor."

"You befriended demons?" Ananel asked.

"No. Not befriended. It was a lie. I was using them. When the opportunity to come into this realm presented itself, I took it. I couldn't wait to escape my responsibilities. But Semjaza knew about the work I'd been doing. When we got here, he tasked me with reestablishing my contacts."

Sariel could hardly believe what he was hearing.

The range of emotions on the faces of the Myndarym was varied, but all were pronounced except for Ezekiyel's. He just grinned and crossed his arms.

"Semjaza kept pushing me and pushing me. He was so desperate to insulate himself from the Amatru that he was willing to accept help from anywhere."

"I can't listen to this," Ananel said. The skin of his upper lip was wrinkled, revealing his massive teeth. He turned and began walking away from the group.

"He's right," Jomjael added. "No matter what threat lies outside these walls, I refuse to align myself with the Marotru in any way."

"Do you really think they would help us?" Danel asked.

Jomjael growled low in his throat as he turned and walked away from the group.

Fyarikel's head shook and swiveled to the side in what Sariel could only assume was the raptor's equivalent of disgust. The feathered Myndar stepped awkwardly away from the group, waddling until he had gained enough distance to use his wings. Then he also left in a flurry of wings and waving grass.

Sariel looked hard at the remaining Myndarym. "When you're ready to discuss a realistic strategy, you can find me working with the men of Sedekiyr, helping them prepare to defend their city and their families."

Sariel turned and walked out from under the roof of the Elder's Circle. In contrast to the Myndarym, who were still looking for a solution that would give them complete victory, their children were working with the men of Sedekiyr to prepare for the imminent attack. As Sariel had instructed, the walls and storehouses had been left alone. All other structures were being torn down and their materials used to either reinforce the wall or be made into weapons. Support poles became spears, their ends sharpened and hardened by fire. The thatch that covered roofs was being wrapped around the ends of smaller poles—torches that would be carried through the skies and dropped onto the plains to set the grass on fire, burning Azael's armies before they even reached the city.

"Sariel," Methu called, sprinting toward him from a nearby street.

Sariel held up his hand in acknowledgment.

"The armies are connected on the west side now. We're completely surrounded." He had just come to a stop in front of Sariel, and his breathless words were barely above a whisper.

"Show me."

\* \* \* \*

THE PLAINS NORTH OF SEDEKIYR

The afternoon sun beat down upon the plains, keeping the mist at bay. The air was warm, but fires were burning nevertheless, being tended throughout the ranks to roast the meat that Yarut had so generously provided. His army was camped to the east, and the night watch had apparently stumbled upon a large group of humans trying to escape Sedekiyr. Hyrren tore the last bite of flesh from the thigh bone and tossed the human remains into the grass on his left.

Savoring the last of his meal, he wiped his hands on the sides of his loincloth and continued moving along the front lines of the northern army. A few paces ahead, he could see his brothers and the other generals standing in a group, while Azael, Parnudel, and Rikoathel waited beside them.

"Welcome," Imikal shouted, stepping away from the group to embrace his older brother. Vengsul was next. His face was beaming as he spread his arms wide. The other siblings lined up behind him to follow his example. When the reunion was finished, Hyrren walked toward Azael and knelt before him. "My king, I have waited many cycles for this moment."

"Welcome, Hyrren. Indeed, these are exciting times. And we have you to thank for that."

Hyrren's brothers cheered.

Azael smiled and waited patiently for the applause to die down. "Rise and look upon our enemies."

Hyrren stood and turned, joining the other generals and Iryllurym as they faced south toward the human city with wooden walls. It was impossible not to laugh at the pathetic sight.

"Yes, go ahead and laugh," Azael said. "The Myndarym and their children take refuge behind a pile of sticks."

"Can we not attack now, my king?" Imikal asked.

"Not yet," Azael replied. "We will let them stare upon our millions while the sun is out. I want them to see their destruction from afar so they have time to consider the depth of their treachery and to mourn it."

Hyrren looked left and right, allowing his eyes to trace the dark boundary of their front lines that formed a perfect circle all the way around the city. He took pleasure in the knowledge that what he saw was not a single row of soldiers, spread thin, but millions of his brethren forming a deep and robust ring around the ones who had betrayed his father. The fulfillment of his vengeance was so close now he could almost taste it.

\* \* \* \*

"What are they waiting for?" Methu asked.

"Nightfall," Sariel replied. "When the sun goes down, the mist will gather. We won't be able to see them advance."

"But we already know they're out there."

"Yes. And the anticipation mixed with the fear of not being able to see them will weaken our resolve. It's a tactic used by the Marotru."

Methu leaned out over the railing and looked west, where the sun was already touching the horizon. Sariel kept his eyes focused to the north, where thin wisps of gray were starting to collect above the grass in the foreground. From what the Myndarym had told him, Azael was somewhere within that dark line of Nephiyl soldiers. Parnudel and Rikoathel were likely standing beside him, discussing the details of their attack plan. They would, no doubt, be leading the winged Nephiylim in the first assault as soon as the land forces were near the walls of the city.

"It won't be long now," Methu mumbled.

Sariel just nodded, but kept silent. As he stared at the contrasting colors between the fields of grass and the dark boundary of the Nephiyl front lines, he saw another contrast—one from his memory. A hand with tiny fingers, reaching out. Black skin, coated in blood, stark against the earthen flesh of Sheyir's inner thigh.

"Are you alright?"

Sariel closed his eyes and realized that his lids felt wet. He quickly reached up and wiped them. "Yes. We need to have Rameel and Fyarikel alert their children. It's time."

"I'll let Father know that it's time to go to the storehouse."

Sariel turned away from the railing and headed for the ladder. "He doesn't know you're going to fight, does he?"

"No. He thinks I'll be in the other storehouse with the rest of my family. And I'm not going to tell him differently."

Sariel didn't say so, but he felt bad about keeping a secret from Enoch. He knew what the child meant to his parents.

Methu's absence had been an open wound to them. But he was an adult, and a headstrong one at that. When he made up his mind to do something, there was little anyone could say to change it. Sariel just hoped that the Holy One was keeping watch over him as with his father.

When they reached the ground, Sariel and Methu headed south toward the center of the city. Enoch could usually be found wandering alone in the crop fields there, like he used to do on the outskirts of Sedekiyr. He said it was easier to speak with the Holy One away from the noise of others. And since Fyarikel's children had claimed a few of the fields as their temporary home, Sariel figured he'd walk with Methu most of the way.

But as they approached the grain crops, the sight of Rameel's dark silhouette moving through one of the fields was immediately alarming.

"What's he doing in this part of the city?" Methu asked, noting the oddity of the situation as well.

Sariel stopped walking. "That's Arakiba over there," he noted, pointing at the other shape moving toward Rameel.

"Who's that?" Methu asked, pointing.

Scanning the field, Sariel noted Zaquel coming from the opposite direction. It looked like the three of them were on a course to converge at the center of the field. "Something's not right."

"What do you mean?"

Sariel ignored the question and began looking around for something to use as a weapon. There was a damaged hut nearby. Its roof had been removed and its walls had been pushed over, but a few of the intermediate support poles were still present. "Here, help me." Sariel ran over to the abandoned hut and began pulling at the grass cords that bound the poles together. "Take that one," he yelled.

Methu grabbed the pole and slid it free. "What are we doing?"

"Your father's in trouble," Sariel grunted, removing another pole before turning around and running into the field.

\* \* \* \*

*Holy One. I ask that You would spare Methu and his family,* Enoch prayed. *His disbelief was my fault. The things that You showed me ... the things You led me through were too amazing to be real. If it required anything of me, it required more from my family. Methu was just a little boy when he saw the tribe turn on his father. Don't hold him responsible for that. It was my fault.*

The grass rustled beneath Enoch's folded legs as he shifted his weight forward. He kept his eyes closed so that his mind wouldn't be distracted by anything.

*In his heart, Methu made the decision to move his family to El-Betakh months ago. He was just waiting for me. I beg You to honor that decision. He doesn't live in disbelief anymore. He believes the things I've told him. He believes in You.*

Enoch felt a stirring in his spirit, that undefinable part of himself through which the Holy One spoke. He immediately quieted his thoughts, focusing only on the memory of being before the throne of his Creator in the White City. He imagined himself kneeling on the transparent floor with flames burning deep within, though it was cool to the touch.

*Fear not, Enoch, my faithful servant.*

Was it an answer? Was it a separate admonition? Or was Enoch imagining it altogether? He couldn't be sure.

*Your legacy will endure.*

Enoch hoped that this was real, and not just a product of his most sincere desire.

*Now open your eyes and stand. The time has come.*

*Time for what?* Enoch wondered.

*Your salvation draws nigh.*

\* \* \* \*

Young stalks of grain lashed at Sariel's legs as he trampled them. Blades of grass sliced at the underside of his arms. He held the pole above his head and ran as fast as possible. "Stop!"

he yelled, trying to distract the Myndarym from what they were about to do.

Rameel, Arakiba, and Zaquel were at the center of the field, and their body language suggested that they were preparing to attack. Enoch was visible now, standing between the Myndarym with his hands up. He must have been sitting down before. Zaquel was shouting. Rameel was holding a spear and his wings were beginning to extend.

"Don't do it!" Sariel yelled.

Zaquel turned her head, finally noticing that they were not alone.

"Leave him alone!" Sariel shouted as loud as he could. The grain was slowing him down, and his legs burned, but he kept running. "Leave him alone!"

The sky overhead suddenly bulged outward and began to ripple like water.

Sariel glanced up.

The blue expanse took on an indigo hue, then violet. Bands of colors seemed to appear out of nowhere as the air itself bent outward. Then a column of white light shot downward to the field, scattering the Myndarym backward.

Sariel covered his eyes. The intensity of the light caused a shooting pain in his head. He stumbled and almost fell, but refused to stop running. When he regained his balance and looked again, his body nearly seized up with fear and awe.

Seven Iryllur soldiers of the Amatru were crouching in a defensive posture, facing outward while surrounding Enoch with their vaepkir drawn. In the fading dusk, their illuminated bodies shone like torches, hotter and brighter than anything in the Temporal Realm. They wore full battle armor, and their weapons gleamed with the power of the Holy One's Spirit. It seemed like an eternity before Sariel realized that these angels had just *shifted* into this realm, which meant they were *Shapers* wearing Iryllur bodies. Sariel was looking at himself as he used to be—the way he had first appeared to Sheyir at the waters of Laeningar. And when this realization came, he recognized the colors in the plumage of the group's leader.

*Tarsaeel!*

"FATHER!" Methu yelled from somewhere behind.

The small figure at the center of protection, now dark by comparison, leaned to one side and looked toward Sariel and Methu.

"FATHER!" Methu yelled again, running past Sariel.

Enoch extended his hand toward his son just as an Iryllur slid an arm around his chest and lifted him off the ground. Massive wings of burning feathers extended in all directions. The Iryllurym shot into the sky in a thick column of streaking light that left stalks of grain bent low in their wake. The sky rippled and bulged, swallowing the column of light.

And Enoch was gone.[22]

The field was silent.

The sky empty.

"NOOO!" Methu screamed. He was at the edge of the bent stalks of grain, hand still extended toward the sky.

Sariel looked up in disbelief as he stumbled forward and put his arm across Methu's shoulders. He had almost forgotten about the other Myndarym when Rameel finally climbed to his feet almost a hundred paces to the south.

"What have you done?" Sariel yelled.

Zaquel and Arakiba rose slowly from where they had been thrown. None of the Myndarym appeared injured, but all of them were clearly shaken.

Sariel stared hard at each of them in turn. "Fools!" was all he could say.

"... saved us the trouble," Arakiba said under his breath.

"What?" Sariel hissed, letting go of Methu to take a couple steps forward. He still had the pole in his hand and suddenly wanted to shove it through someone's chest. "How could you possibly benefit from harming Enoch?"

"Killing him," Zaquel corrected. Her voice was cold and calculating.

"Why?"

"Because we cannot pluck out the eyes of the Holy One, or cut off His ears."

"But we could have silenced His mouth," Rameel added.

Sariel couldn't believe what he was hearing. "Do you really think you can escape His judgment by killing His prophet?"

"His judgment cannot be delivered if there is no one to speak it," Arakiba answered.

A rustling of grass made Sariel look behind him. Methu had dropped to his knees. His body was shaking with sobs, though he wasn't making any sounds. Sariel turned back to the Myndarym. "Enoch was an innocent man, and you tried to kill him!"

"You forget that it was he who took away our power to *shape*," Zaquel hissed.

"The Holy One did that. Enoch was just the messenger."

"The distinction is meaningless," Zaquel replied. "If Enoch did it once, he could have done it again."

Now Sariel realized what this was about. "You're going through with that insane idea. You think the Marotru can give you back your power?"

Zaquel turned and began walking away without another word. Arakiba did the same. Rameel walked across the circle of bent stalks and looked at Sariel as he left. "You'd better hope so, or we're all going to die."

When the Myndarym were gone, Sariel turned to find Methu on his feet again. His eyes were dry, and there was a determined look on his face. "Where did they take him?"

"The Eternal Realm."

"He's not coming back, is he?"

Sariel shook his head. "I don't think so."

Methu clenched his jaw and nodded. Then he turned and walked away.

# 36

A flash of light drew Azael's attention. He looked up from the meeting of generals and watched the walls of the human city.

"What was that?" Parnudel asked.

"I don't know." Whatever he'd just seen from the corner of his vision had occurred above the city, or possibly in the distance behind it.

Hyrren and the other generals had gone silent. The entire war council was now staring across the fields to the south. As they watched, it happened again—streaks of brilliant light flashed upward and disappeared into the sky.

"The Amatru," Rikoathel noted.

"Do you think they're coming to help the Myndarym like they did in Mudena Del-Edha?" Parnudel asked.

Azael shook his head. "There weren't many. And they left."

"My king, have the Myndarym escaped?" Hyrren asked.

Azael kept his eyes on the city and ignored the question. "All of you, return to your armies and wait for my signal."

"Yes, my king," the generals replied.

\* \* \* \*

INSIDE SEDEKIYR

Methu locked the storehouse door and paused to lay his hand upon the wooden frame. He could still hear his youngest daughter inside, crying as Jurishel tried to console her. Methu waited for the crying to subside, but after several minutes, he gave up. His chest felt as though it had been pierced by an arrow, and there was no use subjecting himself to such pain when there was nothing he could do about it. The city needed him up on its walls, with his bow in hand. If he stayed here and the walls were overrun, it would only draw attention to the fact that his family was inside.

The only hope for Methu's family was to maintain the walls and keep the Nephiylim focused on their true enemies—the Myndarym and their children. Taking his hand off the door, Methu inhaled a deep breath to steady his nerves, but a horrendous noise suddenly reached his ears, causing his heart to race. It was a massive and continuous roar like a river going over a steep cliff, and it was so loud it hurt his ears. Methu glanced about, and even up into the sky, which was now dark, but the cause was nowhere to be seen. The noise seemed to be everywhere.

*The Nephiylim are coming!*

Methu turned and began running for the wall on the north end of the city.

\*   \*   \*   \*

Zaquel, Arakiba, and Rameel had all left in the same direction. Sariel wasn't sure how long he had sat in the field before he noticed this. He had been too distracted—lost in his thoughts. The sky had already turned completely dark. But when this realization occurred to him, he got to his feet and started walking in the same direction.

Something had changed within him. He could feel it even before he was able to articulate it in the form of a thought. Earlier in the day, Sariel had been ready and willing to give his life to defend Sedekiyr. But now that Enoch was gone, the war seemed pointless. Sariel had to wonder if his motivation had really been to protect Enoch all along. When this question crossed his mind, he remembered the moment when he had given up on seeking revenge. It had been when Enoch was thrown out of Galah—the sight of him stumbling out of the gate, the citizens throwing rocks at him, the realization that Enoch was not welcome anywhere on the Earth. Not among the Myndarym. Not among the Kahyin. Not even among the Shayetham. Sariel's own desires had seemed so unimportant in that moment. And ever since that day, he had dedicated himself to helping the prophet.

*But now ...*

Sedekiyr seemed fragile. Vulnerable. The Nephiylim were going to destroy everything they touched.

Sariel had allowed himself to hope again. Without realizing it, he had placed his trust in Enoch. The Holy One wouldn't allow Enoch to die in this battle, so there had to be some manner of success waiting at the end. Sariel had done the very thing he told the Myndarym not to do. He secretly allowed his heart to fix itself upon a successful outcome. But Enoch was gone. The Myndarym couldn't hurt him, and neither could the Nephiylim.

And somewhere out in those fields, under the night sky, hidden by the gathering fog, was Azael—the one who had stolen Sheyir's happiness and impregnated her with death. If not for her, Sariel would have died in the Borderlands. It was his love for her that had drawn him into this realm, had given him the strength to go on living. All he had wanted to do was to share a life with her. And just when he thought that dream had become a reality, it was smashed to death upon the rocks.

The idea of allowing Azael to live now seemed unthinkable. Sariel's dedication to Enoch had given him another reason to go on living, but it had been temporary. Commitment? Friendship? Whatever it was, Sariel's vengeance was more powerful. More persistent. More patient. And it could not be pushed aside any longer.

The roof of the Elder's Circle loomed over him now. Zaquel, Arakiba, and Rameel were gathered near the stone seat of Mahalal-el with all of the other Myndarym—what was left of the Council. Baraquijal was standing in their midst. The others were seated around him.

"Is it possible?" Sariel shouted as he walked briskly toward them. "Is it really possible to regain our power?"

Baraquijal looked up at the sudden interruption.

The others turned their heads, shame on their faces, as if they'd all been caught in a lie.

"The Marotru are forbidden from the Temporal Realm," Sariel continued as he reached the circle. "How can they help us if they have no influence here?"

"It's a little late for explanations, don't you think?" said Ezekiyel.

Sariel ignored him and looked directly at Baraquijal. "How does this work?"

"I doubt that you are willing to accept the cost."

A roar of distant noise steadily grew in volume until it filled the air and shook the roof overhead. The Myndarym who were seated began glancing nervously at one another. None of them had ever heard a war cry before. Only Baraquijal remained steady and he never broke eye contact.

"That is the sound of the Nephiyl armies," Sariel explained. "We're running out of time. Tell me! Please."

"Very well. Sit down."

Sariel did as instructed.

"You are wrong about the Marotru having no influence here. Their influence is simply limited by their lack of a physical presence. But that can be overcome. The Evil One was the first to use a creature's spirit as a bridge—a way to reach into this realm and influence it. This is what Semjaza sought to do. He tasked me with finding a way to give the Marotru permission to come here."

As he spoke, Baraquijal knelt to the grass and laid down the cloth bundle he'd been holding. He unwound its layers with great caution until it was laid out flat. Lying on top of the coarse fabric was the golden figurine of an animal.

Sariel's heart began racing. "Where did you get that?"

Baraquijal looked up. "I made it," he said calmly, standing up again.

It was clear that the others didn't know what it was, but Sariel had seen figurines like this one before. The first time had been along the shores of Armayim, the Lake of the Curse. The second time had been in a pit of refuse on the outskirts of Sheyir's village. It was figurines like this one that had allowed demons to take control of a man's body, and Sariel would never forget the effort it had required to expel the demons and rescue the man.

"This idol," Baraquijal continued, "is the property of the Marotru. I gave them authority over it, but it isn't a living creature. Therefore, it is not something they can inhabit."

Ezekiyel leaned forward.

"Don't touch it!" Baraquijal snapped. When he regained his composure, he continued, "Not yet, anyway. This idol is a means of making contact with the Marotru. Even now, I can see that your desires are inclined toward it. This is the very thing that allows the Marotru to influence this realm. When I was under Semjaza, I experimented with idols like this one by giving them to humans. I observed that when a man's desire was great, and he reached out to take hold of the idol, the Marotru were able to cross over and inhabit that desire. In effect, the idol became a bridge. And the desire became temporal property yielded to the Marotru."

"Property which they could inhabit," Ezekiyel said, drawing the conclusion for himself.

"Yes."

"So if we touch it, demons will inhabit our bodies?" Zaquel wondered.

"Not exactly. The strength of the desire is proportional to the amount of control yielded. Touching it without a desire to possess it will only allow for communication, not inhabitation."

Sariel was finally discovering the answer to a riddle that had plagued him for hundreds of years. But the roar of the Nephiyl armies was still loud in his ears, feeding the urgency of the situation. "How can this bring back our *shaping* ability?"

Baraquijal looked up with a scowl.

"When they stop yelling," Sariel added, "they will begin advancing. Perhaps they will come slowly and silently through the mist in hopes of building our fear. Or perhaps they have already grown tired of that strategy and will decide to come running at us. We may only have a few minutes left."

Baraquijal looked down at the idol again. "The desire that we will allow them to inhabit is our desire to survive. We must be careful and diligent to focus only on that desire, because they will take anything available to them. We must make sure to limit their amount of control. Once the inhabitation occurs, we will also have access to the Eternal Realm through them."

"But they only operate in the Borderlands," Satarel pointed out.

"Yes. Just as their access to this realm is limited to us, our access to the Eternal is limited to them."

"To them and their abilities, you mean?" Ezekiyel questioned.

"Then we won't necessarily get our *shaping* powers back," Kokabiel concluded.

"No. I never said we would. What we will regain is some measure of awareness and control in that realm. But all of us know a multitude of ways to exploit that."

Sariel remembered how he had caused the birds to swoop and dive toward the Chatsiyr men who had come to confront him. They thought they were being attacked and they fled. If Sariel could only possess that level of influence over the Eternal Realm again, he would certainly survive this battle. And possibly even figure out a way to destroy Azael.

"What will happen afterwards?" Zaquel asked.

Baraquijal knelt down near the cloth. "When Azael's armies are destroyed and our children are safe, the desire to survive will be ... unnecessary. As it fades, so too will the inhabitation. That is why it is critical to concentrate only on our desire to survive."

All of a sudden, the war cry of the Nephiylim stopped.

Baraquijal looked up from the idol and into the eyes of each Myndar gathered. "Do you desire to survive?"

"Yes," they all answered.

Sariel knew that he desired much more than survival. He desired vengeance, or was it simply justice for what had been done to Sheyir? But he put those things out of his mind and concentrated on survival. Survival was good enough for now. A first step. Anything beyond that would have to wait. "Yes," he answered.

"Good. Hold that desire in your mind as you come near," Baraquijal said, beckoning everyone to come close. "Only survival matters."

"Only survival matters," the Myndarym repeated to themselves.

Baraquijal nodded. "At the same time, everyone reach forward and touch the idol."

Sariel reached out his hand and watched the others, matching their speed. When his fingers came in contact with the cold metal, his vision suddenly went dark and he felt his consciousness slip away from his grasp.

# 37

Methu's fingers were already tired from gripping his bow too hard. It seemed like the Nephiylim had stopped shouting hours ago, but nothing had come out of the fog yet. Visibility was limited to a few dozen paces, but when he glanced up at the dark sky, the silhouette of a giant bird could be seen passing in front of the faint stars. Fyarikel's children were circling above the city, waiting for the first attack. Gigantic wolves and tigers were prowling along the top of the wall, and each time one of them came near, Methu had to concentrate on the sound of his own breathing to keep from yelling out in fear. He still hadn't gotten used to being near such frightening creatures.

For the hundredth time that evening, Methu looked down to the bare soil inside the wall. But this time, the two-legged children of the Myndarym weren't there. They had been standing just inside the wall with their makeshift spears only a moment ago, but now there was only the swirling mist.

"Where did the other Nephiylim go?" Methu called down to the man on his right, just at the limit of his vision.

The man looked back over his shoulder, then suddenly turned around as if he was also surprised by their disappearance.

Methu turned to his left and was about to ask the other man the same question, when he heard a distant yelp. The man on the wall turned his head to the west, obviously hearing the same thing.

"What was that?" Methu called out.

The man shrugged.

The wall under Methu's feet began to vibrate.

He looked down at the timbers below him, watching them sway. He grabbed hold of the railing and when he looked up again, a massive wolf with black fur was running toward him along the top of the wall, its steps shaking the fragile structure beneath it. The wolf's teeth were bared and its eyes were staring past Methu to where the yelp had come from. When it passed him, Methu could feel the wind on his face. He watched it go, feeling relieved that the bared teeth were not intended for him.

All of a sudden, the mist beside the wolf swirled. A large shadow slid through the gray, paralleling the creature just as Methu recognized wings and a blade. He didn't even have time to call out before the wolf yelped in pain and slid off the inside of the wall. When it landed heavily on the bare soil, Methu could see that a deep gash had been opened up along its flank.

"WE'RE UNDER ATTACK!" Methu yelled as loud as he could.

Seconds later, he began hearing similar cries of alarm from all directions. The wall began to vibrate again under his feet, but Methu ignored it and focused his attention outward, into the fog. His eyes searched wildly, locating another swirl of moisture just seconds later. He pulled on the bow string, but his prey was already gone. He kept the string taut and waited, scanning the mist.

A shadow passed along the wall to his left.

He took aim and loosed the arrow, watching it disappear into the gray without the sound of contact. Pulling another arrow from the quiver at his leg, he set it to the string and looked up just in time to flinch. A winged creature passed overhead with an ear-piercing screech, only to disappear just like the arrow had done.

*I can't see anything! Where is the enemy?*

Another yelp sounded to the left, followed by a wicked snarl that made him go weak in the knees. Then a loud scream cut through the air. Methu turned to see the man on his left hit the ground inside the wall. His scream came to an abrupt end as his limbs flailed from the impact. Methu stared for a moment before suddenly realizing that he was exposed. He immediately dropped to a crouch behind the railing. His eyes kept searching. His heart pounded. His fingers ached from the bite of the bowstring. But all he wanted was a clear shot.

\* \* \* \*

*Are you there?*

Sariel tried to open his eyes, but there was nothing to see.

*Are you there?*

He tried to open his mouth and respond, but he didn't have one.

*Sariel?*

The voice was familiar, yet there was no sound to it. *What's happened to me?* he thought.

*Nothing yet,* the voice replied. Only, it wasn't a voice.

*A thought?* Sariel wondered.

*A consciousness,* the other replied.

*You seem familiar to me. Who are you?*

*Come now. It hasn't been that long,* the other replied. *At least, not in this realm.*

Sariel suddenly remembered what Baraquijal had been telling him. What he and the other Myndarym had agreed to. *You're Marotru?*

The other seemed disappointed.

There was no sight or sound to indicate as much. Only an impression. Sariel wondered why any demon would seem familiar to him.

*Now I'm offended.*

Finally, Sariel remembered. The demon he was never able to defeat. A Nin-Myndar more elusive than any he had tracked. One who had killed as many of Sariel's fellow soldiers as Sariel had killed of his. The stalemate had gone on so long that Sariel had eventually given up.

*Yes, that was disappointing. I rather enjoyed our private war.*

The Nin-Myndar who became a soldier. In many ways, Sariel had thought of him as his equal.

*In every way,* the other corrected. *And stop with the ... Nin-Myndar. It's very unoriginal. Did it never occur to you that we have titles of our own?*

Sariel didn't even want to think of the demon's name, but it came into his mind anyway. *Vand-ra.*

*I thought I had made more of an impression on you.*

*It was so long ago,* Sariel replied, before realizing that he didn't need to give a reason.

Vand-ra seemed to smile. *Don't scold yourself. You're an angel. You can't help your honesty.*

*What are you doing here?* Sariel asked.

*I came here to save you from making a serious mistake.*

*What do you mean?*

Vand-ra seemed to shake his head, though there was only consciousness and darkness. No physical manifestation. *Did you really want Baraquijal as your master?*

Sariel was confused.

*I know it's hard for an angel to comprehend, but he lied to all of you. He wasn't helping you regain your shaping ability. He was bringing you under his authority. He's a demon ... and a very powerful one.*

*No. You're lying,* Sariel replied.

*I'm the only one who's telling the truth,* Vand-ra countered, his thoughts suddenly taking on a serious tone. *Allow me to shed some light on the situation ... to borrow a phrase from the Amatru vocabulary. Baraquijal did work with the Viytur. That much was true. And he did try to infiltrate our intelligence organization. But he wasn't the one setting the trap. He was taken over by one of our Seraphim long before he ever met Semjaza.*

*What do mean, taken over?*

*Merged. Two spirits becoming one,* Vand-ra explained.

*That's impossible.*

*No. It's exactly what you were just about to do with another demon.*

Sariel's confidence suddenly drained away.

*That's right. All that talk of inhabitation was intentionally misleading. A demon can, indeed, inhabit the desires of someone, but that's not what was about to happen to you. Baraquijal was offering you up to his underlings, and if I hadn't intervened, you would have merged with one of them and become subject to his rule.*

Sariel tried to think through the logic of it. If Baraquijal had merged with a demonic Seraph, his brilliance would have dimmed, and the Viytur would have noticed it immediately.

*Not necessarily. After a merging, the capabilities of both remain available, if one knows what they're doing.*

If that was possible, the Marotru would be capable of impersonating Amatru soldiers without anyone knowing.

*Now you're getting it.*

*Why would you tell me this?* Sariel wondered.

*You may consider it an act of trust. Others may not respect you enough to be honest, but I hold you in the highest regard. And as a further demonstration of this fact, you should know that this whole conflict was Baraquijal's idea. It was he who first conceived of preying upon the desires of the Myndarym—those who had first sustained and then reshaped creation. Those who were so heavily invested in its success. It was he who sought out Semjaza and suggested the idea of going to the Temporal Realm, not the other way around. After you killed Semjaza, it was Baraquijal who manipulated the Myndarym into aligning themselves with Azael. He played both sides against each other until one became desperate enough to reach out to the Marotru for help. His subtlety is unparalleled. Everyone thought they were seeking their own goals when they were really just pursuing suggestions that he planted in their minds.*

Sariel didn't know how to respond. Lies were the territory of demons. Lies and betrayal. But the explanation made sense. Every question he could think to ask was already answered by it. One after another, they flashed through his mind until there was only one left.

*And you know the answer to that one as well,* Vand-ra replied.

*You intervened because you want me for yourself. You want to merge with me.*

*Yes.*

*Why would you work against Baraquijal, if you're both Marotru?*

Vand-ra seemed to smile at this. *Let's just say, there are many ways to accomplish the same goal. But not everyone shares my broader understanding.*

Sariel thought about the consequences of this proposal. *You would become me, and I would become you.*

*There would be no more distinction between you or me,* Vand-ra clarified. *There would only be us—a single entity. A new creation.*

*With competing interests,* Sariel reasoned. *Full of doubts and second-guessing. Everything I want would be countered by your desire for the opposite. We would cancel each other out. Why would you risk losing yourself?*

*Because I don't see it as a risk. I see it as an opportunity. It's a simple question of whose will is stronger.*

*And you believe the stronger will is yours,* Sariel added.

*I don't believe. I know … just as I'm sure that you know the opposite. And that is the only reason either one of us would agree to do this.*

It was disorienting to hear truth from a demon.

*It happens more often than you're willing to admit,* Vand-ra replied. *But you'll understand that and much more after this merge.*

*Tell me why I should agree to this,* Sariel demanded.

*Because you want revenge, and I can give it to you. Azael is nothing compared to me and what I have at my disposal. If you wish to see his body broken like Sheyir's, you will have it. If you want to keep your promise about ending Semjaza's kingdom, I will give you Parnudel and Rikoathel also. You will have access to the Eternal Realm again, and your imagination will be your only limit.*

*All I have to offer you is this frail, human body,* Sariel pointed out. *Why does that appeal to you?*

*The Temporal Realm has been unavailable to me. With the power I possess in this realm, a frail human body is hardly a limitation. It offers immeasurable potential.*

Sariel knew he should decline. He should go back to Sedekiyr and face whatever fate awaited him there.

*Oh yes. As part of our ongoing demonstration of trust, you should be aware that the Myndarym have abandoned Sedekiyr.*

*What?*

*That's right. There was no discussion between equals, like we're doing now. They already succumbed to their much stronger demonic counterparts. And once their wills were overpowered by Baraquijal, their own desires and interests ceased to exist. There was only his will, and that apparently didn't include wasting his resources on a war with the Nephiylim. The Myndarym of the Council and their children have already exited the east gate and broken through the enemy line. Most of the Nephiylim don't even realize the majority of their enemies are gone. The animals are the only ones fighting now, and they will not last much longer. It is your right to decide which path to take, but you should know that if you go back to Sedekiyr with nothing more than your frail, human body, a swift death is the only thing that awaits you.*

Though there was no such thing as a physical presence in this place, wherever this was, it seemed to Sariel that Vand-ra was extending his hand. He didn't want to take it, but what choice did he have? Merge or death. Those were the only options available to him now.

*The city is about to be overrun, and your physical body will soon be in jeopardy,* Vand-ra added. *If you don't make the choice now, someone might make it for you.*

With every bit of his conscience screaming in protest, Sariel reached out to the demon.

\* \* \* \*

OUTSIDE SEDEKIYR

The Iriylim, led by Vengsul, had been paralleling the walls of the city for hours. With each pass, another child of Ananel or Jomjael would fall. Their teeth and claws had only met flesh a few times, and even those had been accidental. Fyarikel's raptors had proven more deadly, but only slightly so. The fog was so thick that most of their dives had ended with nothing but empty talons.

In all, the first attack had been a complete success. It had frustrated and demoralized the enemy, to the point of exhaustion. But Azael had allowed his winged soldiers enough fun. Their brethren on the ground had been growing more restless with each passing minute. And now they could hardly contain themselves. It was time to release them.

Standing at the rear of the northern front, Azael looked to his Iryllurym on either side and nodded before pulling his helmet over his head. They bowed their heads and followed his lead, taking to the air with their Rada. The trio kept just inside the mist, passing over the ranks of Imikal's army. Azael soared to the front of the line, and when he passed over the general's head, a trumpet signaled the next stage of the attack.

Azael immediately pulled up and out of the gray moisture, rising quickly toward the swarm of birds circling over the city. Parnudel and Rikoathel matched his speed, staying just behind him in a *V* formation.

Fyarikel's birds noticed the trio and began diving out of their swirling formation to meet the threat.

The mist, now far below, seemed to boil as thousands of Iriylim rose from every direction. The effect was startling. Azael could see fear alter the flight paths of his enemies. They hesitated, confused as to which of the millions of enemies they should attack. Azael could have slowed down and let the Iriylim engage, but he was eager to show his soldiers that he was a warrior first and a leader second.

Raptors descended, talons reaching.

Azael rolled left, dragging his vaepkir across wings and feet, severing them clean from feathered bodies. He dipped and rolled right before coming up again, pulling his wings inward as he shot through a void in their ranks. Parnudel and Rikoathel mirrored each movement, taking their own paths when needed, but always returning to Azael's sides.

Feathers filled the air.

Limp heads slumped forward.

Wings folded in the wrong direction.

Birds spun wildly as they dropped from the sky.

A long trail of defeated enemies fell toward the city below, like leaves falling from a dead tree.

As the battle-hardened Iryllurym broke through the other side of the raptors, Azael took a moment to look down. The walls of the city were teeming with his Aniylim. They had already climbed up one side and down the other and were now pulling the fragile walls apart, piece by piece.

\* \* \* \*

INSIDE SEDEKIYR

The ranks of the Nephiylim coming at the city walls seemed endless. There were now so many of them that they were climbing on top of one another in an effort to reach the top of the fragile boundary. Methu set another arrow to the string, pulled back, leaned over the railing, and took aim straight down at a Nephiyl who was only five paces away, climbing the wall like it was a ladder. Methu released the string and the arrow stuck into the center of the Nephiyl's chest. A look of surprise came over his face as he lost strength and fell backward into the teeming mass of his fellow soldiers.

Methu had been releasing arrows as quickly as his arms and fingers could move. His weapons pierced shoulders, faces, arms, and chests. One after another Nephiyl dropped from the wall in front of him, but there were always more, and he was running out of arrows. A quick glance left and right revealed that he was now alone. The impaled bodies of wolves and tigers were strewn along the ramparts. Behind him, at the base of the wall, the few men of Sedekiyr who had defended the walls were lying motionless next to the bodies of Fyarikel's raptors. On both sides, the Nephiylim had overrun the wall and were climbing down the inside of it, snapping supports and tearing bindings as they went.

Methu set his last arrow to the string, but when he looked up the Nephiyl climbing over the railing was closer than expected. Methu pulled on the string and raised his bow just as a spear flew past his head. He flinched, and his arrow flew wide into the shoulder of another Nephiyl who was coming behind the other. The next thing he saw was a massive arm and fist colliding with his face.

# 38

Sariel opened his eyes to find the roof over the Elder's Circle partially caved in. The southern section was on fire, and the smoke was thick in the air. He was lying on the grass, coughing uncontrollably as his lungs tried to expel the acrid odor. Dawn was fast approaching. The Myndarym were gone, just as he had been told. But he wasn't alone. Dozens of demons were standing nearby, waiting patiently to do his bidding. They varied greatly in both size and appearance, depending on their function, but all of them were dark like shadows. Emptiness. A lack of substance confined to an area that could be thought of as a body. But they weren't standing in the Elder's Circle. They were standing in the Borderlands of the Eternal Realm. Sariel could see both places at once—two aspects of the same existence.

The demons were looking down at him with concern in their smoldering eyes. Not concern for his safety, but concern for why he looked different. Sariel followed their gazes, looking down at his own body. In addition to the human form that he'd chosen for Sheyir's benefit, light and darkness swirled around him and through him, like incompatible materials fighting each other for dominance, neither able to absorb the other.

When he looked up again, it seemed that the demons around him were not separate beings but parts of his own body. He could feel them and the authority he had over them. The mysterious structure of the Marotru's solidarity was no longer an enigma, but an innate knowledge. With nothing more than a thought, he willed the demons to turn and push the collapsed roof away. In the Eternal Realm, he watched them obey, crawling and flying forward to attack the crumbling object whose existence they were unaware of until this moment. An object that didn't exist in their realm without Sariel's experience of it. In the Temporal Realm, he saw thick smoke curl away from him, and the smoking timbers bowing outward in obedience. The power was unlike anything he'd ever felt, but seeing two realms at once was incredibly disorienting.

The roof finally gave in to his will and exploded outward, allowing fresh air to come rushing all around him. Sariel's temporal body inhaled the precious substance while he rose to his feet and looked out upon the burning city. The torches that had been intended to set the fields on fire were now being carried by the thousands of Nephiylim that he could see running wild through the streets. He watched, transfixed by the raw power these creatures possessed. Their temporal bodies were more than three times the height of his own. Each muscle worked with minimal effort to propel them in all their movements, with strength in such abundance that they hardly considered it an effort to destroy everything the humans of Sedekiyr had built. And their eternal bodies were a fascinating composite of intense colors. Were these observations his own, or did they come from Vand-ra? The name seemed both foreign and intimate at once. A disorienting yet intriguing thought. And even as he marveled at the Nephiylim, Sariel wanted to reach out and crush them—to squeeze the life from their bodies and watch them suffer.

No sooner had the thought entered his mind than his demons swarmed forward, driven by his outstretched hand. With fangs and claws, they attacked the spirits of his enemies mercilessly. Three Nephiylim were knocked off their feet by the simple gesture of Sariel's hand, and their limbs came apart from their bodies a second later. The swirling colors of their eternal bodies dissipated into the air like the smoke around them.

Sariel felt simultaneous and conflicting emotions. It was satisfying to kill the Nephiylim with such ease, and disappointing to see the end of such useful resources. He knew, without even testing it, that he could reach out and acquire their spirits for himself. His demons could overpower them and absorb them. And yet, the desire to kill them was stronger, as if he had promised himself that he would do so.

*Very well, Sariel. We will kill for now,* he thought as he walked away from the Elder's Circle with his hands extended.

\* \* \* \*

The pain in Methu's ribs brought him back to consciousness. One by one, his senses began detecting his environment. He tasted blood. He smelled smoke and damp earth. He heard the crackling of flames nearby and shouting in the distance. The pain in his ribs was caused by the pole that he could feel jabbing into his side. But there was no sensation of wetness—no blood. It hadn't impaled him. Darkness surrounded him, with only a few points of light. He stared at them, trying to make sense of what he saw.

*Daylight?*

Suddenly, realization flooded in. Methu remembered being struck in the head by the Nephiyl and falling backward off the wall. Before he lost consciousness, he remembered a terrible crashing sound and the feeling of something falling on top of him. Methu tried moving his legs and found that he was able to wriggle forward like a worm. His arms and hands still had enough strength to pull at the crossed poles that he assumed were the remnants of the wall. Minutes later, when he emerged from the rubble, his suspicions were confirmed. In the pale light of dawn, he climbed to his shaking legs and looked out upon what was left of his grandfather's city. Whole sections of the wall had been pushed inward. Flames crawled over piles of timbers, sending thick curls of black and white smoke into the air. Bodies were strewn across the ground, but none of those inside the remnants of the wall were Nephiylim that he could see.

*Jurishel!*

Something about the sight of the battlefield reminded Methu that he wasn't alone. He started running, as if he had just been awakened from a dream. Piles of burning debris passed by in a blur. More bodies. A collapsed storehouse. The arm of a Nephiyl. A torso with a leg attached.

Methu's steps faltered. He suddenly found himself looking down a long street paved with the remains of Nephiylim. Some had been burned. Others looked as if they had been pulled apart. Methu felt his stomach churn, and he covered his mouth before turning down another street. As he neared the center of the city, he began hearing the sounds of battle to the south. The enemy had already passed over the north and central sections and moved on, but the fight was still raging just a few streets over.

Methu scanned the area, now finding it difficult to orient himself with so many of the buildings destroyed. He turned east and finally passed a field that he recognized, which told him that he was still north of where he had left his family. Cautiously, he headed down an alley between burning huts, and when he came to the end, it opened into a field where Sariel was standing.

Nephiylim were fleeing before him. He motioned with his hands, and flames jumped from a burning hut to engulf the soldiers. He motioned again, and three more Nephiylim were knocked backward off their feet as if something had hit them.

Methu tore his attention away from the battle and ran along the field to the next section of buildings. The walls of the storehouse had been pushed in, and the roof was collapsed, but it hadn't been burned. He climbed over the collapsed wall and dropped into the pit where food and supplies were usually kept.

"Jurishel?" he yelled.

All around him were the bodies of dead women and children. They had been run through with spears.

"Lemek?"

Bile was rising in his throat. He gagged as he bent down to look at each face. He tried yelling again, but he heaved instead.

His tears began to flow, but he wiped them away and continued looking. Then he heard something. A muffled scream.

*No. Not a scream. A yell!*

"Hello?" he called out. "Jurishel?"

The yell sounded again. It was faint and coming from the left side of the pit.

Methu followed the sound until he reached the place where a tunnel had been. The earth had collapsed and spilled over the entrance. It wasn't the tunnel where his family had been staying, but someone was inside. With the sounds of battle growing steadily quieter to the south, Methu began digging his fingers into the soil.

"Hold on! I'll get you out!" he yelled, eager to put his hands to the task and avoid the conclusion that burned in his mind like the remains of Sedekiyr—that his family was gone.

\* \* \* \*

OUTSIDE THE EASTERN GATE
SEDEKIYR

Ananel could hear Jomjael roaring, but he couldn't see through the dense fog that was drifting across the field in front of him. He ran blindly into it and had to climb over a section of the city wall that had fallen outward.

"Jomjael?"

The roaring changed to a yelp and then went silent altogether.

Ananel finally came through the mist into a section of clear air. Jomjael was pinned to the ground with a spear, and wriggling violently. The Nephiyl standing over him had deep claw marks running down his back.

Ananel lunged forward and tilted his head to one side. He opened his jaws wide and clamped down as hard as he could on the lower back of the soldier.

The Nephiyl suddenly let go of the spear and tried to straighten his stance.

Ananel wrenched his head in the opposite direction.

The flesh of the Nephiyl tore away, revealing the spine as his body was thrown off his feet, dead even as he hit the ground.

Ananel pivoted and looked to Jomjael again, but the striped feline had gone still. The ground under his body was dark with his blood, and his tongue was hanging out of his open mouth. Ananel lowered his head and nudged his friend, but there was no response.

"This one's mine!" came a voice from nearby.

Ananel spun around.

The field was now clear of mist for more than a hundred paces to the east. A large Nephiyl was stepping away from a group of four others, holding his hand out to indicate that they should stay back.

It only took Ananel a second to recognize the one who had hunted his pack through Kokabiel's lands.

\* \* \* \*

Hyrren moved his spear to his right hand and reached for his knife with the other. He had already killed dozens of the wolf children, but their deaths weren't nearly as satisfying as when he would put a spear through Ananel's chest.

"Go on," he told his soldiers. "I'll catch up. This won't take long."

No sooner were the words out of Hyrren's mouth than Ananel was sprinting forward.

Hyrren quickly lowered his spear tip and jabbed, but the wolf had already gotten underneath it and was coming up with his jaws open. Hyrren barely had time to pull his other arm inward before Ananel's teeth closed around it, pinning his hand and most of his arm against his chest.

The force of the attack threw Hyrren backward, but he curled his other arm around Ananel's neck as he fell. When the two hit the ground, Hyrren yanked the wolf's head sideways and the teeth came free of his skin. He rolled backward and came up to his feet with his spear still in hand.

Ananel shook his head and then licked the blood from his teeth.

Hyrren glanced down at his own chest and the blood pouring from the fresh puncture wounds. "Very good, wolf. But you won't get the same chance again."

Ananel didn't seem to be in a speaking mood. He was crouched low, with his front paws in a wide stance. The hair on his back was standing up. His snout was sticking out level with his spine, and his large teeth were bared. The snarling noise that he was making would have been intimidating if it had been the first time Hyrren had heard it. But he'd been battling and killing Ananel's much larger children throughout the night, and he'd learned how to deal with these animals.

Hyrren kept his spear tip forward and jabbed at Ananel while shifting his stance to the side.

Ananel growled and snapped at the annoyance.

With his left hand behind him, concealed by the position of his body, Hyrren removed his knife from its sheath and held it with the blade was facing upward. He kept jabbing at the wolf's face with his spear to keep him distracted.

Finally, Ananel whipped his head to the side and bit down on the shaft of the spear.

Hyrren tugged at the captured weapon, feigning a look of panic.

Ananel's instincts told him to rush in toward Hyrren's exposed throat. He let go of the spear and lunged forward with his jaws opened wide.

Hyrren pivoted, bringing his knife from behind his body in an upward stab. The long blade sunk deep into the soft flesh of Ananel's throat, sliding upward into his brain. The jaws full of dagger-like teeth came to a stop only a handbreadth from Hyrren's throat. The Nephiyl stood there for a moment, staring into Ananel's eyes as he held the weight of the wolf's body with only the knife in his hand. Then he wrenched it free and let the dead animal fall to the ground.

\* \* \* \*

Methu pulled another armful of dirt away from the pile and a small hole appeared. He shoved his hand inside and someone grabbed onto it.

"Methu?" the voice called out again, this time sounding clear and distinct.

"Jurishel, is that you?"

"Yes. We're all in here. We're safe."

Methu could hardly believe his ears. "I thought you were dead. What happened?"

"The giants began pushing down the walls. I crawled in here after the children, and Lemek caved in the front of the tunnel to hide us. Is anyone else out there?"

"No," he whimpered. "They're all dead."

"Oh, no," came Lemek's voice.

Jurishel began crying.

Methu's dirty grip was still clamped around his wife's fingers. He gently squeezed her hand. "The Holy One has shown us mercy."

She squeezed his hand in reply, but it was several seconds before she spoke, "Where is your father ... and Sariel? Are they safe?"

Methu didn't know quite how to respond. "Enoch was taken up. The Myndarym tried to kill him, but ... the angels of heaven ... took him."[22]

There was a long silence on the other side before Lemek spoke, "Where is Sariel?" His voice sounded muffled and distant.

Methu turned his head and looked up from the pit. The pale sky of the morning was now a deep blue, with streaks of black smoke running across it. "He fights for us still. He commands the fire and the wind with only his hands, and the Nephiylim are fleeing. Father never told me ..." but Methu trailed off. There was so much he didn't know, and now his father was gone.

# 39

Azael, Parnudel, and Rikoathel had taken a less active role in the battle after destroying the raptors, staying above the city and only occasionally intervening. With the rising of the sun, the haze had begun to dissipate. Within hours, the fields of Sedekiyr had cleared. And now that visibility had been restored, aside from the smoke, it was obvious that most of the Myndarym and their children had escaped. The only bodies to be found were the children of Ananel, Fyarikel, and Jomjael. To the east, one of the Nephiyl armies had been decimated even before reaching the city. It was unusual, considering there seemed to be little evidence of struggle. The attempted overthrow of Baraquijal's kingdom had produced a similar outcome, and Azael was now confident that there was much to learn about that particular Myndar. But it was only a matter of time. Once the Nephiylim were finished with Sedekiyr, he would put them to the task of tracking the remaining Myndarym.

As he banked into a turn and headed for the southern end of the city, Azael noted that the Nephiylim just outside of the collapsed gate were scattering.

"Why do they retreat?" Rikoathel asked.

Azael descended around a column of smoke and looked down from a different angle. At the center of the fleeing soldiers was a man walking casually across the fields. His arms were extended outward as if he were reaching. Soldiers were falling to the ground all around him.

"It's Sariel," Azael announced before glancing at Rikoathel.

A nervous look crossed the large Iryllur's face.

"Come," Azael commanded. "It is time to finish what you and Hyrren should have done a long time ago."

The trio folded their wings and dove toward the earth.

* * * *

Bodies crumpled to the ground, pressed by an unseen weight. Others were tossed aside as grain to the wind. Sariel had found a hundred different ways to kill the Nephiylim, and his demons were enjoying every second of it. But it wasn't just mindless slaughter. There was purpose in his actions. He was driving the Nephiylim from the city and drawing attention to himself. Even now he could feel the red, watchful eyes of the Iryllur above, who had finally noticed who had been killing his soldiers so effortlessly.

Azael dropped to the earth in an attack posture with vaepkir drawn. Parnudel and Rikoathel landed only seconds later. Their weapons and breastplates gleamed in the morning sun, reflecting flashes of red from the blood they had spilled through the night.

"Sariel!" the enemy king called across the grass. "Take your Iryllur form so we may fight with honor."

Sariel turned from the direction he'd been going and began walking casually toward the last of Semjaza's soldiers. "I can't *shape* anymore."

Azael's eyes narrowed. He had always hated jokes, and was clearly trying to decide if this was another clever choice of words, or an outright lie.

Sariel didn't wait for him to reach a conclusion. He lifted his right hand, and every demon at his disposal came together into a line and shot forward. Some flew. Others slithered. But all moved with speed that would have been unnatural in the Temporal Realm. Their bodies were bound by a different set of laws, the ones governing a different realm. They hit Rikoathel's spirit and passed through it, clawing and biting and tearing as they went.

Rikoathel's chest caved inward and he fell backward to the ground, dead.

Parnudel took to the air immediately, coming straight at Sariel with his bladed arms ready to strike.

Sariel reached up into the air with both hands. He imagined that his demons were his arms and fingers.

Parnudel came to a sudden stop in the air.

As casually as if he were pruning a tree, Sariel pulled his hands apart from each other.

Parnudel's wings were ripped from his body, flying in opposite directions. He screamed in agony.

Sariel repeated the motion.

Parnudel's arms and legs flew through the air.

Sariel lowered his hands.

The Iryllur dropped dead to the ground.

Perhaps for the first time in his life, Azael appeared to be scared. "Fight me with honor!" he yelled.

Sariel came to a stop in front of the soldier who was almost twice his height. He looked up into the fierce red eyes that glared back at him, and he realized that this was what Sheyir would have seen just before she had been raped. "You have no honor," he replied, speaking for the woman whose voice had been silenced.

Azael tried to lunge forward, but he found that he couldn't move. The vaepkir dropped from his useless hands. His arms rose to either side. Then he fell backward to the ground, his limbs pinned by an unseen force.

"As you have done unto others, so I will do unto you," Sariel said, unsure where these words had come from.

\* \* \* \*

From across the field, Hyrren watched Sariel thrust his hand forward into the air as if in a stabbing motion.

Azael's prone body jolted, and a grunt of pain could just barely be heard.

Sariel pulled his hand backward and then thrust it forward again.

"What is he doing?" Imikal asked.

Hyrren couldn't have answered even if he knew. He was still in shock that this human could possess so much power. To see him kill Rikoathel and tear Parnudel apart with nothing but a few motions of his hands made Hyrren sick with fear. This was the angel who had killed his father, Semjaza—the man whom he had chased into the hills. Hyrren wondered how close he might have come to losing his own life that day. But he couldn't even think of running now. His eyes were fixed on the scene before him.

Sariel thrust his hand forward again. Then his fingers spread out and he seemed to be grabbing hold of something. When he pulled his hand back, Azael's stomach and crotch were ripped open. Cries of agony spread over the field.

"We must retreat," Imikal said, his voice wavering with nausea.

The sight of Azael's torture and his screams made Hyrren's stomach turn. For the first time in his life, he felt like he would vomit.

"Brother!" Imikal pleaded. "We must retreat."

Sariel raised his other hand.

Azael's legs came together.

He lifted his hand.

Azael's body rose from the ground as if hung by the legs.

Sariel threw his hand downward.

Hyrren winced as he felt the vibration of the impact in the ground under his feet and heard the cracking of Azael's bones. He couldn't watch anymore and finally turned to his brother. "Signal the retreat."

Imikal lifted the horn to his lips, and the mournful wail of the instrument pierced the air.

\* \* \* \*

It had been hours since Methu had heard the wail of some powerful creature. The distant sound of marching had followed it, and then nothing but silence. Methu had crawled into the tunnel with his family and cautioned everyone to stay as quiet as possible, but there had been no other sounds.

Lemek was staring intently at his father now. Everyone else had fallen asleep except for Jurishel.

"I'm going to check if it's safe."

Jurishel looked as though she would object, but then nodded.

Methu crawled out of the tunnel and quietly climbed out of the pit. When he stood up, there was destruction as far as the eye could see. The air was clear of mist, and only a few tendrils of smoke were reaching up into the sky. Nothing was moving. Methu walked over to a hut that was only partially damaged and he climbed up to its sagging roof. When he looked out upon Sedekiyr, he knew for certain that his father's words had come true. Sedekiyr was no more.

S.A. 988

# 40

The eyes of the children were wide with excitement, but all of them were completely silent. Some had their hands over their mouths. Others were looking to Zacol to see if she would correct anything Methu was saying, but she only smiled. It was good to see his mother smile again. Methu knew that she was not done mourning the loss of her husband, but it would come with time. He could see it in her eyes. She was a strong woman. And the fact that all of her children and grandchildren were together in one place seemed to comfort her even while she mourned.

"It wasn't a dream?" one little boy asked. He couldn't stand the silent tension any longer.

Methu couldn't help but smile. "No. As soon as Sariel told him these words, my father knew that he had actually been there in the White City. The skin on his hands and face hadn't turned red from the sun. It was from being so close to the Holy One."

"This was the Sariel who lived here? The same one who defended Sedekiyr?" an older girl asked.

"The very same one."

"Where is he now?"

"No one knows," Methu admitted. "Some believe he returned to heaven to be with my father."

Zacol and Jurishel smiled at this. Lemek just crossed his arms.

"I believe that he's still out there, roaming the earth, watching over the people of Enoch and protecting them from the Nephiylim."

"Me too," a young boy agreed.

"And from the Myndarym," a girl added.

Several of the youngest children suddenly looked like they were about to cry.

Methu leaned forward and held out his hands. "I know they seem scary, but you don't have to be afraid. Do you know why?"

The children shook their heads.

"Because I have secret," he whispered.

"What is it?" a little boy asked.

"You have to promise me, if you ever see the Myndarym or the Nephiylim, you won't tell."

The boy's face was blank, as if the possibility of seeing either was beyond comprehension.

"You have to promise, because they're not allowed to know yet."

"I promise," the children said.

"Good. My father told me that, when he was in the White City, the Holy One gave him a very special message. It was a message for the Myndarym, which he called the Wandering Stars. But Enoch was only supposed to tell it to his children, and his children's children. Many years from now, it will be revealed to the Wandering Stars when the Holy One wishes them to know."

"What is it?" asked the first boy, who didn't seem to enjoy anticipation.

"The Holy One told my father all of the terrible things they would do. And then He gave him the message: 'Therefore, I will raise up one from among those you despise. And I will awaken his eyes to the mysteries which I have hidden from men since the foundations of the world. His feet will I make to tread upon the paths of destruction and his hands to make war. He will uproot the seeds of corruption which you have sown throughout the earth. And then you will know that I am the Lord and my justice is everlasting.'"[23]

The older children grinned.

The younger ones looked suddenly disappointed. "What does that mean?"

Methu smiled at their innocence. "It means, one day the Holy One will raise up a warrior who will fight for us. And he will make everything right again."

"Like Sariel," a boy shouted.

Methu nodded. "Perhaps. Or perhaps someone even greater than Sariel. Even my father didn't know for sure. We'll just have to wait and see."

# OTHER BOOKS BY JASON TESAR

## THE AWAKENED SERIES

Over five thousand years ago, a renegade faction of angels abandoned the spiritual realm and began their inhabitation of earth. Worshiped as gods for their wisdom and power, they corrupted the realm of the physical and forever altered the course of history.

Amidst the chaos of a dying world, a lone voice foretold the awakening of a warrior who would bring an end to this evil perpetrated against all of creation. But with the cataclysmic destruction of earth and rebirth of humanity, the prophecy went unfulfilled and eventually faded from the memory of our kind—until now!

In his debut series, Jason Tesar delves into the heart of an ancient legend, embarking on an epic saga that will journey from earth's mythological past to its post-apocalyptic future, blending the genres of fantasy, sci-fi, and military/political suspense.

## AWAKEN HIS EYES | BOOK 1

The physical dimension is fractured. What remain now are numerous fragmented worlds moving simultaneously through time, sharing a common history, connected only by a guarded portal. On a parallel earth, in the city of Bastul, Colonel Adair Lorus disappears while investigating the death of an informant, triggering a series of events which will tear his family apart and set in motion the resolution of an ancient struggle. Kael, sentenced to death after rising up against the cruel leadership of his new step-father, is rescued from prison and trained in the arts of war by a mystical order of clerics. Excelling in every aspect of his training, Kael inwardly struggles to give himself fully to the methods of his new family, or the god they worship. Maeryn, bitter over the disappearance of her husband and supposed execution of her son, fears for her life at the hands of her newly appointed husband. Finding comfort and purpose in her unborn child, she determines to undermine his authority by reaching out to an underground social movement known as the Resistance. After being forced from his home, Kael's former mentor, Saba, uncovers a clue to Adair's disappearance. Sensing a connection to his own forgotten past, Saba begins an investigation which leads to the discovery of a secret military organization operating within the Orudan Empire.

## PATHS OF DESTRUCTION | BOOK 2

Returning to his home city of Bastul, Kael finds the Southern Territory of the Orudan Empire under invasion. As he races to unravel the secrecy of the enemy's identity, he becomes entangled in a brutal conspiracy to gain control of the government. After years of collaboration with the Resistance, Maeryn coordinates the covert exodus of the entire slave population of Bastul. Along their treacherous journey to the capital city of Orud, she is faced with the pressures of leadership as she attempts to protect her daughter and ensure the survival of her companions. Saba, held captive by a mysterious military force, escapes after years of solitary confinement. Propelled by an elusive memory, he chases after the hope of rediscovering his past and learns that everyone's future is in jeopardy.

## HANDS TO MAKE WAR | BOOK 3

After fighting his way back from a paralyzing defeat, Kael resolves to bring an end to the enemies of the Orudan Empire. Enlisting the help of his family and most-trusted friends, he faces off against an ancient evil and embraces his destiny. As Maeryn rises through the ranks to attain a command position within the Resistance, she learns of a conspiracy in her organization and realizes the enormous resources at her disposal. Determined to set things right, she seizes control and sets a new course for the movement. Reacquainting with his closest friends, Saba pieces together the identity and motive of the enemy. Bringing his vast knowledge to bear, he collaborates with Orud's High Council to force the enemy into the open, while waiting to reveal a secret of his own.

## SEEDS OF CORRUPTION | BOOK 4

The All Powerful is dead, but the scars of his influence remain, haunting Kael's memories and discoloring his outlook. Seeking closure, Kael retraces the steps of his past. When he discovers that his father may still be alive, the course of his life once again takes an unexpected turn. Determined to answer the most profound questions of his childhood, Kael ventures across the fractured physical dimension. What awaits him is an advanced civilization of private armies and foreign weaponry, and only one path leads to his goal. Entering a covert war of intelligence and paramilitary operations, Kael must adapt to this new world and confront the possibility that his own destiny is just beginning. The seeds of corruption have taken root, but the Awakened has come.

## HIDDEN FROM MEN | BOOK 5

A powerful adversary is surfacing and Null's covert battle is on the threshold of open war. Reunited with his father after twenty-two years, Kael must find the balance between protecting him and confronting the enemy who stands between them and their home world. The timelessness of the In-Between has stolen the years that separated Kael and Adair by age, leaving them as distant equals. Having glimpsed Kael's destiny from the Eternal Realm, Adair struggles to find his role in the life of a son who no longer needs him. Through a global maze of counterintelligence and espionage, a multinational team of operatives has to survive long enough to turn the tide of war. And a father and son will discover how to rebuild what was taken from their lives.

## Foundations of the World | Book 6

Kael has seen into the mind of the enemy and witnessed an abomination beyond imagining. Thousands of years of collaboration have allowed the Myndarym to construct a vast and complex system for exploiting the earth and its inhabitants. It is an ancient legacy of evil, and for the remnants of Null to destroy it, they must capture the system's last surviving creator. Kael has only one advantage against this ruthless warrior, but leveraging it will take him through a battlefield of the world's most advanced weaponry and expose his greatest weaknesses—patience and trust. The journey will bring them all together in ways they never thought possible, leading to a startling revelation that will shake the very foundations of the world.

## Book 7 and Beyond...

Watch Kael's destiny unfold with the continuation of the *Awakened* series. Visit www.jasontesar.com for behind-the-scenes information and release dates for future books.

## The Wandering Stars Series

Deep in the recesses of the human soul, echoes and shadows survive—remnants of a time long-forgotten. These memories refuse to die, striving for existence by taking the form of myths and legends which continue to shape human history across the boundaries of time and culture.

This is their story—where it all began.

In this riveting prequel to the Amazon bestselling *Awakened* series, Jason Tesar sets in motion a sweeping fantasy epic birthed at the very foundations of humanity when our prehistoric world collided with supernatural forces, spawning an age of mythological creatures and heroes.

## INCARNATION: VOLUME 1

Since the ages before time was measured, the angelic races have existed. Unseen by our eyes, they move through creation, shaping our world, sustaining our existence, and battling demonic hordes. But the war is changing; the battle lines are expanding into new frontiers and the next epoch is emerging.

Seven hundred years after the first humans were exiled from their home, their descendants have pushed eastward into a prehistoric wilderness. In a land shrouded by mist and superstition, primitive tribes struggle to establish new civilizations, unaware that their world is about to change forever.

Weary from unceasing conflict, Sariel, legendary warrior of the Myndarym, crosses into the Temporal Realm in search of the only one who can bring him peace. But he is not the first; others have already begun their inhabitation. As the dominance of their kingdom spreads, threatening to engulf all of humanity, Sariel finds himself standing between his own kind and the one he loves and must embrace the life he abandoned in order to secure her freedom.

## VOLUME 3 AND BEYOND...

Follow Sariel's journey as the *Wandering Stars* series continues. Visit www.jasontesar.com for behind-the-scenes information and release dates for future books.

# ABOUT THE AUTHOR

The third of four children and an introvert from the start, Jason Tesar grew up as an imaginative "middle child" who enjoyed the make-believe world as much as the real one, possibly more. From adolescence to adulthood, his imagination fed itself on a diet of books, movies, and art, all the while growing and maturing—waiting for its opportunity. Then, during a procession of monotonous, physically laborious day-jobs, his imagination leaped into motion, bringing together characters and locations of a world that would someday come to life on the pages of a book.

In late 1998, Jason made his first attempt at writing, managing to complete a whole scene before returning once again to reality. A year and a half later, a spontaneous night-time conversation with his wife encouraged him to take his writing seriously and to keep on dreaming. Over the next seven years, Jason carved time out of the real world to live in an imaginary one of epic fantasy, science-fiction, and military/political conflict. The fruits of this labor became the first three books of the bestselling AWAKENED series.

Due to the amazing support from readers around the world, Jason has continued his trajectory into make-believe, recently jumping from stable employment in the micro-electronics industry into the mysterious abyss of full-time writing.

Living in Colorado with his beautiful wife and two children, Jason now spends the majority of his time fusing the best parts of his favorite genres into stories of internal struggle and triumph, friendship, betrayal, political alliances, and military conflict. His fast-paced stories span ancient and future worlds, weaving together threads of stirring drama and intense action that provoke reader comments such as, "I couldn't put it down," and "I'll read anything he writes."

# GLOSSARY
# AND PRONUNCIATION GUIDE

The following is a glossary of names, titles, terms, places, and characters that are used throughout this and subsequent books of the Wandering Stars series.

The *vowels* section below contains characters, or arrangements of characters, which are used in the pronunciation section of glossary entries. Each vowel sound is followed by an example of common words using the same sound.

The *additional consonants* section also contains characters, or arrangements of characters, which are used in the pronunciation section of glossary entries. These sounds are not used in the English language, but examples are found in other languages and are listed for reference.

Glossary entries contain the word or phrase, its correct pronunciation (including syllables and emphasis), the translation of the word or phrase, its culture of derivation, and a description. The format for each entry is as follows:

<u>Word or phrase</u>  \proh-**nuhn**-see-ey-shuhn\  *Translation* [Derivation] Description

## Vowels

| | |
|---|---|
| [a] | <u>a</u>pple, s<u>a</u>d |
| [ey] | h<u>a</u>te, d<u>ay</u> |
| [ah] | <u>a</u>rm, f<u>a</u>ther |
| [air] | d<u>a</u>re, c<u>a</u>reful |
| [e] | <u>e</u>mpty, g<u>e</u>t |
| [ee] | <u>ea</u>t, s<u>ee</u> |
| [eer] | <u>ear</u>, h<u>e</u>ro |
| [er] | <u>ear</u>ly, w<u>or</u>d |
| [i] | <u>i</u>t, f<u>i</u>nish |
| [ahy] | s<u>igh</u>t, bl<u>i</u>nd |
| [o] | <u>o</u>dd, fr<u>o</u>st |

| [oh] | open, road |
| [ew] | food, shrewd |
| [oo] | good, book |
| [oi] | oil, choice |
| [ou] | loud, how |
| [uh] | under, tug |

## Additional Consonants

| [r] | roho (Spanish) |
| [zh] | joie de vivre (French) |
| [kh] | loch (Scots) |

## Glossary

Ad-Banyim \ad-**ban**-yim\ *First Between Waters* [Shayeth] The first narrow strip of land between two bodies of water which Enoch crossed during his first journey.

Adam \ah-**dahm**\ *Man* [Shayeth] The first human, created rather than born. Husband of Eve. Father of Kahyin, Hevel, Shayeth, and Yahsad. See Genesis 2:19.

Ad-Rada \**ad**-rah-dah\ *First Rule* [Angelic] The first, or highest position of rank among the Amatru.

Aden \**ey**-den\ *Pleasure* [Shayeth] The first place of human habitation on earth. See Genesis 2:8.

Amatru \**ah**-mah-trew\ *Faithful* [Angelic] The combined military forces of the Eternal Realm who have remained faithful to the Holy One. The angelic military. The Amatru is comprised of three original branches—Anduar, Iryllur, and Vidir—with a fourth branch, Saman—being added later in response to enemy tactics. Each branch is comprised of seven unique disciplines: Draepa, Vorda, Braegda, Vaeka, Frysla, Viytur, and Smyda.

Aifett \ey-**fet**\ *Sea Girl* [Angelic, Kahyin] Hyrren's Vidiyl sister (non-biological).

Aleydam \al-**eyd**-em\ *People Above The Mist* [Shayeth] The mountain tribe that accepted Sariel and Sheyir into their village after the war against Semjaza.

<u>Aleydiyr</u> \al-**eyd**-eer\ *City Above The Mist* [Shayeth] The city of the Aleydam.

<u>Anah</u> \ah-**nah**\ *Humbled* [Shayeth] The city of Keynan, firstborn son of Enowsh, so named because he went out to possess the earth and was humbled by many hardships.

<u>Ananel</u> \**a**-nah-nel\ *Unknown* [Angelic] The first angel to befriend Enoch, whom he encountered after the Kahyin took the prophet captive. Race: Myndar (in the form of a wolf). Appearance: golden eyes; pale-gray to dark-gray fur. See The Book of Enoch 6:8.

<u>Anduar</u> \**an**-dew-ahr\ *Land Force* [Angelic] The singular name for a member of the land force of the Amatru. Angel of the land.

<u>Anduarym</u> \**an**-dew-ah*r* im\ *Land Forces* [Angelic] The plural name for members of the land force of the Amatru. Angels of the land.

<u>Aniyl</u> \an-**eel**\ *Fallen of Land* [Angelic, Kahyin] Singular name for a Nephiyl of Anduar and human origin.

<u>Aniylim</u>\an-**eel**-im\ *Fallen People of Land* [Angelic, Kahyin] Plural name for Nephiylim of Anduar and human origins.

<u>Aragatsiyr</u> \**ah**-*r*ah-gaht-see*r*\ *Woven Trees* [Shayeth] The name that Enoch gave to the city of the Myndarym, which they established after their rebellion from Semjaza. See also Senvidar.

<u>Ariyl</u> \ah*r*-**eel**\ *Fallen Raptor* [Angelic, Kahyin] Singular name for a Nephiyl of Myndar and raptor origin.

<u>Ariylim</u> \ah*r*-**eel**-im\ *Fallen Raptors* [Angelic, Kahyin] Plural name for Nephiylim of Myndar and raptor origins.

<u>Armayim</u> \**ahr**-mah-yim\ *Lake of the Curse* [Chatsiyr] The lake in Arar Gahiy, north of Bahyith, where several Chatsiyr men found figurines and subsequently became ill.

<u>Aryun Del-Edha</u> \ah*r*-**yewn** del-**ed**-hah\ *Eyes of the Gods* [Kahyin] Semjaza's fortress or tower within Mudena Del-Edha,

so named for its peak, which rises above the surrounding mountains and allows the gods to observe the actions of man.

Aytsam \**eyt**-sahm\ *People of the Trees* [Chatsiyr] A human tribe, descended from the Kahyin, which attacked the Chatsiyram and took Sheyir prisoner.

Azab \ah-**zahb**\ *Leave, Forsake* [Shayeth] The city of Mahalal-el, so named because he wished to escape the struggles of his father.

Azael \**a**-zey-el\ *Unknown* [Angelic] Former Fim-Rada of Semjaza's Iryllurym and one of Semjaza's personal guards. King of Khelrusa. Race: Iryllur. Size: approximately 11 feet tall. Appearance: red eyes; charcoal-gray skin; sleek, black feathers. See The Book of Enoch 6:8.

Baerlagid \bey-air-**lah**-gid\ *Songs of Creation* [Angelic] The comprehensive, musical language used by the Holy One to bring all things into existence out of nothing. A small subset of Baerlagid was taught to the Myndarym for the purpose of *reshaping* the Temporal Realm to make it self-sustaining after its separation from the Eternal Realm.

Bahyith \bah-**yith**\ *House, Dwelling* [Chatsiyr] The village of the Chatsiyram, situated between the mountains of Bokhar and Ehrevhar.

Benahn \be-**nahn**\ *Unknown* [Shayeth] A citizen of Sedekiyr.

Bilaj \bi-**lahzh**\ *Unknown* [Shayeth] Young man who lives in Sedekiyr, engaged to Tullah

Chatsiyr \**kat**-see*r*\ *Grass* [Chatsiyr] The singular name for a member of the small human tribe, descended from the Shayetham, which used to occupy the valley between Bokhar and Ehrevhar. The people of Sheyir. The residents of Bahyith.

Chatsiyram \**kat**-see*r*-am\ *People of the Grass* [Chatsiyr] The plural name for the members of the small human tribe, descended from the Shayetham, which used to occupy the valley between Bokhar and Ehrevhar. The people of Sheyir. The residents of Bahyith.

<u>Da-Mayim</u> \\**dah**-mah-yim\\ *Unmoving Waters* [Shayeth] The large body of water west of Sedekiyr, named for its contrast to other moving waters, such as the numerous streams and rivers throughout the vast plains.

<u>Danush</u> \\da-**noosh**\\ *Unknown* [Shayeth] A citizen of Sedekiyr.

<u>Eili</u> \\**ey**-i-lee\\ *Eternal* [Angelic] The Eternal Realm. The portion of the creation spectrum that is eternal, in contrast to the portion that is temporal.

<u>El-Betakh</u> \\el-be-**tahk**\\ *God's Safety, God's Protection* [Shayeth] The city of Enoch, so named because the Holy One showed Enoch where his people would be safe from destruction.

<u>Enoch</u> \\**ee**-nahk\\ *Dedicated* [Shayeth] Husband of Zacol. Father of Methushelak. Prophet of the Shayetham. Appearance: pale-green eyes; ruddy skin; black hair and beard. See Genesis 5:18.

<u>Enowsh</u> \\ee-**nohsh**\\ *Men* [Shayeth] Son of Shayeth. Father of Keynan. See Genesis 4:26.

<u>Eve</u> \\**eev**\\ *Living* [Shayeth] The first human female, formed rather than born. See Genesis 3:20.

<u>Ezekiyel</u> \\**e**-ze-kee-el\\ *Unknown* [Angelic] A master *Shifter* and *Shaper* of the Myndarym who taught others how to move beings from the Eternal Realm to the Temporal Realm. See The Book of Enoch 6:7.

<u>Fyarikel</u> \\**fyahr**-i-kel\\ *Far Cry, Far Call* [Angelic] Messenger of the Myndar Council. Race: Myndar (in the form of a falcon). Appearance: dark brown plumage with golden eyes. Size: Approximately 10 feet tall.

<u>Galah</u> \\gah-**lah**\\ *Exile* [Shayeth] The city of Adam, so named because the earth outside of Aden was the place of his exile.

<u>Hevel</u> \\he-**vel**\\ *Breath* [Shayeth] The secondborn son of Adam, murdered by his older brother, Kahyin. See Genesis 4:2.

<u>Hyrren</u> \\**heer**-en\\ *Eyes of Fire* [Angelic, Kahyin] Firstborn son of Semjaza and the oldest Nephiyl. Race: Aniyl. Size: 15 feet

tall at the time of the battle in Mudena Del-Edha, 21 feet tall during the battle in Sedekiyr.

Imikal \\**i**-mi-kahl\\ *Silent Cry, Silent Call* [Angelic, Kahyin] Hyrren's younger Aniyl brother who lived with him in Mudena Del-Edha. Second oldest of Hyrren's biological siblings.

Iriyl \\eer-**eel**\\ *Fallen of the Sky* [Angelic, Kahyin] Singular name for a Nephiyl of Iryllur and human origin.

Iriylim \\eer-**eel**-im\\ *Fallen People of the Sky* [Angelic, Kahyin] Plural name for Nephiylim of Iryllur and human origins.

Iryllur \\**eer**-i-lewr\\ *Air Force* [Angelic] The singular name for a member of the air force of the Amatru. Angel of the sky.

Iryllurym \\**eer**-i-lewr-im\\ *Air Forces* [Angelic] The plural name for the air forces of the Amatru. Angels of the sky.

Jomjael \\**johm**-jey-el\\ *Unknown* [Angelic] One of the three Myndarym whom Sariel encountered while searching for the Aytsam. Jomjael led the freed captive women back to Senvidar. Race: Myndar (in the form of a tiger). Appearance: golden eyes; tan to dark-orange fur. See The Book of Enoch 6:8.

Jurishel \\**joor**-i-shel\\ *Unknown* [Shayeth] Wife of Methu. Mother of Lemek.

Kahyin \\**kah**-yin\\ *Possession* [Kahyin] The firstborn son of Adam, who killed his younger brother Hevel. Also, the singular and plural for the largest human tribe, descended from Kahyin. See Genesis 4:1.

Keruv \\**kair**-ewv\\ *Unknown* [Angelic] The singular name for a member of the Keruvym. See Exodus 25:19.

Keruvym \\**kair**-ew-vim\\ *Unknown* [Angelic] The plural name for the six-winged creatures with human and animal features surrounding the throne of the Holy One, as seen in Enoch's visitation to the Eternal Realm. See Exodus 25:19.

Keynan \\key-**nahn**\\ *Possession* [Shayeth] Son of Enowsh. Father of Mahalal-el. See Genesis 5:9.

Khanok \**kan**-ahk\ *Dedicated* [Shayeth] The home city of the Kahyin tribe. See also Khelrusa. See Genesis 4:17.

Khelrusa \kel-**rew**-sah\ *Dedicated* [Kahyin] The home city of the Kahyin tribe. See also Khanok.

Kiyrakom \**keer**-ah-kohm\ *Place of Meeting* [Shayeth] Formerly, the open-air courtyard or meeting area at the center of the Senvidar (Aragatsiyr). Later, the place of meeting was moved to the peak of the mountain on the eastern border of Senvidar.

Kjotiyl \kyoht-**eel**\ *Fallen Cat* [Angelic, Kahyin] The singular name for a Nephiyl of feline and human origin.

Kjotiylim \kyoht-**eel**-im\ *Fallen Cats* [Angelic, Kahyin] The plural name for Nephiylim of feline and human origins.

Kyrindem \**keer**-in-dem\ *Quiet, Alone, Calm* [Angelic] The city of Kokabiel, so named because it allowed him to be left alone to do his work.

Lemek \le-**mek**\ *Powerful* [Shayeth] The firstborn son of Methushelak and Jurishel. See Genesis 5:25.

Luhad \lew-**hahd**\ *Tongue That Draws Blood* [Kahyin] The elder of the Kahyin in Khelrusa. The tallest and strongest human in the city.

Mahalal-el \mah-**hah**-lahl-el\ *Praise of God* [Shayeth] Son of Keynan. Father of Yered. See Genesis 5:15.

Marotru \**mah**-roh-trew\ *Unfaithful* [Angelic] The combined military forces of the Eternal Realm who rebelled against the Holy One to follow the Evil One. The demonic military.

Methushelak \me-**thew**-she-lak\ *Man of the Dart* [Shayeth] The firstborn son of Enoch and Zacol. Father of Lemek. Also called Methu. See Genesis 5:21.

Mudena Del-Edha \moo-**dee**-nuh del-**ed**-hah\ *City of the Gods* [Kahyin] Semjaza's city, which was *shaped* for him by the Myndarym.

Murakszhug \moo-**rahk**-zhoog\ *Mountain of Watching* [Kahyin] The mountain above Khelrusa.

Myndar \**min**-dahr\ *Shaper* [Angelic] The singular name of a member of the Myndarym.

Myndarym \**min**-dahr-im\ *Shapers* [Angelic] The plural name of the angelic race that was entrusted with a small subset of the Songs of Creation for the purpose of *reshaping* the Temporal Realm to make it self-sustaining after its separation from the Eternal Realm.

Myniyl \min-**eel**\ *Fallen Shaper* [Angelic, Kahyin] The singular name for a Nephiyl of Myndar and human origin.

Myniylim \min-**eel**-im\ *Fallen Shapers* [Angelic, Kahyin] The plural name for Nephiylim of Myndar and human origins.

Nagah \nah-**gah**\ *Mountains of Reaching* [Shayeth] The mountain range east of Sedekiyr, named for its appearance to be reaching toward the sky.

Naganel \**nah**-gahn-el\ *Melody of God* [Angelic] A messenger of the Myndar Council. Race: Myndar (in the form of a hawk). Appearance: gray plumage with green eyes. Size: Approximately 10 feet tall.

Nakh \**nahk**\ *Inheritance* [Shayeth] The city of Shayeth, the thirdborn son of Adam, so named because he saw the earth as the inheritance of his people rather than a place of exile, like his father believed.

Nephiyl \nef-**eel**\ *Fallen* [Kahyin, Shayeth] The generic singular name for any child of angelic and human—or animal—origin. See Genesis 6:4.

Nephiylim \nef-**eel**-im\ *Fallen People* [Kahyin, Shayeth] The generic plural name for any children of angelic and human—or animal—origins. See Genesis 6:4.

Neshil \ne-**shil**\ *Unknown* [Shayeth] The secondborn son of Yered. Enoch's younger brother.

Nin-Myndar \**nin**-min-dahr\ *Unshaper* [Angelic] The singular name for a member of the Nin-Myndarym.

Nin-Myndarym \**nin**-min-dahr-im\ *Unshapers* [Angelic] The plural name for the demonic counterparts to the Myndarym, who have misused and distorted the Songs of Creation for the purposes of destroying the Eternal realm and the Amatru.

Parnudel \\**pahr**-new-del\\ *Unknown* [Angelic] Formerly, one of Semjaza's personal guards. Azael's second in command. Race: Iryllur. Size: approximately 10 feet tall. Appearance: golden eyes; mottled-brown skin and feathers.

Rada \\**rah**-dah\\ *Rule* [Angelic] A title of respect among the Amatru, used to signify one's superior.

Reshaping  The period in creation's history, immediately following *The Great Turning Away*, when the Myndarym used the *Songs of Creation* to *shape* the Temporal Realm so that it could become self-sustaining after it began separating from the Eternal Realm. Also called Omynd.

Rikoathel \\ri-**koh**-ah-thel\\ *Power of God* [Angelic] Formerly, one of Semjaza's Iryllurym. Azael's third in command. Race: Iryllur. Size: approximately 12 feet tall. Appearance: golden eyes; dark-brown skin and feathers.

Sahveyim \\sah-vey-**yim**\\ *Water on All Sides* [Shayeth] The section of land, narrowly connected to larger land masses on the south, east, and west, which sits in the middle of the Great Waters north of Khelrusa.

Sariel \\**sah**-ree-el\\ *Minister Appointed by God* [Angelic] Formerly a Myndar, who became a soldier of the Iryllurym. Race: Myndar (in human form). Appearance: bright-blue eyes, light-tan skin, white shaggy hair and beard. See The Book of Enoch 6:8.

Sedekiyr \\sed-e-**keer**\\ *City of Justice, Righteousness* [Shayeth] The city of Yered, so named for its location on the level plains or flatlands, and not as an indication of morality.

Semjaza \\sem-**jah**-zah\\ *Unknown* [Angelic] Formerly a Pri-Rada of the Saman until his invasion of the Temporal Realm. Size: 13 feet tall. Appearance: dark orange eyes, reddish-brown skin, black hair. See The Book of Enoch 6:7.

<u>Senvidar</u> \\**sen**-vi-dahr\\ *Twisted Trees* [Angelic] The city of the Myndarym, which they established after their rebellion from Semjaza. See also Aragatsiyr.

<u>Seydah</u> \\**sey**-dah\\ *Provision* [Shayeth] The city of Enowsh, so named because the Holy One provided everything they needed through the land of their inheritance.

<u>Shalakh Akhar</u> \\shah-**lahk** ahk-**ahr**\\ *After Exile* [Shayeth] A reference point for measurement of time; also abbreviated *S.A.* The first humans were immortal prior to their exile from Aden, therefore, the passage of time was irrelevant. The practice of referring to events and objects in the past-tense only came into being when there was a noticeable difference between their past and present states. This occurred during the time of their banishment and the translated phrase *after exile* came into use.

<u>Shape</u> The ability of a Myndar to alter its form or the form of another being or object.

<u>Shayeth</u> \\**shey**-eth\\ *Compensation* [Shayeth] The thirdborn son of Adam and Eve. Also, the singular name for a member of the Shayetham. See Genesis 4:25.

<u>Shayetham</u> \\**shey**-eth-em\\ *People of Compensation* [Shayeth] The plural name for the second-largest of the human tribes, descended from Shayeth. See Genesis 4:25.

<u>Sheyir</u> \\**shey**-eer\\ *Song* [Chatsiyr] The youngest daughter of Yeduah. Wife of Sariel. Race: Chatsiyr (descended from the Shayetham). Appearance: light-brown eyes; earthen skin; black hair.

<u>Shift</u> The ability of a Myndar to move its body, consciousness, or another object from one point to another along the spectrum of creation.

<u>Skoldur</u> \\**skohl**-dewr\\ *Shield* [Angelic] Singular and plural name for the heavyweight shield used by the Anduarym.

<u>Smyda</u> \\**smee**-dah\\ *Build* [Angelic] One of the seven disciplines within each branch of the Amatru. The Smyda specialize in the design of weaponry and armor and construction of fortifications.

<u>Svvard</u> \\**svahrd**\\ *Unknown* [Angelic] The singular and plural name for an experimental weapon being developed by the Smyda. Similar to a *vandrekt*, it features a shorter handle and longer blade. It functions as a stabbing or swinging weapon in close-quarters combat.

<u>Tarsaeel</u> \\**tahr**-sey-el\\ *Unknown* [Angelic] Sariel's former friend in the Viytur (Amatru intelligence). Formerly a Myndar who became a soldier. Race: Myndar (in Iryllur form). Size: approximately 10 feet tall. Appearance: golden eyes; mottled brown, red, and tan skin and plumage; chestnut hair.

<u>Tima</u> \\**tee**-mah\\ *Temporal* [Angelic] The Temporal Realm. The portion of the creation Spectrum that separated from the Eternal Realm and became temporal.

<u>Tullah</u> \\**too**-luh\\ *Unknown* [Shayeth] Young woman of Sedekiyr. Engaged to Bilaj

<u>Tuval</u> \\too-**vahl**\\ *Born of* [Kahyin] The head metal worker of the Kahyin in Khelrusa.

<u>Ulfiyl</u> \\oolf-**eel**\\ *Fallen Wolf* [Angelic, Kahyin] The singular name for a Nephiyl of wolf and Myndar origin.

<u>Ulfiylim</u> \\oolf-**eel**-im\\ *Fallen Wolves* [Angelic, Kahyin] The plural name for Nephiylim of wolf and Myndar origins.

<u>Unshape</u> The ability of a Nin-Myndar to destroy the form of another being or object.

<u>Vaepkir</u> \\**veyp**-keer\\ *Arm Blade* [Angelic] The singular and plural name for the arm-blade weaponry used by the Iryllurym. When held in the standard position, it functions as a ramming weapon during air-based attacks. When held in a reverse position, it functions as a stabbing weapon during ground-based, or hand-to-hand combat.

<u>Vand-ra</u> \\vahnd-**ra**\\ *Evil* [Demonic] The Nin-Myndar who was Sariel's greatest adversary in the Eternal Realm.

<u>Vandrekt</u> \\vahn-**drekt**\\ *Air Spear* [Angelic] The singular and plural name for the short spears used by the Anduarym. Each *vandrekt* is fitted with a 12 inch, double bladed tip. It functions

as a stabbing weapon in close-quarters combat, or a swinging or casting weapon on the open battlefield—though casting is typically a last resort.

Vengsul \veyng-**sool**\ *Broken Wing* [Angelic, Kahyin] Hyrren's Iriyl sibling (non-biological) who grew up with him in Mudena Del-Edha. Vengsul is the eldest Iriyl.

Vidir \vi-**deer**\ *Sea Force* [Angelic] The singular name for a member of the sea force of the Amatru.

Vidirym \vi-**deer**-im\ *Sea Forces* [Angelic] The plural name for members of the sea forces of the Amatru.

Vidiyl \vid-**eel**\ *Fallen of the Sea* [Angelic, Kahyin] The singular name for a Nephiyl of Vidir and human origin.

Vidiylim \vid-**eel**-im\ *Fallen People of the Sea* [Angelic, Kahyin] The plural name for Nephiylim of Vidir and human origins.

Vidri \**vi**-dree\ *Feathers* [Angelic, Kahyin] One of the captains of Hyrren's Iriyl soldiers.

Viytur \**vee**-tewr\ *Wisdom* [Angelic] One of the seven disciplines within each branch of the Amatru. The Viytur is a cross-branch force, specializing in the gathering and analysis of information and controlled implementation of its conclusions.

Yahsad \yah-**sahd**\ *Foundation* [Adam] The fourthborn son of Adam and Eve, so named because he would be the foundation of their civilization after Shayeth (the thirdborn) was sent out to start his own city.

Yarut \yah-**root**\ *Iron Hand* [Angelic, Kahyin] One of Hyrren's brothers who commands an army in the east.

Yeduah \**ye**-dew-uh\ *Unknown* [Chatsiyr] The elder of the Chatsiyr tribe. Father of Sheyir.

Yelmur \yel-**mewr**\ *Quiet Mouth* [Angelic, Kahyin] One of Hyrren's siblings who is killed when trying to chase after Sariel.

Yered \ye-**red**\ *Descent* [Shayeth] Son of Mahalal-el. Father of Enoch. See Genesis 5:15. NOTE: according to the biblical account, Yered (Jared) would have lived until S.A. 1422. Due to the context surrounding the judgment of Sedekiyr and its people, I chose to alter the time of Yered's death by including him in the judgment.

<u>Yllfae</u> \\**il**-fey\\ *Grace and Beauty* [Angelic] Kokabiel's eldest daughter, born of a human female of Shayeth lineage who took refuge in Senvidar.

<u>Zahmesh</u> \\zah-**mesh**\\ *Resolute Mind* [Angelic] A guard of the Myndar Council. Race: Myndar (in angelic form). Size: Approximately 10 feet tall. Appearance: Blond hair; pale skin; green eyes.

<u>Zacol</u> \\**zah**-kohl\\ *Strong Voice* [Shayeth] Wife of Enoch. Mother of Methushelak. Appearance: dark-brown eyes; ruddy skin; black hair.

<u>Zejuad</u> \\**ze**-zhew-ahd\\ *Unknown* [Shayeth] A citizen of Sedekiyr. The boy who picks on Methu.

# REFERENCES

1. ... the angels which kept not their first estate, but left their own habitation, he hath reserved in everlasting chains under darkness unto the judgment of the great day ... **wandering stars**, to whom is reserved the blackness of darkness forever (Jude 1:6, 13, KJV).

2. ... for the Lord God had not caused it to rain upon the earth ... But there went up a mist from the earth, and watered the whole face of the ground (Genesis 2:5-6, KJV).

3. ... taught men to make swords, and knives, and shields, and breastplates, and made known to them the metals of the earth and the art of working them ... (The Book of Enoch 8:1)

4. ... Enoch was hidden, and no one of the children of men knew where he was hidden, and where he abode, and what had become of him (The Book of Enoch 12:1-2).

5. There were giants *[Nephiylim]* in the earth in those days; and also after that, when the sons of God came in unto the daughters of men, and they bare children to them, the same became mighty men which were of old, men of renown (Genesis 6:4, KJV).

6. ... whose height was three thousand ells, who consumed all the acquisitions of men. And when men could no longer sustain them, the giants *[Nephiylim]* turned against them and devoured mankind. And they began to sin against birds, and beasts, and reptiles, and fish, and to devour one another's flesh, and drink the blood ... (The Book of Enoch 7:2-6)

7. And Adam lived an hundred and thirty years, and begat a son in his own likeness, after his image; and called his name Seth *[Shayeth]* ... And Seth lived an hundred and five years, and begat Enos *[Enowsh]* ... And Enos lived ninety years, and begat Cainan *[Keynan]* ... And Cainan lived seventy years, and begat Mahalaleel *[Mahalal-el]* ... And Mahalaleel lived sixty and five years, and begat Jared *[Yered]* ... And Jared lived an hundred sixty and two years, and he begat Enoch ... And Enoch lived

sixty and five years, and begat Methuselah *[Methushelak]* ... And Methuselah lived an hundred eighty and seven years, and begat Lamech *[Lemek]* ... (Genesis 5:3, 6, 9, 12, 15, 18, 21, 25, KJV).

8.  And all the others together with them took unto themselves wives, and each chose for himself one, and they began to go in unto them and to defile themselves with them ... (The Book of Enoch 7:1)

9.  And it came to pass, when men began to multiply on the face of the earth, and daughters were born unto them, that the sons of God saw the daughters of men that they were fair; and they took them wives of all which they chose (Genesis 6:1-2, KJV).

10.  ... in the vision clouds invited me and a mist summoned me, and the course of the stars and the lightnings sped and hastened me, and the winds in the vision caused me to fly and lifted me upward, and bore me into heaven. And I went in till I drew nigh to a wall which was built of crystals and drew nigh to a large house which was built of crystals ... (The Book of Enoch 14:8-10)

11.  And Adam knew his wife again; and she bare a son, and called his name Seth *[Shayeth]*: For God, said she, hath appointed me another seed instead of Abel *[Hevel]*, whom Cain *[Kahyin]* slew (Genesis 4:25, KJV).

12.  And Cain *[Kahyin]* talked with Abel *[Hevel]* his brother: and it came to pass, when they were in the field, that Cain rose up against Abel his brother, and slew him (Genesis 4:8, KJV).

13.  And the Lord God planted a garden eastward in Eden *[Aden]*; and there he put the man whom he had formed (Genesis 2:8, KJV).

14.  Therefore the Lord God sent him forth from the garden of Eden *[Aden]* ... So he drove out the man; and he placed at the east of the garden of Eden Cherubims *[Keruvym]*, and a flaming sword which turned every way, to keep the way of the tree of life (Genesis 3:23-24, KJV).

15.  And before the throne there was a sea of glass like unto crystal: and in the midst of the throne, and round about the

throne, were four beasts full of eyes before and behind. And the first beast was like a lion, and the second beast like a calf, and the third beast had a face as a man, and the fourth beast was like a flying eagle. And the four beasts had each of them six wings about him; and they were full of eyes within (Revelation 4:6-8, KJV).

16. And out of the ground made the Lord God to grow every tree that is pleasant to the sight, and good for food; the tree of life also in the midst of the garden, and the tree of knowledge of good and evil *[Tree of Wisdom]* (Genesis 2:9, KJV).

17. And the Lord God commanded the man, saying, Of every tree of the garden thou mayest freely eat. But of the tree of the knowledge of good and evil *[Tree of Wisdom]*, thou shalt not eat of it: for in the day that thou eatest thereof thou shalt surely die (Genesis 2:16-17, KJV).

18. And the serpent said unto the woman, Ye shall not surely die: For God doth know that in the day ye eat thereof, then your eyes shall be opened, and ye shall be as gods, knowing good and evil (Genesis 3:4-5, KJV).

19. And Adam called his wife's name Eve; because she was the mother of all living (Genesis 3:20, KJV).

20. Now the serpent was more subtil *[crafty]* than any beast of the field which the Lord God had made ... (Genesis 3:1, KJV)

21. And they besought me to draw up a petition for them that they might find forgiveness, and to read their petition in the presence of the Lord of heaven. For from thenceforeward they could not speak with Him nor lift up their eyes to heaven for shame of their sins for which they had been condemned (The Book of Enoch 13:4-6).

22. And Enoch walked with God: and he was not; for God took him (Genesis 5:24, KJV). By faith Enoch was translated that he should not see death; and was not found, because God had translated him: for before his translation he had this testimony, that he pleased God (Hebrews 11:5, KJV).

23.   Therefore, I will raise up one from among those you despise. And I will awaken his eyes to the mysteries which I have hidden from men since the foundations of the world. His feet will I make to tread upon the paths of destruction and his hands to make war. He will uproot the seeds of corruption which you have sown throughout the earth. And then you will know that I am the Lord and my justice is everlasting (The Writings of Ebnisha).

# ACKNOWLEDGEMENTS

I would like to thank Mike Heath for his amazing artistic talent. Every cover he designs for me is my new "favorite." I am so thankful to have someone capable of turning a conceptual conversation into a piece of breathtaking artwork.

I would also like to thank Carly Tesar, Cindy Tesar, Marcia Fry, Ronda Swolley, Claudette Cruz, and Nicholas Cowan for their editing inputs that helped me clarify this story and make it more understandable for readers.

16706781R00245